ALSO BY T

'A great debut novel that gradually pulls you in through musical references and intrigue until you are holding your breath to find the outcome.'

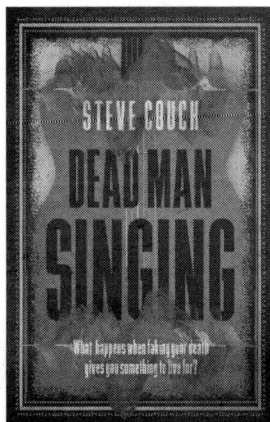

What's a rock star to do when his talent fails him and his career has withered and died?

Fed up with never-ending humiliations, Dave Masters fakes his own death in an attempt to boost record sales, walking away from an industry that turned its back on him.

But what's a dead rock star to do when he realises too late that he can't live without the stage? Dave decides to set up as his own tribute act, and starts all over, soon discovering that building a new life isn't as easy as he might have thought.

Dead Man Singing is a rollercoaster ride through Dave's posthumous life; his brushes with fans, lovers, rivals, stalkers, gangsters, the law and the most dangerous enemy of all – himself.

Can he come out of the other side of death alive?

PRAISE FOR *DEAD MAN SINGING* BY STEVE COUCH

"A great debut novel that gradually pulls you in through musical references and intrigue until you are holding your breath to find the outcome."

Elizabeth Dodd

"*Dead Man Singing* will make you want to cry and laugh in equal amounts."

Matt Shine, FemaleFirst.com

"Funny, unique and engaging. Most of all, I loved the characters."

Alex Oehring

"It's a clever and intriguing story – given total authenticity thanks to the author's impressive musical knowledge of bands, gig venues and the like. Wonderfully written and a real page-turner."

Steve Broadway

"As I got to the end, I speeded up my reading to find out what happens. The ending was spectacular."

Linda Hamilton-Ross

"A brilliant first novel… Every time I thought it might become predictable, another twist in the plot arrived."

Peter Price

"I really enjoyed the twists and turns of the story... The idea of one action causing ripples that just keep spreading fascinates me."

Sarah Minchin

"All I wanted to do was sit and read this riveting tale."

Graham Turner

"A rocking good story which hits all the right notes."

Brian Case, BH Living magazine

FOUL
AND
FAIR

Steve Couch

The Book Guild Ltd

First published in Great Britain in 2024 by
The Book Guild Ltd
Unit E2 Airfield Business Park,
Harrison Road, Market Harborough,
Leicestershire. LE16 7UL
Tel: 0116 2792299
www.bookguild.co.uk
Email: info@bookguild.co.uk
Twitter: @bookguild

Typeset in 11pt Minion Pro

Printed on FSC accredited paper
Printed and bound in Great Britain by 4edge Limited

ISBN 978 1835740 231

British Library Cataloguing in Publication Data.
A catalogue record for this book is available from the British Library.

For Peter and Dan, and their respective team-mates at West Moors Youth Football Club

CHAPTER ONE

As the door slammed closed behind him, James slumped with his head in his hands. There was padding of sorts on top of the plank of a bed, but it seemed designed to provide the minimum possible comfort. He couldn't imagine sleeping easily tonight anyway, not here, not with everything that had happened. How had he let things go this far?

He leaned back against the cold concrete wall of the cell and realised he was shaking. He wanted to blame the security guards, or the police. Mostly he wanted to blame Kieran, but he knew that the only person really to blame was himself. He had been so stupid – how could he have let everything get so out of perspective? It's just kids' football for goodness' sake. Then again, he couldn't let Kieran get away with it, could he? To paraphrase Bill Shankly, football is much more important than life and death. If the last few months had taught James anything, it was that there was some truth in that.

*

SOME MONTHS EARLIER...
James jumped the red light and swore as he swerved to avoid the oncoming traffic. The Audi that he'd just cut up honked furiously and flashed its lights at him.

'Let it go,' he muttered, fighting against the desire to remonstrate. James knew the incident had been his own fault – his head was still back at the pub, back at the committee meeting; he hadn't even registered that the lights were against him.

He pulled over to the kerb when he saw a space and let the Audi roar by, avoiding eye contact with the driver. Handbrake on, he forced himself to take deep breaths: in through the nose, out through the mouth. His heart was pounding against his ribcage, racing like a winger running out of touchline. How had he been so stupid? Why had he risen to the bait?

Kieran, as ever, had been lording it. 'We've lost a few of our players, so we'll need your keeper plus a couple more, just to fill out the bench. Who are your best two?' James clenched the steering wheel as he remembered, indignation pulsing again in his chest.

'What do you mean, you'll have Rory and two others?' James had replied, trying to keep his voice level. 'I've only just got enough as it is.'

'So? Every year, your team feeds my team with your best players. It's easy to find players for your standard; I can only take decent ones. The weaker team always feeds the stronger one.'

James and Kieran managed the two under-twelve sides at the club, but Kieran had always seen his team as the proper representatives of Stoneleigh Youth Football Club in their age group, with James's team an afterthought or a joke to him.

'Stronger team?' James remembered asking. 'We're in the same division.'

Kieran had actually laughed, spilling some of his pint. 'We may be in the same division, mate, but you're still the weaker team; always will be.'

The chairman had intervened at this point. In a completely neutral and impartial manner, he weighed in on behalf of Kieran, who happened to be his son.

'Fair's fair, James, it's what we've always done. The Hawks should never have been relegated last season; that points deduction was a joke.' Kieran's team, the Hawks, usually competed in the top division, while James's Swifts muddled along in the second tier without troubling the top half of the table. Lynn, the club secretary, had stepped in to clarify the flaws in Ron's argument.

'What did you expect?' she had said, briskly. 'I warned Kieran that George Maynard's registration hadn't come through yet, but he insisted on playing him against Belgate Magpies. Once the league found out, forfeiting the match is the standard punishment. If Alison was here, as welfare officer she'd want to point out that the points deduction was also for Kieran's conduct during the game. If I remember correctly, Kieran, you squared up to the ref, called her a cheat and asked what a woman was even doing on a football pitch. Then, when she took your name, you asked for her phone number.'

Kieran grinned at the memory while Ron laughed with paternal pride. Ron was always going to side with Kieran, while James could always rely on Lynn's vote, not least because her son Rory was the Swifts' goalkeeper. With Alison unfortunately absent, James had needed Howard and Dave to side with him too.

Dave was hard to read. He rarely spoke up at committee meetings other than to report on the state of the pitches or to complain about coaches leaving his equipment lock-up in a mess. Howard was more predictable. The longest-serving member of the committee after Ron and another remnant from the previous generation of parents at the club, he was a stickler for going by the book, keeping things as they were.

Lynn wasn't finished. 'We *haven't* always used the Swifts as a feeder team for the Hawks. As under-sevens and under-eights they were in the same division; there wasn't a stronger or a weaker team.'

'Excuse me, love, I don't think so,' interrupted Kieran. 'My Hawks have always been the stronger team. Even then, we ran rings round your lot.'

That was true, but it had been a mistake for Kieran to mention it; Howard had stirred into life. 'That's right, Kieran, we *have* always known that the Hawks were the stronger of the two teams, but Lynn is correct: we didn't start moving the Swifts' best players across until you were promoted to the top division. When you were both at the same level, we let the teams compete as equals, even though we all knew your team was better. Being in different divisions has always been the deciding factor, and this year that's not the case. I think James is entitled to keep his players this time.'

Dave had spoken up next, locking eyeballs with Kieran and asking him a straight question. 'Don't you think your team is good enough to go back up without James's players?'

'Of course we bloody well are. We'll walk this league.'

'Well, what's the problem then? I say we let both teams keep their players for this season. If your team is as good as you say it is, you'll be back up next year and we can go back to the lower team feeding the higher one.'

And that was that. A four-two vote, Butchers versus everyone else. Kieran had sulked over his pint for the rest of the meeting while James tried hard not to look too smug. His good mood hadn't lasted long though. Kieran had followed him out of the Thane of Cawdor at the end of the meeting and caught up with him at his car.

'So what was all that about, you little prick?' Kieran loomed over James, every inch of his six-foot-plenty frame radiating threat. 'You can keep your pathetic little players and your pathetic little team.' Kieran's face was flushing red, spittle flecked at the corners of his mouth. James thought he might even take a swing at him. 'I don't need any of your losers anyway; I'd have to knock all that "it's not about winning" crap out of them before they were any use to me. Face it, I'm a winner and you're not. Your lot call it success if they win a corner.'

James had felt trapped against the car door. If only he'd made it safely into the driver's seat before Kieran had cornered him, it might have turned out differently. As it was, he'd felt he had to answer.

'Wait and see. It could be different this year – we might surprise you.'

Kieran roared with laughter. 'Seriously? You think your lot have got a chance? Go on then, put your money where your mouth is. How about a bet on which team finishes higher? I mean, you'll have to get rid of that lad of yours for a start. He traps the ball further than most of your boys can kick it. The apple doesn't fall far from the tree does it? Crap manager dad has a crap player son.'

The words had rushed out before James could think better of them. 'You leave my Ben out of it. I'll take that bet. What are the stakes?'

'If I win, your team becomes an official feeder side to mine. No, better yet, the loser's team folds, leaving all the players for the winner to pick from. We move up to eleven-a-side in a year's time, so I might need a few extra – not your lad though, obviously.'

Sitting at the kerbside now, remembering the exchange, James tried to focus on his breathing. Waves of anxiety throbbed in his stomach, fighting fiercely against his attempts to calm himself. Why had he agreed to that stupid bet? Why hadn't he pulled back? What were Ben and the others going to do for a team once Kieran cast most of them aside?

Eventually, after a few more minutes of deep breathing, James felt safe to drive on. He was already late starting his shift even before his run-in with Kieran. He logged on to the taxi company's admin system and reported in to work; his first fare was at the train station in fifteen minutes. James noticed the first drops of rain on the windscreen so he flicked his wipers on and headed into town.

*

James didn't get home until 4am. The usual array of late-night revellers had kept him busy despite the foul weather. Tips had

5

been decent and no one had thrown up in his taxi, which was at least something in the wins column. James quickly undressed and fell into bed. Ros, naturally enough, was fast asleep. Since he had started taxi driving, this happened more and more often. Nights when they made it to bed at the same time seemed rarer than a well-timed Paul Scholes tackle. Even though he was shattered, sleep didn't come easily tonight. He considered going back to Kieran, trying to call off the bet, but he knew how that conversation would go. Kieran was right about one thing, James had always cared more about the boys enjoying their football than about winning, but what was so wrong with that? Better that than winning at all costs without a thought for how it affected the boys. Did that make him a loser? He tossed and turned before finally succumbing to a fitful sleep, haunted by dreams of his Swifts conceding goal after goal, with Kieran's touchline celebrations becoming more and more extreme with each one.

CHAPTER TWO

Living the dream. James was grabbing a quick lunch between passengers. He was parked up in Duncan Road with a meal-deal sandwich on his lap, a branded coffee in the cup holder and 6 Music on the radio. Okay, so living the dream was overstating things a bit, but at least he was out of the nightmare of the previous year. His teaching career had been spiralling for ages, but that was all behind him now.

Back when he was an English teacher, he sometimes used song lyrics as a way in to teaching poetry to the lower-school kids. It had just about worked when he started, but as time went on there was more pushback. 'Not being funny, sir, but don't you listen to anything decent?', 'This is English sir, not history.' Or, more prosaically, 'You do know this music is crap, don't you, sir?' On a good day he could turn it round, inviting the pupils to bring in lyrics from their favourite artists for the class to analyse, but as he got older there was less and less cultural common ground with the students. With each passing year he also found he had less patience for the ones who weren't interested, the ones who didn't see the point of Shakespeare, or William Blake, or *Lord of the Flies*; it was harder to engage them and harder not to rise to the bait when they tried winding him up.

A Billy Bragg song came on next, one of James's favourites. He turned the volume up and sang along, though the line about life losing dignity, beauty and passion was a bit close to the bone, summing up his teaching career and his football coaching all at once.

Any further thoughts were interrupted as his mobile sprang into life. James's stomach lurched as he saw the name on the screen: it was Rob. When people said that the worst thing about kids' football was dealing with the parents, Rob was exactly who they meant. James toyed with rejecting the call, but decided to get it over with.

'Morning Rob, how are you doing?'

'Pretty pissed off, to be honest, James. What's this I hear about you blocking Max from switching up to the Hawks?' So much for small talk.

'Well, the committee agreed that as both teams are in the same division now, the Hawks couldn't just take our players. It means we can keep last season's team together and actually build on what we're doing. I thought you'd be pleased.'

'Pleased? My Maxi was looking forward to being in a decent team at last, then he hears that his coach has scuppered his big chance of a move. He's ready to make the step up and it's not fair that you won't let him go.'

'Nobody's stopping him, Rob. If you want Max to switch to the Hawks, that's up to you. Are you sure that Max will be happier though? Remember what happened with Tommy and Fin last year – so excited about the move and then Kieran kept them on the bench all season. They hardly kicked a ball.'

'Are you saying my Maxi isn't good enough?' bristled Rob.

'Not at all, Max is great and if he stays with us, you know he'll get game-time – I make sure everyone does. Kieran doesn't run his team that way, he picks his strongest side every week and he doesn't care if it's the same people always missing out.'

'Well, that's a good thing in my book. You shouldn't give the likes of Ryan and Deepak the same time as Max. Hawks are

8

holding open trials at their training next week and I'm taking Max along.'

'Fair enough, I don't want to lose Max but I'm not going to stand in his way. All I'm saying is you should think about which team is going to give him more of a chance to actually play and enjoy his football.'

'Max enjoys it when he wins. No offence James, but we both know which team is more likely to win games.'

James sighed as Rob rang off and he tried to relax his shoulders, aware of the growing knots of tension in them. Max was one of his best players, although probably not as good as Rob thought he was. As happy as James would be not to deal with Rob, Max was a big part of the team. James also knew that if one boy made the move, others might follow. If he wasn't careful the domino effect could see him lose half his team. He texted Lynn to see what she knew. A minute later she was calling him back.

'Hi James. I thought it would be easier to talk than text, and I've got a few minutes. After that committee meeting Kieran started advertising open trials to fill his gaps. I knew Rob wanted Max to make the move – Clara told me all about it.' Clara was Max's mum. 'Apparently Max has been trying to persuade some of the other boys to go to the trials too, but no one's interested.'

'Are you sure? Who did he ask?'

'Liam, Dylan, Gabe, even my Rory – which is how I heard about it. Rory says that Liam just wants to play with his friends, which means the Swifts. As for Gabe, he wouldn't go back to Hawks if you paid him.' James wasn't surprised to hear that. Gabe had originally started in the Hawks, but had swiftly been cast aside by Kieran after a season of bench-warming. He had almost given up on football but his dad had persuaded him to try the Swifts. In the three years he'd been with them, he'd improved loads on the pitch and really come out of his shell compared to the quiet, unconfident lad who had first turned up to Swifts training. Lads like him needed the Swifts; how could James have put their team at risk like this? He was too embarrassed to admit to Lynn what he'd done with the bet, but he knew she'd find out before too long.

'I think Dylan is wavering,' she continued. 'But Sophie doesn't think Kieran will be as good at managing Dylan's moods as you are; I think they'll talk him into staying.'

'What about Rory, what are his thoughts?'

Lynn burst out laughing. 'Are you kidding? I'd make him give up football and take up ballet if he even considered playing for Kieran. Rory's heard all Gabe's stories about how Kieran treats the boys; he's in no hurry to put himself through that. Anyway, Kieran has set his eyes a bit higher than our boys; he wants to cream off the best players from the second division and run away with the league. He'll upset a lot of other managers, not that that will bother him. Oh, talking of coaches, I think I've found you a new assistant. One of the overseas students at the college heard I was involved in a youth football club and came to find me this morning. He's been coaching for a few years and wants to keep his hand in while he's over here.'

'A student? I'm not sure some kid is going to be much help. I need someone who knows what he's doing.'

'Trust me, he's a bit older than a lot of the students and I think you'll like him. I've told him to come along to training this week. He can get a feel for how you do things and the two of you can talk afterwards. His name is Joao.'

'Joao? What kind of a name is that?'

'Portuguese evidently, what with him being from Portugal.'

James sighed. 'Well, if you've told him already, I suppose I've not got a lot of choice. I'll give him a go.'

'Great. You won't regret it. Wouldn't it be lovely to actually beat the Hawks this year?' It would be lovely. It was also essential thanks to his stupid, rash bet. And it was almost certainly impossible; what had he done?

Any further discussion was cut short when a young man in a smart suit flung open the back door and clambered into the car.

'Forres Street, quick as you like'

James said a quick goodbye to Lynn, then half-turned to face the would-be passenger. The look on his face matched the abrupt tone of his instructions; everything about the man said he wasn't going to make the following exchange easy for James.

'Sorry mate, I can't take you without a prior booking.' The man ignored this, glancing at his watch as he settled into the back seat.

'Of course you can. You're a taxi, I'm a passenger. Forres Street, now.'

James sighed. 'It's not that simple. I'm not a black cab, this is a private-hire vehicle. I'm only allowed to take fares who have booked through my operator.'

'Well, I'm here now. Can't you just make an exception and take me to Forres Street? I'm in a hurry.'

'And I'm not in a hurry to get a fine and points on my licence. This is my livelihood, mate, I can't put it at risk for the sake of a £10 fare.'

The businessman's face twisted into a scowl. 'That's ridiculous. You're not going to get into any trouble, you're just being a jobsworth. Stop bleating and get me to Forres Street.'

James shrugged. 'I'm sorry, and I'd help if I could, but rules are rules, mate.'

'Are you telling me you've never bent the rules before? You don't get anywhere in life playing everything by the book, do you? If the problem is money, I'll even slip you a few quid extra, just get me to Forres Street, pronto.'

For a moment James was tempted, if only for a quiet life. He tried guessing how much extra the bloke would stump up. Even if he got him up to an extra £20 – which was unlikely – it wasn't worth the risk. There was a policewoman directing traffic just down the road; he didn't think she would have noticed the two of them arguing, but who knew? Besides, Raj had let a couple of drivers go in recent weeks for repeatedly taking walk-ups. With teaching closed off to him now, he wasn't in a hurry to tell Ros he had lost his job for the second time in a year.

'You think my problem is the money? Money isn't the problem, mate; my problem is the idiot who isn't listening and won't get out of my car.' Before either man could say anything else, the taxi app beeped, letting him know that his next fare had been assigned. He checked the details, not sure if a location that took him near Forres Street would be a good or bad thing in the circumstances. As it was, he was being sent in the opposite direction.

'Look,' he said. 'You'll have to get out. I've got to get across to Redbridge and I don't have time to argue.'

'That's ridiculous – I was here first. Take me to Forres Street then go on to your next call. I'll give you an extra tenner.'

'I can't do that, mate. Look, I'm going to Redbridge; you can either get out of the car or I can take you with me, but that won't get you to your meeting. The train station is just round the corner; black cabs rock up at the taxi rank every few minutes, or you can phone my head office and they'll send one of my colleagues out for you. If you're really in a hurry, either of those options will get you to Forres Street quicker than arguing with me.' He turned the ignition key and put the car into gear, hoping that his bluff wouldn't get called.

For a moment he thought the bloke was going to dig in and force his hand. The mood James was in, he was ready to drive him all the way to Redbridge, although it might have caused a problem when his legit customer found the back seat already occupied. As it was, the man flounced out of the car, chuntering away under his breath. James thought he caught a few swear words, so he riposted with an airy, 'And you, mate,' before pulling out and getting on with his day. Hopefully it would take a turn for the better at some point.

CHAPTER THREE

Hayley checked her phone and hesitated. It was Andy. She knew she wasn't meant to take personal calls on duty, but she'd been trying to get hold of him for days. She accepted the call and hooked the phone under her chin, continuing to wave the cars past.

'Andy, we'll have to be quick; I'm on duty.'

'What are you up to – clamping down on civil liberties? Oppressing minorities?' Andy had never liked that she was a police officer, and she had often wondered if that was the fault-line that had eventually split their relationship apart. He'd certainly got more vocal about it as time went by.

'Directing traffic actually, on Duncan Road.'

'Ooh, glamorous. Shouldn't you be out catching murderers?'

The driver at the front of the queue was shouting at her, gesticulating for her to let him through. She turned away from him without lowering the hand that was keeping him in his place. 'Look, I haven't got time for this. Did Jayden talk to you about the football team?'

'Yeah, it's not the best idea in the world, is it? How is he going to play on Sundays if he's with me every other weekend?'

'Well, maybe you could take him along to his matches on your weekends. He'd like that.'

Andy huffed. 'He might, but I don't want to spend hours getting cold and wet just to watch a bunch of kids chasing a ball around. There are so many better things I could be doing with him than football.'

'That's not what Jayden thinks. He's really excited about it.'

'He is now, but can't you talk him out of it?' The line of cars on Crown Lane was honking now. She raised her hand to halt the flow on Duncan Road and waved the impatient drivers through. 'Look, his mates from primary school play for Redbridge. That group are going to be split between four or five different secondary schools. Joining the football team means he'll still see everyone a couple of times a week. It's only Sunday mornings – you'll still have plenty of time to take him out on civil rights marches or whatever in the rest of the day.' There was no answer from Andy, so after a pause Hayley carried on. 'He's anxious about changing school, and this will help ease him into the transition. Maybe once he's made some new friends he won't want to keep going with football, but right now joining this team is the biggest thing in his life. That friendship group is a bit of stability when everything else is changing.'

'It doesn't sound like I've got much of a choice.' She could hear the bitterness in his voice. 'Seeing as you've already told him he can join.'

'Well, if you'd got back to me after one of the first half-dozen messages I left, maybe I wouldn't have had to make that decision on my own, would I? This co-parenting thing only works if you can be bothered to communicate. Look, I've got to go. Shall I tell him that you're okay with this?'

'Whatever.' The word was barely out of Andy's mouth before he hung up. She'd take that as agreement, though she wished she could be sure that he wouldn't start backing out once the season started.

It hadn't always been like that with Andy. They had met at a friend's party years ago. She hadn't told him what she did for a job at first, not least because he'd been telling her that the country was becoming a police state, and that people who looked like him were far more likely to be hassled by the police than white lads of the same age. By the time she let slip, they were already getting more serious. Back then, Andy had seemed willing to reconsider his own prejudices, but maybe that was just an act to boost his chances of getting laid. No, that wasn't fair; back then, he really was listening and engaging with what she said. They would never agree on politics, but there was a core of shared values – putting people first, looking out for the ones who couldn't look out for themselves – that they could cluster around, even if they had very different ideas on how those values were best achieved. A lot had changed since then. Their break-up had happened a year or so ago. Jayden had taken it badly at first, but he was doing better now. Hayley would have been happy to have nothing more to do with Andy, but for Jayden's sake she had to find a way to be civil with him. There had to be one grown-up making things work, and in the long term Jayden needed his dad as well as her.

The flow of traffic had eased now. She pushed the talk button on her radio.

'Yankee-Echo Four-Five to Control. Duncan Road looks quiet now. Over.'

'Roger that. I'll let the Sarge know and get back to you.' Hopefully she'd get the okay to return to the station, or at least be given something more interesting than waving cars through. This wasn't what she had come into the job to do. Yes, it was making a difference – a small, trivial difference – in people's lives, but it was hardly inspirational.

'Yankee-Echo Four-Five, this is Control. Over.'

'Go ahead, Control.'

'Sarge says you can leave Duncan Road and head over to the Cawdor Estate to join up with PC Pike.'

'Roger, Control. Out.' Great. She was often paired with Martin – or Pikey as he was mostly known by his colleagues – for beat duty. Though she only stood five feet one in her police-issue boots, she wasn't bothered by the physical side of the job. Even so, it was good to be paired with someone like Pikey, who could handle himself and had been around long enough to have seen everything twice. He saw past the idealism and the pipe dreams too, but still hadn't given up on doing some good. More importantly, he saw her as a fellow officer rather than just some girl who should be pushing paper in an office rather than out on the beat.

'Yankee-Echo Four-Five to Papa-Romeo Five-Three. I've been told to come and join you. Where are you? Over.'

'Received, Four-Five. Just checking in to see how Mr Lock is doing. What's your ETA?' Hayley smiled. Mr Lock ran a favourite café of theirs – Pikey had obviously stopped in for a cuppa.

'I can rendezvous in five minutes.' Hopefully he wouldn't need telling to get her a coffee, but just in case. 'I'm happy to assist with Mr Lock as usual, if you get my meaning.'

'Understood. I'll make the necessary arrangements.'

Sure enough, when she arrived at the café, he was outside with two takeaway coffees. He gave her a quick summary of his shift so far – a couple of low-level disputes but nothing worth writing up – and they started to walk through the estate. She was moaning about being put on traffic duty.

'I mean, what's the Sarge got against me? All the good plod stuff goes to everyone else. He always gives me the worst jobs.'

'Like pounding the beat with me, I suppose? Charming.'

'You know I didn't mean that; I mean stuff like directing traffic while bloody Amber Gould gets the interesting call-outs.'

'She certainly seems to be the Sarge's favourite. I wonder what she'd done to earn that – what kind of favours she's giving out.'

Hayley's eyebrows vanished under her hat. 'Excuse me? Are you seriously suggesting what I think you're suggesting?' As much as she would have liked the excuse to bitch about Amber, there was a limit. 'Why is it so hard to believe that a female officer could make progress on her own ability and not because she was putting out? Unless you know something I don't, that's a disgusting thing to suggest.' She glared at Pikey and then read the smirk on his face.

'I knew you'd bite at that one. No, I've not heard anything – I just wanted to see your reaction. To be fair, Gould has been racking up the arrests just lately. Everything she touches ends up in a cell. She's doing wonders for Sarge's figures, so you can understand why he's looking after her. Maybe you should try to feel a few more collars when you get the chance.'

Maybe he was right, although how she was meant to do that when she was directing traffic, she had no idea. The conversation with Pikey moved on to their respective social lives; she filled him in on her latest conversation with Andy, and he told her about his date the previous night.

'So, it was going fine until I mentioned that I'm a copper. She made the usual jokes about men in uniform and handcuffs, but seemed a little less at ease after that. It was pleasant enough and we said we'd get together and do it again soon, but when I went to message her this morning, she'd already blocked me.'

'Something to hide, you reckon?'

'Maybe. I offered her a ciggie at one point and she paused before checking I meant tobacco, so maybe she's a pothead, paranoid that I was going to nick her.'

'You should have done – someone has to give Amber Gould a run for her money.'

*

Some of the boys were already there, shouting and laughing as they kicked a ball around, when James arrived at training with Ben.

'What are we doing today?' asked Liam after the chorus of greetings.

'Well, it's pre-season, so you know what that means – fitness work!' Josh, Dylan and Deepak groaned, though James noticed Liam didn't seem concerned.

James joined in the kick-about while he waited for the others to show up, exchanging banter with the boys as they played. From time to time, he glanced over towards the gates to see if there was any sign of the mythical Joao. When Lynn arrived with Rory, he threw her an enquiring look. She just shrugged in reply. James sighed, so much for the Portuguese boy wonder.

'All right lads, time to start.' They should have started ten minutes ago, but a couple of the boys had been late. 'Let's get warmed up first: everyone, a quick lap of the pitch. Go!' Liam soon eased away from the pack, running at a comfortable pace, while the others stretched out behind him. Callum and Rory, bringing up the rear, seemed more interested in chatting than actually putting any effort into their running. As the boys slowly worked their way around the pitch, James laid out some cones.

'Put a shift in!' shouted James. 'And don't cut the corners!' Shaking his head at the lack of enthusiasm, he finished laying out the next activity. Once everyone had arrived back, Josh asked if they could do shooting today.

'Shooting? We haven't finished with the fitness work yet! Next up: shuttle runs, between the cones. Keep going until everyone has done it twenty times.' Even Liam joined in with the groan this time.

Once the boys were shuttling, James noticed a young man standing next to Lynn, watching. Presumably this was Joao. He looked like he was in his mid-to-late twenties, with wiry dark hair and a jawline somewhere between a beard and heavy stubble. He looked trim and athletic, which was a good sign. At least he'd approve of James working the boys for fitness. After the shuttle runs (James threw in an extra repetition of ten more, just for Joao's sake), there were press-ups, sit-ups and finally burpees. After that, he set up a passing routine and popped over to Lynn and Joao.

'Hey, Lynn. And I'm guessing you're Joao? Good to meet you.'

'Good to meet you too, Mister Hogan,' replied Joao, nodding deferentially.

'Call me James. Look, I'd better get back to the boys but I thought I'd introduce myself. Have you got time to hang around afterwards so we can chat?' Joao nodded eagerly and James went back to the players. Some of the boys had slipped away from the main group and set up a goal for themselves.

'Ben, Rory, Callum, get back with the others!' shouted James.

'But this is boring!' moaned Callum. 'Can't we do something else?'

'I was going to move on to a match,' replied James. 'But if you lot can't stay on task, maybe we should just go back to more running.' The whole group groaned. The breakaway boys reluctantly trudged back to the passing diamond.

After a few minutes, James called the boys together. He started throwing bibs to the boys as he called names.

'Gabe, Ryan, Dylan and...' he looked around the group, deciding, '... Ben. Get those on. The rest of you stay as you are. We're going to finish with a match.' A brief ripple of excitement ran through the boys.

The match was a glorious shambles. Nobody bothered with positions, apart from the goalkeepers. Ben was playing really well. James just wished he could transfer his training form into matches more than he did; somehow he seemed a smaller, more hesitant figure when it really counted. The bibs were blue and Callum, from the non-bibs team, was wearing a Chelsea shirt almost exactly the same shade. Most of the boys coped fine with the clash, but Ryan kept passing to Callum even though they were on different teams. Each time it happened, Dylan got more and more annoyed, calling Ryan increasingly offensive names. Ryan didn't respond, other than a slight drooping of his shoulders with each fresh insult.

The other big advantage for the non-bibs was Rory in goal, whereas the bibs just switched keepers every few minutes because no one really wanted to do it. That said, when Rory asked to come out, none of his team-mates would take his place. He lost interest after that, sitting down in the middle of the goal when the ball was down the other end and pulling up tufts of grass – not easy in keeper's gloves. Dylan took advantage with a long-range lob which had Rory scrambling to his feet, desperately trying to keep the ball out. Everyone, including James, laughed at Rory's doomed flailing, while Dylan celebrated like it was a cup final winner. A few of the parents had arrived by now, ready to take the boys home, and they all seemed to enjoy watching the chaos.

As the boys helped to collect the equipment at the end, James decided to tease Josh.

'Josh, can you do me a favour? If ever I'm sentenced to death, can I have you in the firing squad? You didn't get one on target all evening!' The boys, including Josh, laughed. Dylan took the opportunity to remind everyone of his more spectacular goalscoring exploits.

'Did you see my lob? Fifty yards at least.'

'You said forty yards last time,' said Josh.

'And it wasn't more than twenty to thirty, tops,' protested Rory, still looking embarrassed about the whole thing.

'It's going up all the time,' added James. 'By tomorrow he'll say it was from a different time zone.'

Lynn offered to drop Ben home, so ten minutes later James and Joao were sat in the Thane of Cawdor – the scene of his showdown with Kieran – with pints in front of them. James told Joao all about how Mac, who had started the team with him, had got a new job a year ago and had to move away. Joao explained that the sporting club he worked for back home was sponsoring him to study Sports Sciences. He was spending two years over here at the local college before moving back to Portugal with his qualification. He coached a kids' team back home and wanted to keep his hand in while he was in England.

'So, what did you think of tonight's session then?' asked James. 'Be honest – I can take it.' He was confident that Joao would approve of the fitness work, and there were some nice touches of skill amongst the bedlam at the end. He sat back in his chair and waited for Joao's praise.

Joao took a thoughtful sip on his pint. 'I see why you look for help,' he began. 'Do you always spend so long just running? Is not good.'

James was taken aback, he had expected Joao to be impressed, otherwise he would never have asked him to be honest. 'It... it's pre-season,' he stammered. 'They've got to build up fitness.'

'Yes, but they need the ball too. Why not fitness with ball? Then they enjoy fitness work. What the point in running, running, running if you can't kick the ball? Half the session with no ball; it... what is your English word...? It madness. It make no sense.'

'We did work with the ball – the passing diamond...'

'What is that? This player passes to that player who passes to the next, all set out just so.' Joao was getting passionate now, flailing his arms around as he spoke too. 'How does that help when opponent closes in and boy has to choose what to do? How does passing diamond help them make choice?'

James was reeling, he felt exposed by Joao's critical assault. He did his best, and it wasn't easy to hear his session being shredded like this. 'But these boys aren't professionals, they need to improve their basic skills...'

'Sim, but all players have to make choices on pitch. And A to B to C with no thought it is, what is word...? Boring. They lose interest. If you make it fun they don't switch off, they work harder for longer. And they improve.'

James had never thought of it like that before. As much as it hurt to admit it, he could see Joao's point: it had been a boring session. Maybe since Mac's departure James had got a bit lazy with his planning.

Kieran's sneering face rose unbidden in James's mind. Competing with the Hawks this season? James couldn't even plan a half-decent training session. Joao had shown him the truth: he was out of his depth. 'You're right, Joao. Maybe I'm just not cut out for football coaching after all.'

Joao's forehead furrowed and he looked James straight in the eye. 'That's… what's your English word…? Bollocks.' He grinned widely when he saw the shock on James's face. 'You belong out there – the boys love you: they laugh with you; they do what you ask even though it's duller than watching England. I would change much, but you and the players…' he clasped his hands together to make his point, 'tight. Without that…' he shrugged and waved his hand dismissively, '…nothing.'

The rest of the evening they talked football. James told Joao more about the boys and Joao suggested some training ideas. James wasn't entirely sure about everything Joao said, but what did he have to lose? By the end of the night they had agreed that Joao would lead the next session. As James walked home, he felt an unfamiliar feeling stirring deep inside. It took him a while to work out what it was; for the first time in a long time, he was looking forward to football again.

CHAPTER FOUR

Stepping into the locker room, Hayley's heart sank. Amber Gould was there, fiddling with the straps on her padded security vest.

'Hi Hayley.'

'Amber. Coming on shift or just finishing?'

'Just starting. Hopefully it'll be another busy one – I had a good day yesterday: a couple of drunk and disorderlies, half a dozen teenagers who had pot when I stop-and-searched them, and I turned up a lead on that car thief. All in all, Sarge was pretty pleased with me.'

Eight collars on a single shift. No wonder Sarge thought the sun shone out of her warrant card. It wasn't Hayley's best start to a day, and it didn't help when she got a text from Andy saying he couldn't pick Jayden up from football training tonight after all. He wasn't a bad dad, but he still wasn't really on board with the football thing. Hayley dashed off a quick message to Flynn's mum, hoping she'd be able to take Jayden for her until she finished work that evening. As for Andy, she'd take this up with him another time. Just because he didn't value what she did for a living, that didn't mean he could expect her to drop everything to suit him. Then again, there were times when she questioned the value of what she was doing. When had she stopped dreaming of being a high-flyer like Amber Gould? When had she stopped feeling that she could make a difference?

*

A couple of hours later, Hayley was hanging around in the shopping centre. Pikey had nipped off to the gents. Hayley was casually checking out the tops in the Next window display while she waited for him, when she heard the cry.

'Stop! Thief!'

She turned in the direction of the shouts, quickly scanning the crowded shopping centre. There was an old lady crumpled on the ground and a young man – black tee-shirt and cargo pants, average height and cropped hair – running away. Away from the lady, but more or less straight towards Hayley, who was hidden from his sight in the doorway. This was her chance; setting her feet to absorb the impact, she got ready to step out and body-check him as he ran past.

Now. She timed it perfectly. The thief was taken completely by surprise, and although both of them were knocked from their feet, Hayley at least had been expecting it, allowing her to recover first. She leapt up, pinned her prisoner and pulled out her handcuffs.

'I'm arresting you on suspicion of theft. You do not have to say anything…'

A babble of voices broke in to interrupt her. 'What do you think you're doing?'

'Not him!'

'I don't believe it – she's stopped the wrong one.'

A crowd of people had gathered, and the mixture of scowls and glares on their faces told Hayley that they weren't pleased to see her. She looked at the man she had brought down; it was definitely the one she saw running; what did they mean the wrong one?

Cargo Pants was still groggy on the floor, his nose bleeding a little from its impact with the ground.

'He was gaining on him as well; might have caught him if she hadn't got in the way.' The voices sounded angrier now. Cargo Pants put his hand up to his nose and saw the fresh blood on his fingers. The crowd had caught up with them now, including the old lady whose bag was snatched, supported by a couple of helpful passers-by.

Hayley had to face the facts: she had brought down the wrong suspect. 'Are you okay, sir? I saw you running and I thought...'

'It doesn't matter what you thought, does it? What matters is you stopped me from catching the thief, and now this old lady has lost her handbag.'

'Not necessarily she hasn't.' Hayley's heart sank as she recognised the voice. She looked up to see PC Amber Gould standing over her, another young man in an arm lock. 'I think this is the one you were aiming for, PC Birnham.' She turned to the old lady, extending a large handbag. 'And this is yours, I think, madam.'

'Oh, thank you, dear! I don't know what I would have done without you. Thank goodness that the boys – well, girls – in blue were on the scene.'

'One of them, at least,' sneered Cargo Pants as Hayley put away the handcuffs, her face burning. Of all the people to clean up her mistake.

'What's going on?' asked Pikey, arriving back from his loo break at just the wrong moment.

'Are you going to tell him or shall I?' said Gould, grinning. 'Hayley created a bit of a diversion while I apprehended a bag-snatcher. Sarge will be pleased with another menace to society brought to heel.'

*

While Amber took the bag-snatcher down to the station – she wasn't going to let anyone else claim her arrest – Pikey and Hayley continued their patrol of the shopping centre.

'It's easily done,' said Pikey. 'I arrested a houseowner once when responding to a reported break-in. I had him in cuffs and halfway into a squad car before he managed to explain he'd just locked himself out.'

'Really?' This was why Hayley enjoyed being partnered with Pikey. Plenty of the blokes wouldn't admit their own mistakes in a situation like this, preferring instead to make her the butt of several jokes.

'Nah, just kidding. I don't think I've ever stuffed up as badly as you just now; what were you thinking?'

'I was thinking I had to stop the bag-thief.'

'And you didn't notice that he didn't actually have, you know, a bag in his hands.'

She shrugged. 'He was running; people were screaming and pointing in his direction. It looked really suspicious.'

'Thank goodness he wasn't black – they'd have you for jumping to racist assumptions.'

'Don't – Andy would have been on my case in a heartbeat over something like that.'

'Imagine the headlines; Sarge would never let you out of the station, just have you filling in forms for the rest of your career.'

Hayley snorted. 'It's bad enough already. And, of course, it had to be the Golden Wonder who swooped in to take advantage. Sometimes I don't think I'm cut out for the job anymore.'

Pikey stopped walking and turned to look her in the eye. 'Don't talk rubbish, Hayley. In spite of what happened in the shopping centre, you're a good copper and you've got good instincts. Just get your head down and keep doing your job; Sarge will come to his senses sooner or later. Amber Gould may have the arrest figures, but I'd trust you over her to back me up any day of the week. Try not to arrest too many innocent people for the rest of the shift though.'

*

Joao was already at the pitch when James and Ben arrived at training.

'Mister James.' Joao greeted him with an enthusiastic fist-bump. Joao took the kit-bag from Ben, opened it up and pulled out the large stack of cones and got busy laying them out.

As the other boys started to arrive, some started kicking a ball around, while others joined Ben in marvelling at Joao's cone layout. Word had spread that they were going to have a new coach for this session, and nobody was quite sure what to expect.

Once Joao was ready, James called the boys over. He noticed without surprise that Max wasn't there.

'Okay lads, this is Joao. He's going to be joining us as a coach, and he's going to be leading today's session.'

'Are you still the manager?' asked Dylan

'Have you been sacked?' Josh grinned.

'You don't get rid of me that easily. I'm still picking the team every week, so it's still me you need to suck up to.'

James turned to Joao, who addressed the group for the first time.

'Hello boys. As Mister James say, I am Joao. Today we play lots of football and have lots of fun. But first, we warm up.' He pointed to the nearest group of cones. 'Get in two lines behind these red cones.' Joao led the boys through a series of stretches as they moved in sequence between the cones. With each new instruction, Joao was explaining the precise movement and making sure the boys understood what was required, correcting them as needed. Some of the boys were more graceful than others, but James was impressed with how good they looked – almost like a professional team.

'Now, we work with ball,' said Joao as the boys took on water after the warm-up. He had them in threes, each group with its own ball. One boy would dribble, keeping the ball close, then at the first line of cones kick the ball further out and accelerate away. Once they hit the second line of cones, they slowed down again before passing to a team-mate waiting opposite who repeated the process in the other direction. The boys were responding well to Joao's encouragement and James noticed a real change of pace as they hit the middle third. Joao caught James's eye and grinned. 'You see, Mister James? Lots of running, lots of fitness, but hidden with ball.'

'Okay,' he said after setting up a goal at each end when the boys took a water break after ten minutes or so. 'Now for the best part of football: scoring goals. We do shooting.' The boys cheered. 'Like before. Start at touchline, dribble to first line, then BANG – speed, speed, speed. Imagine defender at your heel: got to keep ahead. When you reach second line, ready to take your shot. Where do you aim?'

'Duh – at the goal. We know that much,' said Josh.

'Why don't you ever hit the target then, Josh?' retorted Callum, to the amusement of the others.

Joao ignored Callum and fixed his eyes on Josh. 'What part of the goal?'

'Between the posts.'

'Anyone else?'

Rory piped up, 'Away from the keeper.'

'Sim, see where keeper is and put ball beyond his reach – make him stretch.'

Joao split the boys between the two ends of the pitch and told them to fetch their ball after each shot before joining the other line. Gabe and Rory went in goal first, and as the exercise started, Joao was constantly encouraging the boys, urging them to push faster in the middle section and offering comments on technique for the shots. Every few minutes Joao switched goalkeepers, giving other boys the chance to take a breather and making sure Rory and Gabe didn't miss the fun (or the undercover fitness work). The boys laughed whenever someone hit a particularly poor shot, and voiced their approval for the better ones. James smiled to himself. They were running their socks off and enjoying it. Nobody was opting out, nobody was goofing off. Maybe Joao really did know what he was doing.

After another few minutes, Joao called the boys together and asked what was missing from the practice.

'Shots on target when Josh was shooting,' suggested Callum.

'No defenders?' offered Deepak.

'Sim! No defenders – not like real game. Now we make it more real – more good.'

Joao added a defender for each goal and set the attackers to work together to thread the ball behind him for a team-mate to run onto. The boys rotated roles so that everyone had a go at everything. James could see on the boys' faces that they were enjoying the challenge. Ben and Callum were particularly adept with the through-balls. Liam was using his pace to good effect, whether chasing through-balls or defending them. Sometimes Joao got alongside one of the boys, talking intently, at others times he stopped everyone to make a point.

The boys fell happily to their water bottles once Joao called an end to the game. 'You work hard, boys. That was good. What you want to do now? Stop there… or finish with a match?' The boys' response was unanimous and enthusiastic. Joao laughed. 'Okay. We play match. Try to play through-ball and make runs, like we work on.' Joao and James quickly consulted on how to split the teams up and gave out two sets of bibs. Joao told the boys to decide among themselves what positions everyone should play. While they were huddling, he went and put a couple of cones in each goal, one about two feet in from the post at each side.

Joao checked that each boy knew what position they were meant to be playing, and then called out, 'New rule: a goal is worth one point. A goal in the corner – between post and cone – is worth two.'

Joao must have seen James's quizzical look. 'The cones remind them to aim for corner,' he explained. 'Two points give them reason to try.'

James stood back to watch the match. The boys were playing through-balls with some success, although the defenders had got better at anticipating those passes too. Some of the shooting was better than before – Dylan was having a good night, racking up a handful of two-point goals – though Josh was as erratic as ever. When Rory asked to come out of goal, Joao made sure someone else relieved him. Rory hit a couple of well-struck efforts before the end. He was a big lad with a powerful shot, though it didn't look like he was paying much attention to aiming for the corners. Or, for that matter, aiming at all.

James said a few words at the end, and noticed some of the boys thank Joao before leaving, which Joao accepted each time with a gracious nod of his head and a fist-bump. Eventually it was just the two coaches, plus Ben.

'How did I do, Mister James?'

'That was fantastic, Joao. The boys really enjoyed it – I've never seen them do so much running without complaining. I think this is going to be a great season.'

Joao grinned. 'It a good start.'

CHAPTER FIVE

James was happy to get a lift with Lynn; the annual pre-season managers' meeting was in the smaller of the pub's two function rooms – if he didn't have to drive himself home afterwards, he could at least have a drink. Lynn checked her mirrors and negotiated the tricky junction. 'Oh, I meant to ask,' she said. 'How are things going with Joao? Rory tells me he's a hit with the boys.'

'Yeah, it's working well. We'll wait and see what difference it makes when the matches start, but he's certainly made training more fun.' It was true, Joao seemed to have a knack for genuinely enjoyable training ideas – lots of competitive point-scoring, no dull repetition, and nothing that resembled cross-country or organised torture more than football. They had a couple of new players too, Charlie and Hakim. Charlie had been at school with most of the others. He had only ever played playground kick-abouts before, but he was big, fit and keen to improve. He wasn't great technically, but he wasn't afraid of a tackle. Just as well: his first touch was so bad that every second touch seemed to be a tackle. Hakim was the son of one of James's taxi-driving colleagues. They had moved into the area recently and when Amir heard that James coached an under-twelves team, he asked if his son could join. Hakim was a nice, quiet lad with a decent turn of pace. He was much better than Charlie and certainly no worse than some of the existing Swifts. With Max leaving, that brought them up to eleven players: about right for nine-a-side. Maybe one or two more would be handy, but as long as everyone was fit and available, eleven was fine.

The Glamis room was already crowded when they arrived. James bought drinks then joined a conversation with a couple of the other managers. It was the usual stuff – how pre-season friendlies had been going, how many players were signed up – but it was good just to catch up and swap stories. James overheard Kieran boasting about the new electronic ball pump he'd treated himself to, which was able to inflate or deflate a ball at the push of a button. Typical Kieran, not only did he have to have all the best gear, he wanted everyone to know it too.

'I've got a bone to pick with you, James,' came a voice from over his shoulder. James turned to see Alison, the club welfare officer. Fortunately, her smile sent the opposite message to her words.

'Hi Alison. What's wrong?'

'I gather you've got a new assistant coach and didn't ask me to sort out his CRB clearance. This stuff matters, you know. How do we know he's safe with children?'

James's jaw fell. Of course – it was basic safeguarding, everyone working with kids had to be police-checked; he'd completely forgotten about it. Did that mean Joao would have to stop until the red tape was taken care of? He started to stammer out an apology, but Alison cut him off.

'Relax. Lynn told me and the three of us took care of everything. He shouldn't have started before we got clearance, but it's all come through now so no harm done. Just don't forget something like this again.'

'Of course, Alison. Usually I'm all over that kind of thing. I don't know why I didn't think of it. Sorry.'

'What's going on here then?' Kieran joined them. 'Has Hogan been a naughty boy?'

'Not at all,' said Alison, forcing a smile. 'We were just talking about his new assistant, Joao.'

Kieran sniggered. 'Yeah, good luck with that one. Portuguese, isn't he? Not sure he'll cope with a wet Sunday afternoon at Cole Hill. This is real football, not that tiki-taka foreign shit. How many players have you got, Hogan?'

'A couple of new ones, which makes eleven. How's Max getting on with you?'

'Max? Nah, we told him we didn't want him. He came to all three trials, and he wasn't bad, to be fair, but we had better. We've taken Redbridge's keeper, a couple from Melville Dynamos and a striker from Shelley Park Royals. My lads are working on a couple more, but the new ones are really sharp. We've got eighteen already and the competition for places will keep everyone on their toes. Max was your best player, wasn't he? I told him he wasn't good enough. What does that say about your chances with our bet?'

That was typical Kieran – all about making his team the best it could be, and no thought about the feelings of eleven-year-olds. Rob wasn't James's favourite parent, but Max didn't deserve Kieran. Alison looked like she was about to ask what this bet was all about, but Lynn called for everyone to take their seats to get started.

Once everyone was settled, Ron called the meeting to order. They rattled through the various officers' reports and then came to the main business of the meeting: the start of the new season. Ron handed over to Lynn.

'Okay, first things first, here is the league directory and handbook for everyone. All the league rules are in here and I've got one for every team in the club, plus one for each committee member. I know that most of you just shove it in your kit-bag and leave it there all year, but please try to read it at least once and keep it safe for reference. It makes my job easier if you know what you're supposed to do. Kieran, you might want to look at page twenty-seven, which details player registrations.' The rest of the managers, fully aware of the Hawks' points deduction last season, gave a playful cheer. Kieran scowled, while Lynn started running through some new rules; the changes were being trialled with the younger age groups and didn't apply to the under-twelves, so James didn't pay too much attention.

Then the managers each went through how they felt about the coming season, repeating what they had already told most of the people present, just in case they had somehow missed anyone. Kieran was full of it, as usual, boasting about his rebuilt team and saying that the ones who had left were treacherous little shits who didn't have the right character and wouldn't be missed. The 'treacherous little shits' were, of course, the same boys he had been boasting about this time last year.

Finally, Ron stood to speak again. 'As you know, I've been chairman at this club for a long time, building us into one of the best clubs in the area. After twenty years, I've decided to step down at the end of the season and let a younger man take up the reins.' He put his hand on Kieran's shoulder and carried on. 'You won't be surprised to hear that Kieran is my chosen successor. He's come through the ranks as a Stoneleigh player and coach and he's steeped in the history of the club. He's really the only choice. Lynn, can you send out an email to all the parents telling them that Kieran's taking over in the summer?'

'Actually Ron,' said Lynn, 'it's not that straightforward.' The room fell silent and everyone looked at Lynn. 'The outgoing chairman doesn't just decide who replaces him. There has to be a vote.'

'All right then, let's vote now,' bristled Ron. 'The committee is all here, let's get it settled. I propose Kieran as the next chairman.'

'It's not a committee decision, Ron. The whole club membership – all of the parents – vote at the AGM. Unless we need to find someone quickly, that is. You're not resigning now are you?'

'No I'm bloody well not! This is going to be my twentieth year as chairman, and I'm not stepping down until I've passed that milestone. But why wait until summer to confirm that Kieran is taking over? People should know what's happening.'

'Who said it's going to be Kieran?' asked Lynn, a steely look in her eye and a flicker of a smile playing around her lips. 'There might be other candidates.'

'Like who?' asked Ron, contemptuously.

'Like someone who doesn't wind up opposing managers and abuse refs; someone who will enhance our standing as a club rather than constantly get into arguments with the people who run the league.'

'Now hang on a minute,' responded Kieran. 'The best way to enhance the club's standing is by winning, and the chairman needs to stand up to those stuffed shirts at the league, like Dad does.'

'Well, that's a debate that's worth having, but now's not the time. If Ron isn't stepping down until the end of the season, we can hold a vote at the AGM. There's plenty of time for other candidates to come forward.'

*

'Alison mentioned something about a bet with Kieran. What's that all about?' It wasn't long on the car trip home before Lynn asked the question James had been dreading.

How much could he get away without telling her? 'Just a bet on which team finishes higher in the table this season, that's all. I wanted to stop him poaching our players whenever he feels like it.'

'Well, what happens if he wins?' James tried ignoring the question, but Lynn tried again. 'James? What happens if the Hawks finish above the Swifts?'

'I… I agreed we'd fold the team, let Kieran take whoever he wanted for the move up to eleven-a-side next year.'

She took her eyes off the road and glared at him. 'Seriously? And you agreed to that?'

'It was after that last committee meeting. He was goading me;

I was wound up and before I knew it I was agreeing. Watch out – you're drifting.' Lynn looked forwards again and turned the steering wheel, just in time to avoid veering into the oncoming traffic in the other lane. The honking from other drivers didn't improve her mood. 'What were you thinking?' the intensity in her voice made Roy Keane sound placid. 'You can't fold the Swifts – Rory loves playing with his mates. How could you throw that away for him and Ben and the others?'

'We've not lost the bet yet.'

'And how confident are you of finishing above Kieran? Really?' His silence was all the answer she needed. 'What did Ros say when you told her about the bet?'

'I don't know. I haven't told her yet.'

They were pulling up to James's house now. 'Well, good luck with that. I'd tell her tonight if I were you, before she hears it from someone else.'

*

Opening the front door, James could hear the television in the front room. 'Hi love, I'm home.' He poked his head round the door to find Ros in front of the telly, watching *Grand Designs*.

'Oh, hi Jamie,' called Ros in a half-distracted voice, James's arrival not yet tearing her attention away from a man laying turf on a rooftop for some reason. 'How was the meeting?'

James dropped his jacket and keys onto the arm of the sofa, dreading the conversation.

'The usual collection of idiots living out their dreams through kids. Ben and Poppy asleep yet?'

'Just about. Ben's not long since gone up; he wanted to chat for a bit. I think he's anxious about the move to secondary school. It's such a big change, it's a good job he's got the football team to give him a bit of continuity.'

Here we go. 'Yeah, about that…'

*

To say Ros took it badly would be an understatement. Apart from calling him every name under the sun and a few more besides, she had asked how he could be so reckless with their son's happiness. He knew how much the Swifts meant to Ben, how much playing football meant to him, so how could he risk all that on a ridiculous bet? Even James could hear how hollow his excuses sounded. It ended up with Ros stomping up to bed, leaving James and the sofa-bed to watch Kevin McCloud reveal the inevitable budget overspend. James changed channels, found a film that was only ten minutes or so in and settled himself in for an uncomfortable night. Ros was right, of course; the bet wasn't fair on Ben, or Rory and the other Swifts. Suddenly, there was a lot riding on how much difference Joao could make.

CHAPTER SIX

'Please, God, make it stop.'

Ros scowled at James. 'Don't let Poppy hear you saying that.'

'I know, I know, but can you hear it? Whose idea was it for her to learn the violin?' Poppy chose that moment for a particularly harsh rendition of the scale she was practising. James assumed it was meant to be a scale; either that or she had already progressed onto freeform atonal jazz.

'Well, it was you who encouraged her to learn an instrument.' Ros somehow had more tolerance for Poppy's musical terrorism than James.

'Yeah, but I meant the guitar, or the piano, something a little easier on the ear – not the bloody violin!'

'It's a lovely instrument.'

'In the hands of someone who knows what they're doing, yes; but in the hands of a beginner it's a potential war crime that should be banned by all civilised countries.'

Ros at least smiled at that. 'We mustn't discourage her. She may sound awful just now, but she loves it. Playing is the only way she'll get better.'

'Now you sound like Joao; at least you don't want Poppy to play in public yet. There'd be arrests – either us for letting her play, or the audience for what they'd do to shut her up.'

'Just you wait: she'll improve, and when she does you'll be so proud.' James knew Ros was right. Poppy's single-mindedness was legendary within the family; she attacked any new interest with absolute commitment. He loved that about his daughter, and knew it would stand her in good stead as she grew up. But that was in the future. Right now, it was hurting his ears.

Ben came into the room. He slammed the door and threw himself down in one of the chairs.

'How am I meant to do my homework with that racket in the next room?' James suspected that even without the violin, Ben would have another excuse for not doing his homework – definitely his least favourite part about moving to secondary school. He was a bright lad, but hardly the most motivated of students. Realistically, James knew there was plenty of time for Ben to get his academic mojo working, that right now the most important thing was him getting settled, finding a good bunch of mates and starting to feel a bit more secure in his new environment. Ben was gradually starting to mention new names when he talked about school, but it was still Gabe and Liam who cropped up the most.

'Would you rather work down here, lovely?' asked Ros. 'You can still hear Poppy, but it won't be quite so loud.' On cue, a particularly jarring note assaulted their ears, inducing a synchronised wince from all three.

'I'm not sure it will make much difference, Mum. How much longer is she going to be making that racket?'

'Several years,' said James.

'Her violin teacher says she's supposed to do at least fifteen minutes practice every day,' said Ros. 'You know Poppy; she won't stop until she's done the time, and even then she'll want to keep going.'

'How long has she been going – it's been more than fifteen minutes, surely?'

Ros checked her watch. 'No, less than five. I know what you mean though: it feels like a couple of hours. Put up with it for ten minutes more and I'll go and have a word with her, I'll tell her you need peace and quiet while you do your homework.'

'Any chance you could string out that homework, son?' asked James. 'Take one for the team and save the rest of us from violinaggedon?'

Ben grinned. 'Not a chance. But for a fiver, I'll hide the violin once she's asleep.'

James knew he should be encouraging Poppy in her musical endeavours, but he was sorely tempted by Ben's offer.

*

After a couple of pre-season friendlies, Joao had lots of stuff to work on. They spent some time on defensive basics – body shape, jockeying and not diving in, that kind of thing. The boys worked hard, and James could see signs of progress. Charlie wasn't afraid to get stuck in, but his lack of timing and technique meant that there was always the danger of him injuring someone. Joao spent a lot of time helping Charlie to sort that out.

They even got a twelfth player joining – or rather rejoining – the squad. A week or so before the season started, Max had turned up again, telling the other boys how the Hawks had wanted him, but he had decided to stay with the Swifts after all. Lynn later told James that after Kieran's rejection, Rob had apparently tried to get Max into some other teams – Redbridge Town (who had been relegated along with the Hawks), Cole Hill, and Shelley Abbey Royals – but by then everyone good was full up. Never mind, James was happy to have Max back; he'd add some bite to the midfield.

The fixture list had been kind; Swifts started with an away game at Linford Rovers, another team who never expected to find themselves in the top half of the table. It would be great if they could start the season with a win. Mac had always said it was important for the coaches to keep a sense of perspective, not get too worried about results. But the problem with not worrying about results was, well, people worried about results. To be honest, that mostly came from dads like Rob, constantly grumbling at anything less than victory. Some of the boys absorbed that message, leading to heads dropping if things went badly. Over the years James had tried balancing a strong spine of the team with still giving everyone the chance to play. But things were different now: he absolutely had to find a way to finish above the Hawks, which brought him to his first tricky decision of the season. If he was picking his strongest nine, that definitely included Max, but what message would that send to the boys who had stayed loyal all summer? In the end, James decided to leave Max on the bench – he rolled subs on and off regularly, so they wouldn't be without him for long.

The Swifts usually played a three-four-one formation, so who should take Max's spot as a central midfielder? Callum was skilful but lazy, while Deepak was industrious but more limited in ability. Combine the best elements of both and you'd have a great player, so why not try them together? With that settled, the rest of the team fell quickly into place. Playing Josh up front allowed Dylan and Liam to be the two wide midfielders. Gabe was a no-brainer at the heart of the defence, and Hakim had done well enough in training to deserve to start alongside him. Ben could slot in as the third defender: he had a good eye for a pass, which would fit in with the way Joao was trying to get them to play, just as long as he wasn't having one of those days where he was afraid to make a tackle. That left Max and Ryan on the bench… and Charlie, of course. Charlie had struggled in the pre-season friendlies, although Joao was keen to give him plenty of game time ('But Mister James, how will he improve if he not play?'). James could see his point but… no, not this week. The next game was against Weston Park, a team who had just joined the league. Maybe that would be a better starting point for Charlie, particularly coming into a confident, winning team. James knew that Joao wouldn't agree, but he was the manager; it was his call. Just the two subs, Max and Ryan. Charlie would have to wait.

James posted the line-up to the parents' WhatsApp group, along with the match details. He got the usual thumbs ups and thanks from people, although notably nothing from Rob. As James went about his taxi work, collecting old ladies with their shopping, ferrying people to and from the train station, he found that his mind kept drifting back to the coming game. Since he'd given up on teaching – or rather, since teaching had closed the door on him – he found that the Swifts occupied much more of his head space through the week. When he'd been teaching there was so much else to think about that football didn't dominate his week in the same way. Thinking back to his teaching days, those moments when a class – or even just one pupil – caught a sense of wonder, when everything clicked, had made the job worthwhile. He missed that now, but as good as it was, it wasn't worth the aggravation from the likes of Kyle.

You got a Kyle in every school. He would saunter into the classroom like a falcon, towering in pride of place. The other kids paid him plenty of deference, but Kyle seemed to think that the teachers should too. James had run through all his go-to strategies, but Kyle seemed particularly resistant. He just didn't see the point of English and he didn't see the point of Mr Hogan. Somehow Kyle took being difficult to a new level. As for the incident that had brought the whole thing tumbling down – well, the less said about that, the better.

James remembered the first time Kyle had come to his attention. It wasn't their first lesson together, but up until this point Kyle had just been another student in a less-than-enthusiastic year ten group. James had set them close reading of a chapter from *Doctor Jekyll and Mr Hyde*, looking for hints to indicate Jekyll's dual nature. Most of the class were getting on with it, a few were chatting behind their books, but Kyle was just sitting in his place, staring ahead of him. James realised that Kyle was looking straight at him. He walked across the front of the classroom, surreptitiously checking to see what Kyle did. As he had suspected, Kyle's eyes were following him. James briefly allowed his eyes to meet Kyle's full-on and confirm what he suspected. Kyle didn't look away, didn't even flinch. He was trying to stare James out.

There were two options: engage or bypass. If he engaged, there was every chance it would lead to a humiliating climb-down. He had the feeling that Kyle would go all the way if this became a two-sided contest. He wasn't going to give Kyle equal authority in his classroom by joining in his game. James briefly raised his eyebrows in a disdainful show of surprise, then turned away and got on with working his way around the classroom, helping the students who actually wanted to learn something. After a couple of minutes, with Kyle's glare still following him around the room, James walked up to Kyle's seat and crouched down next to him.

'Now look, Kyle,' he said quietly, 'it's entirely up to you; you can get your eyes back on *Jekyll and Hyde* and get on with your work, or you can carry on as you are. If I don't see evidence that you've made reasonable progress in the next ten minutes, I'll put you on report.' Kyle didn't respond immediately, but James ignored him and got on with the lesson. He moved around, helping the others while studiously avoiding Kyle, but making sure to clock him with his peripheral vision from time to time. After a while, he saw that Kyle had returned his gaze to the pages and was writing, albeit only occasionally, in his exercise book. James didn't want to make a big thing about it, but he knew he had won this round. Even then, he had the feeling that it wouldn't always be so simple.

*

Matchday arrived, and even though James hadn't come off shift until around midnight the night before, he was eager to get going. Ben was up and already in his kit when James came down for breakfast. James smiled to see Ben's enthusiasm – there was still another hour before they had to leave.

James had arranged to pick Joao up and give him a lift – Linford Road's car park was notoriously small, so it made sense to keep the number of cars to a minimum. The young Portuguese was waiting outside his front door as James pulled up, grinning broadly once he recognised his lift and exchanging fist-bumps as he clambered into the car.

'Ola, Mister James. Ola, Ben. This Linford Rovers we play – what they like?'

'It's a good game to start with – definitely winnable.'

'Yeah,' piped up Ben from the back seat. 'They're even worse than we are!'

Joao tutted with good humour. 'You not a bad team. Lot of... what is word? Lot of potential.'

James saw Ben's shoulders sag. 'Some of the lads – Liam and Max, maybe – but not me. I'm rubbish.'

Joao turned round in his seat to look straight at Ben. 'Don't say that. I have seen you play; you are good: good touch, good eye for pass, good attitude. You a good player. You show me today – you a good player.'

Ben didn't say much, but in the mirror James could see a quiet smile playing about his mouth as he let Joao's words soak in.

*

Eventually the time came and James was standing on the pitch with the Swifts all around him.

'A new season, lads, and everything to play for. As Alexander Pope said, "Hope springs eternal in the human breast".' Some of the boys giggled because he'd said breast, while Ryan asked who Alexander Pope was, prompting James's response that he played in goal for Newcastle. 'There's no reason we can't make a winning start, just remember what we've been working on in training.' He'd been tempted to give them a different Pope quote, the one about it being better to hope for nothing so that you're never disappointed, but that didn't really strike the right tone. The boys looked eager as they trotted onto the pitch; time would tell whether that would be enough.

'Clear it, Gabe! Put your laces through it!' called James as his centre-back hoofed the ball out for a throw-in. 'Mark up! Callum, get on the eight – goalside! Get goalside!' The ball was thrown down the line, the winger jinked easily around Ben and pulled the ball back to – surprise, surprise – the number eight, who had plenty of time as Callum jogged back with no discernible urgency. The shot was low and hard, and it took a good diving save from Rory to keep it out.

'That was your man, Callum! You have to defend as well as attack.'

Joao's verbal contributions were a little different to James's.

'Great tackle, Hakim. Can you find a pass?'

'Gabe, head up; look and see.'

'Nearly, Dylan; worth a try.'

In truth, it was an entertaining game. Both sides (Callum notwithstanding) were high on effort and low on moments of quality, but play swung from end to end. Rory was by far the busier goalkeeper, and on the occasions that a Swifts move didn't break down before reaching Josh, the striker was having a wasteful day in front of goal. As James was contemplating his first substitutions, Callum received the ball in midfield, spun past the number eight and sprayed a beautiful pass over the full-back's head for Liam to run onto. He easily outpaced his man, looked up and picked out a pass to Josh, arriving on the edge of the six-yard box. Not even Josh could miss the target from that range, surely? Apparently, he could; the ball flew over the bar and Josh threw his head back in frustration.

'Argggh, Josh: no!' shouted James.

'Nearly Josh, get the next one,' added Joao. 'Great passing Callum, Liam.'

James had been thinking of taking Callum off, but that pass convinced him to bring Max on for Deepak instead. Josh came off too, with Ryan going on the wing and Dylan taking Josh's place up front.

'Well done you two,' he said as they trotted off. Deepak seemed okay but Josh still looked sheepish after his miss. James turned his attention back to the match while Joao spent a few moments talking with each boy in turn.

Max made a difference straight away. His approach to midfield play was to chase everything down. Against the better teams he could be given the runaround, but with the likes of Linford Road he could really dominate a game. Almost at once, he started to assert himself. Max exchanged passes with Ryan before feeding Callum, who threaded a perfect through-ball to Dylan, putting him one-on-one with the keeper. Dylan took it closer and then fired it low and hard into the far corner of the net, just like in Joao's first training session. One-nil.

That goal spurred Linford Road on, and they spent the next ten minutes camped out in the Swifts' half. The Swifts defended well, but just as James saw the ref checking his watch, Ben ducked out of a challenge and let his opponent past him. A swift exchange of passes left Gabe and Hakim out of the game and, all too quickly, Rory was picking the ball out of the net. One-one.

'Save it then, you muppet!' stormed Dylan at Rory.

Max was also looking to allocate blame. 'You know that one's your fault, don't you, Ben? Try putting a tackle in.'

The Swifts survived several scares in the second half. James lost count of the times he shouted 'Get rid of it'. Joao never joined him in that, instead encouraging the boys to find a pass in all but the most extreme situations. With only minutes remaining, Ryan dived hastily into a challenge, and once again Rory was faced with a one-on-one. This time he sprang out of his goal to dive at the striker's feet, smothering the ball as the player tumbled over him. The Linford players appealed for a penalty.

'He took the ball, nothing wrong with that. Play on,' barked the ref. Rory got to his feet and looked up before kicking long. The ball hurtled over the heads of the Linford Road defence and into space for the scampering feet of Liam to run onto. Liam got control of the ball on the corner of the penalty box and cut inside. The keeper tried to emulate Rory and dive at his feet, but Liam slipped the ball sideways just before the keeper collided with him. Josh had made up the ground and had the open goal at his mercy. James held his breath. This could be it: the winning goal, the winning start; if only it was any player other than Josh. Judging by the explosion of relief from the Swifts' parents when the ball was tucked safely in, he hadn't been the only one to have those thoughts.

'Focus, lads,' shouted James. 'It's not over yet.' But it was. Linford Road didn't have the heart to mount another comeback. James contained his excitement while he went to shake hands with the ref and the Linford Road manager (who were engaged in a lively discussion about Rory's last challenge), then he went to debrief the boys.

'Fantastic result, lads. You really deserved that today. Well done for battling through. Great character, coming back from their equaliser.'

As he started gathering up the equipment, James heard a voice over his shoulder. 'You got away with that one, didn't you, James?' It was Rob, of course. 'Why wasn't Max on from the start? The game turned as soon as he came on.'

'Yeah, he played well. I just thought starting him would send the wrong message to the boys who had stayed with us all summer without looking for a better option.'

James surprised himself with how bluntly that came out, and he braced himself, expecting Rob to give him a mouthful back. There was a brief pause as Rob gathered himself before replying.

'It would have given them the message that they need to be better at playing football. Still, I guess you've learned your lesson, the way he played. Come on, son, let's get you home.'

As Rob and Max headed across the pitch, James turned to Joao. 'Not a bad start, eh, Joao?'

'Not bad, but lots to work on. Linford Road were, what is your English word?'

'Rubbish?'

Joao smiled again and shrugged. 'There will be better sides to come, no? We must improve this much,' he held his hands way apart, 'to keep winning.'

James agreed. 'It's a good job I've got a great new coach to bring the boys on, isn't it? Anyway, we're playing a new team to the league next week, so hopefully they won't have had the chance to work out what they're doing yet.'

Later that evening, James was checking online for the other results. It looked like Kieran's assessment of the standard of this division might be accurate; his Hawks had enjoyed a five-two victory against a good Cole Hill side. Redbridge Town, unsurprisingly, beat Eastside Diamonds six-one, while the most noticeable result was new boys Weston Park versus regular table propper-uppers Moorlands Rangers. Weston Park had scored fourteen goals without reply. Maybe they did know what they were doing after all.

CHAPTER SEVEN

Hayley smiled as she glanced in the rear-view mirror. Jayden could barely sit still, he was that excited.

'Do you think we're going to win, Mum?' He barely paused for an answer, carrying on before Hayley could even open her mouth. 'Flynn says we're going to walk this league, so that means we should win today, right?'

'Didn't Flynn also say England were going to win the World Cup, that he was going out with a model and that he was European under-fourteens darts champion? You know better than to believe everything Flynn says.'

'That was years ago. Anyway, Flynn says the second-division teams are all rubbish.' He paused for a moment before adding, 'I really want to win today, on my debut.'

Bless him, on his debut. He had all the terminology down pat. Despite what she said to Andy, she wasn't entirely convinced that the football team was such a good idea, but Jayden was insistent. She'd heard stories about kids' football managers ranting and raving on the touchline, which really wasn't what Jayden needed from a male authority figure right now. Other mums had said those stories must be exaggerated, but Hayley's job had taught her not to underestimate just how awful some people were capable of being. Still, Matt had seemed all right when she took Jayden to his first Redbridge training session, and the other parents seemed happy with him.

'Matt says I'm starting as a sub, but if we're doing okay he'll try to get me on in the second half. I've got to earn my place in the team.' He sounded so earnest as he parroted the last phrase. That nagging sensation pulsed in her stomach; she was desperate for today to go well for him.

An hour later, Hayley was on the touchline with the other parents. The dads were shouting their guidance, with lots of footballing jargon that left her bemused. What did 'Line it' mean when it was at home? Some of the mums had settled into little groups, chatting happily and paying the game only partial attention, while others were as invested and animated as the dads. Hayley had exchanged pleasantries with a couple of the others, but she was more focused on the far touchline. Jayden was still waiting for his big moment. The team was five-one up – she thought so, anyway – but there was no sign of Matt calling on his newest recruit.

'How long to go?' she asked Flynn's mum, one of the chatterers.

'Just over ten minutes I think.'

Hayley was reflecting on how ridiculous it was to have dragged her and Jayden out on a Sunday morning for no reason, when she saw Matt move over to talk to Jayden and the other subs. Even across the field she could see the expression on his little face change; he jumped to his feet and started some warming up exercises. Did this mean he was going to get his chance?

Yes. A couple of minutes later the ball was lumped off the pitch and while an opposition player ran to fetch it, Matt shouted to the referee, made a twirly motion with his hands and sent the débutant scampering on. Jayden took up a position near the far touchline (left mid, as one of the dads knowingly informed her, mistakenly thinking she'd know what he was talking about). She just hoped that the fact he was so close to Matt wasn't to make it easier to get him off again. For the next few minutes Jayden hurried and scurried about, with the ball pinging around and never quite going where he had positioned himself. He got a few touches, mostly scrappy, although one intervention drew a comment of 'Good tackle' from a nearby dad. His team let in a couple of late goals, but then scored another themselves. Jayden didn't seem to play any part in the goal as far as Hayley could tell, but he leapt around excitedly with the other boys as they celebrated. When the final whistle went, Hayley joined in the applause, enjoying the sense of relief washing over her. He had played. His team had won and he had been part of it, albeit only for ten minutes. The match was the only topic of conversation in the car going home, with Jayden asking repeatedly if she saw him do the tackle, or the pass he played to Seb, or how he was marking their winger. She said yes, although to be honest she didn't even understand some of the questions. But that didn't matter; Jayden was happy, which was what she wanted more than anything.

*

Jayden wasn't happy the next morning though, and it was all Hayley could do to get him out of the door and off to school without completely losing it.

'What do you mean you can't find your school trousers? I put a load of clean washing in your room at the weekend.'

'Well, I can't see them. You must have put them somewhere else.'

'Jayden, is this going to be another of those times when I walk into your room, move something and find the thing you swear blind isn't there?'

'No! I've told you, they're not here.' Hayley was up the stairs by now, and she strode into his room. He was sat on his bed, still in his pyjamas and eyes glued to his phone. No wonder he couldn't see his clothes anywhere. Hayley looked to his wardrobe, and the pile of clothes she had left there the previous day. Sure enough, the pile was still there, albeit partially covered by a couple of discarded football magazines.

Jayden shrugged. 'They weren't there a minute ago.'

Hayley glanced at her watch: she was already cutting it fine to get into work before the start-of-shift briefing.

A couple of hours later and Hayley's day hadn't improved. Her attempts at slipping unobtrusively into the back of the briefing had been unsuccessful, laying her open to a full dose of Sergeant McGlashan's sarcasm, and a reminder that she now had to provide cake for everyone as a result. She was sure he'd deliberately given her the most mundane, boring and pointless tasks as a direct result, although to be fair, she was never high on his list for the more exciting call-outs. While some of her colleagues were visiting a local jeweller's that had been turned over, or even assisting as backup on a raid to arrest a suspected drug dealer, she was on her way to AbaCabs to follow up a complaint that their drivers had been taking walk-up passengers rather than sticking to pre-booked fares. The local black cabbies were kicking up a fuss, and the Sarge wanted a visit from uniform to remind everyone to stay in their respective lanes.

Hayley paused outside the offices of AbaCabs and peered through the window. Looking past the brightly coloured lettering that covered most of the surface, she could see cheap plastic chairs and a desk at the far end of the room. There didn't seem to be anyone in the waiting area, but maybe someone was out of sight behind the counter.

'Good morning, is anyone working?' she called as she stepped into the room.

'One minute,' came the reply. 'Be right with you, darling.'

Hayley gritted her teeth, as a middle-aged Asian man moved into sight. 'Right then, how can I... oh, I'm sorry officer, I thought you were a customer. Is something wrong?'

'You tell me, sir. I'm looking for the manager,' she checked her notebook, 'a Mister Raj Anand. Would that be you?'

'Yes, yes, officer, that's me. Rajesh Anand at your service. How can I help you?' He was smiling, but it looked a bit forced to Hayley; his eyes were unnaturally wide, and he was shifting his weight from one foot to the other. It could be a guilty conscience, but just as easily a natural reaction to the unexpected visit from uniform.

'We've received a complaint from a member of the public, Mr Anand. Apparently, your drivers have been accepting walk-up passengers, plying for hire at the kerbside. Would you know anything about that?'

'No, no, no, nothing at all. I mean, some private-hire companies do that, but we make it very clear to our drivers we can only take pre-booked customers. They all know they'd be breaking the law if they picked someone up without a booking.'

'So you're telling me that none of your drivers would ever do that?'

Mr Anand frowned. 'I'm telling you that I tell them not to. I'm not saying that none of them have ever done it behind my back, but they all know they'll lose their jobs if I find out about it. Why, who's been complaining?' His eyes had narrowed again now.

'I can't tell you that, sir. Suffice to say we've received a complaint.'

'Is it one of the black-cab guys, accusing us of stealing their customers again?' He looked accusingly at Hayley and she kept her expression as blank as possible. 'I'm not saying my guys are angels, but some of the cabbies aren't above lying to get us in trouble.'

'I can't comment on that, Mr Anand.'

'No, of course you can't. But you decided to believe what the cabbies are telling you and came here to lean on us all the same.'

'Look, if you're right and this is just cabbies making trouble, you've nothing to worry about. But if we catch any of your drivers on the take, please know that we'll take it seriously.'

As she walked away Hayley thought back to how excited she had been when she first qualified as a PC. Like most newbies, she had dreamed of making the streets safer, making a real difference in her community. She still wanted that, but she was a bit more realistic about what was possible these days. Her idealism had been eroded by the daily, repetitive grind of meaningless trivia like taxi disputes or the seemingly unending tide of crime – proper crime – that went unsolved. Each day was simultaneously a new way of letting her down and the same disappointment as ever. It was like walking an endless tightrope with no prospect of reaching the other side. If she was going to make a difference, she had to find a way to get herself assigned to some real crimes rather than taxi disputes and traffic detail.

*

The Swifts were buoyant when they arrived for training on Wednesday. Dylan and Josh were full of their goals, which – if the scorers were to be believed – had been more spectacular than James remembered. Rory's heroics in goal were mentioned (mostly by Rory) and even the usually modest Liam pointed out that he had provided the assist for both goals.

Eventually, James called everyone together to make a start. James and Joao had agreed after hearing the Weston Park result that it was worth spending another week on defending. Before Joao got them started, he said he wanted to talk about something.

'Sunday, we win the game – that good.' A cheery murmur of agreement rippled around the grinning group of boys. 'But there were things I see that were not good. Things that can break a team.' James hadn't been expecting this. Where was Joao going? Why would he want to pour cold water on a winning start?

'When other team scored, we did not react as a team. Players blaming each other for the goal. "You did that; you didn't do this". No. Is wrong. We a team: we win as a team and we lose as a

54

team. When mistake happens, we don't point finger, we support each other. That doesn't mean mistakes don't matter – we learn from mistakes, learn not to keep making them – but turn on one another? No. Not ever. You a team, so act like team. Okay?'

James could see different reactions on the boys' faces. Some of them – the regular targets for their team-mates' ire – seemed happy with what Joao had said. Some of the more vocal ones looked chastened, which boded well, while others were harder to read. James made a mental note to keep an eye on how those boys in particular reacted in future games.

Next, Joao paired the boys up and got them trying to dribble past their partners. Joao focused his input on the defenders' body shape and timing, with James following his lead. There was a constant buzz with everyone trying to get one over on their partner. Joao moved on to how the defence works as a unit, reacting to the movement of opposition forwards as well as each other. That part wasn't as much fun as the one-on-one stuff, but the boys looked a lot better organised in the end-of-session match. James noticed that while Charlie was working as hard as anyone else, he was still a long way behind the others. If Weston Park were as good as they seemed to be, maybe this was another game that wasn't right to throw him into. What was the point of shattering his confidence before he'd even started to build it up?

CHAPTER EIGHT

The grim faces of the three Hogans in the front room could mean only one thing: Poppy was practising the violin again.

'Remind me again why we agreed to this,' muttered James. 'It sounds like someone scraping a cat's guts against the strings.'

'You know that catgut is literally what old violin bows used to be made with, right?' retorted Ros.

'Yeah, but she sounds like she's doing it while the cat is still alive.' Ben smirked at that one, though Ros gave James a reproachful look.

'She *is* getting better.'

'Okay, so she's progressed from sounding like an audible war crime to sounding like a nightmare sequence on a low-budget horror movie.'

'Ben,' said Ros, changing the subject. 'How's school going?'

'The usual. Mostly boring apart from when Robin starts games in lessons.'

'Games in lessons?' James and Ros exchanged confused looks. 'Like what?'

'Like playing "It". We do that in French – Miss Finch hasn't got a clue.'

James was fascinated. 'Doesn't she notice all the ducking and dodging?'

'That's the thing, you're not allowed to dodge – you lose a point if you get found out. If someone gets to you, you just have to take it and try to pass it on to someone else later. If the teacher catches you playing the game, you lose a point.'

'And how often do people get caught? I'd like to think I'd quickly spot something like that happening in my classroom.'

'You'd be surprised – dropped pencils, asking to borrow stuff, Miss Finch accepts most excuses. The other day she even gave Robin an achievement point for being helpful – he offered to hand out the textbooks for her, then tagged Gabe while he did it.'

'And what about you?' asked Ros. 'How far have you gone to tag someone?'

'Oh, I don't take any risks. I just pass it on to someone sitting within reach. But watching what Robin and some of the others get up to passes the time.'

'Shouldn't you be passing the time by, I don't know, learning French?'

Ben just shrugged. James was torn. Part of him knew he should want Ben to be more focused on lessons, but another part wished that Ben had the confidence of this Robin lad. Most of all, he was just glad it wasn't him who had to deal with antics like that in the classroom anymore.

*

Matchday arrived, the first home game of the season. When James and Ben got to the equipment locker they found that Dave, as ever, had everything sorted. James was gathering his goal nets, corner flags and Respect Line markers when Dave appeared from around the corner, his battered Notts County cap shielding his eyes from the sun.

'Morning James, a good win last week I see.'

'Hi Dave. Yeah, nice to be up and running. Expecting a tougher one today though. Many games on?'

'A few. The Hawks and the under-elevens are both away so you can have either of the nine-a-side pitches. The under-sevens have just kicked off; they were at home last week too. They lost six-five, but you'd have thought they'd won by their faces when they came off. Danny seems to be doing all right with them.' Danny Peters was a young lad, in his mid-twenties, who had played for the club ten or so years ago. Unlike most of the managers, he didn't have any kids of his own in his team but he'd recently had to give up playing men's football due to an injury. Volunteering with Stoneleigh was his way of staying involved in the game. James said that he'd try to watch a few minutes of their game once the nets were up.

While they were talking, Joao arrived. He helped James and Ben to carry everything across. Ben went to the supporters' touchline to set up the Respect Line markers while James and Joao got to work on the nets. It didn't take long for Joao to ask the question James had been expecting.

'Mister James, why did you leave Charlie out again?'

'You saw him at training. He's trying hard but he's just not good enough. How could I throw him in against a team who scored fourteen goals last week? He's not ready.'

'But if he doesn't play, how will he ever be ready?'

'Okay, okay, I take the point. Next time, I promise I'll put him in the squad. Anyway, let's focus on today; I think it's going to be a tough one.'

That was an understatement. Weston Park were, quite simply, the best kids' team James had seen. They were all comfortable on the ball, bringing it effortlessly under control with a single touch. The goalkeeper never kicked long, always looking to throw or roll the ball out, with defenders well-drilled in pulling wide to provide passing options as soon as the ball went back to the keeper. James was constantly barking instructions to his players, desperately trying to stem the flood of passes that threatened to wash them off the pitch. By contrast, the Weston Park manager wasn't ranting and raving, simply asking his players questions as the game progressed: 'Can we play?', 'Where's the pivot?', 'Can we create space?' James knew that the Swifts had touched the ball – they kicked off, for one thing – but he couldn't remember many instances of them enjoying possession for more than a few seconds at a time.

Actually, they kicked off a lot, as they were four-nil down by half-time. In fairness, the work Joao had done on their defensive shape seemed to have done some good, and Weston Park had to work to break them down. Max was getting frustrated – his usual ball-chasing wasn't working, and the Weston players had all the time in the world to move the ball on to the next man before he even got close. Max was guilty of leaving a foot in after a challenge more than once. Josh, starved of the ball up front, was drifting deeper and deeper until the Swifts' formation was more of a three-five-zero. James could see that the scoreline was getting to some of his players. Callum seemed to have stopped bothering altogether, while Dylan was getting more and more volatile, ranting at his team-mates for any shortcomings.

'Dylan – remember: we a team,' called Joao more than once.

At half-time, James took Callum off and replaced him with Deepak. Callum reacted badly.

'Fine, but what's the point even being out on the same pitch as that lot? They're like an academy team or something. It's a waste of time us playing against them.'

'If you feel like that, Callum, you don't have to go back on,' snapped James. 'Have a think about it and let me know what you want to do, but I don't want you on that pitch unless you're going to put in a lot more effort than you did in the first half.'

Five minutes into the second half, James was forced into another change. Dylan was losing the uneven battle with his temper. When a Weston player jinked past him on the left wing, Dylan lashed out with a dreadful challenge. His victim picked himself up gingerly, with no apparent harm done, but it could easily have been much worse. James exchanged glances with Ed the ref, Gabe's dad, and he knew immediately what he had to do.

'Sub please, ref,' he shouted. 'Dylan, off you come, mate.' Dylan's eyes were smouldering as he stomped off, fists clenched. He was breathing so hard that James thought he might be hyperventilating. James took him to one side. 'Look, I get it, we're being thrashed, but that's no reason to take it out on the other team. Do you think that lad's parents want to see their son taken out like that? Go and calm yourself down. I'll put you back on later if I think you can handle it, but it's not fair on anyone – least of all you – to send you back out there in this state.' James could see Dylan wasn't far from the point of tears, so he turned back to the game to give him some space. Dylan wasn't a bad lad, but when things went against him he struggled. This wasn't the first time he had needed to cool off in the middle of a game, and James suspected it wouldn't be the last.

With Callum showing no interest in getting back out there, that left James with just the nine on the pitch and no prospect of reinforcements. Ben had taken Dylan's place on the left wing – this wasn't the game to risk his lack of tackling in defence – and was actually playing some nice passes on the rare occasions that the Swifts had the ball to pass. It was him and Liam who looked the most effective going forward for the Swifts, but even that was only relative. Mostly it was one-way traffic and it was a mercy when Ed blew the final whistle (a couple of minutes early by James's watch, but at nine-nil down they had hardly been denied a late comeback).

'Well played,' said James to the Weston manager as they shook hands at the end. 'That was a footballing masterclass. How long have you had this lot together?'

'A few years. We've been playing in the County league, but to be honest there wasn't enough competition. We heard the Town league was stronger so we decided to move over and give it a go. We wanted to go straight into the top division but they said we had to start at the bottom and work our way up.'

'Based on that performance, I don't think it'll take you long. Mind you, there are plenty of teams in this division who are better than us and Moorlands, so hopefully you'll get some more challenging games this season.'

'Thanks. Your keeper's good, isn't he? And I liked the way your number six played – he's got a good eye for a pass.' Number six was Ben. James grinned. 'Thanks. I'll tell him you said that.'

As he walked back to the Swifts, who were sat on the ground with their heads hung low, James wondered what he was going to say to them. What was there to say?

'Well, we tried. Don't be too hard on yourselves. Sometimes you just come across a better side, and to be honest I wouldn't be surprised if no one in this league manages to get a point against them all season. All I ask in a game like that is that you keep going, even when the scoreline means the game is already lost. Keep playing like the next goal will change things. Even if it's a lost cause, I don't want to see people giving up. Do you want to add anything, Joao?'

'Sim, today was hard, but I saw positives. Rory in goal, making save after save. The defence was good.' Joao saw the expressions on the boys' faces and smiled. 'Okay, it funny to say that after we let in so many goal, but you kept your shape, you reacted to one another, you moved and covered: all good. Sometimes, like Mister James say, it not enough because the other team better. That okay. If we defend like that against most teams, we get result.'

James was about to let the lads go, when Dylan piped up. 'I just wanted to say sorry,' he mumbled. 'I got mad and I let the rest of you down. Sorry, guys.' The boys told him not to worry about it but Dylan's face said it didn't make him feel any better. James glanced across at Callum to see if he had anything to add, but Callum was staring at the ground, studiously avoiding eye contact with everyone.

James and Joao went to unhook the goal nets. 'Well done, Joao. I was struggling to find something positive to say about that one.'

'There always something positive, Mister James. Sometime it tiny, but it always there. After a game like that a...' he paused, searching for the word, '...a drubbing?' James nodded a confirmation and Joao carried on, 'it important to give the boys something good to hold on to.'

James sighed. 'Yeah, you're right. It's just not always easy to find it.'

As they made their way over to the equipment lock-up, James saw Danny Peters coming towards them. He introduced Danny and Joao and asked how the under-sevens had got on.

'Great. They're loving every minute of it. We still haven't won a game – lost five-two today – but they just want to play football with their mates and enjoy themselves. I mean, they don't like losing – who does? – but five minutes after the final whistle, they're jumping around and kicking balls to each other without a care in the world. I'm trying not to get too focused on results myself, but it's hard, isn't it? I stayed around to watch your game after ours had finished. How many teams like that do you get at your level?' James admitted that Weston Park were comfortably the best he'd seen, and that gave him the crumb of comfort he'd been looking for: at least there was one team in this division who the Hawks wouldn't just roll over. With Weston Park a shoo-in for one of the promotion places, it only needed one other team to finish above the Hawks to seriously put Keiran's nose out of joint. It was just a shame it wasn't likely to be the Swifts.

*

James was working a late shift the following evening, and after the annihilation his Swifts had endured at the hands of Weston Park, he wasn't in a chatty mood. He had been okay immediately after the match, but as the day went on he found himself increasingly brooding about the game. He kept telling himself that Weston were in the wrong division, that he shouldn't take the result to heart, yet it just demonstrated how hopeless it was to expect his Swifts to compete. James found himself being surly and snappish with the customers, or just opting out of interaction altogether. Unsurprisingly, it wasn't a good night for tips. He was also worrying about the boys' fragile confidence being snuffed out by the humiliation. He thought again about Callum's reaction and wondered what he could do to help him change his attitude.

James's mood wasn't improved by the knowledge of what was waiting for him later in the week. Tuesday night was another committee meeting.

CHAPTER NINE

When James arrived at the pub, the first face he saw was Kieran, who didn't take long to bring up the Hawks' latest result, an eight-nil win against Eastside Diamonds.

'Another three points last weekend, second in the league now. We might have been top if you hadn't boosted Weston Park's goal difference so much. What happened?'

James tried to shrug it off. 'Beaten by the better team. Weston Park are really good.'

'We'll see about that. We play them ourselves next month; that'll put them in their place. No offence, but my boys will give them a better test than you or Moorlands.' James clenched his teeth, frustrated at having to take this, even though he had said much the same himself. It felt a bit disloyal to the club, but he really hoped Weston could beat the Hawks.

There wasn't a lot to discuss at the committee meeting. Howard was happy with the finances and Alison was chasing up a few volunteer refs whose CRBs hadn't been organised yet. Then Kieran rattled through a summary of the various teams.

'Yeah, it's mostly good. Tony's under-fifteens are off to a great start, two wins out of two in the top division. He thinks they might finally win the title this year. Nick's under-thirteens have got four points out of six and should do well. My Hawks, of course are a hundred per cent and even the Swifts have somehow got a win. Mind you, the less said about this weekend the better, eh Hogan? How many was it that you shipped? I'm glad I didn't take your keeper now. The younger teams are a mixed bunch, but one or two promising sides. I'm a bit worried about the under-sevens. So far they've played two and lost two. I'm not sure Danny Peters is the right man to be looking after them.'

Lynn interjected. 'It's not all about winning, Kieran.'

Kieran just smiled. 'Yeah, whatever, love. It's football – what else is it about? Let's see how he does over the next few weeks and we can find someone to take over if results don't improve.'

'I spoke to Danny on Sunday,' added James. 'He said the boys are really enjoying themselves, in spite of the results.'

'So what? They've got no right to enjoy themselves if they keep getting beat. Did your lot enjoy letting in nine goals? I'm not going to be chairman of a club with rubbish teams who just make the others look good.'

'You might not be chairman at all, Kieran,' said Alison pointedly.

Ron interjected before Kieran could respond. 'Of course he will be; I've been getting him ready to take over for years. Anyway, who else is going to do it? Now, let's get this meeting wrapped up – I want to be home in time for the second half of the Chelsea game.' James toyed with introducing lots of new business just to make the Butchers miss their beloved Chelsea, but on balance he preferred being rid of them sooner. Once the meeting had finished and the Butchers had gone, James stayed for another drink with Lynn and Alison.

'We must find another option for chairman,' Alison was saying. 'Kieran doesn't care about the kids' well-being, or if they are enjoying themselves; it's all about satisfying his need to win. Even if you accept his idea that the under-sevens need to start winning – which I don't – it didn't occur to him to offer Danny some help, to support him in his new role.'

'Does Kieran do support?' asked James, trying to recall any time that Kieran had been genuinely helpful to him, as opposed to just palming off players that were surplus to his requirements.

*

The mood at training was more understated than the previous week. The boys were still happy to mess about as they arrived, but when James called them together there was tension in the air. Everyone was waiting to see how the coaches would react to Sunday's demolition. James did a quick head-count and realised there were only eleven boys; someone was missing.

'Has anyone seen Callum?' No one knew where he was, and apparently he hadn't said anything about not coming. James checked his phone for messages from Callum's parents, but there was nothing. Hopefully he was just running late.

Joao started things off. 'In a moment we warm up, then we have much to work on.'

'Defensive stuff I guess, after Sunday,' said Deepak, his voice heavy and flat. The others murmured their unenthusiastic agreement.

'No,' said Joao abruptly. 'Last few weeks you work hard on defence, big improvement. On Sunday we play Eastside Diamonds, for that game we work on our attacking play.' That pepped everyone up, and they threw themselves into Joao's warm-up. The rest of the session was spent on attacking interplay, encouraging the boys to be aware of the options around them and to move the ball quickly. It wasn't as if they were going to become Weston Park overnight, but over the course of the hour James could see definite improvement. James kept an eye on Charlie; there were signs of progress, but was he ready for a competitive game against anything but the weakest of opposition? Probably not. At the end of the session, he called everyone together.

'Great session tonight, lads; well done. You've worked really hard and I think we'll see the benefit of that on Sunday. Joao and I will put our heads together about the team selection and I'll message it out to your parents in the next day or so.'

James was working that evening, so he took the opportunity of a gap between fares to text Callum's mum, asking if everything was okay. She replied within a few minutes saying that Callum had come home from school and said he didn't fancy training this week, but he was okay for Sunday. James was torn: he knew he ought to pick Charlie – who had been at training – ahead of Callum this week, but… it was Eastside Diamonds, definitely a winnable game. When Callum tried, he was a good player. James decided to go with three subs rather than leaving Callum out altogether. Ben could play left midfield, to build on his display last Sunday, and Dylan deserved a chance to start up front – his apology had gone a long way to making amends for his bad temper.

*

It was a rare night out for James and Ros. Lynn had agreed to babysit (Ben had taken great offence at that particular terminology) and James had booked a table at a local restaurant that had been a favourite of theirs in the days before they had their children.

'We should do this more often,' said James as he finished his meatballs and mozzarella starter. 'It feels like we hardly see each other these days.'

'I know. Taxi driving seemed like a good short-term option, but I hadn't realised you'd have to work so many evenings and late nights to make it pay. At least when you were teaching, your evenings of work were spent in front of the telly with me.'

James shifted his feet. Ros was only saying what he thought himself, but teaching wasn't an option anymore. He shrugged, trying to think of a way to shift the conversation on to another topic.

Ros wasn't letting it drop. 'Have you had any more thoughts about going back to teaching?'

'I don't know. After what happened, I'm not sure I could face it. That's if anyone would even have me back. I messed up pretty badly, you know.'

'Yeah, you did. But does that have to define the rest of your life? All of our lives?' They had had this argument so many times. James knew she was right, but the thought of going back into a classroom terrified him. 'Dr North said he'd give you a good reference. He understood that it was just a one-off moment, that you were provoked.'

'He still made me resign though, didn't he?'

'What else could he do? You said yourself, it was either resign or get sacked. Maybe all you needed was a break; things might be different now.'

'Maybe. Or maybe they wouldn't.'

'Well, this isn't working for us, is it? You used to love teaching – I remember you saying how good it felt to be making a difference in people's lives. Can you honestly tell me that you get that from driving a taxi?' She held his gaze while he shrugged. She was right. He had been passionate about teaching, once upon a time. He'd never felt that way about driving.

'Well, if not teaching, what about becoming a driving instructor? You wouldn't have the late nights, and it would build on your teaching skills. Maybe that would be more satisfying?'

'I don't know. I'd have to retrain for that. I've got no idea how long that would take.'

'Six months.'

'I'm sorry?'

'It would take six months. I've looked into it. Oh, don't look so surprised. I've been trying to think of an alternative for ages. You're miserable, you have been ever since you left Brookton. You need to get back on track, to find yourself again. Maybe a new project is what you need. I'd much rather we spent a bit of time and money finding something that satisfies you than see you have a full-on mid-life crisis and start an affair or something. You're a bit of an idiot, but you're my idiot and I don't plan on losing you.' She reached across the table and put her hand on his. 'I'm worried about you, Jamie. You've got to work out what's going to make you happy again before you lose yourself altogether.'

James blinked back the tears. She was right, he had been treading water since leaving teaching, but somehow he knew that becoming a driving instructor wasn't the answer. He didn't want to invest time and money into qualifying for another short-term solution, but what was the long-term answer? Any further discussion was halted by the arrival of their main courses. James made sure to change the subject once the waitress had departed, asking Ros about a new colleague who had started at her work and was ruffling a few feathers, then pivoting into Ben and Poppy and their latest school exploits. Ros didn't bring the subject up again, but James knew he couldn't put off the subject of his future career forever.

*

'How's the season going?' asked James when he saw Iain, the Diamonds' manager, at the pitch on Sunday morning.

'Two losses so far, but Hawks and Redbridge, so no surprise.'

The Swifts players arrived in dribs and drabs, but one of the dribs never appeared: Callum was a no-show. James called them together for the team talk.

'Okay lads, let's get last week out of our system. Who has heard of Billy Bragg?'

'Who?' asked Ryan.

'Singer. His uncle used to play for Red Star Belgrade, apparently. Anyway, Billy Bragg once wrote that he was 'Waiting for the Great Leap Forwards'. Last week was a disaster, but we're only ever one game away from the great leap forwards: let's make it this game. Remember what we worked on in training: keep the ball moving; be positive and attacking; let's play some good football. Eastside are nowhere near as good as Weston. That said, their little blond left winger has given us problems in the past – Liam, try to help the defence on that side; Deepak, don't dive in; don't make it easy for him.'

When they kicked off, Callum wasn't the only absentee. The Diamonds' star winger was missing too, which made life a little less stressful. The defence of Hakim, Gabe and Deepak looked solid. Gabe was doing lots of talking – something Joao had asked him to do – and keeping the others organised. Once or twice the Diamonds tried to play a ball over the top, but Hakim's pace usually cleared things up.

'Away!' shouted James, as Hakim once again outpaced the Diamonds striker. 'Get it clear, Hakim!'

Max was winning lots of possession in midfield, although he was still trying to do too much on his own when he got the ball. James kept bellowing at him to pass it, but he continually ran himself into dead ends. Even so, most of the game was spent in the Diamonds' half. Just as James was contemplating some substitutions, Max rolled the ball in to Dylan, his back to goal on the edge of the box. Dylan held his man off, protected the ball and then slipped a pass with the outside of his foot out to the left. Ben, running in, struck Dylan's perfectly weighted ball past the Diamonds keeper. One-nil. James leapt for joy, the broad smile that instantly spread across his face matching the one on Ben's.

The second half was more of the same, with Swifts on top but failing to take their chances. After a rare Diamonds attack broke down, Charlie found himself with the ball at his feet in the corner.

'Get rid of it!' yelled James.

'No,' muttered Joao. 'Pass to Rory.' Charlie had already put it out for a corner. Diamonds threw their big defender up and, sure enough, his header levelled the game at one-one.

The goal inspired Eastside, and the game lurched from end to end. Hakim replaced Charlie, who Joao immediately took to one side for a chat. A few moments later, Ben, now playing in centre midfield, threaded a pass through for Liam to run onto. Liam's pace took him clear of the Eastside defence and he dinked the ball calmly over the goalkeeper.

There were some hairy moments before the game ended, not least as both Josh and Gabe had to come off with minor injuries. Charlie looked panicked whenever he had the ball, but at least he managed to find a team-mate most of the time. Finally, as the ref was checking his watch, Max burst out of midfield with the ball at his feet. He broke through a couple of tackles, the ball ricocheting kindly, and strode on into the penalty area. One more touch, then he cannoned the ball into the net to seal the win.

The two managers exchanged handshakes, as usual, straight after the final whistle.

'Well done,' said Iain. 'You're doing well this season. I can't say you didn't deserve it either, you outplayed us for most of the game.'

'Thanks,' replied James. 'It might have been a different story if you'd had that left winger of yours. How come he wasn't here?'

Iain's face darkened. 'Don't get me started. I got a text from his dad during the first half. Apparently, he was asked to join the Hawks this week. You didn't know anything about it, did you?'

James shook his head. 'No, first I've heard. Sorry mate, that sucks; it sounds like Kieran though; he's always poaching players from other clubs.'

The boys were jubilant, and Charlie looked happier than James had ever seen him, so pleased to be part of a winning team. Even Rob looked content, telling James that Max had played a blinder and it was a shame they didn't have a couple more like him rather than having to rely on the likes of Charlie.

Lynn, who had been there watching Rory, came over to James as he was carrying the goal nets back to the lock-up.

'I've just heard from Danny Peters.' She grinned. 'His under-sevens won six-four. I didn't know you could get that many exclamation marks into a text message. That should keep Kieran off his back.' James told Lynn about his conversation with Iain.

'That's typical,' she replied. 'Kieran's got more players than he needs, but he's seen a shiny new toy in someone else's hands and he has to take it.' Lynn shook her head despairingly. 'He'd better not have played him today – I know for a fact the new lad isn't registered yet.'

James checked the other results on the website that night. No big surprises: Hawks had had a tough one against Redbridge Town, but they had come through with a three-two win. Weston Park had broken another hundred per cent record, beating Shelley Abbey Royals seven-two. At least someone had finally scored against them. Swifts were one of four teams on six points, just three points behind the leading pair.

James knew that it was early days but was it ridiculous to hope that this season might be something special? They were playing Belgate Magpies, the top division champions, in a cup game next week, so it looked like they were going to have to focus on the league anyway.

CHAPTER TEN

Hayley was trying to be positive on the way home, for Jayden's sake, but something inside her was on the verge of boiling over; it was one of those days on the touchline where she wished Jayden had picked another hobby. The other parents were all saying what a great match it was – Redbridge had lost, but only three-two, with the lead swapping between Redbridge and Stoneleigh Hawks throughout. The downside was that with the game being so close, Matt hadn't given Jayden even a minute on the pitch.

'I wouldn't have made a difference anyway, Mum,' said Jayden from the back seat. 'I mean, I'm sub for a reason, right?'

'Rubbish,' she snapped, sounding harsher than she meant to – it wasn't Jayden she was angry with, it was Matt. If it came to that, the other team's manager had been even worse. He'd been prowling up and down the touchline, shouting at the ref, the Redbridge players, his own players: pretty much everyone, in fact. She had been tempted to go over to caution him for a public order offence, but knew that Jayden would have died from embarrassment. Putting idiot managers to the back of her mind, she managed to find a more soothing tone.

'You've done really well when you've got on in the other games. Maybe if Matt had given you a chance, Redbridge might have won.' She sneaked a look in the rear-view mirror; she wasn't sure that Jayden was convinced by her pep talk, but she had to try. 'And I'd rather you boys lost every week than behave like the other lot, with all the shirt-pulling and back-chat. Why did they spend the last five minutes kicking the ball as far away from everyone as possible?'

'It's just time-wasting, Mum. It's part of the game, it's what the professionals do when they're winning.'

'Yeah, but that's professional football. This is kids on a Sunday morning. Matt doesn't tell you boys to do that, does he?'

Jayden almost grinned, briefly. 'Sometimes.' The smile faded as quickly as it had emerged. 'But I'm not usually on the pitch when the scores are close, am I?' Hayley couldn't argue with that. She just wished that Matt could be a little less obsessed with winning matches. Then again, when Jayden's mates were round their house, she often heard them talking about winning promotion and getting back to the top division, so maybe he was just giving the boys what they wanted. Either way, at the risk of sounding like she was agreeing with Andy, sometimes she felt that Jayden's football was more trouble than it was worth.

*

On Sunday evening James texted Gabe and Josh's parents, to see how the boys' injuries were doing. Ed replied that Gabe was fine, but Josh's mum wasn't sure whether he'd be fit for training. She said she'd keep James posted and thanked him for checking in. He also texted Callum's mum who said that he had woken up feeling poorly but she had forgotten to let James know. Sally could be a bit ditsy, so her story was believable, but James couldn't shake the suspicion that Callum just hadn't liked the idea of being a sub.

The next day was a busy one, with James's taxi criss-crossing town. He snatched at his lunch in instalments, finding pockets of time to eat where he could. By the afternoon when he picked

Poppy up from school, he was exhausted. On the way home, Poppy was telling him all about how cool her teacher, Mrs Hughes, was. Ben had had Mrs Hughes a couple of years earlier, so James knew Poppy was in good hands.

An hour or so after they got home, Ben arrived back from school. He flung his bag across the hallway, got himself a drink from the fridge and threw himself down on a chair in the front room.

'How was school today, Ben?' asked James.

'S'all right. French was a laugh.'

'Go on.'

'Miss Finch went out of the room to get some books, and she left the big walk-in cupboard unlocked.'

James forced himself to smile, but he sensed that any enjoyment he would get from Ben's tale would be a bit hollow. He had been thinking again about Ros' suggestion of returning to teaching, so the thought of students hazing teachers was a bit close to the bone.

Ben carried on with his tale. 'Robin said we should all hide in it.'

'And did you?'

Ben laughed. 'Yeah. It was a bit of a squeeze though. We all tried not to laugh when Miss Finch came back. She stood there in the doorway and I think she swore a bit, under her breath. Once she left, we all burst out laughing and went back to our places. A couple of minutes later she walked in with the deputy head and just stood there with her mouth hanging open. Mr Rice gave her a furious look and said, "Well they seem to be here now, don't they Miss Finch? Can you handle it from here?" and he stomped off. It was awesome.'

'Do you think Miss Finch thought it was awesome?' asked James quietly.

Ben shrugged. 'She seemed all right later. I saw her laughing with Mr Hayward in the corridor. Besides, by the end of the day the whole year group was talking about it – we're legends!'

James could see it from Ben's point of view, but he felt bad for Miss Finch: completely undermined, then humiliated in front of the deputy head. Lessons with that class would be harder, and as word spread, other classes would see her as a soft touch. James knew how it felt for a teacher who lost control.

*

Callum and Gabe both turned up to training on Wednesday, although not Josh. James had agreed with Josh's mum that it was better to give him more recovery time rather than risking him before the weekend.

During a break in training, when Joao was sorting out teams for a match, James beckoned Callum away from the other players for a chat.

'How are you doing, mate?' asked James. 'I was a bit surprised not to see you on Sunday. Was everything okay?' Callum shrugged and muttered something. 'I would have thought you'd have been keen to get back to the football after a frustrating game like Weston Park. We never really talked about your reaction at half-time, did we?'

Callum gave no sign that he was about to open up. James tried a different tack. 'Your team-mates really missed you out there in the second half that day.'

Callum scoffed. 'Yeah, like I would have made a difference – they were way better than us. We'd already lost it long before that.'

'True,' conceded James. 'But how do you think it felt for the others, losing heavily and then one of our better players decides he can't be bothered? How would you have felt if it had been, I don't know, Rory or Liam say, who had done something like that?'

After a short pause, Callum sniffed and said, 'I guess I'd be annoyed with them. I'd feel let down.'

'Yeah, that sounds about right to me. What would you want someone to do in that situation?'

'Keep going, keep trying their best.' He grinned bashfully at James. 'Not throw a strop and give up. Sorry James.'

'Apology accepted. What about last weekend, were you really unwell, or did you just not fancy being sub?'

The shrug again. 'A bit of both, maybe.'

James smiled. 'Well, I appreciate the honesty, mate. If you weren't well, that's fair enough, but if it was about being sub, I think your mates deserve a bit more from you, don't you? We've got another tough game this week, so this will be your chance to start making it up to them. What do you say?'

Callum nodded. 'Yeah, will do. Thanks James. Sorry.'

'All done. Now go play some football – hurry before the others decide you're in goal.' Callum grinned and cantered across to the others, calling out 'I'm in midfield!' as he went.

Well, Callum had said all the right things. Now James would just have to wait and see if it made any difference against Belgate Magpies on Sunday.

*

'Okay lads, gather round. I'm not going to try to kid you; this one's going to be tough.' He'd been thinking a lot about this team talk; how on earth was he going to make them believe they could get something out of the game? 'Magpies won the top division last year, and they're properly good. We've got to keep our heads in the game and at least make it hard for them. I'm not talking about parking the bus – when we get the ball, I want us to attack, to give them a game – but when we lose it, work hard tracking back, closing them down. From start to finish, we have to work together and support each other. Whatever happens with the scoreline, keep playing as if the next goal changes everything.' James looked around the group, he didn't see much confidence in their faces, and to be fair, he didn't blame them. 'There's a famous Welsh poet called Dylan Thomas,' he began, eliciting the now-traditional response from the boys.

'Who?' asked Rory.

'He scored a last-minute goal to win Arsenal the league title at Anfield in 1989. His most famous poem is about not giving in to the inevitable end of things, kicking and screaming to hang on to life in the face of death. It goes something like this.' James recited the lines with as much emotion as he dared. '"Do not go gentle into that good night. Old age should burn and rave at close of day. Rage, rage against the dying of the light".' The boys were exchanging glances, trying to keep the smirks off their faces, but James carried on. 'That has to be us today, whatever happens on the pitch, even if the goals are mounting up, "do not go gentle into that good night". If we're one goal down, or five goals down, or ten, or more: "do not go gentle into that good night, rage against the dying of the light". Right to the end we fight for everything and we make them walk off the pitch knowing that we've given them a game from start to finish. Are we up for that?' The boys responded, although some of the yeahs were more convincing than others. 'That doesn't sound like raging against the dying of the light, that's grumbling about a dim light bulb. Are we up for this?' This time there was more volume, and more confidence. They were ready.

Half-time was a bit more low-key. It's hard to lift a team when they are already seven-nil down. At least they were sticking to the task and working hard – even Callum – which really was all that could have been expected from this game. James noticed that Joao had been more animated on the touchline than in the previous games, constantly calling out encouragement – 'Great tackle, Charlie', 'Yes, Ben, good pass', 'Unlucky, Ryan, keep going; that's the right idea'. The final score of thirteen-two was worse than it sounded. Actually, no, it was pretty much exactly what it sounded like, but James was delighted with the way everyone had kept going. Charlie had looked out of his depth at times, but then again so had most of the others. Liam and Dylan had scored the two Swifts goals, both the result of quick breaks as the Magpies piled men forward with the game long since won. The boys were okay at full time – they had known what to expect, and were just pleased to have got a couple of goals. James made a point of complimenting Callum on his improved attitude.

James wasn't surprised to discover that the Hawks, along with some of the other division-two teams, had won their cup games that afternoon. That meant that in the coming weeks the league table would start to get a little uneven, as league games were dropped to make room for cup matches and some teams would have played more games than others. The good thing about going out of the cup early – something James was very familiar with – was that if they played more games than the teams around them, it might artificially boost their league position, which James could then use to lift the boys' morale.

The Swifts had a tough run of games coming up. Shelley Abbey Royals next week, followed by Cole Hill. Both teams, like the Swifts, were on six points. Unlike the Swifts, at least some of their wins had come against decent teams. After that, Swifts had the return match with Linford Road Rovers to warm them up for the one James had been dreading: the Hawks.

CHAPTER ELEVEN

'So, did you have a good time at your dad's?'

'Yeah, we went bowling and then out for pizza. He wouldn't let me have pepperoni though: meat is murder, apparently.'

'Do you want me to have a word with him, remind him that going vegetarian or not is your decision, not his?'

'Nah, it's not worth it – I don't mind doing without meat for a couple of days at a time. Can we have burgers tonight though?'

'Not tonight, but I'll get some in for later in the week. Was it all bowling, pizza and Xbox with your dad, or did you get any homework done?'

'Yeah, he had some friends coming round, so I got an hour or so in while I was watching the football on telly.'

Hayley glanced across to the passenger seat, trying to deliver one of her maternal glares while still keeping her eyes on the road. 'You know you can't concentrate properly if you're watching TV – we've been through this. When you're doing homework, you should find somewhere with a bit of peace and quiet.'

'How am I meant to do that with Dad and his mates going on about an occupation? At least the football drowns that out. Anyway, I got everything done, so what's the problem?'

Hayley made a mental note to look through Jayden's books later, just to check how thorough he'd actually been with the homework. Then a thought occurred to her.

'Occupation? Can you remember what Dad and his friends were talking about? What exactly were they planning?'

'Something about the local college. There's some lecturer they're not happy with. Dunno what it's got to do with them though – most of them aren't even students.'

Hayley tried another couple of gentle enquiries, but other than the fact that they kept talking about a Thursday, Jayden didn't seem to have taken any other details on board. Later on, once he'd gone to bed, she started googling and soon found a local news story. Apparently one of the staff at the local college had caused a stir with some of the things he had said in one of his lectures, questioning recent criticism of the town's historic involvement with the slave trade. That made sense: Andy and his crowd would be up in arms about it.

*

When she got in to work the following morning, she found Sergeant McGlashan at the first opportunity.

'Sarge, have you got a minute?'

'Make it quick, Birnham. What's up?'

'You know this business about Alaistair Symecock…'

'The slave-trade bloke? What of him?'

'I think the usual suspects are planning a protest: some kind of occupation on Thursday. I don't know any more than that, but there's every chance something will be going down.'

She had the Sarge's attention now. 'And how have you come by this information? I know for a fact that you've not got any registered informants who you're authorised to make payments to.'

'This informant doesn't need paying, well apart from pocket money. My Jayden spent the weekend with his father and his activist pals. He overheard them planning something. I don't know any details – as if Andy would tell me anything like this – but thought I should pass it along the chain, just in case it helps.'

'You never know what the final piece of the jigsaw is going to be. Good work, Hayley. I'll pass that along.'

She felt a little bad about going behind Andy's back, but as long as whatever he was planning was legal – which it generally was – he shouldn't have anything to worry about. It had been tempting to just say nothing; it wasn't as if she disagreed with Andy on this particular issue: what Symecock had said was pretty shocking. Nevertheless, he was still entitled to protection in case things got out of hand. Besides that, it wouldn't do her any harm with Sarge to have found this nugget – she didn't see Amber Gould doing anything to get ahead of this particular potential breach of the peace.

*

Monday was a tough day for James: working all morning and over lunch, off for a few hours to pick Poppy up from school, then a full evening shift and into the night. The morning was brisk, with lots of pick-ups and a steady flow of reasonable tips. During a break between fares, James reflected on how well Callum had responded to their chat the previous week. It was no guarantee that the problem wouldn't crop up again, but at least Cal had backed up his good intentions against the Magpies. Talking things through with kids didn't always get such a positive result though. His mind went back to a conversation with Kyle, a few weeks after the staring-out incident. James had kept Kyle back at the end of another frustrating lesson.

'How do you think our lessons together are going, Kyle?' The question was met with the briefest of shrugs. Kyle's misbehaviour was building into a pattern of disruption, escalating in scale. This was James's attempt to turn things around before the senior leadership team had to be brought in. 'Is there anything I can do to make the lessons better for you? How can I help you, so that everyone can get on with the work?'

'I dunno. Make it less boring?'

James resisted the temptation to wax lyrical about how studying great literature was anything but boring, about the joys of examining the human condition through the minds of wise and insightful authors. Somehow, he knew that wouldn't fly.

'And how do I do that, Kyle? It seems to me that you've already decided the lesson is boring before you even sit down. We get several minutes of disruption before I can start actually teaching the rest of the class. No one has the right to stop other people from learning, and that's what you're doing, isn't it?' Again, the shrug. 'If you don't understand the work, I'm happy to help – that's what I'm there for – but I can't let you disrupt a whole class of students who actually want to do some work.'

'There ain't a whole class wanting to work though.' Kyle finally came to life, stung into speech by James's outrageous claim. 'One or two sweats, maybe, but most of us don't see the point.'

'Well, that's your opinion, and I'm afraid you're not in a position to speak for everyone else in the class. You may be correct about some people, but I suspect that a lot more of them want to apply themselves and get a decent GCSE result at the end of it. I'd like to help you to do that too. Whatever you say about it being boring, English is an important subject: it's one of the ones that employers look for.'

'I don't know why: what's the point of reading? All the good stuff gets made into films and that. Why waste time reading when you can just watch it?'

James decided not to go down the books versus films argument, instead trying another tack.

'Well, I don't necessarily agree with that, but even if you don't see the point in English, employers want to know you can stick at a task and make a good job of it. That's an important skill to develop, and, for you, GCSE English is a great opportunity to do that. When you get a job, whatever it is you really want to do, there will be things about it that you don't enjoy. Being able to stick it out and get the job done will help you get on and be able to do more of the good stuff.'

'Am I one of the parts of your job that you don't enjoy, Mr Hogan?' Kyle looked up at James, and James wasn't sure if this was a joke, a trap, or a genuine enquiry. James resisted the temptation to claim that Kyle was the best part of his day, but decided that mixing honesty with idealism might not hurt.

'Kyle, you're the reason I came into teaching. I wanted to help young people to achieve their potential. You can be so much more than just messing about with your mates. I want to help you to find that.' Kyle stared blankly back at James. There was no response, no hint as to whether he was getting through.

'So how are we going to leave this, Kyle? What do we do next?' Kyle returned to his shrugging. 'Are you going to start knuckling down, or do I need to start getting serious with sanctions? I don't want to remove you from lessons on a regular basis, but if you're interfering with other students' education, I won't have a choice. It's up to you where we go from here.'

'I want to go to lunch; that's where I want to go from here, sir.'

James smiled. That seemed fair enough. 'Yeah, me too, Kyle. Let's leave it there, but think about what we've been saying, you need to decide what you're going to do about it.'

James had actually been optimistic that things might change after that. You'd have thought that five years of managing a kids' football team, let alone fifteen years of teaching, would have made him remember Alexander Pope's warning about optimism. He really should have known better.

*

All of the boys were back in training on Wednesday, and Joao was still focusing on their attacking play. Charlie's mum had told

James that Charlie wasn't available this weekend as they were away seeing family, which saved James telling him he was left out again. James tried to convince himself that he was protecting Charlie's confidence, but he suspected that, deep down, it was really because he wanted to win. The Swifts were definitely improving. Two wins out of three (not counting the cup game) was great, but a win against the Royals would be their best result yet.

*

Sunday arrived and it was a fantastic match. The defence weren't diving in, and when the Royals did make it past them, Rory was in good form, flinging himself across his goalmouth to make save after save. The midfield was battling hard, but for all the good play going forward, the Swifts couldn't fashion a chance worthy of the name. Shortly before half-time, Joao tugged on James's sleeve.

'Mister James, we need more up front. Why not try three-three-two? Push Dylan up with Josh.'

'I don't know, Royals are looking dangerous; I'm not sure about taking a man out of midfield.'

'What do you want: try to win, or try not to lose?'

James pondered those words for the next few minutes. Royals were a good team, a win would be a huge morale booster. If the Swifts could nick a goal…

Ben came off at half-time, despite it being one of his more confident performances, leaving Callum, Max and Liam in midfield. James saw Joao talking earnestly with Max, with the boy nodding his understanding.

'What were you saying to Max?' asked James as the boys jogged back onto the pitch.

'I tell him to sit back, to be anchor, protect the defence.' James nodded, that made sense, though he wasn't sure if Max had the discipline to stay back. Dylan and Josh looked twice as effective up front together than either had on their own. They played off each other, which meant when the ball went up to them it was much more likely to stick. Eventually, Josh slipped a tantalising pass between two Royals defenders and Dylan pounced: jinking past a third man, he drilled the ball hard and low past the keeper and gave Swifts an unexpected lead.

That's how it stayed until just before the end. Max won the ball, slipped a pass to Ben, who had come back on midway through the half, and then surged forward to join the attack. Moments later, the ball was lost and the Royals broke into the space Max had left vacant. Play switched quickly to the wing, and a low hard cross was driven into the Swifts' six-yard box. Gabe raced the Royals striker, just getting his right foot to the ball and denying his opponent the chance to shoot. Agonisingly, though, the ball flew off Gabe's boot and crept inside Rory's far post: an own goal to bring the score back to one-one.

'We were so close!' exclaimed James, his head in his hands.

Most of the Swifts looked just as crestfallen. Max looked furious, while Gabe was crouched down on his haunches, head hanging low. Ben was the first to go to him, offering him a hand to pull him back to his feet. As they lined up for the restart, a haunted expression clung to Gabe's face like it was man-marking him.

Moments after the kick-off, the final whistle went. James accepted the praise of the Royals manager for how much the Swifts had improved from last year, then went to his players. He thought he could see tear-marks on Gabe's mudded face.

'Lads,' James started. 'That was awesome. It's a shame we didn't get the win, because you definitely deserved it, but we've got a point against a really good team, and we'd all have taken a point from this game before the kick-off, wouldn't we?' There was murmured agreement from the boys. 'You've come so far already this season. Let's keep it going. Yeah?'

'I'm sorry, guys,' said Gabe. 'I messed up and cost us the win.'

Before anyone else could speak, Joao jumped in. 'No,' he replied brusquely. 'No, Gabe, you not mess up. If striker get there first, he scores: you had to take that touch, take that risk. You saved the team over and over today.' Gabe grinned sheepishly, looking a lot less burdened than a few seconds ago. By now the parents were coming over, broad smiles all over their faces.

'That was amazing,' said Lynn. 'Best you've ever played, boys. Hard luck, Gabe.'

'So cruel,' added Amir, Hakim's dad. 'You deserved the win.' Even Rob had something positive to say for once, adding that it was a proper football match and that he'd have happily paid to watch it. Josh held out his palm and looked at Rob expectantly, which made the others laugh, and even brought a smile to Gabe's face.

As the boys drifted away, Rob moved closer to James and said, 'Maxi was fantastic again, wasn't he? Shame that Gabe forgot which way we were kicking.'

'It wasn't Gabe's fault, Rob. He had to deal with the danger. The problem was the gap in our midfield when Max surged forward. Once we lost the ball, it was easy for them to play through it.'

'Exactly – that's what I keep telling you. Nobody covered when Maxi drove forward. This team will never get anywhere until you find some better players who can read what the good ones are trying to do.' James bit his tongue, resisting the temptation to say that Max had been asked to hold back and protect the lead. It just wasn't worth it with Rob.

*

When they got home, Ben was full of the game, and couldn't stop telling Ros and Poppy all about it. Ros was happy to hear everything, just enjoying Ben's excitement. Poppy was less enthusiastic. 'Blah-blah-blah-blah football, blah-blah mud, blah-blah-blah smelly boys,' was her considered statement on the occasion. Either that or she was quoting Roy Keane.

A couple of hours after he got in, James's phone pinged. It was a text from Lynn.

Weston versus Hawks result now in… James stared at his phone. For some reason Lynn hadn't sent the whole message in one go, he couldn't understand why. Then a second text arrived, just saying *Wait for it…* When he saw the third text, he understood: *Weston 7 Hawks 0!!!!! Kieran furious and blaming the ref, the pitch – everyone but himself.* James actually laughed out loud when he read that result. For one thing, Hawks hadn't done much better than the Swifts against Weston Park, for another, it meant there were only two points between the two Stoneleigh teams now. If it hadn't been for that own goal they'd be level.

Checking the website later, James saw that Weston and the Hawks occupied the top two positions in the table, Swifts and Royals were just two points behind them on seven points, with the next three all a single point behind that. Equal third; well, fourth on goal difference, but even so. If the Swifts could play like that again next week, they had every chance of getting something against Cole Hill, and then Linford Road the week after should be straightforward. Who knows, they might even be above the Hawks by the time they met next month. James wished there was going to be another committee meeting this week, just to hear Kieran's excuses and see the look on his face.

CHAPTER TWELVE

The canteen queue wasn't too bad, and Hayley had picked out a better-than-average sandwich from the usually meagre offerings, when a voice came over her shoulder.

'It's PC Birnham, isn't it? Let me get that for you: I want to ask you a favour.' Hayley turned and saw one of the detectives from CID. 'I'm DC Morgan. Am I right in thinking it was you who gave us the shout about that college occupation?' Hayley followed Morgan across the canteen to an empty table once he had bought her sandwich and bottle of water. They settled themselves down, and started on their lunches – Morgan had bought himself a pasta salad.

'The thing is,' said Morgan. 'We've been keeping an eye on the Black Lives Matter lot for a while now, and we hadn't heard anything about the occupation until you flagged it up. I gather that you used to be involved with Andy Wood. Is that right?'

Involved with, that seemed a bit weak for near enough fifteen years and a child together. 'Yeah, he's the father of my son, so I'm still in regular contact with him.'

'That can't be easy, sharing parenting duties with a lefty scumbag.' The look on Morgan's face took Hayley aback; as far as she could see, he wasn't joking.

'Well, I don't think co-parenting is easy for anyone, but he's not a scumbag. I mean, we don't agree on lots of things, but he's a decent enough guy; he just has a different point of view to me.'

'I should hope so, with some of the rubbish I've heard coming from that lot. Look, all I know is that he's involved with people who are involved in a lot of things that we're very interested in right now. We'd be a lot better off if we can shut those troublemakers down, so any information about Wood and his friends you can send in our direction will be very welcome.'

'What kind of information?'

'Same kind of thing as last time – what they're getting worked up about, what they're planning to do about it; anything to keep us one step ahead of them.'

Nothing he was asking was unreasonable, but somehow Hayley felt uneasy with the way the conversation was going. 'Look, I got lucky with the occupation. His friends happened to bring something up in front of my Jayden, and Jayden happened to mention it to me once he was back home. I seriously doubt that Andy is into anything illegal – and if he was, he's hardly likely to take me into his confidence, is he? I mean, you wouldn't, would you, what with me being in the job.'

Morgan smiled a thin, tight smile that Hayley wasn't sure was entirely genuine. 'No, I suppose not. Even so, keep your ears open; maybe ask your boy to do the same.' With that, Morgan pushed his half-finished pasta salad aside and stood up. 'Anything you hear could help us a lot. It could be good for your career too.'

Hayley watched him make his way out of the canteen, and didn't notice Pikey until he sat down in the seat Morgan had vacated.

'What was that all about?' he asked. 'High-and-mighty Morgan doesn't usually fraternise with uniform. Was he asking you out?'

Hayley blanched at the thought. 'Hardly. He was asking about Andy; wanting information about what him and his mates are planning next.'

'And?'

Hayley looked blankly back at him. 'And what?'

'And what did you tell him?'

She laughed. 'That I'd let him know if I heard anything, but not to hold his breath. Much as I'd like to see the look on Amber Gould's face if I got a transfer to CID, my finger isn't as firmly on the pulse of the local activist scene as Morgan seems to think.'

The more she thought about it, the more uncomfortable she was with the whole business. The picture that DC Morgan had painted of Andy wasn't the man that she knew. Maybe they knew things about him that she didn't, but she trusted her own judgement enough to know what Andy was really like. If Andy and his friends were actually breaking the law she couldn't just turn a blind eye, but there was a huge difference between breaking the law and legal protest. She didn't agree with everything Andy said – increasingly she agreed with less and less of it – but he was entitled to make his case. If Andy thought she was spying on him, things could get very awkward very quickly, which couldn't be good for Jayden. If it came to that, it wasn't fair to ask her son to spy on his father. This was a tricky line for her to walk, and she'd have to think very carefully about anything she passed on to CID.

*

Dave had messaged on Saturday morning. The rain had been relentless for most of the week, so James had been expecting the cancellation. All of the games due to be played on Stoneleigh's pitches – which included the Swifts' – were off, though the sides with away games still had a chance, depending on how good their opposition's drainage was. Sundays always felt strange when a game had been cancelled. The extra time with Ros and Poppy was nice, but for James and Ben there was something missing. It wasn't the same as the weeks where no game had been scheduled in the first place. For those weeks, plans had been made without football – well, without the Swifts anyway: Ben generally let Sky's premier league coverage fill in the missing hours. It was different when a game was called off, snatched away at the last minute. In those cases the absence was more pronounced; James's mind kept drifting towards the football-shaped hole in his day, like a tongue constantly drawn to the gap left by a newly-extracted tooth.

During the evening, while Ros and Poppy were watching the *Strictly* dance-off, James checked online to see which games had beaten the weather. Two others had also succumbed, but two had gone ahead. Hawks had beaten Melville Dynamos six-one, and Redbridge also won six-one, away to Eastside Diamonds. That meant Hawks were joint top again, although having played a game more than Weston Park, Redbridge had moved into third place on nine points. Checking the following week's fixtures, James saw that Redbridge were playing Hawks, so at least one of them would drop points. If the Swifts could beat Linford Road – which they should – they'd gain ground on one of their rivals. James couldn't see anyone stopping Weston Park, but with Joao's coaching, he was starting to think there was a realistic chance of competing for the other promotion place. They were still to face the Hawks, but beating them wasn't impossible anymore.

Joao texted James that evening, saying he had an idea to talk about. James wasn't working Monday night, so they arranged to meet up in the Thane of Cawdor pub. Joao was already there when James arrived, and he'd got the pints in.

'I remember what you drink last time, Mister James. Hope I got it right.'

James took a sip on his beer. 'Perfect Joao. Now, what's this idea of yours?'

'Last week, against Royals, two forwards work much better than one.'

'It did, but I still think we do better with four in midfield. Three have too much space to cover, especially as most other teams play three-four-one.'

'Sim, they do. So why have three defenders against one striker? Against weaker teams, why not play two-four-two?' James sat back in his chair and took this in. Two men at the back sounded reckless, but as Joao said, if most teams only played one striker, did they need three defenders? Joao expanded, explaining how midfielders could drop in when needed to fill the gap and become a third defender. It would give the team an extra attacking player without exposing them to too much extra danger. James agreed that it was worth a try against Linford Road that weekend, and they could then decide how it had gone. Joao said he'd plan something for training to get the boys used to the system.

On Wednesday, once the boys had done their stretches, Joao got out his tactics board. The boys had been quite excited the first time Joao had used this in training. Even though the novelty had worn off a bit, it still helped to focus their attention on his instructions. He set up nine red discs in the Swifts' traditional three-four-one formation.

'Up to now, we mostly play this. Solid at the back, plenty boys in midfield, but lone striker can be, what is word…? Isolated.' The boys nodded their understanding. 'Against Royals, we try this.' He moved the pieces around on the board into the three-three-two formation. 'Defence still solid, one less in midfield, one more up front.' He pointed out each part of the pitch in turn and summarised, 'Same; weaker; stronger. Good when we attack, but maybe we get overpowered in middle. Most teams play with one up, yes?' The boys nodded again. 'With some teams, we not need three defenders to deal with one forward. So we try this.' He shuffled the counters into the two-four-two formation he had sold to James. 'Weaker, but not weak; strong, strong. When they attack down middle, two defenders protect middle. When they attack down side, this man move to deal with attack.' He slid one of the defenders across to the flank. 'This man, move over to cover.' He slid the other defender into the gap the first counter had left. 'What problem here?'

Gabe was first to answer. 'There's a big gap on the other side.'

Joao beamed. 'Sim! Big gap. Solution?'

Liam spoke up. 'The midfielders could track back and cover.'

'Sim! Sim! You boys know your football! If defence moves over to the left, right midfield has to track runners. If defence moves to the right, left winger fill the gap. Mister James has decided, we try this on Sunday against Linford Road. If it work, great. If not work, we can change. But before then, we practise.'

Joao pulled out his dry-wipe marker and drew lines on the board, corresponding to the cones he had laid out before the session. He quickly explained an attack versus defence game, arranged two teams and got them started. The boys set about it eagerly, with the attackers working the ball down the wide channels and forcing the defenders to reorganise repeatedly. Joao was enthusiastic as usual, but James noticed that his comments focused on the boys' movement and recognising what was happening around them. After a while, Joao switched a few boys around, giving players different roles to try.

At the end of the session, James asked the boys what they thought about the new formation. Everyone was keen to give it a try that weekend. Hakim said that he hadn't been sure at first, but after the practice he could see it working.

*

It was another week of iffy weather, but nothing compared to the previous one. James was confident that the game would go ahead. Swifts were at home again, as were the Hawks, but as Stoneleigh had two nine-a-side pitches, that wasn't a problem. It would mean potentially standing back-to-back with Kieran during the game, but he'd put up with that before.

On Friday, James was making a cup of tea when Ben, arriving home from school, sat himself down at the kitchen table and started talking.

94

'Dad, this new formation; Joao said you wanted to try it against Linford Road. Whose idea was it, yours or his?'

James smiled to himself, there wasn't much that got past Ben – maybe he should be playing in goal.

'That was Joao, I didn't need a lot of persuading though. Do you think it's a good idea?'

'Yeah, definitely. We were talking about it at lunchtime and the others all think you came up with it. Joao never makes it look like he's trying to take over or anything.' That hadn't occurred to James, but Ben was right. For all that Joao had revolutionised the team, he'd been careful not to undermine 'Mister James' with the boys. To think he'd been reluctant, initially, to get Joao involved.

*

Despite a blustery Saturday, James hadn't heard anything about postponements by Sunday morning. Working on the basis that no news was good news, James and Ben headed off to the match. The boys all arrived promptly and started kicking balls around until it was time for the proper warm-up. Strangely, there was no sign of Linford Road. For that matter, there was also no sign of the Hawks or their opponents, Redbridge. It wasn't like Kieran to be late for a game. The under-nines were warming up on one of the seven-a-side pitches, but apart from the Swifts, the nine-a-sides were deserted. James trotted over to the far touchline to talk to Lynn.

'It's definitely a home game, isn't it?' he asked.

'Yes!' she replied. 'I copied you in on the emails with Linford's secretary. Is it worth giving their manager a call?'

John, the Linford manager, picked up almost immediately. 'Hello James, what can I do for you?'

'Hi John. Is everything all right?'

'Yeah, a bit disappointed, obviously, but it can't be helped.'

'Aren't we supposed to be playing you today?'

There was a pause, then John said cautiously, 'Yeah... that's what I'm disappointed about. You guys called the game off, remember?'

Now it was James's turn to pause. 'Sorry, what?'

'You called the game off. Our secretary got an email this morning saying the pitches were waterlogged so you'd have to postpone the game.' James looked at Lynn, who could only hear his half of the call. 'Hang on, John, I've got our secretary here now; let me check with her.' He put the phone away from his mouth. 'He says they got an email from us saying the game was postponed.'

'What? I didn't send any email like that.'

James put the phone back to his face. 'John, who was the email from?'

'Let me have a look... Ron someone I think. Yes, here it is – Ron Butcher, chairman. It says that the nine-a-side pitches haven't recovered from the heavy rain over the last couple of weeks and are unplayable.'

James turned to Lynn and mouthed Ron's name before returning to the phone call. A dark expression loomed over her face.

'Ah, right, yes. Sorry, there must have been a crossed wire somewhere – I think Ron forgot to tell me about it. No worries, I guess we'll do it another time.' He rang off and turned to Lynn. 'Ron emailed them to cancel, said the nine-a-side pitches were waterlogged.'

Lynn's eyes were burning. 'He did, did he? Let's find Dave, see what he knows about all this.' James went over to the Swifts' parents and told them what had happened. Most of them were okay about it, but one or two reacted badly.

'It's a bloody joke!' complained Rob. 'Do you mean we're not even getting a match? There's nothing wrong with that pitch.'

'What can I say, Rob? I'm as disappointed as you. I don't know why no one told us about the cancellation, but I'm going to find out. Look, if anyone wants to clear off, that's fine. If not, I'm happy to let the boys have a kick-about now that they're here. I'm really sorry, everyone.'

Most of the boys stayed and soon a dads versus lads game was in progress. James left them to it and joined Lynn and Dave at the equipment lock-up. Lynn was in the corner, on her phone and Dave looked apologetically at James as he arrived.

'Sorry, mate,' he said. 'No one told me about any cancellations. Look: I've got the Hawks' gear out ready for their game. The pitches are a little boggy in places, but definitely playable.'

Lynn snapped her phone shut. 'I've just spoken to Ron. Apparently, the Hawks have an injury crisis. Three of their best players were off school ill this week and Kieran didn't want to go into such a crucial game with a weakened team. Not content with calling their game off, Ron cancelled yours too so it wouldn't look too suspicious.'

James and Dave exchanged looks, taking in what Lynn had just told them.

'You mean Kieran got his dad to call off our game, just so his team could avoid a potential defeat?'

'Yes,' bristled Lynn. 'That's exactly what happened. He wasn't even short of players – he's got such a big squad that he still had plenty to choose from, but he didn't have his stars so he didn't want to give Redbridge what he called "an unfair advantage".'

'Ron doesn't make the decisions about the pitches,' growled Dave. 'That's my call.'

'And he doesn't contact other teams about games,' added Lynn frostily. 'Ron's gone too far this time. This week's committee meeting is going to be lively.'

James thought about all the work the boys had put in on Wednesday night getting their heads around the new system. He didn't think the Hawks game next week was the right place to try it, so now they'd have to put the experiment on hold. At least the two games following were against weaker teams, so they wouldn't have too long to wait. James trudged back to the pitch to see how the kick-about was going. He joined in on the dads' team, and before long was laughing along with the rest of them. He got clattered by Max at one point after a hospital pass from Rob, and then five minutes later was nutmegged by Ben, much to Ben's glee and James's embarrassment.

One man with nothing to be embarrassed about was Joao, who had the advantage of being younger and fitter than all the dads and older and stronger than all the boys. He also had an impeccable first touch, a great eye for a pass and an endless ability to run from one end of the pitch to the other and back again. At one point, when Amir hit a slightly dodgy corner which went high and behind him, Joao pirouetted in the air and performed a perfect overhead kick that went, as Ben later described it to Ros, top bins. There was a moment of stunned silence before everyone just started applauding. Joao just shrugged and grinned, slightly embarrassed, but clearly enjoying the moment too.

The two Stoneleigh games turned out to be the only victims to the weather. Weston Park had continued their stroll through the second-division defences, beating Melville Dynamos ten-nil; Cole Hill had beaten the Royals two-one and Iain's Eastside Diamonds had beaten the still-pointless Moorlands Rangers for the second time in three weeks. A win for the Swifts today would have put them up to third place; as it was they had dipped into the bottom half, and a defeat to Hawks next week would leave them eight points adrift. James hated the phrase, 'must-win game', but he couldn't remember ever wanting to win a game of football more than the next one.

CHAPTER THIRTEEN

Tension hung over the committee meeting from the moment Ron and Kieran arrived. Lynn's usual playfulness was nowhere to be seen. Everyone knew why she was so brisk and businesslike, and no one was surprised that Ron tried to make light of it.

'Everyone does it: if you're the home team, the weather's iffy and you're missing a few players, you call off the game and blame the pitches. We've had it done to us before, what's wrong with us doing it to Redbridge?'

'So why didn't you ask me to cancel the games, Ron?' asked Lynn, eyes blazing.

'Because you might have said no,' replied Ron, bluntly. 'You'd have got your knickers in a bunch and started bleating about fair play or some rubbish. As I said, everyone does it, so what's the problem?'

'The problem, Ron, is that you went over my head,' responded Lynn.

'And mine,' added Dave. 'I look after the pitches. You never consulted me. More than that, even after you'd told the other clubs, you didn't bother to let me know. I had all the kit ready for your game – for both games.'

Ron shifted in his seat. 'Yeah, well, that was an oversight. I forgot about that.'

'That's why we follow a procedure,' said Lynn. 'So I can make sure everybody is told.'

'No one let me know either,' said James, quietly. He saw Kieran smirking. 'We had a winnable game.'

'Debatable,' dead-panned Kieran.

James ignored him. 'My boys missed their match last week as well; they were itching to play this time.'

'Yeah, well, that can't be helped,' said Ron. 'It was for the good of the club that we cancelled. Your match was a small price to pay to keep the Hawks on track.'

'Never mind that,' said Dave. 'I want to know what happens going forward. Do I have the final say on the pitches or not?'

'Yeah, mostly,' said Ron. 'Unless we need to make another quick decision like this.'

'Not good enough.' Dave spoke quietly, but his voice still bristled. 'Either you let me do my job without interfering, or you find a new ground manager. Do you want to get everyone's gear ready, Ron? You seem to like deciding how playable the pitches are, do you want to do that every week? To spend time picking up dog shit and forking pitches so they'll drain better? If you want me to do it, bloody well keep out of my way.'

Ron shrunk like a scolded child, staring downwards and waiting for the teacher to run out of steam.

'Thank you, Dave,' said Lynn at last. 'I think we should minute the committee's gratitude to Dave Grey for all that he does, and assure him that there won't be any further... what shall we say... misunderstandings about the process for calling off matches.'

James resisted the temptation to join in with the smackdown. Anything he said would seem limp after Dave and Lynn, and frankly the sight of a cowed Ron was quite enough to be going on with. As for the others, Howard looked deeply unsettled with the whole business, while Alison had the hint of a smile playing around the corner of her mouth.

In the car on the way home, James reflected on Dave's handling of Ron. Would Dave put himself up for chairman? He'd be perfect, but James doubted he'd be willing. He was like one of those teachers with great classroom management but no interest in taking a senior leadership role. James would love to see Dave in the classroom though.

That reminded James of another lesson with Kyle. The friendly chat hadn't worked, and on this particular day Kyle had arrived in a boisterous mood. It was the first lesson since James had sat Kyle apart from his mate Richie, hoping that a problem split up would prove a problem neutered. Not so much.

'Yo, Richie.Yo, Richie. Hey, Riiiiiichieeeee!' Kyle was calling out across the room. 'Can I borrow a pen? Lend us a pen, mate.'

'Kyle,' snapped James. 'You don't have to shout across the class to borrow a pen. Try asking someone sat next to you.'

'Good thinking, Mr H,' said Kyle enthusiastically, turning to Olivia, the unfortunate who had been placed alongside Kyle in James's new seating plan. 'Yo, Liv. Can I borrow Richie's pen?' A peal of laughter ran around the class. No learning would be taking place until James wrestled control back from Kyle. He strode over and produced a pen from his top pocket.

'Kyle, here is a pen. You will give it back to me at the end of the lesson. You will be quiet, and you will use the pen to get on with your work. You will not disrupt my lesson any further. Do you understand?'

'Are you calling me thick, sir?'

James sighed. 'No Kyle, I am not calling you thick. I am making sure that you understand what I'm telling you.'

'It's not hard to understand though, is it, sir? It's not as if you used long words or nothing: pen, work, lesson. If you think I can't understand that, you must think I'm thick. That's disrespectful, sir.'

James wanted to show Kyle just how much disrespect he had for him in that moment, but he swallowed it down. 'No disrespect intended, Kyle. I'm glad to hear that you understood my instructions. Now will you follow them and quietly get on with some work?'

'All right sir, seeing as you asked nicely.'

James had barely got back to his desk at the front of the class when Kyle started again.

'Yo, Richie. Riiiiiichieeeeeeeeeeee.'

'Whassup KK?'

'Can I borrow your ruler, mate?'

'Sure. I'll wang it over.' Richie picked up his ruler and made to throw it across the classroom.

James intervened once again. 'Richie, don't you dare throw that thing. Someone will get hurt. Kyle, why do you need Richie's ruler?'

'Straight lines, Mr H; you want me to underline titles and shit properly, yeah?'

The swearing had been the last straw. James sent Kyle out of the lesson and down to the head of year's office. He went, but not without complaining that James had it in for him. This was the pattern that was emerging: Kyle finding increasingly spectacular ways to disrupt the lesson, and James sending him out so the others could get some work done. James sometimes imagined just sending Kyle out in the first minute, a pre-emptive red card before the first offence was even committed. He knew that wasn't an option, even though just about every lesson was like refereeing Robbie Savage – you knew what he was going to be like, but you couldn't book him until he actually started. If James really did have it in for Kyle, he'd do a lot more than just send him out of the class. And then, of course, one day he did.

*

James arrived at training and opened up the equipment lock-up. It seemed roomier than usual, emptier.

'Where's all our stuff?' asked Ben, peering past James. 'The balls are usually right here.' Dave kept the lock-up pretty neat, with every team having their own spot. The Hawks' balls were missing too. James could see plenty of the size-three balls that the younger teams used, but the only size fours were deflated – not just gone a bit flat, but completely hollowed out. He picked up the carry bag and took a closer look. There, written in marker pen were the words *U12 Swifts*. It was their bag all right, but why were all the balls like this? He reached for the bag where Dave kept his ball pump, only to find that the needle was missing.

'What are we going to do, Dad? We can't train without footballs.' Some of the other boys were arriving now, and the murmurs of discontent were growing louder. James decided to make the best of it and reached for the size threes; they'd have to do.

After the boys had kicked a size three around, enjoying the ridiculous pace they could generate when pinging it at Rory, James called them together.

'Look, lads. Sorry again about the balls. I don't know what's happened, but we're going to have to make the best of it.'

'But we're playing the Hawks on Sunday,' moaned Max, with the others muttering their agreement. 'How are we meant to practise with kids' balls? This is a joke!'

'That's right, we're playing the Hawks, which means I just don't think it's the right game for the two-four-two formation. It's a shame we didn't get to try it after you all worked so hard, but I think we'll need three at the back this time around. Everyone agree?'

The boys all nodded, and voiced their approval. James was relieved to have distracted them from the balls fiasco. Then Josh asked, 'But are we going to play with one or two up front?'

James glanced at Joao, who responded with the slightest of shrugs.

'What do you boys want to do?' asked James. There was no clear consensus, with some wanting three-three-two and others preferring three-four-one. After a minute, James brought the discussion to a halt. 'Okay, me and Joao will have a think about that. Let's get on with the session. Joao, what have you got for us today?'

Joao focused on positioning and movement again, but this time he was mostly interested in the runs players made without the ball. He showed boys how to stay onside when making a run, he talked about runs for you and runs for your team-mate – moving a defender to make space for someone else to exploit. The boys, as ever, worked hard and James could see signs of progress by the time they had to pack up and go home. He really felt they had a chance on Sunday.

Once the session was over, James had time to think about the deflated footballs. It couldn't be Kieran, could it? Trying to sabotage their training session before the big game? James didn't know whether to be pleased that his rival clearly regarded the Swifts as a threat, or furious at the lengths he was taking. Either way, it just made him more determined not to let him get his own way.

*

James woke up with an uneasy feeling on Sunday morning. He just wanted to get on with things. At the same time, he was dreading the match, dreading how Kieran might try to throw him and the Swifts off their game. Hawks were officially the home team, so at least he didn't have to get there early to set up. They had eventually decided to start positively with the three-three-two. If the midfield was getting swamped, they could always pull a striker back. Despite James's promise to Joao, Charlie was left out again. To be fair, when he said he'd include Charlie in the next game, the next game hadn't been against the Hawks.

Charlie was looking more like a footballer every week, but 'more like' wasn't going to be good enough for this one. Next week, against Moorlands, definitely.

Opening the boot to load his car, something wasn't right, but James couldn't put his finger on what. Stepping back to take a wider look, he realised the car was sitting slightly low on the drive: all four tyres were flat. Bending down for a closer look, he saw nails driven into each one. It wasn't just bad luck, this had been done on purpose. He felt panic rising in his chest, threatening to engulf him. What was he going to do? He'd be late for the match – how was he going to get there in time? He only had one spare tyre, and even if he had more there wouldn't have been time to change all four. It didn't even occur to him that he needed the car for work the next day, all he could think about was the match.

He ran back inside, his mind railing wildly like a fan on a phone-in show. Ros tried to calm him, eventually getting what had happened out of him.

'Right,' she said. 'Here's what we're going to do. Let's phone Lynn and see if she can pick you and Ben up. While you're out, I'll phone the AA and get the car sorted. You just concentrate on winning your football match.' When she saw that he had eventually taken this in and was starting to calm down, she asked, 'Would Kieran do something like this, or is it just kids and bad timing?'

James wanted to say that not even Kieran would resort to these lengths; he wanted to but he couldn't. First, the footballs, now this; it had to be Kieran.

*

When Lynn got them to the ground, the Hawks were already warming up. Kieran was working with his goalkeeper in one of the goals, and James noticed that the net at the other end hadn't been set up yet.

'Hey Kieran, is there something wrong with the other goal?'

'Nah, I just thought I'd leave you to sort that one out, seeing as we're both at home really.'

'But you're the home team, you're meant to take care of all that.'

Kieran shrugged. 'Well, I've done ours. I suggest you get on with yours if you want to use it before the kick-off. It's not my fault if you leave getting here so late, is it?' He grinned as he saw James do a double take in response to the last comment, before adding, 'You're okay for footballs though, yeah?' With that, he turned to his keeper and got back to barking out instructions.

James gritted his teeth, trying to keep the growing cocktail of frustration and anger in check. Even knowing Kieran, he still found it hard to believe he'd go to these lengths just to win a kids' football match. There was no time to dwell on that though, he had the goal to sort out. With the help of a couple of the dads, James got the net in place a few minutes before they were due to start. Joao was warming up the boys, and James was just making his way across to deliver his team talk when the ref approached him.

'It's James, isn't it?' James recognised him; his son had been in Kieran's team for a few years now. 'I'm Phil, Kieran's asked me to ref today. I gather there's been some ill feeling between the teams, something about you not being happy with last week's cancellations and somehow blaming Kieran for the state of the pitches.' James opened his mouth to answer, but Phil cut him off. 'Warn your lads that I won't stand for any nonsense out there. You tell them that I'm keeping my eye on them.'

'Are you saying this to the Hawks as well?' asked James.

Phil glared back at him. 'Of course. What are you trying to suggest?'

James held his hands up, palms forward. 'Nothing, nothing at all. It's just that my lads aren't really like that.'

'Well, if that's the case we won't have a problem, will we? Ready to kick off in five minutes please.'

James quickly gathered the boys together.

'Okay lads, we all know this is going to be a tough one, but I know you can handle it. Have you heard of William Shakespeare?'

The Swifts grinned at one another.

'Even we know who Shakespeare is,' said Ben.

'Of course you do. He played for West Brom in the nineties then went into coaching. He wrote, "Ambition should be made of sterner stuff". You might think this is going to be a tough game, but if you don't believe we can do this, there's no point going out onto that pitch. It *is* going to be tough, but it's just another game. Play like you did against the Royals and we can give the Hawks a run for their money.' James looked around the boys' faces as he spoke, and was pleased to see a look of determination spreading across the group. Heads were nodding in agreement. 'Remember all the things we've worked on – stand the forwards up, don't dive in to tackles, and when we get the ball we pass and move. Set your ambitions high, and make sure this isn't a game where you come off wishing you'd given just a little bit more. Come on boys, let's do it.'

The game started brightly. Liam's pace was causing trouble down the right, where he was marked by the blond lad Kieran had poached from Eastside Diamonds. Dylan and Josh were carrying on where they had left off against Royals, combining well and almost – almost – opening up the Hawks' defence a couple of times in the first five minutes. There was nearly a third, but the linesman, another Hawks parent, raised his flag before Dylan could take the shot.

Kieran was stalking the touchline, bellowing instructions and berating his players.

'Fin! What was that? Hit it like you mean it. Jack! Make that challenge – it's not netball.'

Max was everywhere in midfield, winning tackles and making good decisions on the ball, playing like he had something to prove. For once he was making simple early passes rather than going for the flashy option. The ref seemed keen to give fouls against him though, and at the same time he let several nasty Hawks tackles go unpunished.

'Referee!' called James as one of the Hawks nearly cut Liam in half right in front of him.

'Nothing wrong with that, ref,' bellowed Kieran.

'Nothing wrong with that,' echoed Phil. 'Play on!'

James made his first substitutions, Ben and Hakim replacing Deepak and Ryan in defence. A few minutes later, Rory caught the ball and rolled it to Ben, in space on the right-hand side of the Swifts' box. James and Joao both shouted to Ben at the same time.

'Get rid of it!'

'Look for pass!'

Ben got the ball out from his feet and looked up to see what was on. Max was in space, calling for a short diagonal ball into midfield, and Liam was dropping back to give an option up the line. Ben ignored both, hitting a screamer of a pass over Liam's head, picking out a cross-field run that Dylan was making from left to right. The ball bypassed the entire Hawks midfield and left their defence scrambling as Dylan turned and ran towards goal. The Hawks keeper charged out of his goal and collided with Dylan as he poked the ball past him. Both boys went down in a heap and the ball trickled into the goal.

'No goal,' called the ref. 'Free kick.'

'What do you mean, no goal?' James shouted. 'It was our advantage, and we scored.'

'It's a free kick to the Hawks, not the Swifts,' replied the ref. 'Your lad followed through on the keeper.'

Dylan put his hands to his head in shock. 'You can't be serious!' he exclaimed. '*He* took *me* out. I had the ball – why would I want to foul him?'

'I saw what I saw,' snapped the ref. 'Now stop arguing. Free kick to the Hawks.'

James and Joao exchanged a disbelieving look, and James noticed Kieran grinning at him from further down the touchline. Dylan was still muttering as he took up his position for the free kick. Joao called his name and made a calming downwards motion with his hands.

'Let's go, Hawks,' called Kieran. 'They can't score without cheating, show them how it should be done.'

The momentum was shifting. The Hawks were getting on top now, but Rory and his defence were holding firm. Rory was having a great game, flinging himself around in the mud like he was looking for a sponsorship deal with a washing machine company, each save ramping up Kieran's frustration.

'Come on! Just put it in the net. How hard can it be? It's only the Swifts for God's sake.'

Joao put his hand on James's arm to prevent him from reacting.

Shortly before half-time, Dylan picked up the ball just inside his own half and set off on a run. He beat two Hawks before exchanging a one-two with Josh that took him past the last defender and through on goal. James glanced across at the dodgy linesman. Dylan had been nowhere near offside, and even this lino couldn't get away with flagging him. Dylan didn't want to risk the keeper coming out again, so he took aim from just inside the penalty box and fired the ball hard and low into the corner. Reluctantly, the ref pointed to the centre circle. The Swifts were winning one-nil.

'Get in!' yelled Dylan as his team-mates leapt on him. 'Let's see you disallow that one!' James heard Dylan's words, because Dylan was facing him when he said them. Fortunately, Dylan had his back to the ref, so the official heard nothing.

'Oi, Phil!' shouted Kieran. 'Did you hear what he just said? What he just called you?' The ref ran over to Kieran, and James quickly joined them. 'He was mouthing off about that one you disallowed before, calling you a cheat. Are you going to just stand for that?' The ref called Dylan over to him.

'Have you got something to say, young man?'

Dylan shook his head. 'No ref, just celebrating my goal.'

The ref turned to Kieran. 'I can't do anything if I didn't hear him.' He turned back to Dylan. 'I'm watching you, though.'

Kieran was getting louder and more red-faced by the minute, his ranting increasingly animated. His players responded with aggression of their own, but still the ref wouldn't give anything the Swifts' way. Wave after wave of attacks floundered on the twin peaks of Gabe at the heart of the defence and Rory in goal. Eventually, the half-time whistle blew with the Swifts still ahead.

'Superb, lads,' began James. 'Even better than against the Royals. Keep going and whatever you do, stay calm. We can't expect a fair shake from this ref, so don't give him an excuse to make a decision against you. Tackles have to be timed perfectly, and you can't afford to react to anything. Dylan, well done for keeping your cool. I'm going to take you off for a bit, but I'll get you back on later. We need you out there, but we need you calm.' Dylan nodded.

Joao spoke now. 'First five, ten minutes, they will throw everything at you. Stand strong. We want a second goal, but they *need* a goal – don't let them have it. Stand strong and remember to play.'

The second half started much as the first had finished, with a spate of Hawks attacks and a ref who only saw fouls from one team. From one of the many Hawks free kicks, the ball was pumped into the box. Rory came bounding out and leapt to gather the ball above the heads of the Hawks strikers. As he was in mid-air, one of the Hawks shouldered into him and sent him cartwheeling through the air. Somehow Rory kept hold of the ball as he landed in a heap. That didn't stop the Hawks from kicking out and in the melee, James heard Rory cry out in pain. The ref, to his credit, blew the whistle and checked Rory, quickly beckoning James onto the pitch.

Rory was holding his right arm gingerly; the colour had drained from his face.

'It's okay, Rory,' said James. 'Does it hurt?' Rory nodded, grimacing. 'Can you move it?' Rory took his left hand away and grimaced again. He shook his head. James turned to the ref. 'We're going to have to take him off.' The boys looked shocked and Max asked the question that was on everyone's mind.

'Who's going in goal?'

CHAPTER FOURTEEN

Gabe was probably the best keeper after Rory, but he was having a great game in defence. James looked around, hoping desperately to see someone else who might inspire some confidence, but coming up blank. He made his decision.

'What do you think, Gabe? Will you give it a go?' Gabe's eyes widened, but he nodded after a momentary pause. Rather than try to get Rory's keeper top off over his injured arm, Phil said it was okay for Gabe to wear a bib over his outfield shirt, ignoring Kieran's complaints about bibs being inappropriate at this level. For a moment, James thought he was going to side with Kieran, as he had done on every other decision.

James reorganised the others. 'Hakim, you go into the centre of defence. Ryan, stay as you are and Deepak, you drop back to join them. Callum goes back on in centre midfield and Dylan, we'll get you on in a little while. We can still do this. Gabe's going to do his best for us, but you've all got to protect him.'

Joao was helping Rory to the touchline and James saw Lynn making her way round to check on her boy. When she arrived James said, 'He can't move it, it doesn't look great. I think you're spending an afternoon at A&E.'

Lynn looked at Rory, concern written all over her face. Then she turned to James and almost spat out the words: 'Just you make sure you beat those dirty bastards!'

The Hawks were still intent on constantly fouling, and Phil was still intent on letting them. Both sets of parents were increasingly animated on the touchline, simultaneously mirroring and feeding the passion on the pitch. Dylan came back on for Josh and instantly became a target for particular attention from the Hawks. After being scythed down for the third time in five minutes, Dylan dragged himself to his feet and roared, 'What do I have to do to get a free kick? Look at the studmarks on my leg!' The ref called him over and gave him another talking to. James couldn't hear what he was saying but he saw Dylan taking deep breaths, trying to regain control. Dylan's dad was getting just as wound up, with Amir trying to calm him down on the touchline.

Eventually, the relentless pressure on the Swifts' goal got too much. After yet another Hawks corner, the ball was bouncing around in the Swifts' box like an unexploded hand grenade. Eventually, inevitably, one of the Hawks pounced to lash it into the net. James could almost see the hope evaporating from the Swifts' faces. They didn't deserve this.

'Yes!' yelled Kieran, raising both arms in triumph. 'Justice! Now go get another. Let's finish the job and beat this useless shower!'

James bit his tongue. If he started to give voice to his feelings, he might not be able to stop. He had to focus on his boys, not on Kieran.

'You can do it, lads. Keep going – not much longer.' He tried to sound convincing, but he wasn't even fooling himself; he couldn't see Phil giving the Swifts anything.

The Hawks were throwing everything forward, looking for the winner. Gabe never looked as comfortable as Rory, but he was doing a good job: saving most of what the Hawks sent his way and getting lucky with a few that whistled past his posts. Liam's pace created occasional counter-attacks, but if it didn't look like the defence could catch him, the linesman was quick to flag him offside.

'How long, ref?' shouted James. Phil looked at his watch and held up four fingers. Funnily enough, when James had asked five minutes ago, he had said five. Clearly, the Hawks were going to be given every chance to grab a winner. The Swifts were playing for their lives. One minute went by, then another, then another.

'How long, ref?' There wasn't even a response this time.

The Hawks surged forwards again. The little blond left winger dribbled his way into the box and then flung himself theatrically to the ground. Deepak wasn't even close to him, but the ref blew instantly and pointed to the spot.

'No way!' All of the Swifts were shouting now. 'He never touched him!' Phil just waved them away and repeated that it was a penalty.

'All those times they tried to break my leg, you give nothing,' fumed Dylan. 'And now, you give a penalty just because someone looked at him. You're the worst ref I've ever seen. You're a cheat!'

At that Phil spun round and glared at Dylan. 'What did you say, lad?'

'You heard!' Dylan was already walking, even before the words 'You're off' were out of Phil's mouth.

Gabe was composing himself on the goal line while Malky, Kieran's son, stepped up and placed the ball on the spot. He looked confident and he hit the ball hard to Gabe's right. Gabe flung himself after it, but never had a chance. The Hawks roared as the net bulged. Kieran joined the celebrations, knee-sliding down the touchline towards James, his face a grotesque mask of triumph and gratification. Before the Swifts could even retrieve the ball, Phil blew the final whistle; he'd got the result he wanted, so now the game could end.

Kieran made a beeline for James.

'That was a great game. You lot are better than I thought. A bit dirty, but not bad.'

'Us dirty? Us? Are you joking?' James could feel the blood pounding in his ears. 'My keeper has gone to hospital and you say *we're* dirty?'

Kieran grinned provocatively. 'The stats don't lie, mate. We had twenty-something free kicks and a penalty. You had one free kick and a man sent off. Seems clear to me. It's a shame your lot had to resort to that, but the better team won in the end. Handshake?'

'Handshake? Handshake?!' James's voice was steadily increasing in volume. 'You sent your boys out to kick my lot off the park, you put my keeper in hospital and you want me to shake your fucking hand? You don't have a clue, mate!'

Kieran laughed. 'Yeah? I've got three points though. I never had you down as a sore loser, Hogan. Surprising you're not better at it, what with all the practice you get.'

For a moment James's brain was flooded with impulses, none of them good. He wanted to go on shouting, swearing; he wanted to go beyond screaming, to make Kieran hurt. He stepped forward, not even sure what he was about to do.

Joao appeared at James's shoulder and pulled him back. 'Leave him, Mister James. He not worth it.' Somewhere amid the fury, James was impressed with Joao's textbook usage of such a cliché of British male posturing. Somehow the incongruity pulled James back from the brink, showing him how ridiculous he was being.

'Mister James,' said Joao. 'The boys.' James looked and his rage vanished, replaced by heart-breaking empathy. The Swifts looked devastated. Some – Ben, Callum, Hakim – were moving around, consoling their team-mates; others – Gabe, Dylan, Deepak – just looked broken. James breathed deeply, trying to find something to offer them.

'What can I say, boys? You were superb, again, all of you. You deserved to win that game, but sometimes you just don't get what you deserve.'

'It was so unfair,' moaned Deepak. 'That ref – I never touched him for the penalty!'

'I know, Deepak. Don't be hard on yourself; I think he was going to play until he could give them a winner.'

'Sorry, James.' It was Dylan. 'I shouldn't have lost my cool and got sent off.'

'To be honest, Dylan, the kicking they gave you, I'm surprised you lasted as long as you did. You were amazing. You know I never comment on referees, and I'm not going to change my principles for that biased, cheating idiot.' At least this made some of the boys smile. 'One team tried to play football today; one team deserved to win and one team should feel proud of themselves – and it's not the Hawks. You boys took them all the way, and with a fair ref you'd have won. Keep playing like that and you'll get the rewards you deserve. One more thing, I should apologise for what you just witnessed with me and Kieran. I can't tell you not to react and then lose it myself. I'm sorry, I'll try to do better.'

Liam spoke up. 'Do we know how Rory is?'

James shook his head. 'Not yet. I'll text his mum and see how they're doing. As soon as I know anything, I'll message everyone's parents.'

The parents had wandered over already. Rob was seething, and he wasn't the only one.

'That ref was a disgrace!' he spat. 'He let their lot get away with murder – almost literally with poor Rory.'

'I wanted to go and lay him out at the end,' fumed Dylan's dad. 'If Amir here hadn't held me back...'

'I know, I know.' James shrugged. 'I've just told the boys how proud I am of them – all of them. Let's try to focus on how well they did. Has anyone heard from Lynn?' There was a general shaking of heads. 'Right, I'll text her now then.'

James sent an *Any news?* to Lynn, and didn't have long to wait for the reply.

Still waiting to be seen. How did it finish? James remembered the last thing Lynn had said before taking Rory and felt guilty. *Lost two-one*, he texted. *Dodgy penalty deep into Kieran-time. Dylan sent off. Apart from that, all good!!!* Lynn responded with an array of angry and sad-looking emojis.

James had been trying to keep his emotions in check while all the other parents were around, but once he got home, he was able to drop his guard and sound off to Ros. James's momentary loss of control had passed, but his righteous anger was still boiling.

'It was so blatant! The worst thing is the way the Hawks tried to injure my players – Kieran must have said something because they definitely got worse after half-time. That man shouldn't be in charge of children; he's an animal.' And so was I, nearly, just for a moment.

Ros soothed and sympathised, coming out with the usual empty lines that were all anyone ever had in moments like this – it's just one game, it sounded like a moral victory – but she soon realised that James just needed space to brood and decompress.

*

James was still livid with Kieran, but almost as angry with himself. He had worked so hard in the last few months not to lose control, and he was embarrassed at throwing that all away. He felt like an alcoholic who celebrates his six-months-sober chip by getting to the bottom of a bottle of whisky. He hadn't reacted like that for ages, not since a day he knew he would never forget.

That day had started well, with an A-level lesson, discussing Ophelia from *Hamlet*. A year 9 group followed: more crowd control than teaching, but nothing out of the ordinary. Then the main act: 10R and Kyle Kettering.

It started like any other 10R lesson: boisterous chatter as he approached the classroom, no discernible change when he walked in. This time something was different, though James couldn't put his finger on what. There was something in the air, as if the students were anticipating something.

'Good morning class,' James started, trying to keep the suspicion out of his voice.

'Morning sir,' the class responded in a ragged chorus, Kyle's voice noticeably more enthusiastic than usual. James put his laptop bag down on the desk and pulled out his chair. And there it was. His chair was covered with what looked like the contents of the room's bin. Dust, chewing gum, a couple of banana peels, and other assorted detritus that James decided he was better off without identifying.

'Who is responsible for this?' he asked, as the class dissolved into sniggers.

'Responsible for what, sir?' It was Kyle, of course, using the last word in a way that stripped it of any sense of implied respect.

'You know precisely what I'm talking about, Kyle. This mess on my chair didn't move itself out of the bin, did it?'

'You don't know that, sir. It might have done.'

'No, Kyle, it might not. The contents of the bin remain in the bin unless some outside agency intervenes.'

'Maybe it was… what was that phrase you taught us the other week: dogs in the machinery?'

'Almost, Kyle, deus ex machina, although as I'm sure you recall, that term applies to an outside agency intervening to provide an artificial or contrived solution to an intractable problem, not to create a problem where there wasn't one.'

Kyle's grin broadened. 'Maybe the bin was intractably full, sir. Maybe the problem was not having enough room to put more crap in it? Someone – some dog in the machine – tipping it out onto your chair would be a solution to that, wouldn't it?'

'Yeah,' piped up Ollie, one of the smarter lads in the class, but with several strands of mischief in his DNA. 'It all depends on the narrative point of view, doesn't it, sir? If you're the protagonist of this story, the bin being emptied on your chair is a bad thing. But what if you're the antagonist? Wouldn't that make it a good thing?'

Kyle took the ball and ran with it. 'Yeah! What he said – you're just an antagonist. All you do is antagonise!'

James had wanted to reassert his authority. 'Well, protagonist or antagonist, I'm still expecting someone to come and clear up this mess, to put it all back in the bin. Kyle, up you come.' That had been the mistake, he had made it into a zero sum game: now whatever happened, one of them had to lose face.

'Why me, sir?' Kyle's playfulness tipped into defiance. 'Are you saying I did it?'

'I'd say you're a prime suspect, wouldn't you?'

Kyle's outrage, whether real or contrived, was growing. 'You can't say that, sir. You've got no evidence – did you see me do it? Did anyone see me do it? How do you know it wasn't like that when we all arrived? How do you know one of the other teachers didn't do it because they all think you're a boring wanker too?'

'That's it, Kyle, out you go. You can't call me that.'

'Why not, sir? You can't punish me for what the other teachers think of you.'

Fight-or-flight hormones swamped James's brain. 'I'm not punishing you for what the other teachers think; I'm punishing you for what you called me. I won't put up with swearing in my classroom.'

'So you admit that the other teachers do think you're a boring wanker, sir?' The triumph in Kyle's voice was unmistakable. He turned to address his peers, to make sure that everyone knew that he'd reduced James to. 'Hogan just admitted that even the teachers think he's a boring wanker!' The class was jubilant: laughing, cheering, mocking James.

'That's not what I said, Kyle. Now get out of my classroom.'

'No.' Kyle sat back in his seat and folded his arms. 'I won't. Are you going to make me? Wanker.'

Blood was pounding in his ears now, he was struggling to keep control.

'Kyle, this is only going badly for you from here. Why don't you make it easy on yourself by walking down the corridor to the head of year's office rather than making me call for a member of the senior leadership team.'

'They won't help though, will they, sir? They all think you're a boring wanker too.' The rest of the class rallied to Kyle's side, a loud buzz of disembodied voices echoing 'boring wanker' over and over again.

And then it happened. The words erupted out of James's mouth in spite of himself. He had the sensation of watching as if he was someone else, as if he was a YouTube video entitled 'English teacher kicks his entire career into touch'.

'Shut up! Shut up! Shut the fuck up!' The room fell into a shocked silence, but James was too far gone to stop now. 'Listen here, you miserable fuckwits. I am not a wanker, boring or otherwise.' He was lost in the storm, adrift in a deep, deep ocean of frustration, resentment and hatred. 'You lot, on the other hand, are a bunch of malodorous wankers with no prospect of getting on in life until you start to show some respect to the people who are trying to help you. As for you, Kyle Kettering, you bag of shit, you miserable cockwomble; get the fuck out of my classroom. And for all I care, you can fuck off and die!'

For a moment, time stood still in the classroom. Nobody – least of all James – could believe things had escalated so far so quickly. It was the longest moment of James's life as everyone took in what had just happened. Once the moment of shock had passed, the class coalesced into a single organism, one that sensed fresh blood.

'Whooooaaaa!' roared the beast, the noise a mixture of delight, astonishment and vindictiveness. Kyle's eyes shone.

'Oh, sir,' said Kyle gleefully. 'I don't think you should have said that, sir. You could get into a lot of trouble for that, calling me names and shit.'

The others were quick to join in, quick to play their part in shredding their prey's carcass.

'Sir, did you call us all fuckwits and wankers, sir? That's not very nice.'

'I thought you wouldn't put up with swearing in your classroom, sir.'

'Do you still want to call in senior management, sir? I don't think they'd like what you just called us.'

'Shall *we* go tell the head, sir?'

'What even is a cockwomble, sir?'

James had lost. He knew the story would be all over the school within minutes, given that the school's rules about mobile phone use were more honoured in the breach than the observance. He noticed a couple of girls in the back row who had already got their phones out and were furtively texting. He felt light-headed, dizzy. All that remained was to leave with whatever dignity he could still scrape together.

He quickly gathered his things, packing up his laptop while talking – if he was speaking, it might stop them from throwing further taunts at him, at least for a moment.

'Well 10R, good luck for your exams; good luck for your lives. I hope at least some of you work out how to be decent human beings. As for you, Kyle,' James paused, still not sure how this sentence was going to end, 'You'll either end up serving fries or serving time. Personally, I hope it's the latter – you'll have the living shit kicked out of you in prison.'

As the beast roared with malevolent glee, James walked out of the classroom, keeping his head high in a last, hollow show of strength. He went straight to the English department office and threw up, ironically enough, in a bin. One of his colleagues, Mandy, was there and once she had got the story out of him she went to take charge of 10R. James just sat in the office trying to make sense of what had happened. Fifteen years of teaching, trashed in a moment. He knew there was no coming back from this. He set up his laptop and dashed out an email to the head, trying to get ahead of the oncoming storm.

Dear Dr North,

I'm very sorry to say that I lost my cool with 10R and Kyle Kettering this morning and said some things that I really shouldn't have done. I'm sure you will hear all the details very soon. I was placed under severe provocation but that's no excuse for what I said. I know that I'll be hearing from you in due course, but I think the best thing all round for now is if I simply go home for the rest of the day.

Apologies,

James Hogan.

And that was that. James's career was over and Kyle became a hero: the boy who pushed a teacher over the edge. In his mind, the faces of Kyle and Kieran morphed one into the other: Kieran was probably somewhere now, crowing about how he had got one over on James, beating his team on the pitch and reducing him to a ranting, impotent fool on the touchline. Would James ever learn not to rise to the bait?

James's musings were interrupted when his phone rang. It was Lynn, calling from the hospital.

'Compound fracture in his forearm, just below the elbow. They reckon he won't be back to playing for a couple of months.'

'Oh, no. How's Rory feeling about that?'

'How do you think? He's gutted. He feels really guilty too – says he let the team down, that it's his fault we lost.'

'That's ridiculous,' said James.

'That's what I said. I told him to stop acting like a bloody idiot and feeling sorry for himself. Then I started crying and gave him a big hug. I got Kieran's confirmation text about the result, by the way. Do you know, he didn't even ask me how Rory was doing? There's no way we can let him take over as chairman, just no way.'

CHAPTER FIFTEEN

'Papa-Romeo Five-Three. We've got a non-compliant, potentially violent shoplifter apprehended by store security at the Quick Stop supermarket on Morgan Street. Can you deal?'

Pikey pushed the button on his radio. 'Roger that, Control. Papa-Romeo Five-Three and Yankee-Echo Four-Five on our way. ETA four minutes.' He turned to Hayley. 'You heard that?' She nodded a confirmation. 'Let's go.'

Once they arrived at the supermarket, they were ushered into a room at the back, away from the public. There was a young woman sitting on a plastic chair, rocking a pushchair and failing to settle a crying baby. The store security guard, a young man positively bristling with energy, was standing by the door – Pikey almost hit him with it as they came in. Hayley wondered whether the guard was making sure the shoplifter didn't make a run for it. She didn't look very non-compliant; she looked too worn out even to try crawling away.

'About time too,' said the guard. 'Here she is. I hope you're going to throw the book at her.'

Pikey took the lead. 'Non-compliant?'

'Well, she's calmed down a bit now. Anyway, you lot don't come if we don't say that.'

'What exactly did she take?'

'It's all here.' The guard pointed to a pile of things on a table by the side of the door, which Hayley hadn't seen as they came in. Baby formula, tampons, a couple of packets of biscuits.

'She was slipping them inside the pushchair when we weren't looking. She bought a few things, but not nearly as much as she tried to smuggle out.'

'So did she actually try to leave the store without paying for these?'

The guard smiled as he answered. 'Oh yes. I made sure that she walked off the premises before I challenged her – I wasn't going to let her wriggle out of this. This isn't my first rodeo. I thought about joining you lot, you know, but I didn't fancy all the paperwork.'

'And is it worth prosecuting her for this lot?' asked Hayley. 'I mean, it can't come to more than £20, can it? £30 tops.' It might be good for her arrest figures, but it was hardly worth the paperwork, and the poor girl looked like she could do with a break.

The guard's shoulders went back as he puffed himself up to his full height. 'That's not the point, is it? Theft is theft. When stuff gets stolen, the cost of it gets put back on the honest customers. Why should everyone else pay just so the likes of her can get a few freebies?'

Hayley was about to argue, but Pikey jumped in first. 'Absolutely, sir. You're right of course.' He half-turned to Hayley and gave her the slightest of winks on the guard's blind side before paying for the stolen shopping, explaining that he needed to take the evidence, and getting a receipt from the security guard so he could be reimbursed. The guard tried arguing at first, until Pikey said they could review the security footage to see just how non-compliant she was, which seemed to clip his wings a bit – Hayley guessed he knew the footage wouldn't back up his version of events. Pikey turned to the poor shoplifter. 'What's your name, love?'

'Abi,' came the sniffed reply.

'All right, Abi. I'm going to have to take you in. Come with us, please.' Hayley quickly gathered up the shopping and followed Pikey, Abi and the pushchair towards the shopfront door.

As soon as the three of them were out of the shop and out of the guard's sight, Pikey stopped walking and radioed the station, who confirmed that Abi had no previous convictions. He turned to face her.

'Do you want to tell me about it, Abi? How desperate have things got?' The poor girl looked terrified, despite the fact that Pikey was using a much gentler tone than when he'd been inside the store. Hayley wasn't sure she was even out of her teens and her face looked drawn and tired. Receiving no more than a shrug by way of an answer, Pikey carried on. 'Here's what we're going to do. We're going to take you and the little one home, and – with your permission – we'll have a quick look around. As long as we don't find any signs of serious criminal activity, I think we can let this one slide. I mean, if this is part of a huge scam in dealing black market baby formula, we might have to take it further, but something tells me that's not what's going on here.'

Sure enough, Abi's flat turned out to be perfectly innocent. It was a mess, which Abi was hugely apologetic about, with a massive pile of washing next to the machine and wet baby clothes drying in the kitchen alongside a sink full of unwashed plastic bowls and plates. Pikey gave the cupboards a quick once-over while Hayley sat and chatted. The baby's dad was long gone even before little Archie was born, while Abi didn't get on with her parents and didn't have any contact with them. After a few minutes, Pikey announced himself satisfied that they hadn't just broken the international puréed apple triad.

'Have you got anyone supporting you with Archie?' Abi shook her head. 'Well, you need help. St John's Church do some great drop-in groups and they'll be only too happy to give you lots of help, no strings attached.' He pulled out his phone and found a number, which he wrote down for her. 'Give the church a ring;

they're good people. And let me put you in contact with social services.' Abi's eyes widened, flaring with fear, so Hayley jumped in quickly.

'They won't try to take Archie away from you – you're a good mother, just a bit overwhelmed right now. You need help and that's what the social workers are there for.' Once Abi seemed reassured, it was time for the two officers to leave. Hayley went to pick up the bag of shopping, but Pikey reached over and took it from her. 'There's no need for us take this any further, so we don't need to keep the evidence. And as the shop has already been paid, I guess that means this is yours now, Abi. If I were you, I'd do my shopping somewhere else from now on, though; I don't think you're going to be very welcome at Quick Stop. And get in touch with social services. Let someone give you a helping hand – for Archie's sake.' He glanced over at Hayley, avoiding eye contact, and slipped some notes out of his wallet. He put them down on the table next to the shopping. 'This should help until they can get you some support.'

*

'That was unexpected – the money I mean,' said Hayley once they were back on the beat.

'Well, the poor kid. How would it have helped anyone for us to prosecute? She's struggling enough just dealing with the kid; the last thing she needs is a criminal record. The way I see it, we'd just be putting more obstacles in their way. Sometimes you have to bend the rules to do the right thing.'

'Martin Pike, you're going soft.'

He grinned sheepishly. 'Nah, I just didn't like that security guard. I'm still the same old mean-spirited bastard I've always been. And if you tell anyone at the station about this, I'll start making up rumours about you and Sergeant McGlashan.' He grinned at Hayley's wide-mouthed reaction. 'I can be very inventive when I put my mind to it – you don't want to know what I'd have you doing.'

*

Training was all about goalkeeping that week, with Joao covering basic technical stuff – handling technique, narrowing angles, collapsing leg dives, that kind of thing – in the hope of finding a decent stand-in. Rory had come along, sling and all, and everyone was pleased to see him. He acted as a third coach, wandering around giving pointers to the others. James was impressed at how patient Rory was, how he brought out positives while critiquing the mistakes. At one point he asked Rory if he wanted to take over as manager, which at least made Rory smile.

As the session went on, a pecking order of goalkeeping talent began to emerge. Gabe and Hakim were quite good, Ben and Callum were awful and most of the others were somewhere in between, though Max made it clear that he had no interest in playing in goal. The two who really impressed though were Ryan and Charlie. James drew them aside towards the end of the session to ask how they felt about playing in goal on Sundays. Ryan shrugged, saying he was happy to give it a go, while Charlie looked less confident but agreed nonetheless. James suggested that the two of them went in goal for the match at the end of training, so he could see how they did in a more realistic situation. Both boys did well, which was a relief, and afterwards Charlie seemed happier than before. Moorlands weren't likely to create too much of a problem, so at least Sunday should be a gentle introduction.

The goalkeeping situation wasn't the only thing James was mulling over. How could he even consider going back to teaching if he could lose it like he had on Sunday? Granted, no student would ever be as provocative as Kieran, and there would be no dodgy refs to deal with in the classroom, but he couldn't afford another Kyle incident. Ros may be keen on him going back, but would she want to find herself picking up the pieces again?

The next day, sitting in the town centre between fares, James was running through possible line-ups in his head – he couldn't risk two-four-two with a stand-in keeper – when Lynn called him.

'Hi Lynn, how's the patient?'

'Complaining a lot. He definitely perked up after training yesterday though. He said it was frustrating not to be able to play, but he enjoyed being out there with all his mates.'

'He was great. It was really useful having him there.'

'Aw, that's nice. Anyway, I've got some bad news. Would you believe Phil told the league about sending Dylan off? He's been banned for two games.' Sending-offs were rare at this level, and there was an unwritten rule that if the game was taken by a parent rather than a league-appointed ref, bookings and sendings off were kept between the clubs to avoid kids missing matches.

'Why did he go and do that?'

'Spite, I think. I gather some of our parents spoke to him after the game and they didn't hold back. Either that or Kieran told him to make your life harder. There'll be a fine for the club as well, probably £15 or £20, which is generally passed on to the parents of the player.'

'Stuff that, I'm not making Dylan's dad pay for Phil being a dick. When the fine comes through, I'll pay it.'

'I thought you'd say that.' James could hear the warmth in Lynn's voice.

The news of Dylan's suspension meant he couldn't continue his partnership with Josh up front. Charlie and Ryan had agreed to a half each in goal, so James decided to start with the strongest possible defence: Hakim, Gabe and Deepak. Why not try Ryan up front with Josh for the first half – it's only Moorlands, after all. That left Max, Callum, Liam and Ben for three midfield spots and one sub. Ben was sub last time, and Max and Callum had both been subs before, so… Liam? James hesitated over this, Liam was possibly the most skilful player in the team, and his pace was a major weapon. Leaving him out would be fairest, but shouldn't they play the strongest team possible, get some goals before thinking about rotation?

His decision-making was interrupted by the news that he had a pick-up from a house ten minutes away. He punched the address into his satnav and started his engine.

His fare turned out to be a young student called Maddie, who was happy to chat as he drove her to the station. She had come home for a few days because her mum had been poorly, but now she was heading back to university. She was studying English, and looked concerned to hear that her taxi driver had done the same degree – probably anxious about her career prospects. She visibly relaxed when James said that he had been a teacher for several years and this was just a stopgap job. They chatted about *Paradise Lost*, which she was studying that term, and discussed Blake's view that Milton was of Satan's party without realising it. She took C S Lewis' side of that debate, while James sided with Blake. She knew her stuff though.

'But come on,' he said at one point. 'Milton paints Satan as the classic epic hero. Deep down, he loves him – he clearly thinks he's great.'

'No, no, no,' Maddie responded. 'Milton *does* paint Satan as a classic hero, but then systematically undermines him. Long before the end, Satan is so diminished there's nothing heroic left. Milton wants us to reassess what makes a hero. The true heroes of *Paradise Lost* are Adam and Eve at the end of the poem, facing the reality of their fall and making the best of things. God and Satan are just a sideshow, the poem is about holding onto what's right even after you've got everything hopelessly wrong.'

James remembered another quote. '"The world breaks everyone and afterwards many are strong at the broken places".' He saw her looking quizzically at him in the rear-view mirror. 'Hemingway,' he added. '*A Farewell to Arms.*'

She grinned. 'I'll use that in my next essay; it fits really well.'

As James helped Maddie with her bags he noticed she was wearing one of those WWJD wristbands – What Would Jesus Do? If she was a Christian, that partly explained her taking Lewis' side over Blake. It also helped with his decision about team selection; in future with decisions concerning matters of fairness, he'd ask one question: what would Kieran do? Whatever the answer, James would do the opposite. That meant Liam starting on the bench this week.

It had been great talking literature with Maddie. As much as teaching could feel like an exercise in having his soul slowly extracted through the most painful metaphysical orifice available, he really missed the other side of it. Challenging students towards fresh insights, seeing them engaging with ideas; that made it all worthwhile. There would always be the Kyles, but he'd forgotten about the Maddies. Was it really too late for him to give teaching another try?

He was pulled out of his thoughts by the sight of a familiar face waving at the side of the road. It was Richard, his former second-in-department from Brookton High, with a couple of bulky bags of shopping. James edged his car forward twenty yards or so and wound down the window.

'Richard, mate; what are you up to?'

'Blimey, James. What were the odds? I'm trying to get this lot home. Any chance you could take me?'

'Well, I'm not meant to pick people up without a prior booking, but as long as I don't charge you, I'm not doing anything wrong. Hop in.' He entered a code into his management app to go off duty as Richard manhandled the bags into the back seat.

'Are you sure this is all right? I mean, I wasn't expecting a freebie – I'm happy to pay.'

'I'm just glad to do a favour for a mate. Are you still living in Devonside Close?' Richard confirmed the address so James set off. 'I mean, if you really want to pay me back, how about buying me a drink sometime? It'd be good to have a proper catch-up one night soon.' A lot of James's old colleagues had melted into the background when the Kyle thing blew up, as if they were afraid of being tainted by association, but Richard had got in touch as soon as he heard about it. Looking back, part of James's problem was that Richard and Lynn had both left Brookton at around the same time, leaving James without the safety net of his most supportive colleagues. James had often thought that if they had still been at the school, things might have played out very differently. Soon the two old friends were swapping stories of mutual acquaintances and what they were up to these days.

*

When James got home, he noticed a familiar car parked up outside his house.

'Hello?' he called as he made his way through the front door. 'Is Madam Secretary paying us a visit?'

'We're in here,' called Ros from the front room. 'Come and join us.' James was surprised to see that as well as Lynn, Alison was there. Lynn and Ros knew each other well from her time working with James, though he hadn't been aware that his wife and Alison knew each other.

'Oh, hi Alison, I didn't know you were here too. What's going on?'

'Well, that's charming, isn't it?' Lynn put on a tone of mock umbrage. 'I thought we'd get a warmer welcome than that. Maybe we should rethink our plans.' Ros and Alison were chuckling, though James didn't entirely understand what Lynn was talking about.

'Sorry, I didn't mean it like that. Of course, you're more than welcome. But what is this? Some kind of sub-committee meeting?'

'Something like that,' said Ros. 'Jamie, darling, come and sit down. Lynn and Alison have got something they want to talk to you about.'

'The three of us have been talking,' said Alison. 'And we're all agreed: you're going to be the next chairman of Stoneleigh Football Club.'

'Hail Hogan,' said Lynn. 'Manager of the Swifts. You shall be club chairman hereafter! We can't let Kieran win.'

'Ron's been bad enough,' added Alison, 'but this is our chance to get someone who will actually put the kids first.'

'But why me? Who says I want to take on Ron and Kieran in an election – they're not going to go without a fight, are they?'

'You leave the election to us,' said Lynn. 'You're the perfect candidate.' She glanced across to Ros who took up the conversation.

'Think about it. We've been saying for ages that you need some kind of a project to get your teeth into, something more than driving a taxi till all hours. You were great at running an English department; running a kids' football club will be a piece of cake in comparison, particularly as Lynn has the admin ticking like a Swiss watch. All you have to be is the figurehead.'

'The frontman,' said Alison.

'The anyone-but-Kieran,' said Lynn. 'Look, all it needs is someone the younger managers will look up to and who won't make the club look bad when he deals with the league. Someone who isn't an arsehole, basically.'

'And you're the closest we can get to that Platonic ideal,' added Ros. 'Anyway, it's not as if you've got a choice: the three of us have agreed, so that's that. You concentrate on winning that stupid bet of yours, and leave the election to Lynn. You know nobody schemes quite like her.' Lynn and Alison started gathering their things and getting ready to leave.

'Lovely to meet you, Ros,' said Alison. 'This was fun.'

'Yes,' agreed Ros. 'We must do this again soon.'

'Absolutely,' said Lynn. 'When can we three meet again?'

James went upstairs to change, leaving the three women comparing diaries. So, not only was he doing battle with Kieran on the pitch, now they were competing off it as well. He wished he could be sure that either campaign would end in success.

CHAPTER SIXTEEN

To say the Moorlands game went badly would be an understatement. The first half was disjointed and scrappy. Ryan kept getting caught offside, and even when Liam came on the Swifts struggled to put anything together. Charlie was nervous in goal, but did okay. He only had simple saves to make, which he made look more difficult than they were, but at least his goal was still intact when the game reached half-time.

Charlie replaced Deepak in defence and Ryan took over in goal, but the second half was more of the same. The Swifts were doing most of the attacking, now with Liam alongside Josh up front, but a mixture of poor passing and inaccurate finishing kept the score at nil-nil. James was prowling the touchline, shouting instructions and trying to direct his players to create something that looked remotely like football. Ryan was easily distracted when the ball was down the opposite end, and eventually his lack of focus led to disaster. A rare Moorlands attack broke down the right wing. Ryan was slow to get into position, and when the Moorlands player sliced his cross, it dipped wickedly under the crossbar and into the Swifts' net. Even though it was a massive fluke, Moorlands celebrated like they had just won the Champions League. Ryan punched the turf in frustration as Max ran to get the ball out of the net and onto the centre spot, ready to kick off again. The Swifts surged forward, desperate to make amends, but it was too late. All too soon, Ed blew a mournful final whistle and the Swifts' humiliation was complete.

As James was taking down the goal nets, Dave Grey wandered over. James had noticed him on the touchline, watching the game.

'That looked tough,' Dave offered. 'One of those days?'

'Yeah, another one.'

'I heard about Lynn's lad, what the Hawks did to him. Are those two keepers who played today the best you've got without him?'

'Looks like it,' replied James. 'I mean, they're not bad, either of them, but they're not proper keepers.' He shrugged. 'What else can I do?'

'Funny you should ask. My brother has just moved into the area. His Sam is a goalkeeper, played to a decent level where they used to live and hasn't found a team down here yet.'

'What age is Sam? Is he year 7?'

Dave hesitated for a moment. His eyes rolled upwards as he thought. 'Yeah, that's right. Just turned twelve the other week.'

'Sounds perfect. See if you can get him to training this week.'

Dave grinned. 'Will do. Text me with the time, and I'll get right on it.'

James caught up with Lynn and Rory in the car park – Rory had come along to support his team-mates – and told her about the conversation with Dave. She said she'd drop the registration forms round to James that evening, for him to pass on to Sam on Wednesday.

'Make sure they get them back to me as quickly as possible, though. If you want to play him next weekend, the registration has to go through by Thursday night.'

James couldn't help but feel that things were looking up again. If Dave's nephew was half decent, they might be in with a chance.

*

Wednesday training; James and Joao were setting out cones and the boys were kicking footballs. Word had spread about the new keeper and everyone was keen to see Sam in action. Ben spotted Sam first, walking towards the Astroturf pitches with Dave. He nudged Liam and soon all the boys were looking. This wasn't what they had been expecting. Sam was tall – at least as tall as Gabe – and had a lean, athletic build. He also had long blond hair tied back and what looked like the beginning of breasts developing. Sam wasn't a he, he was a she. The looking turned into staring, which turned into urgent whispering among the boys.

'Evening James.' Dave grinned as he drew closer with his unexpectedly female companion. 'This is my niece, Samantha, but everyone calls her Sam. You might want to close your mouth, James. I know it's just surprise rather than anything seedy, but it's not a good look, mate.'

James pulled himself together. 'I'm so sorry, Sam. Your uncle never mentioned that you were a girl.'

Sam smiled. 'Yeah, sorry about that. He told me he wanted a bit of fun at your expense. Family, eh, what can you do? It's not a problem is it – me being a girl?'

'God no – boys' football is officially a mixed league, so girls are allowed. If you want to play with this lot,' he indicated over his shoulder to the gaping Swifts, 'you're very welcome.'

'Cool. I'm not late, am I?'

'Right on time. I think Joao was just about to start. Let me introduce you to the lads.'

The boys seemed to be struggling to shake off the shock and were definitely quieter than usual.

'What's wrong with you lot?' asked James. 'Haven't you ever seen a goalkeeper before?'

Joao put the group through the usual dynamic stretching routines. Sam took it in her stride, though some of the boys seemed a little more awkwardly self-conscious than usual. By contrast, others – Dylan and Ryan, for example – seemed to be making an effort to impress their new, exotic team-mate.

James turned to Dave. 'Getting forgetful in your old age, Dave? You never mentioned that Sam was a girl.'

'Must have slipped my mind. Seriously though, I know some people are funny about girls and football. I didn't think you'd be one, but just in case, I wanted you to see her play before you dismissed the idea. She's good, you'll see.'

It didn't take long for Sam to prove Dave's point. She was good – really good. They started with shooting, which after last Sunday was clearly in desperate need of improvement. The standard of finishing was much better, but even so, none of the boys could beat Sam. When they played a match at the end, Joao deliberately put some of the best attacking players – Dylan, Liam, Max – against Sam, and as the game went on swapped Gabe and Hakim out of her defence to give her less protection. It made no difference: she commanded her area, barking orders at defenders, and wasn't afraid to dive at the forwards' feet when needed. In short, she looked fantastic. Towards the end of the session, James asked Joao what he thought.

He smiled broadly. 'She superb. Brave, good decision-maker, good shot-stopper. Gift from God!'

James had planned to ask Sam privately how she felt about joining the team, but when everyone was together at the end of the session, the boys got there first.

'Is Sam signing for us?' asked Ryan eagerly.

'Can she play on Sunday?' chorused the others.

James looked from Sam to Dave and back again. 'What do you think, Sam? Are this lot good enough for you?'

Sam grinned mischievously. 'I don't know about that, but I'll give it a go if you want me.' The boys all cheered. James wasn't convinced they were all thinking entirely about football, but Sam clearly deserved her place on merit. James gave Sam the registration forms and said that her parents had to get them to Lynn as soon as possible. Dave assured James that he'd take care of it. Sam pulled on her sweatshirt and James noticed the club badge on it.

'Ah, so are you a Nottingham Forest fan, Sam?' he asked.

'Not exactly,' she replied bashfully and paused before continuing. 'I used to play for their girls' team.'

James looked over to Dave, whose grin was now so fixed it looked like it had been tattooed on. 'Played at a decent level, you said?' he asked with raised eyebrows.

'It's only Forest,' replied Dave. 'It's not as if they're anything special, but I'll admit they qualify as decent. Just about.'

*

Dave phoned James that evening to fill him in on Sam's history. She had played for Forest's girls' team for a couple of years, and only left because of her dad's work relocation. Although the club were pleased with her, she had been getting fed up with how serious it was: training multiple times a week, football coming ahead of everything else. It was all about commitment, and Sam wasn't sure that she wanted football as the biggest thing in her life. The move had given her the chance to step back, but when Dave had mentioned the Swifts' situation, she had been taken with the idea of playing just for fun again. She had really enjoyed her first session, said that the boys were nice, even if a few seemed a bit awkward with her, and she had liked James and Joao. She was happy to help while Rory was out of action, but she didn't want to upset anyone by taking Rory's place once he was fit again. James hadn't even thought of that. Sam seemed even better than Rory; he would love her to join the team permanently, but he also had to be fair to Rory – reverse WWKD and all that.

*

'…So the bloke turns to me and asks, "And do I get a VAT receipt for that?". Can you believe it?' Richard shook his head, chuckling at James's story. It hadn't taken long to find a night they could both make for their pub-bound catch-up.

'I mean though, it seemed like a good idea at the time, moving into taxi driving: more control of my hours, choose which shifts I work. The trouble is, to make decent money I have to work a lot of evenings and that means I hardly see anything of Ros.'

'Why not come back to teaching? Every school is struggling to find enough good teachers to cover the timetable. We're short at the moment if you fancy it – I could put in a good word with our head and I'm sure she'd give you a chance.'

'Put the old team back together? But with you as department head this time?' It was a tempting thought, particularly after his chance meeting with student Maddie, but maybe he was better off out of it.

James took a long pull on his pint then shook his head decisively. 'I don't think so. I mean, taxi driving isn't perfect, but at least I don't have to put up with late nights marking books and planning lessons, departmental politics and angry parents who think it's my fault that their child is a lazy good-for-nothing who couldn't recognise a subordinating clause if their lives depended on it. And if I pick up someone like Kyle Kettering, I can just pull over and dump him on the pavement.'

Richard put his pint down and looked James in the eyes. 'That was a one-off. We both know there's more to you as a teacher than Kyle bloody Kettering. That shouldn't stop you from coming back.'

'Well, it's hardly a great addition to my CV, is it?'

Richard wouldn't leave it. 'Maybe all you needed was a break. Now that you've had one, maybe it's time to come back to the classroom.'

'Or maybe I don't need the aggravation – idiot kids and idiot colleagues.'

'Thanks.'

'Not you, but you know what I mean.' Richard nodded a concession of the point. 'Maybe I'm better off out of it. Anyway, how are you and Linda getting on – when is the baby due?'

'A couple of months. I'm making the most of nights out like this before he arrives.'

'Got any names picked out?'

'One or two. What do you think of Kyle?' There was a moment's pause, before both men roared with laughter.

'What are you laughing about, Hogan?' A third voice joined their discussion. 'If my team had lost to Moorlands at the weekend, I think I'd be crying. Mind you, my team would never lose to that shower – you must be really bad. Or did you not have a full squad?' Kieran's smirk turned into a long belly laugh.

James could see Richard taking all this in, trying to work out the unspoken part of the conversation. 'I had most of them – apart from the goalkeeper you injured and the lad you got suspended,' said James.

Kieran laughed again. 'The keeper's not much of a loss – he's probably no worse with one arm than he was with two.'

'Your boys couldn't score past him.'

'Biding our time, mate, that's what we were doing. Toying with you. We knew the goals were coming, don't you worry about that.'

'Is that why the ref played so much additional time? You were looking pretty desperate there at the end. If you're that good, why do you have to cheat?'

Kieran's face contorted, and James thought he was going to take a swing at him. Fortunately, Kieran was distracted by his phone ringing. He pulled it out of his pocket and stared at the screen before rejecting the call.

'The wife,' he grunted dismissively. 'Where were we?' In his drunken state, Kieran had already forgotten James's insult.

Richard spoke up for the first time. 'I think you were wishing

James luck for Sunday.' He flashed James a look to steer him away from further confrontation.

Kieran laughed. 'Luck? You'll need it, mate! Melville aren't all that, but they're better than your shower.'

'Well, say what you like, Kieran. I wouldn't swap my Swifts for your Hawks if you paid me.'

'Whatever. I'm going back up to the top division and next season you won't even have a team.' Kieran clumsily tipped the last of his pint into his mouth, a sizeable dribble spilling down his chin. 'Later, losers.' With that he turned and walked away.

'Blimey, what was all that about?' asked Richard.

James sighed before answering. 'Everything that's wrong with kids' football, mate. One of those blokes who sees his team as a reflection of himself. It's all about his ego: if his team wins, it proves he's a winner; if not, they've let him down personally. He cares about his team, but I'm not sure he cares about his players.'

'Why do they let blokes like that anywhere near a kids' team?'

James didn't have an answer for him. Partly because, well, why did they? But also because he had just noticed something. In his inebriated state, Kieran had left his phone at their table.

CHAPTER SEVENTEEN

Acting on impulse, James pocketed the phone. Perhaps he could use it to mess with Kieran; he wasn't sure how, but he could work that out later.

He stayed for another drink with Richard, then started to walk home, trying to push back the nagging thought that taking the phone had seen him cross a line. Once upon a time he would have given it back without thinking twice, but after Kieran's antics on Sunday he didn't owe that prat any favours.

His first task, once he got home, was to crack the phone's password. He hid himself away – better that Ros didn't know – and hoped Kieran had chosen something predictable. He tried all the obvious default settings – 1234, 1111 – and then punched in random combinations until he got a message saying the screen would be locked for thirty seconds, and a warning that five more unsuccessful attempts would lock the phone for thirty minutes. He decided to hide the phone away until he could come up with something more systematic. It wasn't as if he had a plan anyway, not yet.

*

James had already worked out his team for Sunday – with Sam in goal they could afford to play just two at the back, which meant Ryan and Liam as twin strikers. Having two subs would be handy as well. Those carefully laid plans barely lasted a few hours. On Friday morning, Lynn called.

'I'm so sorry, James, I checked this morning and Sam's registration hasn't cleared in time. You won't be able to play her against Melville.'

'There's no way we could just play her and hope nobody notices, is there?'

'I'll pretend you didn't say that – that's the kind of thing Kieran would suggest.'

The bit about sounding like Kieran stung. Of course Sam couldn't play unregistered, and not just because she wouldn't pass convincingly as a Rory or a Ryan. What was happening to him? Six months ago he'd never have even considered that. While Lynn was on, he said to make sure Rory knew his place wasn't under threat once he was fit again – Sam was just keeping the goalkeeper's spot warm for him. Lynn admitted that Rory had seemed concerned by the other boys raving about Sam's goalkeeping – they were calling her SuperSam, apparently – and she was grateful that James had thought to reassure Rory.

'I told him he'd have to use it as motivation to get even better himself,' said Lynn.

'Now who sounds like Kieran?' James laughed.

Almost immediately after Lynn had hung up, Ryan's mum texted. Ryan had woken up with a temperature and was off school. He was desperate to play, but even if he recovered by Sunday, she thought a couple of hours out in the November wind and rain wouldn't help his recuperation. James bit his lip in frustration before dashing off a reply about completely understanding and how he hoped Ryan felt better soon – reverse WWKD again. What he wanted to say was that if Ryan could just keep himself together and play for this one weekend, it wouldn't matter if he got bubonic plague after that. After Sunday with Dylan and SuperSam available they wouldn't miss Ryan half as badly.

The text from Ryan's mum, though, gave James an idea. If he could get in to Kieran's phone, he could message all the Hawks parents as if he was Kieran. Hawks were playing Cole Hill next, a tough game, but what if nobody turned up? If Kieran didn't have a team, he'd have to forfeit the match... oh this was just too good. Or at least, it would be if he could work out Kieran's password.

James took Kieran's phone to work the following day, an afternoon/evening shift, which meant he'd miss out on eating with Ros and the kids again. If Ros stumbled across the unfamiliar phone at home, she might think he was having an affair or something. That would be awful, but maybe less embarrassing than admitting what he was really up to. Waiting for a pre-booked fare, a sudden electronic burst of 'Blue Is the Colour' started bleeding out of his jacket pocket. He might have known that Kieran would even use his ringtone to pay homage to his beloved Chelsea. Glancing at the screen, he saw the call was from a Hawks parent and rejected it. Then a thought struck him: what if Kieran's password had some resonance for Chelsea fans? He tried 2608 (John Terry and Frank Lampard's shirt numbers), then swapped them round to try 0826, but neither worked. How about the first league title under Mourinho, or winning the Champions League for the first time? A quick google on his own phone gave the years as 2005 and 2012 respectively, but neither was the magic number. Scanning through the club's Wikipedia entry, James noticed the year of formation: 1905. Was that the kind of detail Kieran might have picked up on? It seemed less likely than a trophy year – it was all about winning with Kieran, after all – but he'd already tried those. Was it worth risking another lock-out? James was still debating with himself when he heard a tap on his car window.

'Excuse me, mate,' said the smartly dressed man behind the tap. 'Taxi for Harper?' James apologised, tucked the phone back in his pocket and checked where his fare wanted to go. Mr Harper was a regular customer, a local businessman who had started using AbaCabs when he lost his licence for speeding. James always said that you encountered all shades of opinions driving a taxi, and Mr Harper had some of the shadiest opinions going.

Harper was sounding off about foreigners taking all the jobs and sponging off the welfare state. James wanted to point out that if they were taking jobs, they were paying for the welfare state with their taxes, not sponging off it, but he held his tongue.

At last, they reached the industrial estate that was Harper's destination. James checked the meter.

'That'll be £10.40 please.'

'Round it down to a tenner?'

Not a chance, not after the party political broadcast for the English Defence League. 'No can do. You can throw in a tip and round it up to £15 if that's easier though.'

James watched as Harper counted out forty pence in change and tossed it desultorily through the window onto the passenger seat along with a ten-pound note. No tip then? What a surprise.

As soon as Harper was gone, he pulled out Kieran's phone again and tried 1905. He blinked in disbelief as the array of app icons revealed itself. He was in: now he could get busy wreaking havoc.

He quickly found the Hawks' WhatsApp group and started scanning the messages. Kieran had already sent out details for Sunday morning's game, telling everyone to arrive an hour before the kick-off. He'd change that for a start. *Change of plan*, he typed. *Now 2pm ko – arrive at 1.* By that time, the opposition would have been and gone and the Hawks would have lost by default.

Over the next hour, a steady stream of thumbs-up emojis acknowledged Kieran's message. As his plan came together before his eyes, James felt something gnawing in his stomach, but he pushed the feeling away. Kieran had this coming; after he robbed the Swifts the other week, this was just levelling the score, right?

*

Having laid his trap, James was keen to get rid of the phone as quickly as possible. When he arrived for his own match that Sunday he made a point of dropping it at the back of the equipment cupboard where it would be found sooner or later. Coming out with his bag of footballs, he saw Dave waving as he made his way towards him.

'Morning James. Got everything?'

'Yes thanks, Dave. It might be a struggle today though – I wish we'd got Sam's registration through in time.'

Dave grimaced. 'Sorry about that. I told her dad about the deadline but he's never been the most reliable bloke for that kind of thing. Sam's really cross – she barely said two words to him all weekend apparently. She was looking forward to today.'

'Tell her there'll be plenty of other chances. I just hope we manage to get something out of the game without her.'

'Will do. I hear you had some trouble with your kit a while back, something about no balls for training. Everything was ready as usual when I left it, so I don't know what happened.'

'Kieran,' James virtually spat the name out, 'that's what happened. Those balls hadn't just gone flat, they had been fully deflated, the week before we played the Hawks. Does that sound like a coincidence to you? And all the other balls, apart from the size threes – which are next to useless for our lot – were missing.'

'It does sound suspicious, but do you think Kieran is capable of pulling something like that just to win a game of kids' football?'

'I wouldn't put it past him.' Nor past me either, if the last week is anything to go by.

'Well, we'll have to make sure he doesn't get away with it.' Dave grinned at the surprised look on James's face. 'I mean, now that Sam has signed up, I'm a fully-fledged Swifts supporter, aren't I? Get out there and get yourself three points and start reeling the bastard in.'

*

'Okay, down to the bare bones, just nine of you and no subs.' James looked around the faces of the remaining Swifts. 'We're still missing Rory and Dylan, and Sam can't play until next week, but that doesn't mean that we can't get something out of this one. You'll have to work hard, but let's be positive, attack the hell out of them and go for the win. Louisa May Alcott – Theo's mum – once said "I am not afraid of storms, for I am learning to steer my ship". Last week was horrendous, a perfect storm of a match, but you guys kept going right to the end. You showed your character, like you did against the Hawks, and I've never been prouder of you. Let's show that same character today; let's go out and play our football. Take the game to Dynamos right from the beginning; test their keeper, let him know he's in for a busy game. When we defend, give Charlie lots of protection. The last thing we want is someone curling a worldy into the top corner because we haven't closed them down.'

The Swifts started well, cruising to a two-goal lead by half-time. Liam, up front alongside Josh, scored the first and made the second for his strike partner. They both missed several more, but at least the team was creating chances. More of the same was the half-time message.

The second half, however, was a different story. Deepak miscontrolled the ball in the first couple of minutes, allowing the Dynamos winger to surge past him. Despite the best efforts of the others, the ball ended up in the Swifts' net. Sam or Rory might have saved it, thought James, but Charlie never had a chance. Max started moaning at Deepak for the mistake, but Ben shut him up, saying Deepak hadn't done it on purpose.

The goal gave Dynamos fresh belief and had the opposite effect on the Swifts. The first half had been full of positive runs and penetrating passes, but now they were struggling to escape their own half.

'Looking forward! Can we play?' asked Joao repeatedly, but the boys were falling back on old habits and just hoofing it clear. Eventually, the pressure told; Hakim was slow to close down on the edge of the box and it was exactly what James had warned about. The Melville player had space and time to set himself and he curled the ball into the top corner. He could have tried it twenty times without getting it right, but he'd done it when it mattered.

Joao was clapping his hands and rousing the team. 'Come on, Swifts. Remember what worked before. Play your football – confidence, attack, enjoy.'

The Swifts did rally after that, but the Dynamos were also chasing a win and the game swung back and forward. The decisive moment came when Charlie moved out from his goal to gather a misplaced cross. With no one challenging him, he fumbled his catch and saw the ball drop from his hands in the direction of the goalmouth. Him and Gabe both scrambled for it and when Gabe attempted to lash it clear, the ball rebounded against Charlie and into the net. Not long after that, the ref blew the final whistle.

'It's so unfair,' James muttered to Joao. 'They've deserved more from the last few games.'

'Is football,' replied Joao. 'Like life: not always fair, but there's always another game.'

'Can you do the post-match talk today, Joao? Right now, I've got nothing.'

Joao did a decent job. He reminded each of the boys of the good things they had done – in both halves, not just the first. He mentioned a couple of decent saves Charlie had made when it was nil-nil, saying Charlie kept them in the game before they scored themselves. In truth, the saves weren't anything special, but at least Charlie looked less miserable.

The rest of the day, James grumped about the house and avoided everyone. A few weeks ago, he'd been within touching distance of Kieran; now the gap was growing week by week. Hopefully Hawks would have dropped points today, but he'd still missed the chance to close the gap. When he finally checked the other results, he got a surprise. Weston Park and Redbridge had both won, but the game showed as a walkover for the Hawks, not the other way round, meaning they were eleven points ahead of Swifts now. James phoned Lynn to find out what had happened. Apparently, the opposition had scratched on Saturday evening – a flu bug had gone through their team and they only had five fit players. Lynn tried consoling James with the fact that Linford Road weren't likely to have troubled the Hawks, but she didn't know what he had done. James tried to sound convincing as he agreed, but inside he was screaming. All his subterfuge undone by a stupid flu bug. First Ryan, now Linford Road. Was it too much to ask for auto-immune systems to be more robust? All the stress of his scheming, the fear of being found out; was it worth it? His rivalry with Kieran was making him do things he never thought he was capable of.

*

Tips were down the next couple of days, possibly because of the sullen mood in James's cab, and he was aware of Ben, Poppy and Ros tiptoeing around him at home. On Tuesday night, he arrived home after a late shift and found a note on his pillow. Ros was fast asleep, but she had obviously left it there when she went to bed. He unfolded the message and read it:

Pull yourself together and snap out of it, you idiot. You're worrying the kids.

He thought back to the last months of his teaching career and its impact on his mental health. Poppy had been too young to understand what was going on, but his relationship with Ben had certainly been affected. His current mood was nothing compared to what he experienced back then, but James knew he couldn't let it escalate. Perhaps the brooding time between fares didn't help.

As he climbed into bed, James resolved to make some changes: for one, he'd make more effort to relax at home, for Ben and Poppy's sake. He'd obsess less about Kieran too. Then again, he had to find a way to claw back the gap between the Swifts and the Hawks.

CHAPTER EIGHTEEN

'You have got to be kidding, Sarge. You want me to pay a visit just for a stolen phone?' Sergeant McGlashan met Hayley's disdainful glare with a blank slate of a face.

'I certainly do. The word from on high is that we're to improve our response stats, so we're following up every complaint, even when there's little chance of getting a result. Go and talk to the victim. Who knows, it might even lead somewhere.' Hayley took the call sheet from his outstretched hand and walked away, resisting the temptation to say that all it would lead to was pointless paperwork. She glanced at the name and address: someone called Kieran Butcher.

In the car on the way to Mr Butcher's house, Hayley found herself reflecting on her career. She had been so full of dreams and ideals when she joined the police. Back then she couldn't understand why so many of the longer-serving officers seemed so cynical about everything. Now, fifteen years in, she had long since started to see it from their point of view. If it wasn't ten-a-penny trivia like this lost phone, it was an unending stream of toe-rags doing the same nasty things over and over again. The burglaries, the muggings, the domestic abuse cases; they all merged into one after a while. Hayley was suffocated by the sense that she wasn't actually doing any good.

'Good afternoon, Mr Butcher. You called us about your stolen phone.' There was something familiar about Mr Butcher when he opened his front door, but she couldn't immediately place him. Kieran looked her up and down before replying. 'Yeah, but I was hoping your lot were going to take this seriously.'

'Excuse me? You reported your phone stolen and I've come round to take the details. I can assure you we're taking this seriously.'

'I mean, it's great that someone's come out, but I was hoping to get a proper copper, not some girl on work experience or something.' Hayley managed to stop her hands from balling up into fists, but she could feel redness burning on her face.

'Mr Butcher, I am a proper copper, with several years' experience in the job. I can assure you, a stolen phone is well within my capabilities. Now, what makes you think the phone was stolen?'

She was still fuming over Butcher's casual sexism and only half listening as he yabbered on. Something about running his football team and someone using his phone to send fake messages to the players' parents. She forced herself to switch back into professional mode.

'And which football team is this?'

'Stoneleigh Hawks under-twelves.'

Hayley looked at him again. That was it: he was the ranty man from Jayden's football match a few weeks ago, the one who had seemed on the verge of bursting a blood vessel at any moment. He was quieter now, but he didn't seem any more pleasant removed from the touchline.

'So why would someone want to do something like that? I mean, it's only kids' football, right?'

Mr Butcher's nostrils flared. 'Only ki... I suppose this is what you get when you send a girl to do a man's job. Someone tried to sabotage my team, probably the manager of one of our rivals, and I want to know what you're going to do about it.'

'That's a bit far-fetched, isn't it? More likely you just left it somewhere? Maybe some kids found it and were having a laugh.'

She was trying to wind him up now, and he bit. 'I don't think you know how big a deal my team is around here, how jealous people are. You need to get on to the other managers and shake them down, see what you get out of them.'

By now, Hayley just wanted out, so she told Mr Butcher to let the police know if the phone turned up down the back of a sofa or somewhere and took the details of the managers he thought might have something against him. Matt from Redbridge was on this list, so maybe he'd be a good first port of call for her. If nothing else he could tell her more about Butcher, although she rather suspected that she knew enough already.

*

James was walking Poppy home from school, when he had a moment of role reversal: Poppy brought up the subject of football.

'Daddy, Ben said there's a girl in your football team. Is that true?'

'Yes, sweetheart. Sam – Samantha – is playing in goal while Rory's injured. She's really good.'

'Do you mean good for a girl, or properly good?' asked Poppy, her tone conveying that she wouldn't be impressed if James meant the first option.

'I mean she's *really* good; good for a boy, a girl or an orangutan. The best I've seen at this age, to be honest, boy or girl.'

Poppy giggled. 'Or orangutan?'

'Definitely – most orangutan goalkeepers just eat the ball and take naps during the game; Sam's way better than that.'

Poppy giggled some more, then changed the subject to what Amy had done with her nails this week and how it looked totally amazing.

Ros was out at a work thing that evening, so James had made sure he didn't have a shift. Poppy had gone to bed but Ben was still up, doing some homework in his bedroom. Flicking through the channels James had a choice between a documentary on Dostoevsky or an old Eddie Murphy film. Just as he was about to change channels for the documentary, Ben appeared at the door.

'I'm bored, Dad. What are we watching?'

James hesitated. He'd quite enjoy chilling with Ben, but he knew the first question Ros would ask when she found out.

'Have you done all your homework?' he asked in her place.

'Everything that's due tomorrow.' Ben looked hopefully at him.

'Good enough. *Beverly Hills Cop* – it's an old one, but you'll like it.'

The film was more sweary than James had remembered, so he'd probably get it in the neck from Ros, but Ben had enjoyed it. He'd probably enjoyed it that little bit more because of the swearing, truth be told. Ben wanted to know if a banana in a car's exhaust would really stop it from working and James had to warn him not to find out by experimenting in the staff car park at school. Ros really would blame him if that happened.

*

Despite Hayley's reservations about mixing her family life with work, this business about the phone was forcing her hand. The far from comfortable conversation with Matt would be easier kept as informal as possible – she didn't want to approach him in uniform – so she made sure to catch Matt when she picked Jayden up from training.

'Can I have a quick word, Matt?'

'Oh, hi Hayley.' Matt put the stack of cones in his kit-bag and gave her his full attention. 'Sure. Is everything okay with Jayden?'

Well, not really, thought Hayley, but this wasn't the moment to bring up the subject of his minimal playing time.

'Yes, he's loving being part of things.' That much was actually true, to the extent that he was part of things. 'But that's not what I need to talk to you about. It's, erm, it's a work thing.'

She could see the confused look on Matt's face. 'Work? Why do you need to talk to me about your work?'

'You don't know what I do, do you? I'm a police officer.'

Now Matt was looking worried. 'Police? Why do you need to talk to me? I've not done anything wrong.'

Hayley tried to smile reassuringly. 'No, not at all – at least, I doubt it. But there's something I've got to follow up on. How well do you know the Stoneleigh Hawks manager?'

Matt rolled his eyes. 'I don't know him at all outside football. Were you there when we played them the other week?' Hayley confirmed that she was. 'Well, you'll have seen for yourself what he's like. That wasn't even him at his worst.'

'His phone went missing the other week, and I got called out to talk to him about it. He's convinced that someone stole it in order to sabotage his football team. Apparently someone was messaging his players' parents so they'd be late for kick-off.'

'Seriously? Which game was it – it wasn't when they played us, was it?'

'No, Linford Rovers. As it happened, Linford scratched the game, so the Hawks won anyway, but if it had gone ahead they wouldn't have had a full team.'

Matt started laughing. 'Linford Rovers? He'd have been furious to lose by default to them. Shame it didn't work.' He stopped abruptly, his brow suddenly furrowing. 'Wait, why are you telling me all this? You don't think I had something to do with it, do you?'

Hayley held her hands up placatingly. 'Not at all, I'm just following up my leads.'

'Well, it wasn't me.' Matt's tone of voice was firmer now. He clearly wasn't happy with the way the conversation had gone. 'And I'm surprised you needed to hear me say that. For one thing, I can't imagine any football manager would go to those lengths to win a game. For another, even if Kieran is right, there's no shortage of other people who don't like him. I know your lad hasn't been part of Redbridge Town for long, but I would have thought you could see I wouldn't stoop to something like that.'

This is what Hayley had been afraid of: she didn't want her investigation to rebound on Jayden and affect his standing with Matt.

'I can, Matt. I think it's ridiculous that I have to follow this up, but it's my job and I have to be able to say that I've spoken with you about it. Now I have, I can tell my sergeant you've got nothing to do with it. I'm just doing my job.'

She could see Matt's anger deflating, which was a relief. 'Yeah, I get it. Sorry I took it like that. The cheek of the bloke though, assuming that everyone else in the league is as bad as him. If you catch whoever was behind it, tell them well done from me.'

Hayley grinned. 'If I was on duty, I couldn't possibly condone that. As it is, I'll see what I can do.'

*

Sunday morning came around and James and Ben went to set everything up. The Hawks were also at home, playing on the other pitch. James steeled himself for his encounter with Kieran, dreading the possibility that his rival had started to suspect him over the phone. Kieran more or less ignored James though, until he spotted Sam warming up.

'Are you serious, Hogan?' Kieran roared with laughter. 'Playing a girl? You'll be the laughing stock of the league, mate.'

'Well, we needed someone, after Rory got so badly injured.'

Kieran just grinned. 'Yeah, that was a shame. He did well to keep the score down for you.'

'We were winning before your striker trod on his arm and broke it.'

'Whatever. Justice was done in the end.'

James just turned away, shaking his head. He was determined not to let Kieran wind him up. That said, someday, somehow, he would wipe the smile off Kieran's Neanderthal face.

Cole Hill were a good side, but the Swifts were matching them. Sam made a couple of good saves early on – James could hear Dave on the touchline, cheering his appreciation – and her performance spread confidence through the rest of the defence, including Charlie, who was back in the starting line-up as a defender.

It was nil-nil at half-time, with Josh having missed two or three really good chances, and Dylan having a fine shot tipped over by the Cole Hill keeper. Early in the second half, Max got the ball in midfield and bulldozed forward. He bundled through tackles and found himself on the edge of the box, pulling back his right foot and letting fly. The ball rebounded off the right-hand post, hit the diving goalkeeper on the back of his head and trickled into the net. It had taken a lucky break, but the one-nil lead wasn't undeserved.

'Come on, Cole Hill!' roared the other manager. 'Show 'em what you've got!'

'Keep playing your football, lads,' yelled James.

'What about me?' retorted Sam mock-indignantly, prompting much laughter from the other Swifts.

'And you, Sam. You keep playing your football too. Sorry!'

Cole Hill's striker was a big, strong lad and he was giving Gabe a hard time. Gabe wasn't often beaten in the air, but the striker was winning most of their duels. At one corner, he outmanoeuvred Gabe and sent a free header speeding towards the Swifts' goal. Sam flung herself across, just managing to tip the ball wide of the far post.

'What a save!' Even the Cole Hill manager was impressed. The striker put his hands on his hips and shook his head despairingly.

James knew how he felt – he couldn't believe that Sam had kept that one out either.

Cole Hill threw more and more players forward, becoming increasingly desperate in their search for a goal. Making his last changes, James thought the breakthrough was bound to come. Josh and Charlie came off, replaced by Ryan and Deepak. Dylan dropped into midfield to make a three-four-one, with Liam as the lone striker. The extra midfielder would help absorb pressure, and Liam's pace gave them the best chance on the break.

Five minutes from time, Cole Hill's striker was denied by Sam yet again. As he flung his arms in frustration, Sam looked up the pitch and then threw the ball out to Dylan on the left. Dylan skipped past his marker and spotted Liam's diagonal run. One driven pass took out three defenders and put Liam one-on-one with the Cole Hill keeper. Liam's dancing feet left the keeper flat-footed, tucking the ball past him into the net.

'Well played, mate,' said the Cole Hill manager after the final whistle. 'I won't lie, I thought this was going to be an easy one today, but your lot are good. That keeper of yours is fantastic – although our lads won't let big Connor forget he couldn't get the better of a girl.'

'Thanks,' said James. The Cole Hill manager usually exuded an air of superiority over teams like the Swifts, lording it a bit even before a match, so it made a change for him to talk to James as his equal.

James saw Kieran looking thoughtfully towards the Swifts players at the end of the game, but then was distracted when Iain, whose Eastside Diamonds had been playing the Hawks, came over to say hello. They chatted for a minute or two, James being careful not to give too much away – they were playing each other the following week.

When James and Ben got home, Poppy was uncharacteristically enthusiastic. Having enjoyed a couple of hours with no male presence in the house, she generally wanted their return to cause as little disruption as possible, and to Poppy football represented the pinnacle of corrupting male influence. Today was different.

'How did you do? How did you do? What was the score? Did you win? Didyoudidyoudidyoudidyou?' James wasn't sure how Poppy expected them to reply in the face of her unrelenting barrage of questions. When she finally paused to take a breath, James jumped in.

'We won two-nil. They played great.'

'What was Sam like? Did she make lots of saves? Was she good?'

'Sam was brilliant,' answered Ben. 'They just couldn't get past her.'

'She didn't let any in? None at all? Against boys?'

'Not just against any boys, Cole Hill's centre forward was one of the best strikers we've faced all season.'

'But even he couldn't score past Sam?'

'That's right.'

'Yay!' Poppy started bouncing around, celebrating the blows that had clearly been struck for the sisterhood that morning. 'Girls can play football too, just as well as boys can. Even the best of the boys, he can't score against Sam,' she chanted in a sing-song voice.

James, Ros and Ben just looked at one another and even Ros couldn't help but burst out laughing.

For the rest of the day, Poppy asked endless questions about Sam. When James and Ben settled down to watch the Premier League game in the afternoon, Poppy climbed up on the sofa and watched with them.

'Which one is the goalkeeper, like Sam?' she asked.

'The one with a different coloured shirt to the others.'

'Is that why Sam plays in goal, because girls are more fashion-conscious than boys and she likes wearing something that makes her stand out?'

Ben and James exchanged a glance before Ben answered, 'Yes, that's the reason.'

'Or,' countered James, 'it could just be that she's a good goalkeeper. I'd say it's almost certainly one of the two.'

'I think all teams should have a girl in goal,' said Poppy decisively. 'From what you've said about Sam, we're clearly better at it than the boys are.'

CHAPTER NINETEEN

Tuesday night was another committee meeting, the first since the infamous Hawks versus Swifts match. Lynn was particularly tense.

'I don't want to even be in the same room as him,' she admitted to James when he phoned her on Monday night. 'The way his boys set about my Rory. He still hasn't asked me once how Rory is doing.'

'Just ignore him, Lynn. Whatever he says or does, don't let him rile you.'

'That's just it, he riles me at the best of times. And this is so not the best of times.'

'Keep it low-key. Kieran's not worth the aggravation.'

Kieran, along with Alison and Dave, was already there. There was no sign of Howard or Ron yet, so the prospect of small talk with Kieran loomed large. Lynn went to the bar, delaying the moment she would actually have to engage with him.

'Bit of a result for you on Sunday, Hogan,' said Kieran as James took a seat at their table. 'Beating Cole Hill is not bad at all, particularly as you resorted to a girl in goal!' Kieran didn't manage – probably didn't try – to hide his disdain. 'Does she wear high-heel football boots?'

'Her name is Sam and she's really good,' replied James calmly. 'Did you see any of the saves she made? She was brilliant.'

'Is it even allowed, playing a girl?' Kieran continued, ignoring James's answer. 'I mean, I've never looked it up because, well, why would I? We're a serious team, not a knitting circle. Wasn't there even one boy who could fill in, rather than you having to play a useless girl?'

James tried to read Dave's reaction across the table. He never gave much away, but James suspected that he wouldn't appreciate Kieran being so dismissive of his niece. 'It's not that we couldn't find a boy,' said James. 'Sam's a great keeper. She's in the team on merit.'

'Yeah, right, whatever. You keep telling yourself that. You look ridiculous playing the likes of her.'

'What's that supposed to mean?' asked Dave, who had finally had enough: 'The likes of her?'

'Well, it's a boys' team and she's a girl. I mean, it's great that girls are getting into football now, but girls' football isn't proper football, is it?'

Alison looked horrified, though it was Dave who spoke up first. 'What about the Lionesses? They've been more successful than the men in the last few years.'

Kieran just shrugged. 'Yeah, they've won stuff, but only against other women. That's hardly a proper test, is it? Anyway, it proves my point: they stay in their lane and don't try to mix it with the blokes, do they? Football's a man's game; always has been, always will be.'

'Well, Sam and I would disagree with you on that one. You just watch what you say about my niece in future, Kieran, okay?'

That knocked Kieran momentarily out of his stride, but only momentarily. 'Look, here's my dad.' Ron came through the door just as Lynn returned from the bar.

'Evening everyone. Did you get me one in, son?'

'Right here, Dad.' Kieran indicated the pint in front of the empty chair he had saved for Ron.

161

'Is everyone here then?'

'Everyone except Howard, and he texted earlier to say he might not be able to make it.' It was the first thing Lynn had said since arriving at the table, and her tone was clipped and businesslike.

'Right, let's crack on then.'

Lynn was uncharacteristically quiet at the meeting, particularly when Kieran had anything to say. When they got on to how all the teams were doing, Kieran was moaning about being short of players for his next game against Shelley Abbey Royals.

'I thought you had, what was it, sixteen? Eighteen players?' asked Alison.

'We started with eighteen, yeah, then we picked up a cracking lad from Eastside Diamonds to make nineteen. Since then we've had two or three leave because they weren't getting a game. No real loss, to be honest; there's a reason they weren't getting picked. Of the others we've got one lad injured and, would you believe, lots of the others away at Scout camp this weekend. I asked if they could come home early to play, but the parents weren't having it. I said they should get their priorities right, put the team first, but none of them budged. Anyway, long story short, we've only got ten players this weekend, just the one sub. Some of the regular lift-giving parents are missing too, so I'm taking a couple of the lads along with my Malky.'

James started summarising the Swifts' change of fortunes when, without warning, Lynn interrupted.

'Rory's doing fine, Kieran. Thanks for asking.'

'You what, love?' He looked genuinely puzzled.

'I was telling you that Rory, my son, the boy whose arm was broken by your players, is doing fine. Your concern on the day was touching, or would have been if you'd shown any.'

James, Alison and Dave exchanged glances. This wasn't what James had meant by low-key, but with Lynn stewing all through the meeting it had to come out sometime. At least she seemed to be in control of herself.

'Okay, good to know,' replied Kieran slowly.

'Don't you even feel a little bad about it?' challenged Lynn. 'About your boys making him miss two months of football?'

'It's all in the game, isn't it? We didn't set out to break his arm, we were just trying to get the ball. Anyway, he's not my player, so it's not my problem.'

Alison put a hand on Lynn's arm, though James knew it would take more than that to restrain her if she really got going.

'While we're talking about that game,' said James. 'Why did your ref notify the league about Dylan's red card? You know fine that most teams keep that kind of thing off the books. With Rory's injury as well, we had real problems with numbers after that. Would it have killed him to keep it within the club?'

Kieran shrugged. 'Don't ask me, ask Phil. I think he was annoyed at your players' appalling attitude. He said you were bolshie with him before the game, so it's clear where they get it from. If you can't control your players, you can't complain when they get suspended.'

James was too stunned to reply. Lynn opened her mouth, but Alison jumped in first.

'I think it's a shame that someone who is standing as chairman, who wants to represent the whole club, can't see past his own team.'

'Let's move on,' said Ron decisively. 'This isn't getting us anywhere.'

James wondered how the minutes were going to read, given that Lynn hadn't been writing much down and was clearly still livid. She had a good rant about it in the car on the way home.

'I could have killed him! He talks about struggling for numbers when he's got a much bigger squad than us and the only reason we've been missing Dylan and my Rory is because of his hooligans. We've got to beat him, James, we've just got to.'

James knew exactly what Lynn meant. After hearing Kieran twist everything to portray the Swifts as the bad guys, he was even more determined to stop him.

The next day was like running through tar: everything took longer and more effort than it ought to. James kept returning to the fact that this week it was Kieran who was low on numbers: there had to be a way he could use that to his advantage.

At the end of his shift his phone rang. It was Raj.

'Hate to say it, James, but I've had a complaint about you. Apparently, a week or so back someone saw you picking up a passenger who just hailed you down in the road. You know it's only the black cabs that are allowed to do that; we only get the pre-booked fares.'

'I know, that's why I never take walk-ups.'

'Really? I've checked the records and you went off shift for fifteen minutes at about that time. Then when you logged back in you were in a different location.'

For a moment, James was confused. What was all that about? He knew he hadn't taken any walk-up, unless…

'Oh, wait, no: I did pick someone up but it wasn't a fare. It was an old friend with loads of bags. I told him I wasn't allowed to take his money but I could give him a lift as a mate; that's why I went off shift.'

'Are you sure about that? You didn't just clock off and keep the cash? It all looks pretty sus to me.'

James bit his tongue before replying. 'Are you saying you don't believe me?'

'I'm saying you wouldn't be the first driver to try something like this and then deny it when they got found out. You know the pressure I'm under. I had the police in a few weeks back complaining about walk-ups; I've got to think about keeping our licence.'

'Yeah, I know, which is why I never take walk-ups.' James realised that his voice was increasing in volume, so he took a deep breath and tried to keep his composure.

'Unless it's an old friend?'

'Look, I went off shift and I didn't take any payment. What else was I supposed to do?'

'Say you couldn't help him and drive on. Or get him to call through to the office to arrange a pick-up. Or at least tell me about it at the time to cover your back. As it is, you can see how this looks. I'm going to have to write this up. Consider this an official warning. You're a good worker, James, but I'll let you go before I risk the business.'

*

That night, sleep again eluded James, but he found something else instead: an idea to scupper the Hawks. It would involve him crossing lines he'd never crossed before – never even imagined crossing – but if it worked, it would be another precious three points clawed back in the battle to win the bet and save the Swifts.

CHAPTER TWENTY

James wasn't working on Saturday night, yet here he was driving around at 2am. He parked up round the corner, trying to convince himself that this wasn't a huge mistake. His heart felt like it was trying to escape his ribcage. He hadn't actually done anything wrong at this stage. Nevertheless, all he could think about was not getting caught in the act. At the first sign of trouble, he would call it off and walk away. Part of him wanted an excuse to abort, but there was too much at stake to pull out lightly.

As he walked to the house, he saw the car there on the drive, just as he had hoped. He recognised it from the Stoneleigh car park, and the faded sticker (a delightful one showing a Chelsea fan urinating on a Spurs shirt – classy) confirmed the owner's identity. The lights in Kieran's house were all off, so hopefully everyone was asleep. He was go for launch. James walked past the house without breaking stride. He carried on down the road, doubled back round the block and went back to his car for his backpack.

James had remembered to wear dark clothing to blend into the shadows. The bag on his shoulder felt much heavier than its actual poundage; how would he explain its contents if he got caught? A few deep breaths brought a little calm, but not much.

Approaching Kieran's drive again, James looked all around. Still no lights, not in Kieran's house or any neighbouring ones, and no sign of pedestrians. It wasn't the kind of road that got a lot of through traffic at the best of times, and 2.10am on a Sunday morning was hardly rush hour. With a last look all around, James stepped off the pavement and made his way to the back of Kieran's car. Halfway up the drive, security lights flickered into life, presumably triggered by motion detectors. The driveway was lit up like a midweek Wembley international, and James threw himself into the bushes, his heart pounding so loudly now he thought it would wake the whole street on its own. He waited for a full minute, eyes glued on the upstairs windows, satisfying himself that everyone was still asleep. His hands were shaking, but he knew he had to go through with this. At least now he could see what he was doing.

James crept gingerly from his hiding place and opened up the bag. He had checked the equipment several times during the course of the day, but there was still that nagging fear that something crucial had been left at home. No, it was all there. No bananas, but a little googling had found an improvement on Eddie Murphy's technique. He tipped a generous helping of powder into the plastic bowl from the back of the kitchen cupboard – he hoped Ros wouldn't miss that bowl – then added water and stirred it in. In just a minute or so it looked thick but pliable, like the instructions said, and he got started. He only had ten or fifteen minutes before it set, so he had to work quickly. James took handfuls of the mixture and shoved them up Kieran's exhaust pipe. Fear battled with excitement as he crammed in as much as he could, ramming it in with the sawn-off end of a broomstick (another thing he hoped Ros wouldn't miss). If it wasn't airtight, the engine wouldn't seize and all this would be for nothing. Once he was satisfied that the job was done, James quietly gathered everything he had brought with him – minus the sizeable dollop of quick-drying cement now blocking Kieran's exhaust pipe – and hastily headed to his own car. He was trying to look natural, but he was sure anyone passing by would see the guilt written large on his face, in his gait, in every fibre of his being.

James's nerves were in shreds as he pulled his car out from the kerb and drove away. His heart was racing, his palms were sweating, and his hand trembled on the gear stick. It had been a textbook operation as far as he could tell, but he just wanted to get away as quickly as possible. He was certain nothing had been left at the scene of – he gulped at this realisation – the crime. Arriving home, he was about to deposit the evidence in the dustbin when the thought struck him that he might be better leaving it a little further from home. He left it in the boot, ready to dump it somewhere convenient when he was next working. That was a problem for another day, though; it was far too late already and he had to be up in the morning for the match.

Sleep was as absent as – hopefully – Kieran at kick-off time. If he'd got everything right, the car should start normally then seize up after a few minutes. Hopefully Kieran and his carful of players would be stranded somewhere and miss the start of the match. The Royals were a good team and he didn't fancy the Hawks' chances against them with only seven players. James reflected on what a strange evening it had been. He'd thought the mobile phone was a one-off flirtation with crime, but was it the beginning of a slippery slope? He couldn't imagine what Ros and the kids would think about him committing an act of criminal damage. Actually, Ben would probably see it as a brilliant prank, but James was starting to realise that it was much more serious than that.

What if the car didn't just conk out harmlessly? What if his actions caused a road accident, if someone got seriously hurt? There would be innocent people (plus Kieran) involved. Whatever Kieran deserved – and even James could see that didn't extend to death at the wheel – no one else deserved to be caught up in all this. He was ashamed of the lengths he had gone to. He wasn't sure he recognised himself; he was acting like those idiots who treat kids' football like the Premier League. He tried convincing himself he was doing it for his players, but was that really what was driving him? He just didn't know anymore.

*

Sunday morning came and James woke up bright-eyed and bushy tailed. No, that's a lie. Sunday morning came and Ben had to drag James out of bed.

'Come on, Dad, get up – we'll be late if you don't get a move on.'

'Wassatime?'

'Gone eight. It's a ten o'clock kick-off and you told everyone to be there by nine-fifteen.'

Ben pushed his dad into the bathroom. One quick shower later, and James was dressed and downstairs for breakfast. The porridge reminded James of quick-drying cement, and he couldn't bear to even look at it. He pushed it away and had toast instead. He almost jumped out of his skin when Ros came into the kitchen without warning; James realised he was half expecting the police to burst in at any moment. As he loaded equipment into the back of his car, he saw the detritus from last night and his conscience throbbed again. Please don't let anyone get hurt.

The game with Eastside Diamonds was finally a chance for the Swifts to try their two-four-two formation. Hakim and Charlie started at the back, with Gabe having a rare visit to the subs bench (reverse WWKD). Max had been meant to play, but James had received a text the previous evening saying he was unwell. In all the nerves over his late-night sabotage operation, he hadn't given it much thought.

The game started brilliantly. Right from the word go, the Swifts took control. Ben was looking confident, and together with Deepak he made sure that the defence had very little to do, just picking up hopeful through-balls that were never likely to reach the Diamonds' attackers. Ben's passing was as good as James could remember and before long the Swifts were cruising with two goals (Dylan and Ryan) without reply. At half-time, James reminded the players of what had happened against Melville Dynamos and warned against complacency. He needn't have worried. With Gabe, Hakim and Charlie rotating as the back two, Sam and her defenders never looked troubled. Meanwhile, the attacking players were creating lots of chances, putting a few away too. Josh, Liam and Ben all added their names to the score sheet.

'I had a feeling I'd be in trouble today when I saw your result against Cole Hill,' said Iain as the two managers shook hands at the end. 'Well done, mate; nice to see someone taking on the usual suspects. You deserve it, too, all the years you've stuck with your team and done things the right way.'

James felt sick. Last night certainly didn't qualify as doing things the right way. He just hoped nobody had got hurt, and that it had made a difference this time – he didn't think he could bear the knowledge that he'd gone to such lengths for another failure.

James texted his result to Lynn, asking her to let him know how Kieran got on. Ben chirped away excitedly in the car, talking about the game and particularly his goal. James tried to smile as Ben rambled on, hoping his distraction wasn't too obvious.

An hour or so after they got home (and after SuperSam's fan club had insisted on a detailed account of every save her heroine had made) James received a text from Lynn:

Hawks lost 3-1 to Royals. Kieran had car trouble and they were 2-0 down before he got there. Furious isn't the word! A string of laughing emojis made Lynn's lack of sympathy clear.

James grinned to himself; it sounded like only Kieran's pride got hurt. More than that (he was a little embarrassed about what that reaction said about his priorities), the Swifts were closing the gap. Three points made up, but what had those three points cost him? Was that worth it?

The Stoneleigh grapevine soon carried the story back to James. Kieran's car had given out on the way to the game and by the time he managed to get there, it was nearly half-time. Phil had taken charge of the team in Kieran's absence, but with only seven players it was a case of damage limitation. Once the other three players arrived, it was a much closer game. The Hawks pulled one goal back and threw players forward in search of an equaliser, only to be caught on the break for the decisive third goal. Kieran was fuming at the end, telling the boys that even playing with two men down, they should be able to deal with any team in this lousy division. Not only that, he had cancelled the team's Christmas party, saying that if they couldn't beat also-rans like the Royals, the last thing they needed was to lose their focus. They could celebrate at the end of the season, he said, once they had secured their place back in the top division.

*

On Monday, working the first half of a morning/evening split shift, James took an unexpected phone call from Rob.

'Hi James. I'm going to just come straight out and say this: Max has decided to leave the Swifts. He's been training with another team and he wants to go with them.'

James was stunned. For one thing, hadn't they already been through this in the summer? For another, the Swifts had been playing so well and Max was right at the heart of things in midfield.

'Are you still there, James?'

'Yeah, yes. I was just taken aback, to be honest. I thought Max was enjoying it this season – him and the boys have been playing really well.'

'Well, most of them. You're still finding room for Charlie, which is ridiculous. Charlie's a nice enough lad but he's not up to this level, is he?'

'Charlie played really well yesterday,' protested James.

'Did he? Whatever. This other team approached Max and said that having seen him play, he'd get lots of game time if he came over now.'

'Which team is it, Rob?' asked James, suspecting that he already knew the answer.

'It's the Hawks, mate. Kieran said he was really impressed when we played them the other week. He's getting rid of some of the deadwood in his squad and he thought Max would fit in really well now. He said Max has improved since the summer and now he was easily good enough to make the Hawks' first team.'

'And you don't think that improvement is because of Joao's coaching?'

'He's certainly helped, but in the end it's down to the boys themselves, isn't it? If Max wants to keep developing, he needs to be in a better team. At the Hawks he'll have good players around him, rather than the likes of Charlie, Ryan and Deepak. I mean, you and Joao have done great to get him to this stage, but he's got to think about what's best for him, hasn't he? The Hawks will help him get to the next level.'

'Well, I'm sorry you feel that way, Rob. I'll be honest, I expected Max to show a bit more loyalty to his mates, particularly after what they've achieved together this season.'

'Achieved? You're still mid-table, mate. That's your trouble – accepting mediocrity as achievement. That's why Max needs a better team. He's ready for a new challenge.'

James could feel his face reddening, and decided to bring the call to an end before saying something he might regret. 'Well, let's agree to differ. Tell Max good luck with the Hawks.'

'Fair enough.' Rob even sounded a little embarrassed. 'Good luck to you too, and thanks for all that you've done for my Maxi.'

With that, he rang off, leaving James fighting back the urge to punch the steering wheel. The way Rob had put it: Max being ready for a new challenge? He's an eleven-year-old-boy, for God's sake. Kieran was no better, going behind his back to sabotage his team. Then again, James could hardly complain about sabotage, could he? James's earlier misgivings about how far he'd gone were forgotten now. Frankly, whatever it took to bring Kieran down was not only justifiable, it was a moral imperative. He simply couldn't let Kieran win: whatever it cost, James was going to beat Kieran.

James barely said two words to his next fare, grunting an acknowledgement when she confirmed where she wanted to go and knocking back any conversational gambits she attempted. The one after that was Mr Harper, with his dodgy views about immigrants. James had been booked to pick him up at ten-thirty, but the traffic on the High Street was particularly busy and James was running a few minutes late. Harper was waiting outside the building when James pulled up. He strode over to the car and bustled in before James could offer an apology.

'At last. You were meant to be here at ten-thirty.'

'Yes, sorry about that Mr Ha…'

'That Paki in the office said ten-thirty. It's now ten thirty-seven.' James could see him glaring accusingly in the rear-view mirror.

'As I said, I'm sorry about that. The traffic…'

'The traffic is your problem, not mine. If you're booked for ten-thirty, you should be here at ten-thirty on the dot. It's not good enough. I'm not surprised that curry-muncher can't organise his business.'

'Curry-muncher? Paki? Seriously? You can't go around calling people that kind of thing these days.'

'Stop changing the subject. I'll expect this trip for free to make up for your incompetence and lateness. If you don't like it, I'll take it up with Gunga Din in the office.'

'Take it up with who you like, you racist arse. Get out of my car – I'm not taking you anywhere.'

Harper visibly bristled. 'You can't talk to me like that.'

'Yeah? Guess again. Now get out. I don't drive racists, certainly not ones who throw terms like that around when they are talking about my colleagues.'

For a moment the two men just sat there glaring at each other. Eventually Harper reached into his jacket pocket and pulled out his wallet. 'Look, I need to get to this meeting. I'm sorry if I overreacted.' The last words were almost spat out. 'How about I give you an extra tenner to smooth things over and we just get going. How does that sound?' James was tempted to refuse, forcing the issue and kicking Harper onto the pavement, but he knew Raj would want him to keep the peace.

'Okay. I guess we both got a bit heated. It's the Cullip industrial estate you wanted, isn't it?'

Conversation was muted in the car, to the point of being non-existent. Neither man seemed inclined to start the ball rolling, which was just fine by James. The sooner Harper was out of his hair, the better. They arrived at the destination and as James checked the money Harper gave him, he wasn't entirely surprised to see it was the exact fare. 'What about that tenner you promised?'

'What about it? You didn't really think I'd give you a tip after you turned up late and called me a racist, did you? No wonder the only job you can get is working for a Paki. You've not heard the last of this.' With that, he spun on his heel and marched off to his meeting. James was tempted to chase after him, demand his payment and give him another mouthful, but what would it achieve? Better to let it go.

CHAPTER TWENTY-ONE

According to Ben, the boys all knew about Max's departure. Max had already left the Swifts players' WhatsApp group. Once he did, Ben said the others had weighed in with their thoughts. Some were angry, calling him a traitor, others worried how they would cope without him. Apparently Liam had been the coolest, pointing out that the whole team had improved, playing well with or without Max. That had calmed a lot of the anxiety, although not necessarily the ill-feeling. James was genuinely sorry to hear about the resentment; Max had been friends with the boys for years; it was a shame if that had been spoiled.

He was getting ready to go out for his evening shift when his phone rang again. It was Raj. James checked the time and realised that he was cutting it fine for his first fare.

'What can I do for you, mate? I'm just on my way out the door for my 7pm pick-up.'

'Yeah, about that, James. I've asked Amir to cover your shift tonight and he's already on his way.' James hesitated. Why was Amir covering his shift? 'I've had a phone call from one of your morning fares: Mr Harper. He says you lost your rag when he challenged you for being a bit racist.'

'What?' James couldn't believe what he was hearing. 'No way, it was the other way round – he was the one being racist and I called him out on it. How long have you known me? You know I'm not a racist.'

'Well, yeah, I do, but it seems like it's one thing after another with you these days – first, the rogue pick-ups, now getting into a row with one of my best customers…'

'Best? In what universe is Hate-Crime Harper one of your best customers?'

'In the one where people pay their bills. He's threatening to start using another company unless I fire you, and as much as I'd love to tell him where to shove his business, I can't afford to lose him.'

'But you can afford to lose me? Even though I've done nothing wrong?'

Raj had the decency to sound embarrassed. 'That's pretty much the size of it. Look, I feel rubbish about this, but it's business. You get that, yeah?'

James could hear his voice getting louder now, becoming steadily shriller as he spoke. 'I was sticking up for you, Raj. You should have heard the things he was calling you.'

'I have, hundreds of times, from him and others like him. I've learned to turn a deaf ear to it and just take their money. You should have done the same – there's no reasoning with the likes of Harper. It sucks, but that's all there is. Look, good luck, mate. I hate doing this but you're a good bloke and I'm sure you'll find something else soon enough.'

For a moment, James just stood there, the phone still by his ear even after Raj had hung up. He'd done it again, gone and lost his job. The fact that this time he hadn't done anything wrong didn't matter; he'd let Ros and the kids down. Again.

He couldn't face telling Ros what had happened, not yet, so he went out anyway. At first he just drove, his mind bouncing as aimlessly as the random route he was taking. The car was going nowhere in particular, and now so was his career.

Driving down Northumberland Street, James noticed an alleyway that seemed to have become a magnet for fly-tippers. Mattresses, broken furniture, bin bags full of God knows what, they were all heaped randomly inside. There was still a pathway through the garbage, just about, but not one that would make for a pleasant walk. It struck James that it would make the perfect place to dump his incriminating leftovers: let them hide in plain sight with the rest of the discarded junk, with nothing to link them back to him. He drove around the block and pulled up alongside the alleyway. Glancing around, just in case anyone was watching, he opened the boot and carried it all across. There was a sofa far enough back to be unobtrusive, so he dumped everything onto that. He'd thought that getting rid of all this evidence would make him feel better – one less thing to worry about – but with the new problems he had just gained, it didn't seem to make all that much difference. What was he going to do for work now?

*

'Do you want another call-out, PC Birnham?' Hayley toyed with saying no, just to see what happened. Another pointless visit was the last thing she wanted, but she could hardly tell Sergeant McGlashan that.

'What is it this time, Sarge? Bank robbery? Kidnapping? Someone breaking into 10 Downing Street to steal the nuclear codes? Or has someone dropped their wallet on the way out of the supermarket.'

'Do I detect a note of cynicism, Hayley? Even the small crimes matter when you're at the wrong end of them. We owe it to the public to do what we can. And there's something odd about this one; I've got a bloke who claims someone has sabotaged his car. Go and pay him a visit, see what you make of it.'

It took Hayley a moment to join the dots when she saw the name on the call-out sheet: Kieran Butcher. The angry man from

Stoneleigh Hawks with the supposedly stolen phone. Maybe he had a point after all, maybe someone did have it in for him if his car had been vandalised – no, not vandalised: sabotaged. That's what Sarge had said. Maybe this one might be interesting, even if the victim didn't deserve much sympathy.

*

Butcher's face had been a picture when Hayley turned up at his door. She pulled up in a parking space a couple of doors down from his house and rang the doorbell. She had got one of the community support workers to let him know that an officer would be calling round, but not to use her name.

'Afternoon, Mr Butcher. Nice to see you again, although obviously it's a shame the circumstances aren't better. I gather you've been having some car trouble.'

Butcher's eyes narrowed as he recognised her from last time. 'Oh, it's you again,' he said. 'Are all the male officers busy or something?'

'Yes,' she snapped back, 'it's their time of the month. Tell me all about your car.' Butcher actually managed to avoid being too patronising as he explained how he had initially assumed it was a random fault, just one of those things at the worst possible time, until the garage came back to him.

'They had to take the whole exhaust system out, it cost me £450, but Donny got it running again and I had it back the next day.'

'Donny?'

'The mechanic, from Jupp's garage. But then a few days later, he phones me up and says there's something odd in the old exhaust system. It wasn't that something broke, it was that the whole pipe was completely solid. Totally blocked, like someone had filled the whole thing to stop it from working.'

'Not the kind of blockage that could occur naturally?'

'What do you think, darling? Stuff's meant to come out of the exhaust, so there's no reason that much crap would get inside. A car exhaust is a finely tuned piece of engineering; it's not like a handbag that you stuff everything into.' Hayley shrugged off the comment. It wasn't like she hadn't expected it from Butcher; take the moral high ground and stay professional.

'You're saying someone deliberately blocked your car exhaust?'

'Damn right. My first thought was those two young lads down the street at number 17, but them and their parents were away visiting family that weekend. At least, that's what their dad said when I went round to demand he picked up the bill for the repairs. But then I realised, all this happened before a matchday.' He looked meaningfully at her.

'You mean you think it was a rival manager who sabotaged your car?' She didn't even bother keeping the scepticism from her voice.

'Of course; it stands to reason – who else would have a reason to mess with my car like that?' Anyone who had ever met you, thought Hayley.

'So have you any idea which of your rivals it was? Should I be paying a visit to Jürgen Klipp? Pop Guardiola perhaps?' She was quite pleased with that one: all those hours listening to Jayden regaling her with the latest Premier League news was finally paying off. Butcher scowled; if he was impressed with her football knowledge, he wasn't letting it show.

'No, but we were playing Shelley Abbey Royals, so that puts their manager right in the frame if you ask me. It's either us or Weston Park for the title, so I wouldn't put it past theirs either. As for the rest of the league, they're not likely to catch us even with stunts like this, but I suppose pure jealousy could be behind it. Now, I want to know what you're going to do about it.'

'I'll certainly make some calls, Mr Butcher. Can you let me have some names and, if you've got them, phone numbers. Let's start with your mechanic and the managers you just mentioned.'

'When you find the bastard who did it, you tell him that he owes me £500.'

Hayley checked her notebook. 'I thought you said it was £450.'

Butcher hesitated just long enough for Hayley to see that he was flailing for an answer. 'Yeah, that's right. £450... plus VAT. Round about £500 all told. And I want to see him prosecuted: he cost me three points that weekend as well as the money.'

'Don't you mean, you want him prosecuted because he endangered the lives of a carful of children?' Butcher didn't answer, but his sneer told Hayley which consequences he was more worked up about.

*

Donny the mechanic confirmed much of what Butcher had said about the car. He was a young lad, but seemed to know his way around an engine and was patient with Hayley's questions. In his professional opinion, there was no way a blockage like that could have just happened; he was convinced that it was done deliberately.

'Look, I kept the exhaust to show the lads – I've never seen anything like it before.' He wandered over to a workbench and pulled out something that even Hayley recognised as a car-exhaust unit, albeit one that had been opened up. Sure enough, the pipe was jammed solid with a grey mass. 'Cement,' added Donny. 'That's my best guess. If not, something pretty similar. It's clever: the car would still start, but after a few minutes as the gases build up with nowhere to escape, the engine seizes. Whoever did this would have had to pack it all in tightly, shoving a big stick or something to ram it down and make sure it sealed the tube tight. It's definitely been done on purpose by someone.'

'Is that a confession then? Is cementing exhausts on the sly your new way of drumming up some extra business?'

Donny grinned, correctly reading Hayley's playful tone. 'Hardly. I mean, I was happy to take the money but I've got plenty of work coming in. But whoever did this knew what they were doing.' They had to have the motive to actually go through with it as well, thought Hayley. It was hard to imagine a kids' football manager, like Matt, going to these lengths though. Still, she had to do the legwork and start chasing down some leads.

*

'I still can't believe Raj would fire me over this – he knows Harper was making the whole thing up.' James and Ros were discussing – again – his departure from AbaCabs.

'Can't you?' asked Ros. 'It makes a lot of sense to me. It might not be doing the right thing by you, but Raj has to think about his family, doesn't he? He relies on that business to put food on the table, and if it's a case of selling you short or seeing them go without, what parent wouldn't do what it takes to keep their own kids safe?'

'I know, but I'm no racist, and Raj knows that. It just rankles that he's sided with a human cesspit like Harper over me.'

'No, he hasn't; he's sided with keeping his family safe. I'm sure he'd love to tell Harper what to do with his business, but principles and morals are sometimes a luxury that people can't afford.'

James stopped what he was doing and looked directly at Ros. 'Do you really believe that?'

She shrugged. 'It doesn't matter what I believe, it matters that that's how Raj saw it. You weren't happy in the job anyway, and if this has given you the push you needed to give teaching another go, it might even be the best thing to happen to you all year.' It was a fair point. Once James levelled out after Raj's bombshell, he had got in touch with Richard and arranged another pub night – that night, as it happened – to talk through his options. A couple of hours later, sitting in the Thane of Cawdor, he was nursing a pint with one eye on the door.

Richard arrived and greeted James warmly. Once he had got himself a drink and settled down in a chair, James outlined what had happened and asked whether there was still a chance of work at Cole Hill with Richard.

'Definitely. We're two teachers down in the English department, and in January we've got another going on maternity leave; we're pretty desperate. After our last meeting, I mentioned you to the head, Mrs Cranbrook, and she said to let her know if you had a change of heart. She knows about the incident, so expect to answer questions about that. You'll need to convince her it won't happen again.' Richard paused for a moment. 'It won't, will it? I mean, you are ready to come back, aren't you?'

'Yeah, I've had it easy driving taxis for too long; what I need in my life is stroppy fourteen-year-olds who can't tell their Austen from their elbow.'

*

James wondered how Max's departure would affect the mood at training, but everything was fine. The atmosphere was good and if anyone was dwelling on the departure, they didn't show it.

Joao had another new training idea. He marked out a pitch with a halfway line, and divided the players into two teams. Apart from the goalkeepers, the rule was that everyone had to be in the same half as the ball. The ball could be passed or dribbled across the halfway line, but once it crossed, everyone had to follow. The aim of the exercise was to work an opening to play a through-ball from your own half to put a team-mate in behind the opposing defence. Joao encouraged and challenged the players to use their movement to create the space for their side to play the killer pass.

At first, play was scrappy. The main goalscoring chances came from tackles and interceptions deep in the opposition half. As the game went on, players became more adept at protecting the ball, making passes that enabled team-mates to beat the game's inherent offside trap. Sam, when playing outfield, was particularly good at shielding the ball from the opposition until her team-mates gave her good passing options, and Callum and Ben emerged as kings of the through-ball.

At the end of the session, James gathered all the players around.

'Cup game this week, against Little Dibbing.'

Joao looked perplexed. 'Mister James, I thought we already went out of the cup back in October. No?'

'That was the Town Cup, just for the teams in our league. This is the County Cup. It's a different competition.'

'What are Little Dibbing like?' asked Ryan.

'Are they good?' added Deepak.

'No idea. That's the thing with the County Cup. Some of the teams aren't from our league, so we won't find out until we play them. It's a home game, and an afternoon kick-off for once, 2pm. Let's just enjoy ourselves. If we win, we get a cup run; if we lose, it hasn't cost us anything.' James knew more than he was letting on; Little Dibbing was a small rural village on the other side of the county. They probably struggled to attract players who didn't actually live there, so it may well be that they weren't that good. He didn't want to tell the team though, just in case they got complacent. He wanted to keep the momentum going with another good win.

As James was picking up the bag of balls to take back to the lock-up, Sam approached him.

'Just to let you know, James, Kieran asked me if I wanted to join the Hawks as well.'

James could hardly believe it, after everything Kieran had said about girls playing football. 'Seriously?'

'Yeah, I know. He came up to me after the Cole Hill game and said I belonged in a much better side than Swifts.'

'What did you say?'

Sam grinned. 'I told him I was happy with the Swifts and I wasn't interested in moving. He said that just proved I didn't know the first thing about football. Is he always like that?'

'Yeah, that's Kieran. Thanks for not making the move.'

'Are you joking? Uncle Dave told me some of the things he says at committee meetings – I don't want to play for someone like that. Besides, it's fun with the Swifts. I'm not sure I'd enjoy playing for the Hawks.'

'I think you're right, but I'm still grateful to you for helping us out. By the way, my daughter seems to be turning into your biggest fan.'

Sam giggled. 'Yeah, Ben has been telling me about her. What can I say? She must be a young lady with great taste!'

Sam said goodbye and made her way over to the car park where her mum was waiting. James was left reflecting on how treacherous Kieran had been. Again.

CHAPTER TWENTY-TWO

'Fly-tipping, seriously Sarge?'

'It was still a crime last time I checked, Hayley.'

Hayley sighed. This old argument – that she knew she couldn't win – again. 'Well, yes, but we almost never get anyone for this kind of thing, and even if we do the courts will give them a slap on the wrist at most. There are more important things for us to focus on, surely?'

'Not more important to the residents of Northumberland Street; and certainly not more important to one Mr Newson, who phoned in to make the complaint. Can you arrange to meet up with him at the site and make all the right noises? Let him feel that we're taking this seriously.'

'Even if we're not?'

'I'll pretend I didn't hear that. If you want to impress me, stop complaining and see if you can turn this situation around.'

She could understand that fly-tipping was unsightly, unhygienic and antisocial, but she also had a fairly clear idea of what kind of person was going to be complaining about it. She phoned Mr Newson and arranged to meet him at the alleyway in half an hour. First impressions from the call did little to change her preconceptions: he huffed and harrumphed, berating her as if she was personally responsible for the mess. This wasn't what she'd joined the force for.

'It's just round this corner, officer.' Nuisance Newson was an older man, late sixties as far as she could tell. He was still quite spritely, and Hayley had to walk a little quicker than she would have liked to keep up with him as he bustled towards the offending site. As she rounded the corner, she could see why he was complaining. The alleyway was full of discarded items, ranging from binbags and small boxes of junk to bigger appliances. There was even an old washing machine and a rusted, mangled bicycle.

'You see, once there's a couple of things left here, everyone else thinks it's the place to dump their rubbish. The other day I saw a couple of kids playing in the pile. Now that can't be right, can it? Would you want your kids doing that?' Hayley bit back her response that she wouldn't have Jayden playing on his own out on the street.

'No, absolutely not, Mr Newson.'

'So, what are you and your colleagues going to do about it, then?' He looked expectantly, almost defiantly, at her.

'I can assure you I'm taking this very seriously,' she lied. 'For a start, I'll make arrangements for a council clean-up team to come and collect it all. Unfortunately, there are no CCTV cameras on this road, which means it's unlikely that we'll be able to identify any culprits, but I'll certainly pass on the word to my colleagues to keep a close eye on this area for any reoccurrence.'

'Is that all you can do?' Hayley couldn't decide if he was really disappointed, or secretly pleased that he had something else to complain about. Maybe what he really wanted was a project, something to occupy his retirement.

'I'm afraid so. Of course, the council could put up signs warning people not to leave their rubbish on the street, advising them about the fines they could incur; that might help deter would-be reoffenders. And you could always ask for CCTV to be set up. That would be the biggest deterent and hugely improve our chances of catching someone in the future. The council is more likely to listen to you than us on that kind of thing.'

'Really?'

'Absolutely. You're a voter; individual councillors know that they're only ever one election away from losing their position. I'd phone the council staff if I was you, but also make contact with your elected representatives. It only takes one voice to start things moving.' It also only takes one crank to start a revolution, but she suspected Mr Nuisance wouldn't take kindly to that phrasing. He bustled away and Hayley thought she saw a new sense of purpose in his stride. She wouldn't want to be the council official that he landed on next.

Right, time to head back to the station then. Hayley turned and made to walk away, casting a final eye over the pile of junk. It was amazing the things that people thought they could just dump in public. She took a few steps past the pile, in the direction of the police station, before something made her pause. She couldn't put her finger on what it was, but something was drawing her back to the rubbish. She scanned the assorted detritus, searching for what was bothering her. She had been in the job long enough to know when to trust her instincts, and something was telling her to take another look.

She walked back to the alley and stepped past the rusted fridge and disgusting-looking mattress, picking her way through the burnt-out kettles and hair-dryers, carefully looking all around. She was just about to write it off as a false alarm when her gaze fell on a collection of discarded items clumped together on top of a tatty sofa. There was a bag – still half-full – of quick-drying cement. Alongside it was a plastic bowl half-encased in grey clumps of solid matter and a short wooden pole with one end similarly covered. Donny's description of how the exhaust must have been blocked came back to her mind, and it occurred to Hayley that this was exactly the kind of kit the saboteur would have needed. Maybe it was just a coincidence, but what if it wasn't? Another day she might not have bothered, but Sarge's words about impressing him were still ringing in her ears. He had just meant getting Nuisance Newson to back off, but what if she could actually get a collar out of this? If she was going to change his mind about her, it was at least worth a try. She quickly slipped on some latex gloves and started filling evidence bags to send off for fingerprints checks.

*

The Little Dibbing game went much as James had hoped. They were a classic village team, a couple of good players, but also a few younger lads making up the numbers. James had started in a three-three-two formation, but quickly switched to two-four-two, moving Deepak into midfield. The Swifts calmly passed the ball around, while Little Dibbing ran themselves ragged chasing after it. Ben and Callum were playing defence-splitting through-balls on a regular basis, and Dylan, Liam and even Josh were filling their boots with goals. They walked off the pitch nine-nil winners in a game so one-sided that Sam would probably have had time to have taken her homework onto the pitch and still not looked like conceding a goal.

All things considered, James was delighted with how the team was doing, but he knew he'd need more than that to narrow the gap and catch Kieran and the Hawks. Despite the success of the car trick, he knew he couldn't risk it a second time. For one thing, his nerves wouldn't take it, and for another it had only made a difference because he had known that Kieran was short-handed. Most weeks, the Hawks' battalion of subs would step in and all it would achieve would be to irritate Kieran (so not entirely pointless then). Even so, he wasn't sure his conscience could take it if his luck ran out and someone got hurt.

In the meantime, James's thoughts were turning again to his return to teaching. The end result of his meeting with Mrs Cranbrook was an agreement that she would give him supply work in January up until the February half-term, with a view to extending that if James showed that his past issues really were behind him. She was sympathetic, seeming to accept that the Kyle incident was out of character, but she was also clear that any repetition would see the end of James at Cole Hill. That was fair enough; James knew he was lucky just to get this chance.

*

Sunday morning, and Hayley was roused from her sleep by her phone beeping with a new text message. Jayden was at Andy's for the weekend and she wasn't on duty, so she had planned a rare lie-in. Drowsily stabbing around for her phone on the bedside table, she pulled it towards herself and found the message: it was from Matt, letting the Redbridge Town parents know that the game against Stoneleigh Swifts had been called off due to the snow. Hayley paused as she read the message, wondering why the name of the opposition was ringing bells. Of course, Stoneleigh – wasn't that Mr Butcher's team? No, his were the Hawks, weren't they? She wondered whether the other Stoneleigh manager was cut from the same cloth as Butcher. If he was, maybe it was just as well Andy hadn't had to witness the match today: it would just give him more evidence to support his theory that football reflected everything that was wrong with capitalist society. On the other hand, Jayden would be disappointed not to have a game, whatever the conditions were like.

Awake now, she climbed out of bed and made her way to the bathroom for a pee. She looked out of the window as she washed her hands and, sure enough, saw a blanket of white lying across the road outside. A brief sortie downstairs to make a cup of tea and some toast, and she was soon back in bed and wrapped up warm. She supposed she had better let Andy know.

The phone rang a few times before Andy answered.

'Hey, what's up?'

'Bad news,' she replied, knowing he'd see it as anything but. 'Jayden's match has been cancelled because of the weather.'

'Yeah,' she could hear the smile, 'I thought it might be when I got up and saw that the snow was looking like a police enquiry.'

She bit. 'How's that?'

'Oh, you know: a complete cover-up.' He was very pleased with himself for that one, she could tell, but she wasn't rising to the bait. They chatted for a minute, with Hayley reluctantly conceding that Andy's alternative plan, which involved a snowball fight in the morning followed by a cinema trip and a pizza, sounded like something Jayden would enjoy. The film was one that she had been planning to take Jayden to herself over the Christmas holidays, but she didn't say anything. Andy wasn't actually doing anything wrong – all he was doing was trying to give Jayden a nice day. Hayley settled back with her tea and toast and Radio 2. She must look in on old Mrs Lewington down the road once she got up, see if she needed anything from the shops. There was no way the old girl should be out and about in conditions like this.

The weather didn't improve, and most of the following week saw snow enveloping the town. Word came through that the league had decided to call off all of the weekend's games in plenty of time. Jayden tried explaining to her how Redbridge's position in the league table was better than it sounded.

'So you're fifth, right? Out of how many?'

'Out of ten. But we've got two games in hand. If we win both of those, we'll go above Stoneleigh Swifts and Shelley Abbey Royals and we'll be third, just one position out of the promotion places. And if we can beat Stoneleigh Hawks, we'll pull level with them for second.'

'So it's just between you and Stoneleigh Hawks then?'

'No. The Royals are good, and Cole Hill in sixth have got two games in hand as well, so they're in just as good a position as us. Stoneleigh Swifts have picked up some good results, but Matt says we ought to be able to beat them. No one's going to catch

Weston Park – they haven't dropped a point all season – but there's at least five teams still chasing second place. Matt says it's in our hands.' Hayley wondered how many minutes of game time Jayden was likely to get next year with the higher standards and tougher opposition of the top division. If it came to that, how much was he going to get this season with so much at stake? At least Jayden was still excited about his football, even if he was spending much more time watching than actually playing.

*

Across the other side of town, James was performing similar calculations about the league table, although with less enthusiasm than Jayden. Before his feud with Kieran had escalated, fourth at Christmas would have sounded great, but the stakes had been raised since then. The lost games against Melville and Moorlands still rankled; wins from those games would put Swifts just two points behind the Hawks, and he blamed Kieran completely for those defeats. As it was, instead of being masters of their own fate, all he could do was to keep going and hope the Hawks slipped up several times. Either that or take matters into his own hands again.

CHAPTER TWENTY-THREE

It wasn't exactly the Christmas Day of Hayley's dreams. She remembered when Jayden was small, his excited little face as he burst into her and Andy's bedroom, shaking them awake to come and see what Santa had left. Jayden, with all the worldly wisdom of an eleven-year-old, was a bit cooler about the whole thing now, but he was still fun to spend the day with. Not that Hayley would get to do that this year: he was spending the day at Andy's because she had drawn the short straw and got the early Christmas Day shift at work. It was 6.45 now, and she was swinging her car into the station car park, giving her just enough time to get changed and come on shift at 7. It took Hayley a minute to gather all her bags. She had a load of sausage rolls for the bring and share Christmas lunch, though past experience said the skeleton staff were unlikely to all be there for it at the same time.

The day started quietly enough, but before too long everybody was out and about, responding to the usual array of Christmas Day call-outs. A young man on his own, whose solitude had triggered a mental health episode; a blazing row between a middle-aged couple whose simmering marital unhappiness had finally, inevitably, boiled over somewhere between lunch and the King's speech. Saddest of all was a young couple whose Christmas had involved turkey, lots of alcohol, and an unusual exchange of gifts: a black eye for her and the prospect of a night in the cells for him.

It was closer to 5pm before Hayley managed to get away. She had arranged with Andy to call in at his once she finished, to at least see Jayden and give him his present in person, but Jayden was staying with his dad until after lunch on Boxing Day. Standing at Andy's door, ringing the bell, she wondered if this would be a happy easy-going encounter with Andy or another tense stand-off. Fortunately, it was a cheery, relaxed Andy who opened the door and invited her in. She had thought it was just going to be Andy and Jayden, but some of his mates were also there – she recognised Neil and Amy among the group, but none of them seemed enthusiastic to see her. They all knew what she did for a job, and none of them had the benefit of having previously shared a bed with her to change their preconceptions about the police.

'Relax everyone,' joked Andy. 'It's not a raid. She's just here to see Jayden.'

'Good job we've finished with the weed already', said one of the guests, a big ginger-haired man with an impressive beard. Judging from the lack of tension in the way the others reacted, it was just a joke, possibly to test her out (of course, if it hadn't been a joke, that might be another explanation for the lack of tension in the room). She decided not to bite, contenting herself with a raised eyebrow in Andy's direction.

'Oh please. Marcus is joking. As if we'd be doing that kind of thing in front of Jayden.' The eyebrow remained in place, prompting Andy to add, 'Or at all, *officer*.'

She didn't stay long, just an hour or so – long enough to spend some time with Jayden and to let him show her his other presents. She gave him his – a new Town football shirt – and got her usual box of chocolates from him, but she was wary of outstaying her welcome. Marcus made a couple of barbed remarks about whether she'd managed to oppress anyone during her shift that morning, so she decided to quit while she was ahead. Christmas Day was one of the hardest days for co-parenting. Hopefully her shifts would be kinder next year and she'd be able to take her turn of having Jayden for the whole day.

*

All too soon, Christmas passed and James had to get his head around the schemes of work that Richard had sent him. The prospect of teaching literature again was exciting; getting face to face with a classroom full of would-be Kyles, less so.

James was due to start on Monday 4th January, and with no matches on the 3rd, he spent the Sunday going over lesson plans, checking and rechecking that he was on top of everything. Ros found him at the dining-room table and held something out to him.

'A little late Christmas present, to say good luck for tomorrow,' she said. It was a new pack of whiteboard pens, tastefully decorated with a ribbon and a bow.

'Such extravagance! You really shouldn't have.'

'What can I say? You're worth it.' She gave him a kiss as he took the pens from her hand, and whispered, 'Good luck, Jamie. You'll be great.' James appreciated the gesture, but he wished he could be so sure. What if there was another Kyle? Who was he kidding: sooner or later there was always another Kyle. The real question was, how would he react?

Lynn dropped by that afternoon with a good luck card and a nice bottle of wine – something for James to look forward to after his first day. Ros promised to help James out with it, which the others agreed was very generous of her. James asked after Rory, who had an appointment with the consultant in a week's time. Lynn said he was champing at the bit to get back to football, which reminded James of a problem deferred; he was desperate to keep Sam in the team, but didn't want Rory pushed out. Maybe she could play outfield? She certainly held her own against the lads in training, although James knew that she was the better goalkeeper.

Still, reverse WWKD said he had to look after both players, and he was determined to find a way to do that.

*

The big day came and James made sure to arrive in plenty of time. There was a staff meeting at 8.15, and as he sat with Richard in the staff room they were joined by a woman in a smart business jacket and matching pencil skirt, her hair tied severely back as if she was ready for battle.

Richard introduced the would-be Amazon as Claire, his second-in-department. She held out her hand, angling it to be on top when they actually shook.

'James, hi, good to meet you. Richard has told me everything about you.' Was the way she emphasised the word 'everything' a reference to his chequered past? Fair enough, James had always known the rumours would follow him.

'Yeah, great to meet you too. I'm really looking forward to working with everyone.'

Richard stepped in. 'You'll meet the rest of the department soon enough – remember, there's a department meeting tonight after school – but if you need anything and I'm not around, Claire should be able to help.'

The head called the meeting to a start, mentioned James as well as another couple of new staff members, and went through all the usual start-of-term stuff. James kept glancing at the clock behind Mrs Cranbrook's head; he just wanted to get on with his first lesson – the sooner he was back on the horse, the sooner he'd know if he could still ride.

After walking back to the English department with Richard and Claire, James arrived at his classroom and went inside, ready for his first class. As he was getting himself organised, a young slim woman poked her head out of the walk-in cupboard he shared with the next-door classroom.

'Hiya – are you James? I'm Josie. I think we're neighbours.' She grinned as she said this, her elfin features accentuated by the smile. James quickly tried to recall what Richard had told him about Josie: fresh out of teacher training college that year, full of talent and idealism but finding it more of a struggle than she had expected.

'Hi Josie, yes, I'm James. Nice to meet you. Who have you got first period?'

'Top set year 7, which should be a nice one. How's your morning looking?

'Year 8s first, then *Macbeth* with year 10s. What could go wrong? I mean, have you ever met a teenager who didn't enjoy Shakespeare? How better to spend the first day back after Christmas than grappling with iambic pentameter?'

She rolled her eyes, still smiling. 'Good luck, though I'm sure you won't need it.' With that, Josie headed back through to her classroom, leaving James to face the year 8 horde alone.

The lesson started well, but several minutes in, James became aware of a low buzzing noise permeating the room. James looked up, but all of the students' eyes were fixed on their work, which was suspicious in itself.

'Very funny,' said James. 'Now knock it off.'

'Knock what off, sir?' asked one of the lads.

'What's your name?' asked James.

'Gary, sir, Gary Cobb.'

'Well, Gary, you're not the first class to try the mass humming routine on me. Knock it off now.'

'I'm not humming, sir – I'm talking to you. How can I hum when I'm talking?'

'Indeed, and yet the humming continues. It's as if there's several of you who are all in on it.' James was out of his chair and walking around the class. The hum was definitely operating at a reduced capacity now – some of the less daring students had decided to cut and run – but as James walked around, he got a good sense of who was still in the game.

He got back to his seat and pointed out a few individuals, asking for their names, which he wrote up, on the whiteboard.

'Right, I'm certain that you four, plus Gary of course,' he added Gary's name, 'were all part of the great Humming Choir. Here's the deal: everyone gets on with some work and doesn't try anything like that again, and I'll rub out your names come the end of the lesson. Keep this going and I'll give negative behaviour points and the next time you step out of line in my lesson, we'll go for detentions.' There were a few protests, but only half-hearted ones. James held up his hands to quell the dissent. 'This isn't up for debate. To be honest, I'd rather we all got back to the uses of a simile, but if you'd prefer to take me on, you'll find it's as much use as nailing water to a wall – that's another simile, by the way. Do you see what I did there?'

*

At lunchtime, James walked in to the department office to find several of his new colleagues already present. Claire was washing her hands in the office sink before setting about the raw materials of the salad she was about to chop.

'"Is this a dagger which I see before me?",' quipped James as she picked up the knife. The others laughed, but a scowl from Claire suggested that she didn't care for his literary allusion.

'How was the first morning?' asked Simon, an older teacher who Richard had described as already counting down to retirement, even though it was still several years away.

'Okay, to be honest. 8B were a little playful at first, but they soon settled down.'

Simon snorted. 'I don't like it when they co-operate – it makes me wonder what they're really up to.'

'You don't like it any of the time, Simon,' chided Claire. 'You moan when they're quiet, you moan when they're playing up. Is there any time you do like the students?'

'I like it when the little bleeders go home at the end of the day.' This prompted more laughter, though not from Claire.

The door opened and two more teachers came in. The first was a smiley lady, a little older than James, who introduced herself as Moira; the second was Dean, a younger man. Moira had been at Cole Hill for several years, while Dean had been at the school since leaving teacher training college a couple of years ago. Moira seemed quietly spoken – Richard had described her as the rock of the department – while Dean seemed to be brimming with confidence.

The rest of the day went smoothly enough. A few of his classes did the usual testing-out-the-new-teacher stuff, but James was happy that he'd got the right balance of establishing his authority without coming across as a humourless tyrant. At the department meeting, James did more listening than talking. There wasn't any real controversy, although he again saw signs of tension between Claire, who wanted everything done yesterday, and Simon, who didn't want to have to do any of it. James was happy to just get his bearings and get home to Ros and his well-earned bottle of wine.

*

As well as school was going, James couldn't wait for training with the Swifts on Wednesday. As the players arrived, James spotted Sam and called her to one side for a quick chat.

'Rory's seeing his consultant next week, so we should know more about when he'll be back.'

Sam's smile dropped away. 'Does that mean you won't want me in the team anymore?'

'Not in the slightest! I need to be fair to Rory, but I want to be fair to you too. Once we hear how Rory's recovery is going, we'll know more, but I was thinking maybe the two of you could share the goalkeeper's position, take it in turns or something. How does that sound to you?'

Sam nodded, looking happier. 'Yeah, that would be okay. I mean, I prefer to play in goal, but I'd be happy to play outfield if it helps – only if you've got room for another outfield player: I really don't want to push anyone out.'

'I know, and I appreciate that, but you're part of this team too, and you're every bit as important as the others. Anyway, Rory hasn't got the all-clear yet, so for now I definitely need you in goal.'

Sam grinned and headed over to the rest of the players. James was glad that she seemed okay with all that. As for her playing out on pitch, she could more than hold her own against the boys, so it was a definite option.

*

The rest of the week at Cole Hill went well. There were some ups and downs with his classes, but nothing out of the ordinary. Mr Marshall, one of the deputy heads, observed a year 9 lesson, but that was fine. Richard was going to look in on a lesson the following week, and Mrs Cranbrook and Claire were both going to watch him as well. John Marshall's feedback was minimal but broadly positive. James had avoided swearing at any kids, for one thing, so that had to be a plus.

CHAPTER TWENTY-FOUR

'First match of the new year, guys.' James had settled on guys as a gender-neutral term that Sam wouldn't object to. 'You've all heard of Jane Austen, yeah?' A few blank looks, but mostly nods. 'Centre forward, played for Burnley and QPR, among others. Austen said, "It is a truth universally acknowledged that the New Year always looks better when it starts with three points", so let's go out and get the win. We attack when we get the chance; we work hard to defend when we lose possession. We play as a team – lots of talking, helping each other. A win today and we draw level with the Royals and start reeling in the Hawks. After that, who knows where we can finish?'

The game started well, with Ben confidently winning tackles in midfield. Along with Callum, he was controlling the game, spraying passes around to move the team up the pitch. Up front though, Josh's finishing was woeful, and Dylan seemed sluggish after the Christmas break. No matter how many opportunities the midfielders served up, the forwards found new ways to miss them.

With Sam and her defence in good form, the game was deadlocked. As the ref checked his watch for half-time, Callum misplaced a pass to Liam and the Royals swept forward. A quick exchange of short passes and the Royals' winger had the chance to run at Charlie. A few months ago, Charlie would have dived in recklessly, but this time he held his ground, jockeyed his man… and then dived in recklessly, bringing down the opponent and conceding a penalty. Sam went the right way, but couldn't stop the ball from flying past her. One-nil to the Royals.

In the second half, with Liam now up front, the Swifts had the better chances, but still couldn't take them. James switched to two-four-two for the last fifteen minutes but no matter what they tried, the equaliser wouldn't come.

'Never mind guys,' said James. 'Great effort – you were really unlucky. We're still in there fighting for second.' He said it, but deep down he was struggling to believe. Three lost points, and the chances of finishing above the Hawks growing more distant with each one. They hadn't been unlucky, they'd been wasteful. Josh and Dylan could have had a hat-trick each today, if only they had a striker they would have won handsomely. James suggested to Joao that maybe they should work on finishing again on Wednesday night.

There were no surprises when James checked the results that evening. Weston Park had won, along with Cole Hill and Redbridge. Hawks had scored twenty-one goals against Moorlands. James could just imagine Kieran's attitude, going all out for goals galore rather than easing off once the game was sewn up. The Swifts had suffered a few heavy defeats over the years, but nothing like that; how do you pick a team up after twenty-one goals? At thirty minutes each way, that's a goal every three minutes of football, for a whole hour. He couldn't imagine how soul-destroying that must feel for the losing side. The two teams were playing each other again the following weekend – something for the Moorlands boys to look forward to.

*

That week, Richard observed one of James's lessons, and the two of them were going over the feedback when they became aware of an argument brewing across the department office.

'I saw Mark Rylance's first run in the late eighties, and he was incredible,' asserted Simon. 'No one has bettered that.'

Claire's withering tone did as much to express her disdain as her words. 'What a surprise – Simon opts for a performance he saw when he was young. You'd go back and live in 1989 if you had the chance, wouldn't you?'

'Frankly no: we still had Thatcher, CDs were winning the war against lovely old vinyl and the charts were full of Jive Bunny. The fact that I was young when I saw Rylance's Hamlet doesn't mean it wasn't brilliant.'

'No, but it means you saw it when you still cared about things. If someone gave the same performance now, you wouldn't be interested. When was the last time you heard a new idea and didn't immediately dismiss it?'

'It's not like that at all,' said Simon testily, immediately dismissing Claire's comment. 'Nobody has brought out Hamlet's madness quite so well, before or since.'

'But there's more to Hamlet than just the madness,' said Moira, her voice commanding attention despite being little more than a whisper compared to Simon's bluster and Claire's shrill staccato. 'Simon Russell Beale's Hamlet was quite profound: a study of intelligence in the face of mortality. When he said, "The readiness is all", you believed he understood what it was to face death fully prepared.'

Richard grinned at James. 'This often happens. This lot disagree over everything. If Dean was here, he'd probably argue for a more recent high-profile production with a big name from TV – David Tennant or Andrew Scott – which would enflame Simon and Claire even more. Do you want to weigh in? Who's your choice as the best Hamlet?'

'I'm still waiting for the Chuckle Brothers' take on the role – "To me or not to me, that is the question". No, as the new boy,

I'll stay on the sidelines and let the others fight it out; no point in putting anyone's back up.'

'When did you get so wise?'

'Sadly, not before I told Kyle Kettering what he could do with himself. Which brings us back to my lesson observation; you were saying?'

'Relax; I thought it went well. There were a couple of moments when students might have gone off-topic or tried disrupting things, but you handled them well and brought things around without any need for confrontation. I know that's one of the things the head most wants to hear about, so that's why I've included it in the write-up – you and I know you're up to the job, I just need to convince her to keep you on.'

James smiled, grateful for Richard's support. The truth of it was that James didn't know whether he was still up to the job, although he was beginning to suspect that he might be.

*

That evening, James took a phone call from Lynn.

'Hi Lynn, how did it go at the doctor's?'

'Well, there's good news and bad news. The good news is that Rory has been cleared to come back to training – and to playing matches too, if you want him. The bad news is that the doctor said not to play in goal for a few months. His arm is still a bit stiff, and the bone needs time to strengthen. Playing in goal is asking for another injury.'

'Oh no, poor Rory. How did he react to the news?'

'About as well as you'd expect: he's gutted; although at least he gets to come back to training. Have you got room for another outfield player?'

'Of course we have. Will we see him on Wednesday evening?'

Lynn sounded relieved. 'Just try keeping him away – he's been nagging me to let him play for weeks.'

James spoke to Sam before training on Wednesday. She made all the right noises about being disappointed for Rory, but James could see she was delighted to keep her place in goal, for now at least. Rory seemed to be having a smashing time, chasing around the pitch with all his mates. James checked in with him a couple of times after he was knocked to the ground by challenges, but both times he got up grinning. Joao had prepared some shooting games, with input to help the boys add accuracy without sacrificing too much power. Rory unleashed several absolute cannonballs, albeit often wayward ones, but by the end even his accuracy was improving. It was years since he had played outfield for the Swifts, but James didn't think he would embarrass himself.

*

The Swifts had a week off, so James caught up with his marking on Sunday. Although Ben, as ever, was disappointed not to be playing, it was Poppy who kept asking why there was no game. She wanted her regular report about SuperSam's heroics. Checking the league website that evening, James saw that the Hawks had enjoyed an even bigger win over Moorlands – thirty-four-nil. Ouch.

*

James walked into the department office at lunchtime on Monday to hear Dean and Simon in another heated debate.

'Rubbish,' said Dean decisively. 'Tennant's was the definitive performance of his generation; he brought a fresh comic touch, without losing the intensity of all the best portrayals.'

James caught Moira's eye and mouthed the question, 'Hamlet again?' Moira just laughed and shook her head.

'And I say,' replied Simon, 'none of the modern portrayals – none of them – can hold a candle to Tom Baker. Baker *is* Doctor Who, end of argument.'

James went to sit with Moira and Josie, as Dean spluttered his response to Simon's statement. 'It's the end of the argument all right: you've just destroyed your own credibility. Any real *Doctor Who* fan knows that the Doctor isn't called "Doctor Who", he's just "The Doctor". If you can't even get the character's name right, why should we take you seriously on the rest of it? You can't just dismiss all the modern Doctors because you get a warm nostalgic glow about hiding behind the sofa when you were in short trousers.'

Josie screwed her face up and leaned in to Moira. 'Euuwwww – Simon in short trousers. I've got an image. Bleuh!' James and Moira erupted with laughter, briefly drawing the attention of the dissenting Whovians.

James set up his laptop to print off some worksheets, and saw an email from the head of PE. The year 7 football team had a match after school the following week, and some of the 7E boys had been selected. James had them last thing on the day of the match. To make the most of the fading daylight, the kick-off was close to the end of the lesson and Mr Parker was asking if the boys in the team could be dismissed early. They would get changed at lunchtime, then turn up to afternoon lessons in their football kit. All they would need to do afterwards was put on their boots.

'Email about year 7 football,' said James.

'You've got 7E haven't you?' asked Moira.

'That's right.'

'Kenny Harrison, the school hero,' she said knowingly. 'I'm guessing he's been picked.'

James checked the team list and sure enough Kenny Harrison was there, along with a couple of others from 7E, who coincidentally also played for Cole Hill on Sundays.

'Yes. What's so special about Kenny?'

'He's signed up to Town's academy. The PE staff were falling over themselves when they found out. Mr Parker has high hopes of winning trophies with Kenny in the team. Town don't let him play for anyone else, but they're not allowed to stop him from playing for the school. You're into football aren't you?'

'I manage a team of under-twelves, yeah.'

'Maybe you can use that to connect with him. I know his form tutor doesn't want Kenny's education to suffer with his football commitments. I think the poor lad gets pulled in lots of different directions; the club want him to focus on his future career – not that there's any guarantee they'll keep him on; Mr Parker wants him to win things for the school and his parents want him to work hard in lessons.'

'What does Kenny want?'

Moira smiled at James. 'That's the right question. I knew there was a reason I liked you.'

*

Teaching 8B later in the day, James was at the whiteboard when he felt a vibration in his breast pocket. He forced himself to ignore it until he had finished his account of how nothing was wasted in Hemingway's lean prose. Then, once he had settled the class into their work, he surreptitiously took out his phone. It was a text from Lynn: *Check the league table: Moorlands have withdrawn from the league: all their results have been wiped!* James stared at the screen trying to take it in.

'Oi, sir, I thought we weren't allowed our phones during lessons!' It was Gary Cobb, grinning all over his face.

'You got me,' replied James with a smile, putting his phone away. 'I throw myself on the mercy of the court. Now, let's get back to streamlining your own prose, like Hemingway does with his.'

James forced himself to focus on the lesson, but all he wanted was for the bell to go. When it eventually rang – ask not for whom it tolls, it tolls for Moorlands, thought James – he headed next door to the department office to check the FA website. It was true; all of Moorlands' games had been removed, with the points from the games removed too. That was great news: the Swifts were the only team to have dropped points to Moorlands, so they had nothing to lose. Most teams lost three points while Hawks, gloriously, lost six points. Swifts were still lagging, but the gap had been slashed. The impossible task had just got possible.

CHAPTER TWENTY-FIVE

It was another committee meeting, and Kieran was voicing his sense of injustice over Moorlands' demise.

'If you enter a league, you should see the season through. We've lost six points and nearly sixty goals from our goal difference. How's that fair?'

'They can't finish the season with no players, Kieran,' said Alison. 'It sounds as if the two games against you were the last straw. If you hadn't shattered their morale, maybe they would still have a team and you'd have your six points.'

'They turned up with only seven players for the second game,' added Dave, 'and rather than go easy, your boys set about humiliating them.'

'What are we meant to do?' asked Kieran. 'Make them feel better about being crap?'

'Your supporters didn't help,' continued Dave. 'That chant of "Who are ya?" was out of order.' Alison and Howard's faces looked horrified at this detail. 'Some of their players were in tears by the end.'

'I don't see why we can't keep the points,' said Ron. 'When Whitecross folded a couple of years ago, all their results stood. Can't we appeal or something?'

'That was different,' said Lynn. 'It was near the end of the season. The results only stand if a team has already played at least three quarters of their matches. Moorlands were still a long way off that, so their results get wiped.'

'Since when has that been the rule?' asked Kieran. 'First I've heard of it.'

'It's all in the league handbook,' retorted Lynn pointedly. 'Which you never read.'

'What does the handbook say about poaching players?' asked James. 'Talking of which, Kieran, how's Max getting on?'

Kieran smiled maliciously. 'He's doing fine. I even let him play against Moorlands. He's not really Hawks material, to be honest, but I think him and his dad were embarrassed about playing with girls.'

Lynn sighed before answering James's first question. 'Well, it says you can't approach another team's players during the season, but it's always hard to prove that the club approached the player rather than the other way around.'

'Rob said Kieran invited Max to move over to Hawks,' snapped James.

'That's not how I remember it,' said Kieran, sitting back smugly and folding his arms. 'And you can't prove otherwise.'

'And, of course,' added Howard, 'We can hardly complain to the league about ourselves. Perhaps we should accept that what's done is done and move on.'

'Damn right,' said Ron decisively. 'I declare the matter closed.' James could barely focus on the rest of the meeting. There were times when Ron treated the club as his personal fiefdom, and if Kieran won the election, it would be even worse. At least they couldn't get their own way when it came to the league's decision-making.

*

James was working through some marking when Poppy wandered into the front room.

'Daaaaad,' she said, in the drawn-out wheedling voice that meant she wanted something. Past experience told James this conversation would either end with him quickly agreeing, or it would go on for a very long time. 'Is Ben's team playing football this Sunday?'

'Yeah,' James replied, still with half of his mind on his marking. 'We're at home in the County Cup.'

'Could I come and watch?'

James put his marking down and gave Poppy his full attention. 'You want to come and watch? I thought you hated football?'

Poppy shook her head decisively. 'No, I love football now. I want to see how good Sam is. I want to see her keeping the boys out.'

James smiled. 'Well, you know you wouldn't be able to stand with me, don't you? All the supporters go on one side of the pitch, and the coaches and subs go on the other. Have you spoken to Mum about this?' Poppy shook her head. 'It would only work if she was there to look after you.'

'Okay.' Poppy's sing-song response indicated she was satisfied with this outcome – she hadn't been told no, just given a new person to wear down. James chuckled. He didn't think Ros would be wild about the idea, but at least it wasn't his problem now.

*

James had another observation, with Claire sitting in on his lesson with 10C. James thought it went well, but Claire was more critical than John Marshall or Richard had been. She pointed out missed opportunities for extension tasks to help with differentiation, and said that he was giving the students too much leeway to go off-topic. She couldn't give him more than 'satisfactory'. James felt that was a bit unfair, but knew better than to argue. He thanked

Claire for the comments and assured her that he'd reflect on them and incorporate them in future lessons.

James was still brooding over Claire's feedback when he went into the department office at lunchtime. Most, if not all, of the criticisms were matters of teaching style rather than actual failings. She had a point about the extension tasks, but other than that he stood by his lesson. He took an empty seat next to Moira and Simon, glad that Claire wasn't around.

'Are you all right, James?' Moira's gentle tone gave the enquiry a suitably soothing energy.

'Yeah, just a bit frustrated, that's all.'

'Ah! I know that look,' Simon interjected. 'The look of a man who has just had a lesson observation with Lady Macbeth.'

James's forehead furrowed, and Simon smiled broadly at James's confusion. Moira explained.

'Simon has dubbed Claire "Lady Macbeth". It's become quite the joke between him, Josie and Dean. I can't imagine why.'

'Ambitious, manipulative, ruthless,' listed Simon. 'It's hard to see what they have in common.'

'That's a little harsh, Simon. Claire's certainly ambitious, but that's not necessarily a bad thing.'

'She shafted you over the second-in-department job.'

Moira rolled her eyes. James didn't know the history behind it, but she didn't seem overly troubled by the memory.

Simon turned back to James. 'So, the lesson observation; let me guess: she said your lesson was satisfactory.' Moira joined in with the final word; both of them had knowing looks on their faces.

'Er, yeah,' said James. 'How did you know?'

'Take it as a compliment – she never gives any higher than satisfactory,' said Simon. 'She's marked my lessons as poor on more than one occasion. Mind you, my groups still punch above their weight with exam results, which really irritates her – she'd love to paint me as a failing teacher and get rid of me.'

'Wait a minute, does she know you call her Lady Macbeth?'

Simon laughed. 'We didn't think so, but after her reaction to your "Is this a dagger" quip, who knows?'

'That might explain why she doesn't seem to like me very much. I mean, I think I'm getting on well with everyone else, but...'

'James, James, James,' interrupted Simon. 'You're missing the point; you're a perfectly good teacher and a perfectly splendid fellow.'

'A very good teacher from what I've heard,' added Moira.

'It's not that Lady Macbeth doesn't like you. All she cares about is deciding which people will help her to get where she wants, and which might get in her way. She's probably trying to decide if you're going to drag the department down, or if you might conceivably be competition for her. Either way, her starting assumption is that you're a problem to be solved. I'd watch your back if I were you.'

*

For the County Cup match, at home to Farthing Rovers, James and Joao decided to go for it and start with the two-four-two formation again. At training Joao set up a pitch with two wide channels marked with cones. They played an attack versus defence game, where the attackers had to keep one player in each wide zone at all times. Joao said this would help the wingers to remember not to get sucked inside and kill the team's attacking width. As ever, they rotated positions, and James was struck by how well Rory did when he switched from defence to up front. He seemed to have a knack for popping up in just the right place, and his finishing was a lot better than James remembered. Maybe they should try him as a striker? James decided to stick with Dylan and Josh, but to make sure that Rory got his chance from the subs bench.

Sunday arrived, and James headed over to the equipment locker to collect his nets from Dave. James chatted with some of the other managers, including Danny Peters, whose under-sevens were having a fantastic season. 'Still more losses than wins, just about, but they're getting better week by week and loving every minute of it,' as Danny put it. Remarkably, Poppy had persuaded Ros to bring her along. James wouldn't let Poppy go and bother Sam before the game, but he promised to introduce her afterwards.

When the game kicked off, Farthing soon showed themselves to be a decent team. They attacked from the word go and the Swifts' wingers, Liam and Ben, were soon pegged back helping out the back two. Deepak and Callum were getting overrun in midfield and the forwards were barely getting a touch. Sam performed her usual heroics, with each save sparking delirious excitement from one particular supporter.

James was more concerned with what was happening in front of Sam. 'Dylan, drop back into midfield, on the left. Tell Ben to go central and Deepak to drop into defence. We'll go three-four-one.' Dylan relayed James's instructions to the other boys and the team reorganised itself.

The changes made a difference. The extra defender relieved the pressure on the wingers and even with one less up front, the Swifts started to put together some attacks of their own. Josh was having another poor game in terms of his finishing, so James decided to give Rory his chance. He pulled him to one side on the touchline.

'Right, I'm going to stick you up front. Try to make the ball stick until support arrives. And if you get a chance to shoot, what do I want you to do?'

Rory grinned. 'Hit the target rather than boot the cover off the ball.'

'Yes, make sure you hit the target.' James paused, reflecting on the power he knew Rory could generate. 'Boot the cover off the ball too, by all means, but hit the target. On you go.'

Soon Rory was galloping about like a headless chicken tied to the back of a stampeding elephant, so keen to be back in action at last. He received the ball from Callum with his back to goal, shielded it from the defender, laid it back to Ben and then spun to chase the through-ball. Ben threaded the pass, angling it to favour Rory's run. Rory took a touch as it reached the edge of the area, got it out from his feet and let fly. The keeper barely moved as it whistled past him. One-nil to the Swifts and the grinning Rory was mobbed by his jubilant team-mates.

Farthing raised their game. Sam was kept busy, and shortly before half-time even she couldn't keep the ball out as Farthing bundled in an equaliser from close range. James wondered how Poppy would react to the blessed Sam actually conceding a goal. He knew there was nothing Sam could have done, but he doubted that Poppy's appreciation of football was quite that nuanced.

James gave lots of instructions at half-time, but as the team headed out for the second half he realised that everything he had said was covered by Joao's contribution: 'Keep playing football, boys. You can do this.'

And keep playing football was precisely what they did. They were dogged and organised in defence, throwing themselves in front of the ball without a thought of self-protection; the midfield – Ben in particular – were probing and penetrative with their passing, and Rory took aim at the Farthing goal at every opportunity. As they approached the last fifteen minutes, James and Joao discussed their options.

'Keep it as it is, or push another striker up and go for the win?' James asked.

Joao grinned. 'You know me, Mister James, let's go for the win. Three-three-two?'

Josh, who had been on the wing since coming back on at half-time, was pushed up alongside Rory. Quickly, the new forward line seemed to click, with Rory only denied a second goal by a mixture of good goalkeeping and bad luck. With just a few minutes to go, Josh put Rory one-on-one with the keeper. Once again he pulled back his sledgehammer right foot, but this time he jinked gracefully to the side. The keeper was already committed to blocking the shot and was left sprawling, clutching at the air as Rory took the ball past him and rolled it into the empty net. The Swifts' fans, including Poppy, were cheering, with Poppy leaping in the air, having obviously decided to overlook the fact that the goalscorer was a muddy, smelly boy.

Joao reminded the boys to focus, and despite a couple of late scares they saw the game out. For the first time ever, the Swifts had made it to the third round of the County Cup. James was in no hurry to leave the scene of such a great triumph, but he thought he ought to rescue Sam. Poppy was eventually dragged away, with Sam laughingly agreeing to Poppy's demand that she keep showing the boys how it's done.

*

That night, James asked Ros how she had enjoyed her trip to the football.

'Actually, it was good fun. I'm not sure I want to go every week, but it was all right.'

'Poppy might think differently about "not every week". I think she's got the football bug now.'

Ros grimaced at the thought – they both knew how persistent Poppy could be. 'I'll tell you what though,' said Ros thoughtfully. 'I could see the difference in Ben from the last time I saw him play.'

'Well, when did you last come and watch him – a couple of years ago? Of course he's improved in that time. Even without Joao, I'm not that bad a coach.'

'That's not what I meant. It wasn't his skills; it was his whole bearing on the pitch. He used to be such a frail-looking thing when he played football, so awkward and hesitant. Seeing him out there jostling with the other team, standing up to challenges: he looked like a different boy. He's more resilient now. You can see it in him outside of football too.'

James hadn't thought about that before, but he suspected Ros was right. There was something different about Ben, even compared to a few months ago.

CHAPTER TWENTY-SIX

Monday was the day of the school year 7 match, and Kenny and Jonah from 7E arrived at James's lesson wearing bright-yellow football shirts and blue shorts under their blazers, with Tom in a green goalkeeper's shirt.

'It's just like watching Brazil,' observed James, pointing to the shirts. 'When do you need to go, lads?'

'Mr Parker wants us in the changing rooms by 3.15,' replied Tom.

'Okay, if I let you go at five past, does that give you enough time?' The boys nodded. 'Fine, if I don't notice the time, one of you stick your hand up and remind me. Good luck for the match.'

Once the lesson was over and the non-footballing portion of the class dismissed, James quickly packed up his things and made his way out to the playing fields. He was intrigued to see what was so special about Kenny. None of the Stoneleigh players – Swifts or Hawks – had ever had a sniff of a place at Town's academy, and he wanted to see just how big the gulf was.

The game had already started. In the first few minutes of James watching, it became apparent that Kenny was running the game. He always seemed to have time and space, and even on a mudbath of a pitch, his balance and touch was immaculate. In the fifteen minutes that James stood and watched, Cole Hill scored several goals, all of which owed much to Kenny. Big Connor was playing up front for the school, and he notched up a couple of goals, not that the opposition keeper was a patch on Sam.

*

The next day, 7E were filing out of James's classroom at the end of another lesson, when James caught Kenny's eye.

'You played well the other day, in the school match.'

Kenny's face lit up. 'Oh, thanks sir, I didn't know you were there.'

'Yeah, I heard that you played for Town, so I thought I'd come and see for myself what you were like. I came and watched for a bit before heading home. I saw you score a couple, and set up a few more.'

Kenny took this in his stride, James imagined that he was used to getting attention for his football. 'You manage – is it Stoneleigh Swifts?' asked Kenny. 'Some of the others were telling me about your game a few weeks back. Aren't you the team with a girl in goal?'

'That's us. She's good too.'

Kenny laughed. 'That's what Connor keeps saying, though I think he's just making excuses for himself. See you later, Mr Hogan.'

'You seem to be building bridges with 7E pretty well.' It was Josie, emerging from the walk-in cupboard as Kenny was leaving. 'Have you got a minute?'

She was having problems with some of the stroppy year 11 girls. Just when she needed to gear everyone up for the mock exams at the end of the month, two of them had become even more disruptive than usual. James suggested getting the girls one-to-one and asking how she could support them in the run-up to the mocks. It might help to head off the negative behaviour, or at least show she had tried other options before taking more drastic measures.

'Thanks, James. That's pretty much what Moira said. I'm never sure if she makes that stuff work because it's smart, or because she's just so brilliant. I don't think I'll ever get a class to behave the way she does.'

James reacted with mock-indignation. 'I see how it is: Moira's too good to copy, whereas I'm sufficiently flawed that my advice could work for mere mortals. I'll try not to take that personally.'

Josie put her hands to her face in mock-panic and gasped theatrically. 'Was I that transparent? No, I didn't mean it like that, honest!' They were both grinning now.

'And don't be so hard on yourself,' said James. 'Moira is brilliant, but don't forget you're still an NQT. Everyone makes mistakes when they are starting out – I bet Moira did, like the rest of us.'

'I'm not so sure, I think she just entered into the world of education like Botticelli's Venus: perfectly formed, emerging pearl-like from a shell.'

James laughed at the image. 'I don't think that fits the current department of education guidelines for teacher training, even if it was something we could recreate.'

The laughter soon fell from Josie's face. 'However she got there, I could never be as good a teacher as she is. I'm not sure I'm cut out for this.'

'Well, other people are sure about you. Give yourself time and don't worry about not being as good as Moira – I can't think of a better role model for a young teacher to learn from. But, if you have any questions that require a lesser, mortal frame of reference, I'm more than happy to help. I'll try to live up to Moira's Olympian ideal.'

Josie looked down at her shoes and spoke hesitantly. 'This wasn't what I meant, but we all heard about why you left your last job. Do you mind me asking about that?'

James paused. It was never a comfortable subject, but there was no point hiding from it. 'No, go on.'

'What happened?'

James sighed. 'I just snapped. It had been coming for a while. I was fed up and struggling with the workload. I was tired from too many late nights marking and getting more tired by the week. Then Kyle Kettering came along and pushed all the wrong buttons. That's just the background though – it was my mistake. I mishandled the situation, putting myself into a corner where if Kyle didn't back down I would have to, and I just lost it. I went the full Malcolm Tucker on him and the class. It was purely verbal, nothing physical – otherwise I'd have been in a lot more trouble – but it was appallingly unprofessional.'

'Don't you worry about something similar happening again?'

'Absolutely, I worry about that every day. But I've also tried to learn from what happened so as not to repeat the same mistakes. I'm no different from any other teacher – making mistakes and learning from them is the only way to get better.'

Josie smiled. 'Thanks James. Richard said I could learn a lot from you. I can see why he was so keen to get you into Cole Hill.'

*

'Flynn was really buzzing this morning, he's well up for this one. Was Jayden the same?' Flynn's dad was chatting with Hayley as Matt led the Redbridge boys through their pre-match warm-up. Hayley thought back to Jayden at breakfast – all withdrawn and nervous. Just before they left the house, he'd turned to her and asked, 'What if I'm the one who messes it all up, Mum? Matt says this is a really big one.' She'd tried reminding him that it was meant to be fun, but she wasn't sure she'd helped.

'Pretty much.' Flynn's dad didn't give the impression of a great emotional hinterland, so she wasn't going into Jayden's pre-match anxieties with him. At least Jayden looked a bit happier now, haring around with the other boys and kicking the ball whenever it came to him. She would never understand the capacity football had for tying him up in emotional knots one minute, then giving so much pleasure the next.

'Hey, look at that.' Flynn's dad nudged Hayley with his elbow and pointed. 'They've got a girl in goal. That looks hopeful – we might score a few goals today.'

'How can you tell she's not good? They've not even started yet.'

'Yeah, but they wouldn't have a girl in goal if they had a decent boy, would they? It stands to reason.' Hayley was immediately torn. Obviously, she wanted Jayden's team to win, but now she was also rooting for the Swifts' goalkeeper.

Matt was pretty pumped up on the touchline, calling for decisions from the ref and giving a constant stream of instructions for his boys. They were playing the other team from Stoneleigh, which had worried Hayley in terms of what to expect from the coaches. As far as she could tell it was a close match, and that was showing in the reactions of the adults on the far touchline.

'Flynn!' shouted Matt. 'Get into them – you've got to close them down quicker than that! Billy, that should have been yours; get your head in the game, mate.'

There were two coaches for the Swifts, one about Matt's age and a younger man.

'Superb play, boys. Keep it up!' called the older one. 'Liam: awesome run.'

'Hey Ben,' added the other in an accent Hayley couldn't quite place. 'What a ball. What a ball!'

At least these Stoneleigh coaches weren't as bad as Kieran Butcher, not that Hayley could imagine what worse than Kieran Butcher would look like.

'Yay! She's saved it again. SuperSam is brilliant.' There was a younger girl on the touchline with her mum, standing just on the other side of the halfway line to Hayley, probably the goalkeeper's sister judging from how focused she was on her performance.

Much to Matt's frustration, the young girl's analysis seemed spot on. To be fair, Redbridge's keeper, a lad that Hayley thought was called Luke, seemed to be doing just as well, and it was nearly half-time before either team broke the deadlock.

One of the Swifts players broke down the wing, skipping past Flynn like he wasn't there and then whipping the ball into the box, pulling it behind the Redbridge defenders who were haring back. It went straight to a team-mate arriving in the penalty box. He took a touch to steady himself and then whacked the ball high into the net before the desperate defenders could get to him.

'No!' Matt's hands went instantly to his head. 'Who was on him? You can't give them that kind of space. Sort it out, Redbridge.'

Matt was just as animated at half-time, waving and gesticulating and urging his boys on. Jayden, who hadn't been called on, had his head down, avoiding eye contact. Hayley had the feeling that this was going to be another morning where he came home without actually getting onto the pitch.

Redbridge did seem to improve in the second half, but one of the Swifts defenders was having a great game, winning tackle after tackle.

'Yes, Gabe. Brilliant!' shouted the older Swifts coach.

The boy called Gabe went up for a header with Milo and seemed to land awkwardly, twisting his ankle or something. The ref called the Swifts coach on and the poor lad was soon being helped off the pitch while a sub trotted on in his place.

'Good, hopefully the sub won't be as good as that lad.' Flynn's dad didn't seem overly concerned with the injury, and within a few minutes he got his wish. The ball bobbled off the new boys' boot and rebounded into Milo's path. He moved in on goal and slotted it past the girl like she wasn't there. A few minutes later, the keeper jumped to pluck a high ball out of the air and inexplicably dropped it at Milo's feet. He eagerly thumped the ball into the net and ran away joyously, soon to be engulfed by all his team-mates. The Redbridge parents were all celebrating, but Hayley couldn't help but look at the goalkeeper. She was sitting on the ground, hands on her hips. Some of the other Swifts players were going over to her and offering consolation. The tall lad in midfield – Ben? – went to offer a hand to get her back on her feet. Hayley was impressed at the lack of blame directed at her, either by her team-mates or the coaches. She'd seen enough of Redbridge to know how different it would have been if someone had done that while playing for them.

The game was almost over – Flynn's dad kept shouting 'Ref! How long?' – when the tall lad got the ball in midfield and threaded a pinpoint pass through the Redbridge defence to the big striker with a strapping on his arm. The Redbridge defenders seemed afraid, backing away as he ran towards goal and giving him the time and space to lash the ball past Luke.

The Redbridge parents reacted with disappointment, but Hayley was secretly pleased – she hadn't wanted SuperSam's mistake to be the moment that decided the result. Sam seemed to see it the same way, running the length of the pitch to celebrate with her team-mates.

Matt had the boys gathered around him for a post-match debrief. Hayley was waiting with the other parents on the far touchline, shifting her weight from one foot to the other. It had finished two-two. Was that a good thing or not? They hadn't won, but they hadn't lost, so how would Matt react? More to the point, how would Jayden be about it?

Jayden trotted over with the others and he seemed happy enough as they headed to the car park. Hayley knew better than to ask any questions until they were in the car going home – there had been other games where he seemed perfectly happy and then dissolved into tears once he was safely away from his mates.

Eventually, the moment came to question the witness. 'So, how was Matt after the game?'

Jayden paused for a moment then smiled. 'He was all right, to be fair. He lost it a bit when they equalised, but after the game he said we did well. He's usually calmer after the game than during it.'

Hayley bit her tongue. Jayden had said we, but of course he hadn't played any part in the game itself. At least that meant he was out of the firing line when Matt was telling everyone what they did wrong, but she still felt that he was entitled to being more than a permanent reserve.

CHAPTER TWENTY-SEVEN

The last week of half-term was as chaotic as ever. With everyone looking forward to the break, most classes needed extra coaxing to actually get down to work. Mrs Cranbrook had extended James's contract through to the summer, and was making positive noises about a permanent appointment after that. Although plenty of students had tried it on, he had never even felt close to another meltdown. With the obvious exception of Lady Macbeth, James was getting on well with all his colleagues, and loved the department office at lunchtimes. All in all, his move back to teaching seemed a resounding success.

James had a free period the first lesson after lunch that Thursday, so he stayed in the department office, chatting with Moira as they tapped away on their laptops.

'The other week, when Simon said Claire stitched you up over the second-in-department job, what did he mean by it?'

Moira pushed her laptop away and turned to face James. 'Oh, that wasn't anything really – I think Simon and Dean were more bothered than I was. Richard wanted me to apply for the job, and the boys nagged me to go for it, so I gave in and applied. Anyway, Claire evidently made a good impression at the interview.

'From what Richard said afterwards, the head wanted to give me the job and offer Claire a regular teaching post, but Claire made it clear that she wouldn't leave her current job for anything less than second-in-department – which is entirely reasonable, despite what Simon says. The head knew I would stay either way, so she made the sensible choice: the one that brought in another good teacher. Simon was furious when he found out, but none of that is Claire's fault. The way she's got at Simon since is another matter, and we've lost a few people since she arrived who felt she didn't give them the support they needed, but I'm sure she has her reasons.'

'Are they the ones Simon says – ruthless ambition?'

Moira shrugged. 'Maybe, it's hard to tell; she doesn't give much away. What about you – you were a head of department before; any plans to go back to a leadership role?'

'I haven't really thought about it, to be honest. I'm just enjoying being back in the classroom. Never say never and all that, but I'm happy as I am. The best thing about being department head was supporting colleagues, and I don't need a title to do that.'

'Talking of which, how is Josie getting on?'

'She's great. Some of her lessons sound like she's really got the kids engaged.' James paused. 'Other times it sounds like she's struggling.'

Moira nodded in agreement. 'That's exactly what I think. Not everyone in the department agrees, but the children can tell that she genuinely cares. She needs to get better at recognising when someone is taking advantage of that, but I think she's going to be the rising star of the department before too long.'

*

Sunday came around, and the Swifts had another County Cup match, this time against Birchdale Albion, one of the stronger teams from the top division. Checking their results online, James saw that they had beaten Belgate Magpies three-two, making them precisely ten goals better than the Swifts. James reluctantly decided that they would need the extra midfielder for this one, so Josh dropped down to the bench. Gabe's knee kept him out, but at least he wasn't missing a league game.

The final score of five-two flattered Birchdale, with the last two goals coming after Swifts switched to two-four-two formation for the last ten minutes to chase the game. Rory had opened the scoring, before three second-half goals from Birchdale. The tactical switch brought another Rory goal then two late Birchdale goals finished the game.

The other manager was complimentary afterwards, coming over to the Swifts to tell the players personally how impressed he'd been. 'I'll be honest with you,' he said to James. 'The Magpies manager said you shouldn't be too much trouble. Either his team is a lot better than mine – which they're not – or you've improved hand over fist since you played them. You wouldn't be out of place in the top division from what I saw today.'

James could hardly take it in. For years the Swifts had been one of those teams who just made up the numbers. Now, they were going toe-to-toe with the big boys.

'Well, you heard him,' he said to the players as the Birchdale coach walked back to his own players. 'Who fancies the top division?' Loud cheers confirmed their approval. 'Right then,' continued James. 'Keep winning games, let's see where this takes us.'

*

The Swifts, individually, were being taken all over the place the following week: it was half-term and several were away with their families. James had forgotten how nice half-terms could be – a week to regroup without facing classes. There was marking and lesson preparation, obviously, but he could spread it out and still have plenty of time with Ben and Poppy, the latter spending most of the week nagging the former to invite Sam round, despite the fact her parents had taken her for a week staying with grandparents back in Nottingham.

Training was sparsely attended. Ben was there, of course, along with Josh, Hakim, Deepak, Ryan and Dylan. Joao focused on individual skills, then finished with a three-versus-three match with smaller goals and no keepers.

Although the Swifts weren't playing the following Sunday, a few of the other teams were. Weston Park beat Redbridge and the Hawks beat Linford Road. Neither of those results were shocks, but it meant the Swifts were now thirteen points behind the Hawks. Even winning their game in hand would mean they needed the Hawks to lose four times. James could count on Weston Park for one of those, and the Swifts were capable of beating the Hawks with a fair ref, but Kieran was unlikely to drop the extra points without some outside interference. No law-breaking, and no putting lives at stake this time, but he had to come up with something.

*

School returned, as it always does, and James was soon back in the routine of teaching lessons, marking books and listening to bizarre discussions in the English department office. Dean, Simon and Josie were arguing about the relative merits of chocolate bars.

'So you'd have Bounty ahead of a Wispa?' asked Josie incredulously.

'Yes,' replied Dean. 'Wispa is twenty per cent air; I want one hundred per cent filling. I'm not paying anyone for air.'

'And ahead of Double Decker?'

'Definitely, I can't stand Double Deckers.' This caused uproar, but Dean made his case. 'Double Deckers contain nougat, which is an abomination. End of.'

'Whaaaat?' Simon was appalled. 'It's bad enough defending

the crime against humanity that is Bounty, but preferring them to the sublime perfection of a Double Decker? Are you out of your mind?'

'Double Decker makes my top five,' said Josie. 'Along with Wispa, Twirl, Twix and Snickers.'

'Snickers?' Simon's outrage flared again. 'I have vowed to shun them because of the ghastly counterfeit name. It was once a Marathon, and to me it shall always be a Marathon.'

'It was Snickers before it was Marathon, in America,' said Dean. 'Apparently, when they subsequently introduced it to Britain, they worried it sounded too much like "knickers", so they changed it. If anything, Marathon is the counterfeit name.'

'I don't care,' said Simon stubbornly. 'To me it's a Marathon. I haven't eaten one since they changed the name and I won't eat another until they change it back. Principles that cost you nothing mean nothing; sometimes you have to take a stand.' James had to admire Simon's commitment to his principles, even if chocolate bars weren't the hill he'd choose to die on.

Simon continued. 'My top five would be Mars, Tunnock's Caramel Wafer, Double Decker,' he looked pointedly at Dean as he said that one, 'Cadbury's Fruit and Nut...'

'Any bar that tries to smuggle fruit in with my chocolate can do one,' interjected Dean. 'If I wanted healthy, I wouldn't be eating chocolate.'

'...and Fry's Chocolate Cream.'

'Whaaaat?' exclaimed Josie. 'I have literally never seen anyone buy one of those. Talk about old-fashioned.'

'It's the world's oldest mass-production chocolate bar,' huffed Simon, 'and there's a reason why it's lasted. My grandma bought them for me when I was a boy and I still buy them now.'

'They had them when *you* were a boy?' asked Dean. 'I know they're old, but not that old, surely. When did they start making them – the seventeenth century?'

The Swifts, the Hawks and the under-elevens were all at home. Three games into two pitches won't go, so kick-off times had to be staggered. The Hawks and the under-elevens were starting at 10.30 – according to Lynn, Kieran had made a fuss about not getting the late one, as Chelsea were the lunchtime game on telly and he had to get back in time to watch it – and the Swifts were kicking off at 12 against Linford Road Rovers. At least the goal nets would already be up.

Arriving at the ground, James went to set up some cones behind the pitch. The Swifts would need to warm up there until the other games finished. Afterwards, he decided to watch a bit of the Hawks' game.

Kieran, as usual, was strutting and ranting on the touchline. Hawks looked on top, although Redbridge were making a good fist of things. Then a Hawk went on a mazy run from deep in midfield all the way through the Redbridge defence, weaving his way past challenge after challenge before calmly slotting the ball into the net. There was something naggingly familiar about the boy's gait, his impeccable balance. It wasn't until he turned around to celebrate that James saw the scorer's face – it was Kenny Harrison. For a moment, James struggled to take it in. Town didn't let their academy boys play for Sunday teams. Had Kenny been released by Town? That seemed unlikely – he'd have heard on the school grapevine. James certainly hadn't noticed any Kenny lookalikes among the Hawks before now. He fumbled for his phone and fired off a couple of photos. If Kieran was playing a ringer, it wouldn't do any harm to have some evidence.

As the Hawks were making their way off the pitch at full time, James accidentally-on-purpose put himself near Kenny. Feigning a look of surprise, he pointed at the boy and quizzically inquired, 'Kenny? What are you doing here? I thought you played for Town.'

Kenny grinned sheepishly. 'Shhh,' he said, 'it's not Kenny. Apparently today I'm Max Furlong. You're with Stoneleigh so I can tell you; my dad asked me to play for your lot today – he's friends with the manager. It's a must-win game, apparently. I'm playing next week as well, but don't tell anyone. It's all a bit iffy but, hey, I get to play football; that's all I'm bothered about.' That settled the matter, Kieran was playing ringers. This could be the break that James had been waiting for.

*

The Swifts game was straightforward. Rory got them off to a great start, scoring from the edge of the penalty box in the first few minutes, and after that the goals came in a steady flow. Josh was playing his best game of the season, setting Rory up for numerous chances, and even getting a goal himself to go with four for Rory, two for Liam and one apiece for Ben and Gabe – the last of those coming during Gabe's fifteen-minute cameo as centre forward after James switched the positions around to make it less embarrassing for Linford Road.

James sent the match details through to Lynn as usual. Later in the evening, he got her usual response thanking him. He went upstairs, away from Ben and Poppy, and quickly called her back.

'Hey James, everything all right?'

James told her all about what Kieran had done.

'If only we had some evidence.'

'What, you mean like a photo of Kenny wearing a Stoneleigh shirt with Redbridge players clearly visible in the background? Like the photo I took before our match kicked off? That kind of evidence?'

'You didn't!'

'I bloody did.'

'Oh, yes! We can really fix Kieran with this. Can we prove who the lad really is?'

'Well, I can't get his ID photo from school, that's covered by data protection. But if we can get a photo of him in his Town kit, that should do it.'

'How do we manage that?'

'Dunno, but I'll work something out. Leave it with me.'

James tracked down Kenny's social media accounts, but the security settings kept him out. James knew he should be glad Kenny was taking cyber-security seriously, but one photo was all he needed to skewer Kieran. He resolved to work on the problem at school, see what he could come up with.

*

As luck would have it, James had another lesson with 7E the following day. As the students were coming into the classroom, he took his chance.

'Morning Kenny – it is Kenny today, isn't it? Not Max?'

Kenny grinned, and put his finger playfully to his mouth. 'Shhh, it's a secret.'

James carried on chatting, subtly pulling more and more information out of Kenny until he knew when and where training sessions with Town took place. After that, he got on with the lesson, even though he would rather be plotting the perfect surveillance mission than teaching about the First World War poets.

That evening, James phoned Lynn and told her his plan. She wasn't convinced, but couldn't suggest a better way to get the evidence they needed. James made her promise not to tell Ros; somehow he knew she wouldn't agree to what he had in mind.

CHAPTER TWENTY-EIGHT

James pulled into the car park, his fingers tapping restlessly on the steering wheel. What kind of security would there be? On the one hand, Town were a well-run, professional club. On the other, this was only their under-twelves – it wasn't like he was trying to spy on the actual professionals. James had a cover story ready, but was relieved to discover no one checking names on the gate.

He kept his head down and joined the handful of kids and parents making their way to the Astroturf. That familiar knot of nerves gripping his stomach was there again, but he tried reassuring himself that there was no risk of anyone dying this time. While the boys went onto the playing surface, the parents remained outside the wire-mesh fencing. Some stayed to watch while others went back to their cars or the tea bar. James spotted Kenny and half-turned away to keep his face hidden. Fortunately, Kenny's mum didn't linger – it could be awkward if she recognised him at a future parents' evening. Kenny greeted the other players and coaches and headed onto the pitch.

James made his way around the outside of the fence, desperately trying to look casual and fighting a shiver not entirely due to the cold. Once he was happy with his position – away from the parents but close enough to the players for a photo – he slipped his phone out of his pocket. The boys were doing a gentle warm-up, similar to the one Joao used for the Swifts, so James snapped a couple of quick shots then put the phone to his ear, as if he was talking to someone. After a while he finished the non-existent call and swiped into his gallery. A blurry Kenny filled the screen, it wasn't great; he'd have to try again. Nobody seemed to be paying any attention, so maybe he could be bolder. If he took the time to let the phone properly focus, he could take his photo and make his escape before anything went wrong.

He waited for the players to turn his way again, then lined up the photo. Once the autofocus kicked in, he snapped away. He took several shots then repeated the phone-to-ear trick. After a brief non-conversation, he flicked through the latest photos. Jackpot: there was Kenny, beautifully framed with the club badge clearly visible on his top. Now all James had to do was slip away unnoticed.

Nice and casual. James forced himself not to hurry as he made his way back to the car. Past the tea bar, into the car park; nearly there.

'Excuse me, sir.' James turned around and saw a high-vis jacket wrapped around a burly security guard. There were two more hurrying to join him.

James suppressed his instinct to break into a run.

'Hi.'

'Can I ask what you're doing here, sir?'

'Oh, I'm a grassroots coach, I was invited to come along and watch training.'

'Is that right, sir? Who invited you exactly?'

James had researched this, digging through the club website for the names of academy staff. 'Johnny Ashford, I met him at the coaches' event last week.'

'Is that right, sir? And why are you leaving so early?'

James shrugged. 'Phone call from my wife, my daughter has been taken ill and I need to get home.'

'I'm sorry, sir, but I don't believe that. I happen to know that Johnny has been off work ill himself and didn't take part in the coaches' event. Could we see your phone, to confirm that you received a call in the last few minutes?'

James's stomach flipped. The other high-vis jackets had reached them now, positioning themselves to cut off his line of escape.

'I'm not giving you my phone!' he blustered, desperately trying to come up with a new plan.

'The thing is, sir, someone reported a man taking photos of the boys while they were training, and you fit the description. Can we see your phone please, sir?' As the first guard was saying this, James could see one of the others speaking urgently into a walkie-talkie on his jacket.

'This is ridiculous. My little girl is ill and you're banging on about my phone. Let me go – I need to get out of here right away.' James turned to go, and found the largest of the three guards standing right behind him, blocking his path. The first one put a hand on James's shoulder.

'The police are on the way, sir. It's best all round if you come with us and we let them sort this out.' The guard gestured James in the direction of a prefab hut marked *Security*. James was running out of options.

'Look, I get that you're just doing your jobs, but I wasn't doing anything wrong. I'm sure you're all hard-working blokes, and underpaid for what you do – am I right? How about I sort you all out with a nice drink, you let me go and we leave it at that? You can tell the police it was a false alarm, that my story checked out, and we can all just forget about this. What do you say?'

'I'd say that I'm sorry, sir, but trying to bribe us won't help your situation and it certainly doesn't make you look innocent. We are hard-working blokes and we don't turn a blind eye to possible facilitators of child abuse.'

'Child abuse? What are you talking about?'

'Strange man, taking photos of young boys in sports gear? It doesn't take Sherlock Holmes to join the dots on that one, sir.'

James deflated like a punctured football. How could he have

been so stupid? He'd been afraid of being thrown out, but arrested as a child abuser? That hadn't even occurred to him. He meekly followed the security guard into the hut. A few minutes later, two uniformed policemen arrived.

'Evening. Is this the happy snapper?'

'Yeah, this is him.'

'Thanks lads, we'll take it from here.' The lead policeman had closely cropped hair and was shorter than James expected, but stocky with it. He looked like he could handle himself. 'Now then, I gather that you've been taking photos of young boys.'

'Look, officer, I can explain...'

'Oh, I'm sure you can, and you will – down at the station. I'm arresting you on suspicion of taking offensive images of children. You do not have to say anything, but it may harm your defence if you do not mention when questioned something which you later rely on in court, anything you do say may be given in evidence. Do you understand that?'

James nodded weakly and let the second officer put him in handcuffs. They led him back to their car, did that thing James had seen on telly where they push your head down, and they took him away.

It was a short drive to the police station, but for James it felt like longer than additional time when you're hanging onto a lead. He wanted to explain that he was just an obsessive football coach, not a pervert. He wanted to scream and shout, to plead and beg, but he couldn't even form words. That part of his brain had shut down, gone numb, while the rest of it was free-falling through nightmare scenarios. What if they didn't believe him? What if this ended up in court? That really would be the end of teaching for him. He'd be on a register, so he wouldn't be allowed even to carry on coaching. And Ros... he swallowed hard. What would Ros say about being married to a convicted child abuser? What about Ben and Poppy?

They arrived at the police station and James was taken for fingerprints and mug-shots – at least they took the handcuffs off for that. His belongings were taken and itemised in his presence. His phone was placed in a plastic evidence bag and they even removed his belt and his shoelaces. By now he was fighting back the tears. The officers weren't particularly sympathetic, but James couldn't blame them for that – as far as they were concerned he was a paedophile; he wouldn't be inclined to offer consolation in their position. He meekly allowed himself to be led to a holding cell.

*

As the door slammed closed behind him, James slumped down with his head in his hands. There was padding of sorts on top of the thin plank of a bed, but it seemed designed to provide the minimum possible comfort. He couldn't imagine sleeping easily tonight anyway. How had he let things go this far?

He leaned back against the cold concrete wall of the cell and realised that he was shaking. He wanted to blame the security guards, or the police. Mostly he wanted to blame Kieran, but he knew that the only person really to blame was himself. He had been so stupid – how could he have let everything get so out of perspective? It's just kids' football for goodness' sake. Then again, he couldn't let Kieran get away with it, could he? To paraphrase Bill Shankly, football is much more important than life and death. If the last few months had taught James anything, it was that there was some truth in that, though not in the way most people took it. It really didn't matter if you won or not – if football was all about winning trophies, then ninety-five per cent of players at any level were failures every season. Football wasn't about winning, but what you gained from trying to win was priceless.

James thought about the Swifts and what football gave to them: enjoyment, self-confidence, self-esteem. He thought about how Ben had blossomed this year, how Joao's words of praise and encouragement had helped Ben to relax, to start realising his potential. If people like Kieran were left in charge of football, kids like Ben would be snuffed out rather than nurtured, and then where would they find that kind of encouragement? The problem with the "it's all about winning" brigade is that they never understood that not everything that counts can be counted. That was why he'd been taking those photos. How could he make the police understand he was fighting for the future of his club, for the soul of the game, not just snapping dodgy photos to sell to perverts?

CHAPTER TWENTY-NINE

James had regained some of his composure a few hours later when he was led down a maze of corridors, but he still felt a little like he was hanging by a thread. For some reason he was expecting the interview room to be dimly lit and tatty, but it was modern, bright and clean. James's eye was drawn to the sleek table in the middle of the room. There were three chairs around it, one on its own facing the other two. James was directed towards the solitary one.

'Sit there and wait,' said the officer who had escorted him from the holding cell, his tone bristling with hostility, before leaving James on his own.

Obediently, he sat. He quickly spotted the CCTV camera high in the corner of the room and wondered how best to make himself look innocent. After ten minutes or so – though it felt much longer to James – two people strode in. One was the shorter officer who had arrested him, the other a harsh-faced woman of about James's age in a smart, dark suit rather than a uniform. She had blonde hair, cold eyes and a fierce expression on her face. She took a seat opposite James. The uniform sat down beside her, put a recording device onto the table and started it up. He had also brought in the evidence bag with James's mobile in it. He pushed buttons on the recording device and spoke clearly.

'Interview with James William Hogan at Westerham Police Station, 4th March. Present are Constable Martin Pike and Detective Sergeant Julianne Hails.'

Sergeant Hails began. 'So, Mr Hogan. Would you like to explain what you were doing at the Town training complex?'

James had been reassuring himself that although he had been stupid, he hadn't been up to anything wrong. His best chance of getting out of this was to just be really, really honest.

'It's a long story,' he began.

Hails interrupted. 'Well, why don't you get started telling it then? You're not going anywhere until we've heard it.'

James told them everything. He told them about Kieran, about Stoneleigh YFC, about how the future direction of the club hinged on which of them finished higher in the league.

'And what does all this have to do with you taking dodgy photos of young boys?' snapped Hails, evidently losing patience with all the irrelevant information.

'Sorry, sorry, I'm getting to that. Kieran has been playing ringers, well, one ringer. One of the boys who trains with Town played under a false name for Kieran last week. I wanted a photo of the boy in his Town kit so I can prove that Kieran is cheating.'

'Do you expect us to believe that?' snorted constable Pike.

'It's true – please, check any of it. Check my phone. I can show you the photo I took at the Hawks' game last weekend and you'll see the same boy in the photos from tonight.'

'We haven't looked at your phone yet. It might help if you gave us the password.' James told them his password and Pike put on some latex gloves and removed the phone from the bag.

Pike started flicking through the phone, holding it so that Hails could see the screen. Frustratingly, James couldn't see what they were looking at and was desperately trying to remember if there was anything on his phone – photos, text messages – that might look bad out of context. He wondered whether his internet browsing history would show up his research into making cars break down – that might be difficult to explain.

'Who's that?' asked Hails. Pike held up the phone to reveal a half-term photo of Ben and Poppy.

James sighed. 'Those are my children. Ben is twelve, Poppy is eight.' The tears were close to the surface again. How would he explain it to them if he was convicted?

'Is there anything else you can say that might persuade me that this ridiculous tale is actually true? Can anyone corroborate your story?' Hails was dissecting James with her glare.

'My wife doesn't know. Well, she knows about Kieran, but not what I was doing tonight. No one did. Wait – that's not true. Lynn knew.'

'Who is Lynn?' asked Hails, 'and why does she know more about this than your wife?' James didn't like the accusing look in Hails' eye.

'She's the club secretary; her son plays in my team. Look in my text messages, Lynn Carpenter. I sent one earlier today.'

Pike jabbed at the phone and brought up the message to Lynn.

'"I'm off. Wish me luck!". And Lynn replies, "Be careful" plus a fingers-crossed emoji.' He looked at James, then across at Detective Sergeant Hails.

Hails scrutinised James for what seemed even longer than a tight VAR decision. Her stare seemed to burrow into him, searching out and exposing his secrets. 'Do you know what?' she said eventually. 'I actually think you're telling the truth, Mr Hogan. My brother played football as a kid and there were plenty of managers who were either self-important bell-ends, or idiots with petty rivalries. And I can't imagine anyone trying to think of a plausible excuse and coming up with something as ridiculous as this. I'm going to let you go, but I'm giving you a serious warning. Don't go taking photos of kids you have no business taking photos of. If your name crops up again for anything – anything – you won't get the benefit of the doubt.'

*

By the time they let James go, it was closer to morning than midnight. Hails arranged a lift home for James – he'd have to get his car back from the training ground later. Ros had left a light on for him but he crept into the house, desperate not to disturb anyone. Once the police returned his phone, he saw numerous missed calls from her, the latest of which was around midnight. He was going to have a lot of explaining to do.

Ros was fast asleep, which was a relief. He quickly got ready for bed and was so mentally drained that in spite of all the tension, he fell asleep almost immediately.

The next thing he knew, he was being shaken roughly awake. He turned over in bed, sat up and saw Ros glaring at him.

'Where the hell were you last night?' James tried blearily to de-fog, but Ros was making no allowances for the fact that he'd had – he checked the bedside clock – barely two hours' sleep. 'Why didn't you answer any of my calls?'

'I couldn't get to my phone.'

'What do you mean, you couldn't get to your phone? Where was it?'

'I… I was arrested last night. I was at the police station. They took my phone away.' None of this got the shocked reaction James expected. Ros was staying calm, but James could see her anger simmering, just below the surface.

'Go on.'

'I went to the Town youth training ground, to get evidence that Kieran's ringer wasn't who he said he was.' Ros was still glaring. 'And someone saw me taking photos of the boys, put two and two together…'

'And came up with pervert!' finished Ros. 'Oh, for heaven's sake, Jamie, how could you be so stupid? What were you thinking?'

'I was thinking I could stop Kieran, get the Hawks a points

242

deduction. You said I should take him on.' Even as he said it, James could hear how ridiculous he sounded.

'I did, but I didn't mean for you to get yourself put on a register!'

'I'm not on a register!' he protested. 'I told the police everything and they let me go. I'm not being charged. It took a few hours, but it's all sorted now.' His indignation was melting into sheepishness. 'I should have asked them to let me phone you, but with everything going on I just wasn't thinking straight. It wasn't until I finally got to explain my side of the story that I even thought about anything outside of the police station.'

Ros gave him that look, the one that said he wasn't out of the woods yet, but there was a hint of sunlight breaking through the canopy of trees. 'So, you're saying that not only am I married to a jailbird, I'm married to one who doesn't even think about me when he's in the clink. Thanks a bunch, I must mean so much to you.'

'It's not like that. I was too embarrassed to call you.' He lifted his head again to see how she was reacting.

'Don't you ever do anything so stupid again.' Her voice had a softer tone now, just. 'From now on, everything has to be completely, indisputably and utterly legal. I know this business with Kieran is important to you, but it's not worth ruining your life – or Ben and Poppy's lives. Do you hear me?'

James nodded meekly.

'When you weren't answering, one of the people I phoned was Lynn,' said Ros. 'She told me everything and we suspected something like this might have happened. We couldn't phone the club or the police, just in case they didn't have you. Can you imagine that conversation? "Hello officer, I'm phoning on the off-chance that you've arrested my husband as a potential paedophile". Actually, I'd better text Lynn – she made me promise to let her know you were okay, no matter what the time was.'

As Ros was texting, she asked if James had got the photos he was after.

'Yeah, look.' He flicked through the images on his phone until he found the best one of Kenny. 'That's the lad. And here,' he flicked through again, to the ones from Sunday, 'this is him playing for the Hawks.'

James's phone rang at that point. He looked and saw that it was Lynn. He answered and after a brief pause, music blared out: the opening riff of The Clash's 'I Fought the Law'.

'Very funny,' said James, raising his voice to be heard over Mick Jones' guitar. 'Ha bloody ha.'

'Sorry, couldn't resist. Ros says that you're free. Was it a tunnel? Are you now someone's bitch or did you gain the hardnuts' respect in a bare-knuckle brawl?'

'This is going to go on for a while, isn't it?'

'I would have thought so. Is Ros there? Put me on speakerphone.'

James did, and Ros said hello.

'Hi Ros. Is he still in the doghouse?'

'He's through the worst of it, but I'll keep bringing this up for weeks to come, whenever I need a little leverage. You know how it works.'

'Of course. Have you given him the talk?'

'Too right I have.'

'But did he get the photos? Did you get them, James?'

'Yes,' James answered. 'Clear as day.'

'So we've got him – brilliant. When are you sending them into the league?'

'I'm not. I don't want anyone to know it's me dropping Kieran in it. I'm going to send the photos to the Redbridge and Royals managers after Sunday's game, so the complaints can come from them.'

'Good thinking,' said Lynn. 'Wait – you're going to let Kieran do it again?'

'Well, yeah. He'll get more of a punishment if he's done it twice, won't he? And, if Kenny plays, Hawks will lose the three points whatever happens; without him they still might beat the Royals. Why take the chance?'

'Cunning. I like it,' responded Lynn.

'When did my husband get so sneaky?' added Ros.

'Ah, just something us hardened criminals pick up when we're doing stir.'

*

James was late for work the following morning. He missed the staff briefing, but at least he made it for his first lesson of the day. He didn't tell his colleagues how shattered he felt, as he didn't want to have to explain why. He changed his lesson plans to include more independent work or reading around the class – anything to avoid hands-on teaching and make the day a little easier for himself.

Dean, Simon and Josie were arguing playfully at lunchtime, but James was too tired to join in, or even to follow the argument. He just wanted to get through the day and catch up on some sleep. The afternoon dragged like summer without a World Cup, but eventually he was able to get away.

*

Sunday came and went smoothly. The Swifts had another week off, so James went to watch the Hawks play the Royals, surreptitiously snapping another photo of Kenny. At the end of the game he complimented Kenny – who had been brilliant, again – and played nice with Kieran.

Checking the table later, James saw that the Hawks were now sixteen points ahead of the Swifts, but had played two games more. Once their last two wins were reversed, that would be down to ten points. If Swifts won the games in hand and beat Hawks, they would be within one result of overtaking them, and that was all without the inevitable points deduction; with that factored in, the Swifts just had to keep on winning and they'd win James the bet.

James had found the Royals manager's phone number on their club website, and he already had Matt's from the Swifts' match with Redbridge the other week. He reached for his phone and started sending copies of photos, asking the other managers not to say where they got them. Matt replied within a few minutes, thanking James and saying that he thought Kenny had looked a bit good. The Royals manager, Mike, called James back, curious about James's motives. James told him the history between himself and Kieran (though not the bet) and how he hated to see anyone, even his own club, cheating to gain an advantage. This seemed to satisfy Mike, who thanked James and promised not to blow his cover. Fuse duly lit, James sat back and enjoyed a Sunday night of quality BBC police drama, pointing out procedural inaccuracies to Ros, citing his extensive experience of such matters.

*

James was getting changed for Swifts training on Wednesday when his phone rang: it was Lynn.

'I got the email from the league this afternoon,' the words tumbled eagerly from her mouth, 'the club has got two weeks to respond to allegations that the Hawks fielded an ineligible player on Sunday 28th February and Sunday 7th March. We can accept the charge and await punishment, or we can contest it, either in writing or by requesting a personal hearing. Ron has called an emergency committee meeting for tomorrow night.'

CHAPTER THIRTY

'It was wonderful.' Lynn, Ros and James were sitting around the Hogans' kitchen table, and Lynn was holding court, delightedly recounting the events of the committee meeting after bringing James home. 'Kieran tried saying it was all rubbish, until I reminded him about the photographic evidence. When he asked how the league had got hold of photos, Alison pounced.'

'Now we're talking.' Ros' eyes gleamed. 'Did she go for his throat?'

'She was forensic. She kept asking questions and it gradually became clear that Kieran knew there was something that might have been photographed. From there, she forced him to admit to fielding a ringer. Kieran claimed it was a misunderstanding, but then Howard stepped up.

'He can get a bit holier-than-thou can old Howard,' continued Lynn. 'I think the idea of lying to the league appalled him. When Kieran tried the misunderstanding line, Howard destroyed him.' Lynn put on a rough approximation of Howard's pompous tones: '"It's one thing to play a boy whose registration hasn't come through yet, but to deliberately play someone else's player under a false name, deceiving club officials into unwittingly participating in the lie, and then repeating the offence a week later, to do all that and then claim it was a misunderstanding, defies credulous belief".'

'"Defies credulous belief",' repeated Ros. 'Did you get him on loan from the eighteenth century or something?'

'I'm not even convinced he's human,' replied Lynn. 'No, that's not fair. Howard's a nice man, just a bit… uptight, closed off, you know? When his wife died, the club filled the void. It's the biggest thing in his life now and I think he's starting to see Kieran as a threat to the whole club. He mentioned not wanting to second Kieran as chairman. Ron blustered a bit, saying it was too late, but I think you can count on his vote now, James.'

Ros looked thoughtful. 'If Jamie wins and becomes chairman,' she said, 'would that make me the First Lady of Stoneleigh YFC or something?'

'Sure, why not?' Lynn laughed.

'Do I get a dress allowance?'

'Ros,' said Lynn, putting down her wine glass. 'Promise me you'll ask Howard and make sure I'm there to see the look on his face.'

*

Swifts were playing again on Sunday, a home game against Melville Dynamos. James trotted out a pre-match quote from Wilfred Owen, informing his players that Owen had gone from being the most exciting young striker of his generation and a Ballon d'Or winner, to one of the dullest pundits in history. Rory continued to lead the line like Alan Shearer in the days when he still had hair, and it was another comfortable win. Despite the fact that Sam barely had anything to do, Poppy still maintained she had been the star.

James looked up the remaining fixtures on the FA website. Hawks had three games left: against Melville Dynamos (an easy win), Weston Park (almost certain defeat) and finally against the

Swifts. Swifts, on the other hand, had games against Weston Park, Cole Hill, Hawks and then Redbridge. No easy games there, but the way they were playing anything was possible.

James thought back to that September game against Weston Park. Weston had been so composed: always playing out from the back, always with time and space on the ball. The other managers in the league – including him – talked as if they were unstoppable, but what if someone worked out how to take them on? The Swifts could never match Weston at their own game, so how best to counter their threat? He wasn't willing to go down the Hawks' route and kick them off the pitch, but there had to be something legitimate they could do. Packing the defence wouldn't be much fun, and probably wouldn't work; he needed something else, but what? At least he had a couple of weeks to come up with something – a quirk of the fixture list meant they didn't have another game until the beginning of April.

James raised the issue with Joao at training on Wednesday night.

'They good side,' Joao replied. 'When they get the ball, they play, play, play.'

'Max tried closing them down in midfield last time, and they just passed round him. They'e always got the time and space to play, and the players to use it. How are we meant to compete with that?'

'I don't know, Mister James. Is big problem.'

*

It was Tuesday morning and James had a free period. Rather than going to the department office, he stayed in his classroom with some marking. Josie was teaching a year 9 class next door, and it sounded lively. Josie sounded increasingly agitated as she battled with the class. James considered looking in to see if she needed backup, but decided against it; he didn't want to undermine her and make things worse.

Later on in the department office, Josie came over to where James and Moira were sitting. She dumped her bag on the table and flopped down next to Moira, looking utterly fed up.

'Bad day?' asked Moira.

'9C gave me hell this morning. Once Becca Elliott and Rachel Darbyshire get going, there's no stopping them. It always starts with those two, then more and more of them join in. By that stage, I just can't rein them in. What should I do?'

'You need to take the initiative to cut out the distractions,' said Moira. 'Don't give them the chance to get started; plan your lesson really thoroughly and then keep it moving quickly. If you keep it going from A to B to C, it won't give them time to even think of disruptions.'

Josie looked to James, to see if he had anything to add.

'What she said,' he added. 'Seriously, that's great advice. Get them off balance, don't give them time to get started.' James grinned as he spoke, because he realised that Moira had just given him an idea for Weston Park.

*

'Kenny, have we got a problem?' James had asked Kenny to stay behind after the lesson.

Kenny shrugged. He had been in an uncharacteristically sullen mood from the moment he walked in.

'Well, here's my problem. You spent the whole of that lesson without doing a stroke of work. You've never been like that for me before. What's changed?'

Kenny just shrugged again.

'Is everything okay at home? Is something worrying you?'

Kenny's eyes started glistening. James suspected that he might be about to cry. Eventually Kenny opened up, and the words rushed out in a torrent. 'It's football, sir. I had a right rocket from my coach last night. They found out about me playing for Stoneleigh. They're talking about throwing me out of the club.'

'Seriously?' This had blindsided James; when he took aim at Kieran, he hadn't thought Kenny might get caught in the crossfire.

'They said I'm not taking my responsibilities seriously, not sticking to the agreement I signed when I joined the academy. I'm on my last chance – if I step out of line again, I'm out.'

'Well at least you're getting another chance. They didn't have a problem with you before, did they?'

'I didn't think so. Maybe I've been a bit cocky at times, but...' Kenny shrugged as he let the sentence tail off. James could see that this had really rocked him.

'Why do you play football, Kenny?' asked James.

Kenny looked confused. 'What do you mean, Mr Hogan? I just love playing.'

'You know that girl from my Sunday side?' Kenny nodded uncertainly. 'She used to play for Nottingham Forest girls.'

Kenny's eyes widened. 'Really? I mean, I know you said she was good, but I didn't know she was that good.'

'Really. But it was all getting a bit too serious for her. She just wanted to enjoy playing football, for it not to be the most important thing in her life. When her family moved down here she decided to take a step back. Now she just plays for fun and she's loving it.'

Kenny's brow furrowed. 'Do you mean I should leave Town and play for a Sunday side?'

'Not at all! Well, not unless that's what you want. My point is, if what you want is just to play football, you can do that for anyone and no one can take that away from you. But if what you want is to be as good as you can be, to maybe get a shot at being a professional, then you're in the right place with Town, so make the most of it. There are plenty of boys who would love the opportunity you've got. That doesn't mean you can't walk away if you decide it's not what you want, but make sure that's your choice, not someone else's.'

'It is what I want to do,' asserted Kenny. 'It's all I've ever wanted.'

'Well then, show them that; be a model trainee. You've got the talent, now put in the work to go with it. If you don't make it, you don't want to look back and realise it was because you didn't take it seriously.'

Kenny grinned. 'Thanks Mr Hogan. That makes a lot of sense. I'm going to sort myself out – no more favours for my dad's mates; no more mucking about in training.' He picked up his bag to leave, then turned back to James. 'The thing I can't get over, though, is how it all came out – someone had got hold of photos of me playing for Stoneleigh in both games, and then another one in my Town training kit. Why would someone go to those lengths to ruin my life? I don't know who, but some sad little loser was trying to take my dream away from me.'

James didn't say anything at first. He hadn't been trying to take it all away from Kenny, but he had wanted to take Kieran down – and if he was honest, he still did. Perhaps the sad little loser tag wasn't far from the truth. Looking back, there were moments recently when he didn't recognise himself.

'The thing is, Kenny,' he said at last. 'You'll probably never know who it was. Don't keep dredging up the past and looking for someone to blame. It's done, move on.' Please move on. Please don't go digging. 'Focus on getting your head down and showing them what you're capable of. That goes for my lessons from now on too. Okay?' Kenny grinned sheepishly and nodded his head.

*

'We had an odd one the other night.' Hayley was on the beat with Martin Pike again, and he was catching her up on work stories since the last time they were on together. 'We got called in because some bloke was taking photos of the kids at Town's training ground. We thought we'd caught ourselves a pervert, but it turns out it's just the manager of a local team trying to prove that one of his rivals has been cheating. Who'd go that far over kids' football?'

'Oh, you'd be surprised. Anyway, what happened?'

'Hails let him off with a warning, but he looked terrified.'

Hayley chuckled. Hails had a reputation as one of the toughest interrogators at the station, so she could imagine even Kieran Butcher wilting under her onslaught. Talking of Kieran Butcher... 'You don't remember his name, do you? And which team he manages?'

Pikey reached for his notebook and flipped over a few pages. 'Here it is. James Hogan, Stoneleigh Swifts U12s. The rivals were another team at the same club, would you believe. Why?'

'No real reason, just curious – they're both in the same league as my Jayden.' Hayley had given up on the car sabotage case – they found some good fingerprints on the bowl, but they didn't match anyone whose prints were already on file – but mention of Stoneleigh made her think about it again.

At that moment, the radio sparked into life. 'Papa-Romeo Five-Three, this is Control. Reports of a road-traffic collision on Crown Lane. Ambulance has been called, but we need feet on the ground, immediate priority. Are you nearby?'

Pikey responded straight away, turning in the direction of Crown Lane as he spoke. 'This is Papa-Romeo Five-Three. Yankee-Echo Four-Five and I are two minutes away. Responding now. Over.'

The next couple of hours were spent at the crime scene, dealing with the messy aftermath. By the time the ambulance arrived Hayley had managed to stabilise the most badly injured of the occupants, but one young man had lost a lot of blood and she wasn't entirely sure he was going to make it. Once the paramedics took over, she joined Martin in keeping the gawpers back and taking names and addresses of anyone who might have seen what happened. It pushed all thoughts of James Hogan to the back of her mind.

*

'James, have you got a minute?' James was on his way home at the end of the day on Friday when he heard Richard's voice. He turned and saw Richard and Claire in Richard's classroom. James went in and joined them.

'What's up?' he asked.

'We were just chatting about the department. You teach next to Josie; how's she doing?'

James looked from one to the other. Richard's expression was open and questioning; Claire's, as ever, impossible to read.

'I think she's a good teacher,' replied James. 'Still learning obviously, but I think she's going to be really good. I know that Moira thinks the same, for what it's worth.'

'Moira's judgement is worth a lot, and I agree,' said Richard, pointedly looking to Claire. 'I think she's one of the best NQTs I've seen in years. She could be something special.' James suspected that Richard and Claire had been disagreeing, and he'd just come down on Richard's side; that wouldn't endear him to Claire.

'I'm not saying she doesn't have potential,' snapped Claire. 'But she's too weak. Unless she starts taking control of her classes, she'll be done for. All the potential in the world is no use if it isn't realised, and I'm not convinced that she's got what it takes to develop discipline – she's too concerned with being liked by the students.'

Richard turned back to James. 'Again, you're closer to her lessons than us. How does it look to you?' James hesitated; he had to choose his words carefully – he wanted to get more support for Josie, but without confirming Claire in her view that Josie was irredeemably weak.

'She's having a rough spell, struggling a bit, but I think she'll work through it. She's been asking me and Moira about things and I know she's acting on our advice. Her attitude is spot on: recognising problems and looking for solutions, reflecting and learning all the time. She'll get there, we just need to make sure she's supported along the way.'

'Thanks, James,' said Richard. 'That's exactly how I see it. Have a good weekend – good luck on Sunday.' James said goodbye to them both – Claire barely acknowledged him – and headed for home.

CHAPTER THIRTY-ONE

The morning of the Weston Park game arrived, and James couldn't wait to get going. He buzzed around the house, struggling to stay still for more than a few minutes. Ben seemed equally restless; both of them just wanted to get on with it and get to the game.

The plan was a simple one: three-two-three formation and don't let Weston build from the back. As soon as the ball went to their keeper and the defenders split wide, the Swifts' wingers would close the defenders down, cutting off the options. Two ball-winning midfielders to fight for everything in the middle and a striker intent on forcing the keeper to rush his clearances. If Weston couldn't make that first comfortable pass, then much like the disruptive girls in Josie's class, they wouldn't be able to get started. The team had liked the idea at training – it wasn't as if anyone expected anything from the game, so what did they have to lose?

'George Bernard Shaw…'
'Who?'
'Left-back. Plays for Man United and England. Anyway, Shaw said that life isn't about finding yourself, it's about creating yourself. We're doing things a bit differently this time and some of you will

be in unfamiliar roles, but we can do this: we can recreate ourselves and give Weston a surprise. Here's the line-up: Sam in goal; Gabe in the centre of defence with Ben and Charlie either side of him. Deepak and Dylan in midfield, fighting for everything; Rory centre forward with Hakim to his left and Liam to his right.'

'That's not right,' said Hakim. 'I'm not a winger – I'm a defender.'

'No,' Joao interrupted. 'You not a defender. You are a footballer.'

'Too right,' continued James. 'You're made for this role, Hakim, you've just got to make it happen. Use your pace to put the defender under pressure; use your tackling to get the ball off him, and then use your ability to put the ball into dangerous areas. You've been great all season stopping goals; today you can help us score some.'

James knew that the plan depended on a good start. If it didn't seem to be working, the boys' confidence could dissolve as quickly as media support for an England manager. He needn't have worried; the game started perfectly. After Weston's first patient, probing attack was rebuffed, one of their midfielders turned to play it back to the goalkeeper and recycle. Immediately, the two outer defenders split wide. Hakim and Liam sprang into action while Rory charged towards the keeper. Seeing Rory, the keeper calmly switched play to his right. The defender twisted and turned, protecting the ball from Hakim and looking for a way out. Rory was now cutting off the return ball to the keeper, while Deepak was covering the channel to the nearest midfielder. The defender tried taking Hakim on, but was quickly dispossessed. Hakim cut inside and curled a high, dipping cross over the now-crowded penalty box and found Liam, arriving late at the far post. From just a few yards out, Liam bundled the ball inside the post and over the line. Swifts were one-nil up.

The Weston boys looked at one another in disbelief, they hadn't expected this from the team they beat nine-nil back in September.

The Swifts, on the other hand, were jubilant and energised. For the next few minutes, Weston struggled to get a foothold in the game. Deepak and Dylan fought for everything in midfield, while the defence held Weston at bay whenever they made it that far forward, limiting them to long-distance efforts that failed to test Sam. The Weston keeper even resorted to kicking long a couple of times, losing possession for his team both times.

Ten minutes into the game, Ben won a tackle and slung a long through-ball beyond the midfield for Liam to chase. Liam scampered forwards, knocked the ball ahead of himself and checked to see who was in the box. Having set his sights, he hit a perfect cross for the onrushing Rory, whose header powered past the Weston keeper. Two-nil: Swifts had added to their shock early lead.

The game continued in similar vein. The Weston players looked stunned, but their manager stuck to his principles, calmly encouraging them to play their football and pass their way out of trouble. They got their reward after twenty-five minutes, when their striker finally hit a long-distance shot good enough to trouble Sam. She turned it onto the post, but another Weston player was first to the rebound, turning the ball into the net before anyone else could react.

Straight from the kick-off, Dylan ran with the ball deep into the Weston half. Their defenders, still rattled, backed off, and soon he was on the edge of the box. He pulled back his foot as if to shoot, then slipped a diagonal pass to his left. There was Hakim, cutting in from his wing at top speed. Without breaking stride, he hit the ball first time, like a mirror-image of Carlos Alberto in the 1970 World Cup final, and watched as it flew into the Weston net.

The Swifts players absolutely buried Hakim. Sam was the only one to stay in her own half, and she was punching the air gleefully. James was just as pumped: it was working; it was actually working.

At half-time, Joao warned the Swifts to expect Weston to regroup and come out strongly. As predicted, they looked a lot more composed, using their movement off the ball plus an extra man now deployed in midfield to deal with the Swifts' pressing. As a result, they started to play their way out from the back again and establish their dominance.

'They work around us, Mister James. Maybe go three-four-one and try to hold?'

James agreed, shouting for the wingers to drop deeper, but still to be ready to burst forward when Swifts won the ball.

Charlie was having a fantastic game at the back, but he was guilty of diving in for one challenge, missing the ball as the Weston player's quick feet whipped it away. He caught the player's ankle and the ref blew for a free kick. Some of the Weston players wanted Charlie sent off. Charlie looked anxiously at the ref who just smiled.

'Relax, lad,' said the ref. 'I know it wasn't deliberate. I'm not even booking you; it's just a free kick.'

Weston's captain took the free kick and curled it perfectly over the Swifts' wall and into the top corner, just beyond Sam's grasping fingertips. At three-two, the game was in the balance again.

Weston had the momentum now. James made one last set of subs, moving Hakim into defence with Gabe and Charlie. More and more chances fell to the Weston players, with Sam making save after save, including two that were as good as she had made all season. Swifts made sporadic breaks into Weston territory, but never looked as dangerous as before.

Then Ben found a yard of space in the midfield battle-zone and slipped the ball through to Rory. Rory played a one-two with Callum and hit the return ball first time, slotting it past the keeper. Swifts had restored their two-goal lead.

Weston reacted again, like a long-distance racer kicking to stay with the front-runner. The ref gave them a penalty when the ball rebounded off Ben's arm in the crowded Swifts box. James had to hope Sam could keep out the damned spot kick.

But no; the Weston captain took the responsibility for the

penalty, making as good a job as he had with the free kick. At four-three there was everything still to play for.

'How long, ref?' asked James.

'Four minutes,' came the reply after the ref had looked at his watch.

Whether it was the goal or the knowledge of just how quickly time was running out, Weston seemed to go up another gear – how many gears did they have? Swifts gave up thoughts of attack, dropping all nine players behind the ball. When the final whistle blew four minutes later, the Swifts exploded with joy while the Weston players slumped to the ground. The Weston manager made straight for James with his hand outstretched.

'Fantastic game, well done. You worked us out brilliantly in the first half. That was the best anyone has played against us all season – no one else has even scored more than two. You've got a great little side there.'

'Thanks. Coming from you, I really appreciate that.'

Some of the Weston players were magnanimously congratulating the Swifts, although one or two were a little surly about their post-match handshakes. James was glad to see their manager scolding them for it.

Eventually James gathered his grinning, jubilant team around him.

'Brilliant; just brilliant. If you can beat Weston, you can beat anyone in this division. Three games to go, three more wins and who knows – maybe even promotion.' James was starting to believe it himself. Royals had dropped points the week before, so the race for second was getting even tighter. Why shouldn't the Swifts come out on top if they kept playing like that?

After the game, as they carried the goal nets back to Dave's lock-up, Joao's voice took on a serious tone. 'Mister James, can we speak?'

'Of course, what's up, Joao?' James noticed that Joao's forehead was furrowed; whatever it was, he seemed concerned about something.

'My course at the college was meant to be two years, but I receive phone call yesterday asking me to cut it short and return to Portugal.'

James stopped and put down the nets. This was terrible: he'd come to depend so much on Joao, how would the Swifts keep their winning run going if Joao went home? He wondered what had happened to make Joao change his plans.

'Is everything all right, Joao? No one's ill are they?'

A smile cracked Joao's troubled face. 'No, no, no, nothing like that. In fact, is good thing for me. My employers want me to come home early for new job – like Swifts, I going for promotion.'

James wanted to be pleased for his friend, but all he could think about was how much the Swifts were going to miss his influence. James had learned so much from Joao, but it was still the young Portuguese who planned and led training. How was he going to take up the slack and keep the steady improvement going?

'Well, I'm really going to miss you with the Swifts, Joao. You've made all the difference this year. When do you have to go?'

'Not until after end of season.' As the words left Joao's mouth it was all James could do not to punch the air with delight. 'Then I finish my studies part-time at home. It will take extra year, but my new job is – what is word? Good opportunity.'

'Sure, sure. What's the job?'

Joao looked a little bashful. 'The academy head coach has moved on. His replacement at sporting club want me as assistant.'

'Wow, well it sounds like a fantastic opportunity for you. Congratulations.' He held out his hand to shake Joao's. 'I'm really pleased for you. You must be made up.' Joao looked confused, so James rephrased. 'You must be delighted, very happy.'

Understanding swept over Joao's face. 'Sim, sim – very happy; very… made up.'

'I just don't know how I'm going to cope without you next season.'

'You be fine, Mister James. You and the boys – strong together. Just don't get like Kieran. You better than that.'

*

'Mum, you know that friend of Dad's, Marcus?'

Hayley paused for a moment, matching up the names and faces of Andy's mates. 'Big bloke with ginger hair and bad taste in Christmas jumpers?'

'Yeah, that's the one.' Jayden paused and seemed intent on gazing at his own shoes. Whatever he had been about to say, he seemed to be having second thoughts.

'What about him, sweetheart?' Hayley was worried now. Whatever Jayden had to say about this Marcus, it clearly wasn't an easy subject for him to bring up. She forced herself to stay quiet, to let him find the words for himself rather than subjecting him to a torrent of questions. Whatever it was, she just hoped it wasn't as bad as the wild possibilities racing unbidden to the front of her mind.

'He was round at Dad's last weekend, along with a few others and, er…' The silence could only have been a couple of seconds, but it felt a lot longer to Hayley.

'And?'

'He was smoking in the flat… Smoking, but not cigarettes.' Jayden's eyes widened meaningfully, as if he was hoping she would join the dots and save him from actually saying it.

'Do you mean weed?'

'I think so. It smelled funny, and people were getting a bit giggly.'

'Did your dad know about this?'

'Well, they lit up when he was out in the kitchen, and I think Dad was a bit annoyed about it when he came back in – he said something about me being there. But later on, when he went out to collect the takeaway, Marcus asked me if I wanted to try some.'

Hayley's heart felt like someone had just placed it in a freezer. She forced herself to keep her voice as calm and level as she could. 'And did you?'

'No way! After everything you've told me about what drugs can do to people, why would I want to get mixed up in that? I just… I didn't really know what to do about it. I made an excuse and went up to my room until Dad got back. I didn't really feel safe. Did I do the right thing?'

Hayley leaned over and gave him a big hug. 'Absolutely. You did the right thing in saying no and getting away from the situation, and you've done the right thing in telling me. Does your dad know about this?' Jayden shook his head. 'Right, well he's going to find out. I'll have a little chat with him about what kind of environment he's exposing you to.'

'Don't be mad at him – it wasn't his fault, it was Marcus.' Jayden looked more worried now than at any point in the conversation. Hayley ran her hand affectionately through his hair.

'Relax, I'm not blaming him, but your dad should be made aware that his friends are offering you illegal drugs behind his back.' She settled down with Jayden and let him choose a film for them to watch together. As they watched a bunch of superheroes saving the world against impossible odds, Hayley kept thinking about what he had told her. It wasn't only Andy she'd wanted to talk to; once she got into work, she'd be having a word with the drug squad and marking their card about Marcus. While she was at it, she'd have to look into this James Hogan character that Pikey had pulled. If a rivalry with Butcher could make him do something reckless once, maybe he'd been that stupid before; maybe he had something to do with the car-tampering. It was certainly worth cross-referencing the fingerprints from when he was arrested with the ones she had found on the fly-tipped rubbish. Who knew where that might lead her?

CHAPTER THIRTY-TWO

'How the hell did your lot get a win against Weston Park? Were they short of players or something?' It was another committee meeting and Kieran was indignant, almost angry, about the Swifts' achievement. 'I mean, they're a good side – any team good enough to beat my lot...'

'To beat your lot by – how many goals was it, Kieran? Seven, I think,' threw in Lynn, not even bothering to hide her smirk.

'...should brush your rabble aside.'

James smiled. 'What can I say? We had a plan; we stuck to the plan; the plan worked.'

'But what was the plan? What plan could possibly enable your lot to get a result...'

'Not just a result, Kieran, a win,' interjected Lynn.

'...against the best team in the league?'

James just spread his palms and shrugged. 'I think the phrase I'm looking for is, "the boys done good". And the girl as well, of course.' He acknowledged Dave. 'She done good too.'

'She always does,' said Dave as Kieran paused to mentally regroup. James knew what Kieran wanted and had no intention of giving it to him.

'Look,' said Kieran, 'we're playing them this weekend, so for the good of the club, if you tell me how you beat them, we can beat them too.'

'For the good of the club,' echoed Ron, the words somehow carrying the air of a threat.

James looked confused. 'Hang on a minute. Are you asking me for help?'

Kieran sucked his teeth.

'Not just help,' Lynn cackled, 'tactical advice – no, a tactical masterclass!'

'Doesn't that suggest that you see me as your equal?'

'No, not his equal, James; I think he's admitting you're a better manager than him.'

'This is ridiculous.' Kieran was looking daggers while the rest of the committee, apart from Ron, seemed to be thoroughly enjoying the show. 'Just get on with it and tell me what you did.'

'Yeah,' added Ron. 'For the good of the club, as chairman, I insist that you tell Kieran.'

'Okay, okay, here's how we did it.' James paused, looking elaborately from side to side, as if checking for eavesdroppers. 'You know those big white things at either end of the pitch, the ones with nets hanging off them? We made sure we put the ball in their one more often than they did in ours.' He held Kieran's increasingly frustrated gaze for a moment before adding, 'No, really, that's what we did. If you do that, I reckon you'll win.'

'This isn't a bloody comedy club, and you're not bloody funny. Are you going to fucking well tell me, or not?' exploded Kieran, slamming his pint down and sending beer cascading over the table.

James could see that Lynn was trying not to laugh, so he decided it was time to play it straight. 'Face it, Kieran. We're a better team than we were at the start of the season. Joao's a fantastic coach who has made a world of difference to the boys, and they've worked really hard.' Not for the first time, James pushed back the thought that once Joao left it could all fall apart. 'And, even though you dismissed her for being a girl, Sam is the best keeper in the league. Our game plan worked brilliantly up until half-time. After that, they worked us out and, if I'm honest, in the second half we rode our luck. Another day it could have gone differently, and if we played them again, they'd know how to deal with it. Play to your strengths and find a way to not let them play to theirs, that's the best advice I can give. If you and your Hawks are as good as you say, it shouldn't be too hard.'

Kieran didn't seem entirely satisfied with James's answer. 'We'll see who's better in a couple of weeks, when we give your Swifts another footballing lesson.'

'About that,' said Ron. 'I know there was some dispute about the ref last time the Hawks and Swifts played.'

'You mean Phil Gatwood was completely and utterly biased throughout, let the Hawks kick lumps out of us and left my Rory with a broken arm? Is that what you mean by "some dispute"?' retorted Lynn acidly.

'Maybe, in the interests of fair play,' continued Ron, ignoring Lynn, 'instead of a Swifts parent reffing the game, perhaps someone neutral should take charge.'

'You what?' said James. 'Kieran benefits from a dodgy ref last time, so I don't get to have my ref – who, by the way, has never given a crooked decision in all the years I've known him – when it's our turn?'

'I'm not making any accusations about your man, James, I'm just saying that a neutral ref would avoid any appearance of bias, seeing as tempers seem to be running high between your two teams.'

'Did you have anyone in mind?' asked Dave.

'Well, you can't get much more neutral than the club chairman. It's been a while since I took charge of a game, but I don't mind lending a hand.'

There was a moment's silence, before Lynn, Alison, James and Dave all started speaking at once. Perhaps it was a good thing that they drowned each other out, because the few words that James heard from Lynn really weren't what could be described as diplomatic. Or, for that matter, anatomically possible.

'It was just a thought,' said Ron. 'I'll take that as a no. Never mind; let's move on. Lynn, is there any news from the league about the two disputed matches?'

Lynn composed herself, taking a deep breath before answering. 'Well, they're not disputed matches any more, are they, Ron? We've admitted the charge, so there's nothing under dispute. But no, I haven't heard back yet. When I spoke with the league secretary, she said we can definitely expect the points for those games to be awarded to the other teams, and any further punishment will be decided when the management committee meets next week. She did say that as it wasn't the Hawks' first offence, there will almost certainly be something more: possibly a fine, probably a further points deduction, maybe even both. Either way, we should hear next week.'

'Did she say what size the fine might be?' asked Howard.

'She didn't, but the scale of fines in the handbook range from £5 to about £50. I'd expect something towards the top end of that scale.'

'And if we get a fine, will the club pay it, or is the manager responsible expected to meet the cost?'

'Let's worry about that if there is a fine,' interjected Ron, cutting off Howard when he tried to continue the discussion. 'No point getting worked up about it yet. So, it's the management committee who decides, and they meet next week, is that right?' Lynn nodded a confirmation.

'Good to know. Right, has anyone got any other business to introduce, or shall we call it a night?'

'Just one more thing, Ron.' It was Lynn. 'I've provisionally booked the Dunsinane function room here for the AGM, on Tuesday 11th May. No point in hanging around much past the end of the season.'

'The Dunsinane?' asked Ron. 'We usually have the Glamis room, don't we? That's plenty big enough for the committee and the managers.'

'Ah, but we've got a contested election this time, with a lot more people likely to come along. You should be pleased – we'll get a good crowd in for your send-off.'

Alison chirped up. 'Do we need to agree to the AGM as a committee, or is it okay for Lynn to just go ahead and confirm?'

Ron hesitated, so Lynn stepped in. 'Either, but as the committee is all here, there's no harm in voting to confirm. Ron, as chairman, would you like to call the vote?'

'Oh, all right. All those in favour of… what was the date again, Lynn?'

'Tuesday 11th May.'

'Tuesday 11th May as the date for the AGM, raise your hands.' Lynn, Alison, Dave and Howard's hands all went up as one. Kieran and Ron exchanged looks, then sheepishly followed suit.

'Right. That's that then. Meeting over.'

Kieran and Ron bustled away, and Howard spoke tersely to the others. 'I know we're off the record now, and this won't be in the minutes, but if we get a fine over this unregistered player business, I feel very strongly that Kieran should be made to cover the cost of it. He deliberately played a boy who had no right to be on the pitch, invalidating the club's insurance if anyone had been injured. He did it knowingly and he's admitted as much. It would be a scandal if we let him get away with that.'

'Relax, Howard,' said Dave. 'Everyone around this table agrees with you on that. Next time we meet, we'll know what's going on and if the Butchers don't like it, we'll vote them down.'

Howard made his farewells and strode out of the pub, still clearly agitated by the whole business.

'I'm not sure quite when it happened,' said Alison. 'But Kieran has really made an enemy out of old Howard.'

'Of course he has,' said Dave. 'I'm surprised it took him so long. Howard's old-school, he likes things done properly. Once he realised Kieran wasn't going about things fairly, that really offended him. It's a good job you're so squeaky clean, James, otherwise he wouldn't know where to turn for the next chairman.' James forced a smile while avoiding Lynn's eye, knowing his behaviour in recent months had been anything but squeaky clean.

'Never mind Howard, what about Ron?' said Lynn. 'The nerve of that man, offering himself as a neutral peacekeeper. Back when he was Kieran's regular ref, we had so many complaints about him from the other clubs – he was worse than Phil. Can you believe they even suggested it?'

'Frankly, yes,' retorted Alison. 'They're desperate to finish above the Swifts, and I think your result last week has scared them.' She paused, then asked, 'How did you manage to beat Weston Park? What was this plan of yours?'

James looked at her with mock-regret. 'I could tell you, Alison, but then I'd have to kill you, which might damage my squeaky-clean image for Howard.'

*

Hayley toyed with rejecting the call. Even before she looked at her phone's screen, she had known who it was going to be.

'Hey Andy, what's up?'

'As if you don't know,' the words tumbled out of his mouth in a rush. 'It's just a coincidence, is it? Marcus getting busted by the feds? Haven't your lot got better things to do than harassing law-abiding citizens?'

'Law-abiding? He offered Jayden weed! If he was law-abiding my colleagues wouldn't have found illegal drugs on him, would they?'

'Well, it should be legal – it's less harmful than alcohol. Anyway, I told you I was going to take care of things with Marcus and make sure it never happened again. Don't you trust me?'

Hayley made a conscious effort to soften her voice – they had both been getting louder and more heated since the call started. 'Of course I trust you, and I know that it wasn't your fault. But that doesn't mean that I trust all of your friends. If this sends a message about staying away from Jayden, then that's fine by me. They all know I'm a police officer, what did they expect me to do?'

'Well, I don't know about them, but I expected you to have a sense of proportion, and maybe a bit more consideration for the position you've put me in – there's even been talk about keeping me out of planning groups, just in case things get back to you. Couldn't you have turned a blind eye and just let me deal with it? Frankly, there are bigger injustices for your lot to focus on ahead of a bit of weed. And don't tell me you'd have done the same if it had been someone powerful that had been caught with a bit of blow. It's one law for the powers that be and another for the likes of me and Marcus, isn't it?'

'Look, Marcus only got a caution. It's not like he's going to do time over it or anything. The amount we found on him made it clear it was for personal use. We're not doing him for dealing.'

'That's not the point. He's got to declare his caution at work, and that's going to cause problems. He could lose his job over this – is that what you wanted?' It wasn't, but she certainly wasn't going to lose any sleep over it. 'It's yet another instance of the establishment – that's you, by the way – harassing political activists and making our lives more difficult just because you can. I hope you're feeling proud of yourself.' With that he rang off, without giving her the chance to respond. Hayley hadn't meant to make Andy's life difficult with his friends, but at least now they all knew to be more careful around Jayden. Then again, what might they be planning that they didn't want getting back to the police? As much as she didn't want to make life harder for Jayden – or Andy – it might be worth her keeping her ears and eyes open on this one.

CHAPTER THIRTY-THREE

Buoyed up by the great result at the weekend, the Swifts were in perky form at training. James and Joao had agreed to keep Joao's imminent departure to themselves for now; they didn't want anything to disrupt the positive mood of the team. Ryan was missing – his mum had texted James to say that he'd hurt his knee. She didn't think he would be fit for Sunday, but she would get him to the doctor that week and let James know. James hoped it wouldn't keep Ryan out for too long, but at least it meant he didn't have too many players for Sunday – trying to give everyone fair game-time with three subs to juggle could get a bit disruptive to the team at times. The rest of the Swifts threw themselves into everything Joao asked and the standard was high from everyone. They were unrecognisable from the team who couldn't find their way to goal at the start of the season. Liam in particular was tearing up and down the right wing, terrorising whichever defenders had the misfortune to be up against him. Even Hakim, who was his match for pace, struggled to contain him. James couldn't wait to let him loose on Cole Hill. This game had become something of a local derby for James, as he knew that the lads from 7E would keep reminding him about it for the rest of term if they came out on top.

At the end of training, Liam's dad came over to James for a quick word.

'I'm really sorry about this, James, I should have told you sooner. Liam's not going to be around this weekend. We've got a family wedding and there's no way we'll be back in time. Gemma reminded me of it last night.'

'Tim, no; don't do this to me,' stammered James. 'Did you see him tonight? How well he did against Weston Park? We really need him.'

'Sorry mate, Liam's gutted too – he'd rather be playing – but there's no way we can miss it. He'll be back for the Hawks game.'

'But, but – we need to win this one. If we lose on Sunday, the Hawks game might not make any difference. We've got to keep winning if we want to catch the Hawks…'

'They're all playing well, it's not just Liam. You and Joao have worked wonders with them. I'm really sorry but I'm sure you'll do fine without him. Don't forget, it's just kids' football, mate.'

Afterwards, James started shoving equipment back into his kit-bag with surprising force. Just kids' football? Didn't Tim understand how important this was? Didn't he know how much was on the line here? Never mind bragging rights at school, it was all about keeping up the pressure on the Hawks.

'Whoa! You all right, Dad?' asked Ben, responding to the vigour of James's packing away.

'No I'm not. Bloody Tim has just told me that Liam can't play this weekend. They're putting some family wedding ahead of the team.'

'That's a shame, Liam's flying right now.'

'Yeah – what's the point in us beating Weston Park if we then lose to Cole Hill with a weakened team?'

'What's the point? Sunday was brilliant – best game we ever played. And what was it you always used to tell me, Dad: some things are more important than football.'

James bit his lip. He wanted to say that he was well aware of that, and that getting one over on Kieran was one of them –

possibly the biggest one in James's world right now. Why couldn't people understand that this was for the sake of the kids, for the sake of the club? Losing Liam was a punch to the gut, just when he was starting to believe that they really could pull it off. Liam's pace was a major weapon against the better teams, enabling them to break quickly and counter-attack. What would they do without it?

In the car on the way home, Ben was chatting away about training. James, still brooding, wasn't really listening.

'What do you think, Dad?' asked Ben.

'Sorry Ben, I was miles away. What do I think about what?'

'About trying Hakim on the wing again. He was great against Weston, and he's our only player with anything like Liam's pace.'

James opened his mouth to explain to Ben why that wouldn't work, but then stopped. Why not? Ben was right about Hakim's pace. And while he wasn't as tricky as Liam, he wasn't a bad technical player by any means. If he could cope in attacking situations against a team like Weston, surely he'd be okay against Cole Hill.

'He'd be more comfortable on the left than the right,' said James thoughtfully. 'But Dylan is just as happy on either wing, so he could swap across. Do you know, that's not a bad idea, Ben.' He paused, before playfully adding, 'I'm glad I thought of it.' James didn't see Ben rolling his eyes in response, but he knew it had happened, all the same.

*

'We're going to beat you this time, Mr Hogan.'

'Yeah, we had training last night and everyone agreed this is a must-win game.'

Tom and Jonah from 7E had arrived early for James's lesson, just for the banter.

'How are you going to do that, lads? Have you got some new players? I seem to recall when you played us with your usual ones, my Swifts won – what was it now? Two-nil?'

'Yeah, but that keeper of yours…'

'Sam? Yes, she's great. I bet you wish you had a keeper as good as her, don't you, Jonah? Who is your keeper by the way – oooh, sorry Tom – bit awkward.'

The boys were laughing, and once they all got past the false bravado, they actually had a sensible discussion about the match. James admitted that the previous game could have gone either way and said he was looking forward to this one now that he actually knew a few of the Cole Hill players. He decided not to mention Liam's absence – no point in giving them advance warning – and he tried to subtly find out if they were missing anyone. At the end of the lesson, as the boys were leaving, Tom called out, 'Good luck for Sunday, Mr Hogan,' and James returned the good wishes. He meant it, but he'd be just as happy for them to be struck down with every misfortune football could bestow if it meant another three points gained on the Hawks.

*

'T S Eliot said…' James was starting his team talk in traditional fashion.

'Who?'

'T S Eliot: young Liverpool player, started his career with Fulham. Eliot once said, "April is the cruellest month". You lot have been brilliant this season, so let's not have a cruel let-down now. If April is going to be cruel, let's make sure someone else suffers, not us. Keep doing what you've been doing. First thought: can we go forward? What's the attacking option? And when we lose the ball, we work hard to get it back. We've beaten Cole Hill before, let's do it again today.'

The game kicked off, and Cole Hill seemed a touch more cautious than last time. Connor, the big striker, was looking lively, and as with their previous encounter, Gabe looked like he was in for a difficult match. Cole Hill were making the best chances, but Sam was equal to everything they threw at her.

'Come on, Swifts, get into the game!' shouted James as Connor tested Sam with another powerful drive from the edge of the penalty box.

Ben and Callum were struggling to feed Rory and Josh up front. Dylan was getting some joy against his marker – Jonah from 7E – but Hakim looked hesitant and uncertain on the other flank. He wasn't having a bad game, but he wasn't using his pace or going at the Cole Hill defence in anything like the way Dylan was on the right.

Deepak came on for Charlie in defence, although James had considered taking Hakim off and moving a central midfielder into his place. He still wanted to see if Hakim could get behind Cole Hill and make his pace count. A couple of times, Ben played inviting balls behind the defence, but Hakim was always too far back to take advantage.

'Hakim!' roared James. 'That's the ball we want you on the end of – you've got to gamble sometimes.'

At half-time, the score was still nil-nil, although in fairness it was Cole Hill who looked closer to scoring. James brought Charlie back on for Hakim, pushing Deepak into the centre of midfield to make room for him in defence, while Callum switched on to the wing.

'How was that for you, playing left midfield?' James asked Hakim as the other players trotted out for the second half.

'I didn't know where I was supposed to be – I'm never sure if I'm too far forward or too far back. Against Weston I was a wide attacker, staying up. This time in midfield it's harder to get the balance right.'

'You'll work it out. Are you up for having another go once you've had a breather?'

Hakim nodded, looking pleased at the prospect of going back on in the same position.

'Okay, watch Dylan and Callum for the next ten or fifteen minutes. See what they are doing; try to learn from what works and what doesn't.'

Hakim watched intently for the next few minutes, and Joao, who had overheard the conversation, stood next to him, pointing things out and asking Hakim questions about what Dylan and Callum were doing. Despite the best efforts of the midfield, the Swifts just couldn't fashion anything for Rory or Josh to get on the end of. James couldn't help wondering what difference Liam would have made had he been there. With fifteen minutes to go, James put Hakim back on for Callum.

'Go make us a goal, Hakim,' called Joao. Not for the first time, James found himself admiring Joao's optimism without necessarily sharing it. Eventually Ben fed Dylan on the right. Dylan ran at Jonah, twisting and turning and ultimately beating him on the outside. He swung in the cross, which flew over Rory's head. Josh was half a pace too far back to reach it and it looked like it was going to bypass everyone. Then Hakim arrived at the far post. He had cut in from his wing when Dylan started taking on the defender and was in precisely the right place to poke the ball across the goal line.

James and Joao leapt for joy on the touchline. As the boys ran back for the restart, Hakim looked across to the coaches, beaming.

'Great run, Hakim, perfectly timed,' shouted Joao. 'I knew you would do it.'

Cole Hill didn't have long, and they threw everything at the Swifts in search of an equaliser. When they got a corner in the last minute, even Tom lumbered forward from his own goalmouth, but it came to nothing. The referee blew for full time and Swifts had notched up another vital three points.

Later that evening, James checked the results. As expected, Weston Park had defeated the Hawks, winning four-one. James was desperate now to find out how many points Hawks were going to be docked. The Swifts might already have enough points to finish above them, but regardless, James wanted to win the next game more than he'd ever wanted to win a game of football in his life. He'd do anything to secure victory.

*

The mood when Andy dropped Jayden back to Hayley at the end of a weekend was always hard to predict. Sometimes it would be relaxed, sometimes a bit more awkward and snappy. As soon as she opened the door and saw the look on Andy's face, she knew this wasn't going to be an easy encounter, although she wasn't sure why. Jayden dashed past her and scampered up the stairs. Hayley suspected that he made a point of getting out of the firing line, just in case it all kicked off. Even before Jayden was halfway up the stairs, Andy launched into a rant.

'Did you see that story in the papers?' There was an expectant look on his face, like he already had the conversation planned out. 'The one about your lot losing evidence.'

She should have expected this. It had been all over the news; some politician caught drink-driving, only for his breath-test readings to go missing. The usual suspects were making a mountain over it, accusing the establishment of looking after their own. The thing is, sometimes this stuff happens; people get fired for mistakes like that, but sometimes they are just mistakes. But Andy and his fellow travellers would never believe it was just a coincidence in a case like this. She had tried not to engage with him at first, but he'd kept on going.

'Imagine my surprise to discover that our finest boys in blue, who think of nothing creating evidence to bang up peace protesters and activists, bend over backwards to keep the ruling class safe from the consequences of their own actions. It's disgusting.'

'Shit happens, Andy. Evidence gets lost more often than you'd think. It's just that you never hear about the cases where it happens to someone unimportant.'

His eyes widened and she knew immediately the mistake she'd made. 'Unimportant? So, the little people are unimportant are we?'

'That's not what I meant and you know it...'

'I don't know how you do it. It's bad enough the state only cares about the people with money and power – the important people in your eyes, apparently – but at least I'm not propping it up and doing their dirty work for them. How do you sleep at night, knowing that you're a part of all that? It's about time someone called your lot to account. Next Saturday can't come soon enough.'

'What's Saturday got to do with anything? Have you got something planned?'

'Massive protest march, right through the town centre and up to the council building. We're going to make sure that our lords and masters know we're watching and we're not going to let them get away with it.' He caught the look on her face. 'Relax, it's all legal. We've notified everyone we're supposed to. No need for you to get your knickers in a twist.' With that, he left, leaving Hayley fuming at the patronising tone of that last remark. If a male policeman had told one of Andy's female comrades not to get her knickers in a twist, Andy would have been the first to cry sexism. She'd certainly look into the details for Saturday's march, just in case they hadn't got all the notifications in place.

*

On Tuesday evening, James had a call from Lynn.

'Hi James. I don't know where to start with this.'

'Um, okay. How about the beginning?'

Lynn sighed. 'I've had two emails from the league: one with the management committee's verdict on the Hawks, one concerning the match on Sunday.'

'Why are they emailing us about the match? I thought they usually left the arrangements to the two clubs' secretaries – which in this case is you and you.'

'That's what I thought, but they've appointed a referee for the game.' The news came out of nowhere, taking James's legs away from him. The league almost never appointed a ref for the younger age groups.

'There's more. I queried it and the referees' secretary said that *we* had requested one, due to the ill-feeling between the teams.'

'And I'm guessing you never made that request, did you?'

'Of course I didn't; this has got Ron's fingerprints all over it,' agreed Lynn. 'But you haven't heard the half of it. The management committee has awarded the two ringer games to the other teams, as expected. But they haven't imposed any further points deduction.'

The knot of tension in James's stomach gripped hard. 'What?'

'The club gets a fine – £30 for each offence, £60 in total – but they decided that's enough of a punishment. I suspect this is Ron's doing too. He must have friends on the management committee.'

'£60? They're practically letting them get away with it. Kieran is cheating and they've barely given him a smack on the wrist!'

'It's not all over, James. I've checked the table. You can still finish above them; you have to beat them and win your other game, but it's still possible.'

'They should have thrown them out of the league,' James fumed, 'or at the very least hit them with a points deduction. Kieran's not getting away with this, I'm fucking well not going to let that happen.'

'Calm down, James.'

'*I am calm!*' James was shouting now, which even he could see rather undermined his claim. He took a breath and tried again. 'I'm sorry Lynn, it's not your fault – I shouldn't be taking this out on you.'

'No, you shouldn't,' she snapped back. 'And it's not good for you to let it get to you like this either. I'm saying this as a friend, James: get a grip. I feel the same as you about Kieran – I haven't forgotten what his animals did to Rory – but don't you lose yourself in all this.'

When Lynn rang off, James could barely contain himself. His heart was racing and his sense of frustration had nowhere to go. Lynn was right, he did need to get a grip, but in that moment, beating the Hawks and finishing above them was everything. He didn't want to live in a world where the likes of Kieran and Ron got away with dodgy refs and ringers, with poached players and back-room deals. Whatever it took, James had to beat them; had to.

CHAPTER THIRTY-FOUR

Arriving for her Saturday evening shift, Hayley heard her name being called. 'Prisoner in cell three is asking for you, Hayley.' She thanked the desk officer and made her way to the holding cells, wondering who it was. It took her a moment to recognise the name on the door in such an unfamiliar context.

She opened the hatch in the doorway and saw him look up. 'Hey there,' she said, 'fancy meeting you here. Andy Wood: when did you drop the double-barrelled surname? You were the one who said that we should both take it on so we're the same as Jayden.'

'I could ask you the same, PC Birnham. When did you stop going by Birnham-Wood?' That was a fair point; she was just as guilty as him on that one. Not necessarily on whatever had landed him in this cell though.

'Never mind that, what kind of trouble have you got yourself into?'

Andy grimaced in response. 'This is ridiculous. Can you do anything about it? I wasn't doing anything wrong – I've been completely set up. At the very least, can you let Paul Lloyd know what's happened and where I am – he'll get a lawyer down here for me.'

'Of course. Let me look into it and see what I can find out.'

Back at the desk, the duty officer filled her in. Andy had been on the protest march and things had got a little heated. Apparently bricks were thrown and the officers on the scene moved into the crowd of protesters to make arrests. Andy, among others, had been pulled out, though he swore blind that all he'd thrown was clever slogans. Hayley believed that, for what it was worth; Andy had always been one of the calmer heads in this kind of situation. Hayley checked the forms and when she saw the name of the arresting officer – Amber Gould – it made her even more inclined to do what she could to help Andy.

*

The chance to do something about it came sooner than she anticipated. She was changing into her gear for her shift, when the door to the locker room opened. Hayley looked up to see Gould herself coming in at the end of hers. They nodded greetings at one another.

'Hey,' said Hayley. 'Were you the arresting officer at that protest march? Did you nick Andy Wood?'

Amber smiled. 'Yes, once the bricks started flying we put together a grab squad and got hold of the ringleaders. Wood had a loudhailer so we headed straight for him.'

'But did you actually see him throwing bricks? I know Andy: he's a serial protester, sure, but I've never known him cross the line into violence.'

Amber shrugged. 'You said it, he's always at protests – he's a troublemaker. He was one of the main organisers, so it stands to reason he was behind things.'

'But that doesn't make him guilty. He can't control what everyone else gets up to.'

Amber turned to face Hayley full on. 'Whose side are you on, Hayley? He's a troublemaker and if we get him on something like this it'll make him think twice in the future. He's got it coming, the bloody Trot. Anyway, it's another result, isn't it? That's what counts at the end of the day.'

Hayley had finished changing by this point, but she forced herself to wait until Gould had left for home before heading back to the cells to see Andy again.

'I've got good news and bad news,' she said once she was back with him. 'The good news is that I think you can get out of this. Tell your lawyer to request the bodycam footage from the arresting officers. They didn't see you throwing anything, so if you're telling the truth...'

'What do you mean *if*?' The tension of the last few hours was obviously hanging heavily on Andy, so Hayley ignored his terse interruption.

'...which I'm sure you are, they won't have anything on you. Your lawyer should be able to make something out of the possibility that you were picked on because you were one of the march's organisers. The bodycam should confirm your version of events, and if they didn't have the bodycam switched on, any half-decent lawyer will have a field day with that.'

Andy looked relieved to hear that. 'Thanks Hayley, that's great. What's the bad news?'

'You'll be out of here in no time, so you're not going to be the next Nelson Mandela. We'll have to cancel the tribute concert.'

*

As she headed for the staff car park, Hayley smiled to herself. She was glad to have been able to help Andy, but also glad to have got one over on Amber. Of course, she still had to start getting more collars herself if she was going to change Sarge's opinion of her. She should definitely follow up on that Hogan bloke.

*

Even without the tension headache that he woke up with, Wednesday wasn't a great day for James. For one thing, it was hard to keep his mind on his teaching rather than Sunday's game. For another, he couldn't shake the feeling that his classes had it in for him.

There it was again, that odd intermittent rumbling noise that James just couldn't place. He turned around and the members of 8B were all facing him: eyes forwards, smirks on a few faces. There was mischief afoot. He eyeballed the most likely ringleaders – Tracey, Ethan, Nick, Gary – but no one was giving anything away. He was sure he wasn't imagining it though.

He turned back to the whiteboard and continued to write, talking as he did so about how to pick up subtle, implied meanings in a text. He definitely heard the noise again; he didn't react, hoping that if it carried on he might work out what it was. After a couple of seconds he spun around, to be met with the same sea of not-so-innocent faces.

'Gary Cobb, what's going on?'

'I don't know what you mean, Mr Hogan.'

James cast his eye around the classroom. He picked out a snigger in the back row... wait a minute; Nick Cusack was in the back row all right, but there was an awful lot of space behind him, much more than usual. One quick glance around the room confirmed James's suspicion: it was a whole-class desk race. Every time he turned his back, the students had been shuffling their chairs and tables forward, getting closer and closer to the front of the class. Some of the less daring kids were getting hemmed in as those behind them pushed up at a faster rate, and Tillie, who sat at the left-hand side of the front row had actually managed to reach the end wall and was blocking the door.

'Very good,' he said flatly, hoping that they had picked up enough about implied meaning to notice his unimpressed tone. 'Now, get all the tables and chairs back where they belong and if you're not all focused on your work for the rest of the lesson, there'll be trouble.'

'What do you mean, sir?' asked Gary, prompting an outburst of laughter from the back of the room.

James felt his face redden. His snarling delivery meant that his feelings were more than just implied now. If he was still in control, it was a close-run thing – he was winning on goal difference, maybe, but only just.

'I mean I've had enough of this nonsense. I mean that I want you all to work in silence for the rest of the lesson. I mean that anyone who speaks to anyone other than me, and anyone who speaks to me about anything other than the work I've set, is going to get a detention. Is that understood?'

Gary made the mistake of trying to argue; he didn't get far. 'But Mr Hogan, we thought…'

'Right, Gary Cobb, that's the first of the detentions. I'll see you tomorrow lunchtime. Anyone else want to join him? There's plenty of room, even without moving the furniture.'

James was furious. He thought he had a good enough relationship with 8B now that they wouldn't try this kind of crap with him; maybe he had been too easy-going with them – well, that was about to change. The rest of the lesson passed uneventfully, save only for the scratching of pens in books and an oppressive, resentful silence.

*

The next couple of days were a struggle. He was aware that his fuse in lessons was shorter than usual, dangerously short. The perfect example came on Friday afternoon.

James's headache didn't make a lesson of *Macbeth* with 10C the most appealing prospect. Still, it was what it was, so he might as well get on with it.

'Right, the theme of destiny in *Macbeth*. Let's start with a question: all the deaths, all the murders; should we blame Macbeth?' James looked across the sea of faces, hoping and failing to spot a glimmer of response. 'Let's put it another way. Why does Macbeth try to become King?'

'Because his wife nagged him into it?' suggested Justin Skinner, to a smattering of laughter.

'Yes, and that's the reason behind many, many things that men find themselves doing, from visits to IKEA to murdering monarchs. Lady Macbeth urges Macbeth on, driving him forward when his resolve is wavering, but what started their ambition? What makes them think he should be King?'

'The witches?' said Justin.

'What about them?' asked James, nodding his encouragement.

'They tell him he's going to be King, right at the beginning of the play. Before that he hadn't even thought about it.'

'Exactly. So, whose fault is it? Should we blame Macbeth or should we blame the witches for everything that happens?'

'The witches – they set him up,' said Christian Bulpitt. 'Yet again, everything is the women's fault!' The other boys in the class started cheering and thumping desks to show their approval at Christian's interpretation of the play.

'You're saying it's our fault that Macbeth is too pathetic to stand up for himself?' asked Isla Dodds, her voice cutting through the bedlam. 'Men should grow a backbone and stop blaming us for everything.'

Christian kept going. 'Seriously though, if the witches had just kept their mouths shut, Macbeth would have been happy as he was – he didn't even think about becoming King until they mentioned it. If they had kept out of it, he'd still be alive by the end of the play and we wouldn't have to read this rubbish.'

'It's not rubbish, Christian,' snapped James, before consciously taking a softer tone and trying to stay on track with the lesson. 'But you raise an interesting point. Should we blame the witches rather than Macbeth? Isla?'

'The witches didn't tell Macbeth to start murdering people, they just said he was going to be King.'

'Precisely. In Shakespeare's world, you can't do anything about your fate – if Macbeth is meant to be King, then come what may, he's going to be King. But his destiny is all about the choices *he* makes. His fate is to be the King of Scotland; the fact that he chooses to go on a killing spree to make it happen means that he's destined to come to a bad end. By way of contrast, Shakespeare gives us Banquo. Banquo is told that his descendants will be Kings, but he doesn't start butchering people. And Shakespeare's audience – his original audience, when the play was first performed – would have known that Banquo was an ancestor of their current King, James I. Banquo shows us that the prophecy will come true, whatever Macbeth does about it. Macbeth had a choice, and once he makes that choice, it gets easier and easier for him to go on killing, until his hands are sopping with blood.'

'So it's Macbeth's fault that we've got to study this bloody play!' The class roared at Christian's latest response.

'Watch your language, Christian.'

'But it is a bloody play, sir; you were the one who said he had blood on his hands – bloody Macbeth and his bloody decisions!'

The class was coming to the boil now and James had the sense that he was losing control of the situation.

'Enough!' he roared. 'Stop calling it a bloody play. It's an enduring masterpiece from the greatest dramatist in literary history.'

'More like an enduring bloody snoozefest.'

'Yeah, Mac-bored-to-death.'

'Enough! The next person to criticise *Macbeth* is in line for a detention.'

The smirk on Christian's face was taunting James before the words even escaped from his mouth. 'But sir, I thought literary criticism was the point of English lessons – make your mind up!'

James had the feeling that he was watching what happened next like an action replay, seeing himself from the outside as the volume of his voice steadily rose. 'You know fine what I meant, so grow up and shut up, you…' Don't swear at him. Not this time; don't swear.

'I was just saying…'

'*Shut up*! I've had it up to here with you today, Kieran.'

There was a long pause, more Pinter than Shakespeare, and then Justin asked, 'Who's Kieran, sir? Why did you say Kieran instead of Christian?'

Why indeed? Was James getting so obsessed that Kieran was even haunting his lessons? He hadn't been himself for a while and only he knew just how close he had been to another Kyle-like meltdown. Somehow he had to get the lesson back on track and make it to the end of the day.

'Never mind that. Are there any questions – any serious questions?'

Georgia Price, not a student renowned for the finer points of literary study, spoke up. 'Yeah, I get that, sir; but what's going on with the stuff about the forest marching? That's just weird.'

'Birnam Wood,' said James, picking up his copy of the play and flicking through the pages. 'The prophecy in Act 4 where Macbeth is told he can never be vanquished until Birnam Wood comes against him to Dunsinane. What's the problem with that happening?'

'Woods don't walk,' said Justin. 'Not unless you've taken a whole lot of drugs.'

James let the laughter die down before responding. 'No, they don't, heavy weekends notwithstanding. So how does Macbeth interpret this statement? Anyone?'

'He thinks he's safe: if woods don't walk, it can never happen.'

'But of course, we know better. Malcolm's army, marching on Dunsinane, disguise their numbers by carrying branches cut from the trees of, you've guessed it, Birnam Wood. Macbeth fears the game is up, but resolves to go down fighting. Remember, in Shakespeare, our darkest acts always have to be paid for. He's doomed, and he was doomed from the moment he took matters into his own hands.'

Judging from the faces, most of them had followed his line of argument. It occurred to him that, like Macbeth, he had found it easier and easier to do the wrong thing, getting deeper and deeper into the dark side in his ongoing battle with Kieran.

'Okay, homework: plan an essay outline on the following topic: how is the theme of destiny depicted in Macbeth? I want the structure of the essay, plus the quotes that you would use to illustrate your argument. Due in for next Tuesday's lesson.' He hoped he hadn't already sealed his own bloody destiny, even if he didn't have to worry about Birnam Wood closing in on Dunsinane. One way or the other his day of reckoning would come on the pitch on Sunday. Thinking of another great Elizabethan drama, James began to understand how Faustian pacts made sense – if Mephistopheles appeared to him now, he might be willing to trade his mortal soul for a guaranteed win against the Hawks. Maybe that was a bit steep, but he'd at least consider swapping his rekindled teaching career for it.

CHAPTER THIRTY-FIVE

James barely managed any breakfast on Sunday; even looking at food made his stomach turn. He had confidence in his players, but didn't trust Kieran not to try something.

They arrived at the grounds and found that Dave had already got the goal nets up.

'Don't tell the other managers about me doing this,' he dead-panned. 'I have my reputation as a miserable curmudgeon to maintain. But I wanted you to be able to just focus on getting the team ready. Sam has heard all about the first game from the boys. I've never seen her so intent on winning a game. She won't let you down.'

'She never does. Thanks, Dave. I appreciate it.'

As the players arrived, their usual chatter was more subdued than usual; nerves or focus? James couldn't tell. When he saw a man in referee's kit walking across the pitches towards them, James went to introduce himself.

'James Hogan,' he said, offering his hand. 'Swifts' manager. Are you Mr Thornley?'

'That's me, Rhys Thornley,' the ref replied with a smile. He was a similar age to James, with a face that was hard to read.

'Happy to have you,' said James. 'The last time we played them, things got rather heated and the ref – one of their parents –

didn't do anything to rein the Hawks in.' No harm in getting the idea of the Hawks as a dirty side into the ref's head.

'Though it was one of your players that was sent off, I gather.' A raised eyebrow accompanied the observation.

'Yes, that's right. Sent off for complaining after numerous fouls went unpunished. It was also my goalkeeper who ended up in A&E with a broken arm.'

Rhys held up a hand to stop James. 'Okay, I get it. Whatever happened last time won't happen again. You tell your boys I'll make sure both teams are protected from foul play, and I won't put up with any back-chat. If they think I've made a mistake, they should keep that to themselves.'

'Understood,' replied James. 'That's all I wanted to hear. By the way, it's my boys plus one girl: our keeper.'

Both of Rhys' eyebrows went up this time. 'Really? I'll not give her any special favours, but I'll keep an eye on things. Was she the one who ended up in A&E?'

'No, she joined us afterwards. The old keeper plays centre forward now.'

'Versatile. I like it. Have a good game.' With that Rhys went to introduce himself to Kieran, and James went to give his team their final instructions.

'Gather round guys, listen in. Shakespeare's play *Macbeth* – which is about the Scottish ancestors of England's Beth Mead – includes the line "So foul and fair a day I have not seen". That's what we can expect today: the Hawks will do the fouling, but we're going to play it fair. Don't get drawn in to playing them at their own game; we're better than that. We would have beaten them last time with a proper ref, and today we've got a proper ref. Don't retaliate, just stay calm and play your football. Be brave – I don't just mean be brave about the physical stuff, I mean be brave in your decision-making, in the passes you try, in being willing to take a shot. Let's show them who the best team in the club really is. Are you up for that?'

James was expecting a chorus of yesses, either rousing or half-hearted. Instead, he saw expressions of quiet focus on all of the Swifts' faces. One of two of them were nodding, some were looking around locking eyes with one another. They looked ready for anything.

The ref blew the whistle and the Hawks kicked off, knocking the ball around and giving everyone a touch. Rory and Josh, the strikers, hared around after it, but the other six outfield Swifts kept their shape. Back in September, they would have been a disorganised mess already. When the ball finally came forward, Dylan chased his opposite number and managed to poke the ball back to Hakim. Hakim calmly stepped upfield, feeding the ball into Ben's path. Max came hurtling in and completely cleaned Ben out.

'Ref!' shouted James instinctively. 'What was that?' Mr Thornley had already blown the whistle. Gabe took the free kick, and Deepak fed Liam on the right, but his marker toed the ball out for a throw-in as Liam tried to go past him.

The game continued in similar vein for several minutes. Hawks' tackling was skirting the borders of fair play, but the ref was quick to blow if it went too far. James noticed that Dylan was attracting verbals from the Hawks, as well as more than his share of fouls.

Hawks won a corner. When the cross came in, their centre forward collided with Sam after she caught the ball and sent her tumbling to the ground. The ball broke loose and Max – who else – was on hand to bundle the ball into the net.

'That's the way!' howled Kieran. 'Show her to leave football to the boys.' James could see Rob on the touchline leaping about in celebration, but then he noticed that the ref wasn't running back to the centre circle.

'Foul on the keeper, free kick.'

Kieran didn't agree. 'Whaaaat? Are you having a laugh, ref? It's a man's game. If she can't take the knocks, she shouldn't be out there.'

The ref ignored Kieran's protests, shooing away the complaining Hawks. He said something to Sam, who was still sitting in her goalmouth, taking deep breaths. She nodded and got to her feet. Gabe offered to take the free kick for her, but she waved him away.

Mr Thornley was taking no nonsense from either side. He gave some free kicks for the Hawks – Liam mistimed a challenge and brought down the blond winger, Ben took Max out in what James suspected wasn't entirely an accidental foul – but most of the decisions were going to the Swifts. Kieran, of course, wasn't happy about that, and wasn't afraid to let the ref know.

'Are you sure, referee? Nothing wrong with that one.'

'Ref, no! He never touched him!'

'I can give you the number of a good optician if you like, ref.'

That last comment brought the ref over to the touchline to talk to Kieran. James edged closer to listen in.

'I get that there's history between these teams,' said the ref. 'But I will not have you questioning my decisions, and I certainly won't have you questioning my ability. One more outburst like that, and you'll be going in my book. Clear?'

Kieran was nodding, but he didn't look impressed with the ref's show of authority. James doubted that Kieran would be able to stay quiet, and hoped for another decision against the Hawks before too long.

Sure enough, Kieran started to react the next time Liam was scythed down, but after a meaningful look from Mr Thornley, he controlled himself. The free kick was on the right-hand side of the box. Ben and Liam stood over the ball, while Gabe and Charlie loped forward. James shouted for the two defenders, pointing out that they were leaving Hakim on his own with two Hawks, but before either could go back, Liam ran in to take the free kick. The keeper caught the cross and quickly kicked long for the counter-attack. The two Hawks made good use of the extra man, leaving Hakim in an impossible situation, and within moments the ball was past Sam and in the Swifts' goal.

'Yeeeeesss!' Kieran was ecstatic. 'Totally deserved. Well played, lads.'

James tried to rally his players. 'Come on, Swifts, heads up.'

'Remember: play your football; play, play, play,' added Joao.

Gabe, Callum and Sam circulated, encouraging their team-mates to get back into the game. The Swifts kicked off, but other than a few more fouls from the Hawks, there wasn't much else to report before the ref blew for half-time.

James was about to start his half-time talk, when Gabe beat him to it.

'Come on,' said Gabe. 'For years that lot have boasted about being better than us. Let's show them that's not true anymore. Keep playing your football, like Joao and Mister James always say. With this ref, there's no reason we can't win. We outplayed them last time, and we're even better now – what's stopping us? Let's go and win this.'

The other players roared their approval of Gabe's words, and a few looked questioningly at James.

'Yeah,' James couldn't think of anything to add, 'what he said.' As the players turned to go out, James grabbed Ben's arm. 'No more with Max,' he said. 'Don't go down to his level.'

As soon as they kicked off, the Swifts tore into the Hawks, who just kept fouling. After giving five Swifts free kicks in as many minutes, the ref trotted over to Kieran on the touchline. James moved in again.

'Have a word with your lads, manager. The constant fouling has to stop. I've kept my cards in my pocket, because it's a kids' game and it shouldn't need bookings, but if it goes on like this, I won't have a choice.'

'What fouls, ref? They were perfectly good challenges!'

'Okay, if you won't stop the fouls, then I'll have to.'

From the latest free kick, Dylan swept the ball into the box. Rory leapt for a header and the keeper sprinted off his line to challenge for it. Fist foremost, he leapt at the same time as Rory and connected perfectly. Unfortunately, not with the ball; Rory went to the ground clutching his head. As a Hawks defender hoofed the ball upfield, the ref put the whistle to his lips and blew.

'Penalty!'

'Whaaaaat!' screamed Kieran. 'You've got to be joking – he went for the ball!'

To be fair to Kieran, James didn't think for a moment that this one was deliberate, but a punch to the head, even by accident, was certainly a foul. The ref ignored Kieran's ranting and ran straight to Rory. He was sitting up now, groggily shaking his head. The ref beckoned for James to come and see to him.

'He seems pretty woozy,' said the ref. 'I think he should go off – we can't take any chances with head injuries.'

'Can't we wait and see if he's okay?' James was thinking about how much better the forward line worked when Rory was leading it.

'Take him off for five minutes and see how he is, but any signs of a concussion and I won't let him back on. I get that this game means a lot to everyone, but it's not worth risking the boy's health, is it?'

Of course it wasn't. What had James been thinking? Chastened, James helped Rory to his feet and led him to the touchline. Joao had already got Liam ready to take Rory's place, and quickly reorganised the team. While all this was happening, the ref had been speaking tersely to Kieran.

James usually left the boys to sort out who took penalties, but he certainly hadn't expected Josh to be the chosen taker: Josh, who had missed more chances than the rest of the team put together this season; why Josh to take such a vital penalty?

Josh placed the ball and took five, six, seven steps back. James couldn't bear to look but couldn't look away either. Josh started his run-up. As he reached the ball, he pulled back his foot and suddenly slowed its movement right down, waiting, waiting but always keeping his foot just in motion. The keeper blinked first and threw himself to his left, prompting Josh to return to normal speed and slot the ball into the unguarded opposite side of the goal.

'He can't do that!' bellowed Kieran. 'He's not allowed to stop and start in his run-up.'

The ref trotted over. 'He didn't,' he replied. 'He slowed down, but he didn't stop. Now, you can accept that or you can go in my book.'

Kieran was still chuntering to himself as the boys lined up for the restart. James was talking to Rory and Lynn, the latter having made her way around from the other touchline to check on her son.

'What do you think, James?' she asked, looking concerned.

'Put me back on,' pleaded Rory. 'I'm fine.' His face was very pale and what looked like an egg was emerging from his temple; he certainly didn't look fine.

'I don't know, mate. I'd like you back, but it's a head injury… better safe than sorry.' Lynn mouthed a 'Thank you' to James and led Rory away to find an ice pack.

A draw was no good to the Swifts. Shots rained in on the Hawks' goal. The pace was frenetic, but the Swifts still produced some lovely, intricate passing movements, in between being cut down by the Hawks. The ref even produced a couple of yellow cards for Hawks players, but it made little difference. James briefly considered throwing Rory back on for the last few minutes, but one look at the bump on his head made up his mind. They'd have to find another way to get the goal.

Ben picked the ball up just inside the Hawks' half, exchanged passes with Callum and drove forward. Max – who else? – was on an intercept course at full speed. He collided with Ben, taking ball and man together in one crunching moment. The ball was swept clear, but Mr Thornley's whistle rang out again: another penalty.

'Nooooooo!' screamed Kieran. 'You are joking! Nothing wrong with that challenge, nothing at all. Are you going to take the penalty for them as well? You've been on their side all day!'

Ben was getting to his feet, helped up by his team-mates, so the ref calmly walked across to Kieran. Kieran was still ranting and raving, and as the ref drew close he put his hand to his breast pocket and pulled out a red card.

'I've had enough. You're off. Name?'

'Oh, fuck off, you're sending me off for what? For knowing a good tackle when I see one? 'Cos you clearly don't.'

'Persistent dissent, foul and abusive language directed at a match official, calling my integrity into question: all of those. Name?'

'Kieran, Kieran Butcher. And I know your name too, Rhys Thornley. I'd watch your back if I were you.'

'I'll bear that in mind, and I'll put that threat in my match report with all of your other comments. Now, go on, off you go.'

Kieran quickly conferred with Phil, who was on the touchline with him, then stomped away to the car park. His route took him past James, although he was avoiding eye contact. Lynn, on the other hand, called out as he passed her: 'Bye Kieran. Leaving early to beat the traffic, are we?'

The ref went back over to the penalty box and showed a yellow card to Max. Josh didn't look keen to take a second penalty, and Liam, Callum and Dylan all seemed to fancy it. They were still arguing when Gabe stepped forward, pushed past them and picked up the ball. The others just accepted this, despite the fact that a moment earlier none of them had been willing to back down for one another. Gabe placed the ball on the spot. The Hawks keeper was right in front of him, saying something to Gabe and refusing to back off. The ref ushered him away, but the keeper persisted with his mind games, taking as much time as he possibly could. As Gabe paced out his run-up, the keeper started pointing to his right, daring Gabe to put it there. Was he bluffing? Double bluffing? Would it put Gabe off? Not a chance: Gabe ran up and absolutely leathered the ball into the net. The keeper barely had time to move before it was past him. Swifts were in the lead.

With Kieran gone, the Hawks weren't the same team. When the final whistle went, the Swifts' parents burst into applause, joined by some – but by no means all – of the Hawks' supporters. Phil refused to shake hands with either the ref or with James, but James didn't care. He thanked the ref, who gave him a rueful smile and asked if Hawks had played like that in the first game.

'Exactly like that, except they were allowed to get away with it,' replied James. The ref just shook his head.

'Seeing their manager, I can understand where they get it from. How's the lad with the head injury?'

'He seems okay, but we decided not to risk it.'

'Good decision.' Rhys then walked over to where the Swifts were gathering and congratulated them on playing a great game of football and for keeping their composure without resorting to the same tricks as the Hawks. He caught Ben's eye and threw in a 'Well, most of you,' with raised eyebrows. James saw him talking with Lynn and Rory afterwards.

'Brilliant, guys,' said James to the Swifts. 'I'm so proud of you. Eleven heroes – or ten heroes and a heroine if you prefer, Sam.'

'Nah, it's okay. I'm happy to be a hero with the others,' replied Sam magnanimously.

'Very gracious of you, I'm sure. One more game to go, let's see out the season with one more win.'

*

'What about Gabe's team talk?' asked James as he and Joao carried the nets back to the lock-up. 'The hairs were standing up on the back of my neck.'

'Sim, me too. Did you notice, Gabe called you Mister James?'

'Did he? I missed that. What of it?'

'The other week, Gabe asked why I call you Mister James.'

James realised that he had never thought to ask Joao that. It was just something that Joao had always done.

'My country learned football from yours. The first Portuguese teams were formed by Englishmen, and the first coaches who taught us to play were Englishmen. In Portugal, managers aren't called gaffer or boss or a Portuguese word; we call them Mister – the English "Mister", not the Portuguese "Senhor". It is a term of respect, used for someone to look up to. He must have decided you deserved that respect.'

James didn't know how to respond. The idea that Gabe – or any of the Swifts – might see him in that light was completely humbling. Thinking over his recent behaviour, he was sure he didn't deserve the compliment, but he would try to live up to it from now on.

That night, once the league table was updated, James took a long look at how things were shaping up. Most of the teams had finished and there were only two games left to play: Swifts versus Redbridge and Weston Park versus the Royals. Whatever happened, Hawks were staying down. Royals had won that morning, and now the Hawks couldn't catch them. More than that, if the Swifts could beat Redbridge, they would finish above the Hawks too. But that wasn't all: if the Royals lost to Weston Park, which seemed likely, the winners of Swifts versus Redbridge would claim second place ahead of the Royals. As much as James knew not to take any result for granted, one more Swifts win should be enough for promotion. What a reward that would be for the way the team had turned the season around. And how galling would it be for Kieran to see 'his' promotion place going to the Swifts? One more game, and everything still to play for.

CHAPTER THIRTY-SIX

In spite of herself, Hayley was getting caught up in all the excitement. Jaydan actually played most of the game, and the team had even won. He was absolutely buzzing for the rest of the day, talking about how they might win promotion: if they won their last match, they should get second place. Based on the comments of the dads around her on the touchline, Jayden had done all right, so she hoped that might encourage Matt to use him in the decisive match. Then again, maybe it would be better if he wasn't in the firing line if things went wrong. She never knew what to hope for where Jayden and football were concerned.

Another tricky one was what to do about those fingerprints. The remnants of the sabotage on Kieran Butcher's car had proved to be a match with James Hogan. She found it hard to believe Hogan would do something like that – she'd have believed it of Butcher in a heartbeat – but she'd been in the job long enough not to be surprised by what people are capable of. This might be her chance to turn a no-hope assignment into a win, to show Sarge that she could deliver results just as well as Amber Gould. She hadn't any proof linking the rubbish to the car, so without a confession it was circumstantial evidence at best, but she was pretty sure now that Hogan was the guilty party. Maybe she should make an opportunity to talk to him and see what he had to say about it. If he incriminated himself, she had everything else she needed to make the charge stick.

*

James felt like a new man on Monday morning. All the pressure, all the worry that had weighed him down for the previous week – and longer, if he was honest with himself – was gone. Even if the Swifts didn't win their last game, at least he'd got his own back on Kieran. He felt freer, happier than he could remember feeling in months. In the post-victory afterglow, he was even feeling more positive about life after Joao. His young assistant had been encouraging him to take the Level Two coaching course next season. Joao had opened his eyes to so much, but maybe it was time he took the next step in his own coaching education.

When he arrived in the English department office, he regaled Richard and Dean with the story of the match, enjoying their reactions to Kieran's various explosions. Josie seemed quieter than usual when she arrived, and as James was expounding on his footballing triumph he noticed Moira taking her aside and talking intently. He made a mental note to check in with her between lessons, to see how she was doing.

His first lesson of the day was with 8B, and although they seemed wary at first, probably anticipating a return of last week's snarling James, they soon sensed that he was in a better mood and the lesson went fine. The previous week was behind him now, consigned to the dustbin of history along with his Kieran-inspired tension headaches.

James had a free period after 8B, and it sounded like Josie was having a rough time with her year 11s. When the bell went for the end of the lesson, most of the class departed, but James could hear that someone had lingered behind and Josie was giving them a thorough dressing down, her voice becoming increasingly shrill.

'Look, I've offered extra support, I've tried getting tough – what will it take before you make an effort to rescue your English GCSE?' James couldn't make out the response, whatever was said didn't seem to go down well with Josie. 'And do you think that's good enough? Do you?' Then James heard a boy's voice, loud and angry, before Josie shrieked, 'Don't you walk out when I'm talking to you.'

James went in and what he saw momentarily stunned him into inaction. Josie and a year 11 lad were physically grappling. Josie was between the boy and the door. James couldn't tell if he was just trying to get past, or trying to hurt her. One of Josie's arms was pinned between their bodies, and the other flapped ineffectively as she tried to break free. The boy seemed happy to take advantage of his size and strength, so James had to act. He bounded across the classroom and pulled at the boy's shoulders, heaving him off Josie and pushing him away from her.

'Are you all right?' he asked, helping Josie up.

'Yeah, just a bit shocked… oh my God – look!'

James followed Josie's gaze and saw that the boy was now slumped on the floor, a small pool of blood slowly spreading around him. Judging from the fresh red on the table above him, he must have caught his head on its corner.

'Quick, call down to the office and get some help.' James barked the instructions as he went to see what he could do to help the lad. Kneeling down, he recognised him: Chris Marlowe. 'Stay with me, Chris,' he muttered. Chris was unconscious, but breathing. James put him into the recovery position and confirmed what he already knew: Chris was bleeding heavily from the back of his head. James looked around for something to stem the blood and saw that Josie was just standing there, clearly in shock.

'Josie! Get help – now!' he shouted. This shook Josie out of her daze and she fumbled in her bag for her phone. James slipped off his jacket, balled it up and held it against Chris' head wound. It was his best suit as well, but now wasn't the time to worry about that. Once Josie finished on the phone, she came and knelt down with him. James noticed that she was trembling. 'It's okay,' he said reassuringly. 'Help's coming, isn't it?' She nodded, still unable or unwilling to speak. She looked terrified, poor kid. This was probably the first time she'd seen an incident like this. 'It's not your fault, Josie.'

'Yes, it is,' she whispered. 'I made him lose his temper. Then when he went to leave, I got in his way – I forced the confrontation. When he grabbed me, I panicked. I didn't know I had the strength to push him away like that.'

'Whoa there – it's not your fault if a student gets physical. And you didn't push him: I pulled him off you.'

'What if he dies?'

'It's not going to come to that. Help is on the way and he'll be fine. You'll be fine. We're all going to be fine, okay?' James just hoped that was true.

Students were congregating at the classroom door, whispering and speculating. Some had tried to come in, but James shouted them out again. The commotion drew Claire and Dean out of their nearby rooms. Once they established that an ambulance had been called, Dean took charge of shepherding the students to an unused classroom, while Claire came across to where James, Josie and Chris were huddled together by the desk. Avoiding the pool of blood, Claire briefly and efficiently checked what classes each of them were supposed to be teaching next and what each class needed to be getting on with. After sorting the logistics, Claire asked what happened. James gave a quick account, jumping in first to make sure that Josie didn't falsely incriminate herself. Chris was starting to stir, groaning and moving his head a little. James told him to stay still, that he was all right and that help was on the way.

More people were arriving to help. First came staff from the school office, then the paramedics. James quickly filled them in on what had happened, how long Chris had been unconscious and then let them get on with it.

'Good job, mate,' said one of the paramedics as they helped Chris to his feet. 'It sounds like you did all the right things – you did well to stop him losing too much blood.'

'Come on, Chris,' said the other one. 'Let's get you to hospital to get checked out. Can you walk with us? Just until we get you downstairs, then we can get you on a stretcher.'

Claire came back in as the paramedics helped Chris out of the door. 'The school will need incident reports from both of you. Do them now, while it's fresh in your memory. Don't worry about your other classes, we're taking care of them, just get this written up.' She turned and walked briskly away, in full crisis-management mode and, James suspected, in her element. This wasn't a terrible accident as far as Claire was concerned, but a chance to demonstrate leadership skills.

'We're fine, by the way,' muttered James to her back. 'Thanks for asking.'

*

As soon as Richard heard about it, he came to find James and Josie in the department office.

'What happened? Is everyone okay?' he asked.

Josie nodded. Her face was very pale and James thought she was still in shock. He had written up his account of the incident but Josie had barely touched her laptop since turning it on. Moira had insisted on making them cups of strong tea, but Josie hadn't so much as looked at hers. James took Richard through what had happened and asked if there was any news about Chris yet. When Claire arrived in the office at lunchtime, she asked how the statements were coming on. Hearing that Josie still hadn't got anything down, she insisted on taking her to a quiet classroom and helping her with the write-up. Dean and Simon arrived too. James didn't really want to keep going over it, but he was forced to repeat his account each time someone else arrived.

James left his bloodstained jacket in the office and went to teach his afternoon lessons in his shirtsleeves. Once Josie, with Claire's help, finally finished her statement, Richard arranged for someone to take her home – she was in no state to drive, let alone to take charge of a class.

*

The next day, James was called to a meeting in the head's office. When he arrived, Richard, Claire and the head were already there. None of them were smiling.

'Come in, James, I'm sure you know what this is about,' said Mrs Cranbrook crisply.

'Chris Marlowe, I'm guessing. How is he doing?'

'He's going to be fine. He needed stitches and he's staying off school for now, so his parents can keep an eye on him in case there's any concussion, but other than that there doesn't seem to be any permanent damage. I want to hear your side of what happened.'

'Well, I don't really know what to add to what I said in my incident report.'

'That's the thing,' said the head, a serious look on her face. 'Your incident report doesn't quite match up with what Josie and Chris have each told us, so I thought if you talked us through it, we might be able to work out where the problem is.'

James froze. The reports didn't match up? Maybe Chris was covering his back, downplaying his fight with Josie, but surely Josie's account would be along the same lines as his own.

'Okay,' said James slowly. 'I heard Josie telling Chris off from my classroom. When things got more heated, I looked in and saw them wrestling near the door. Josie looked like she was in trouble. I called out and went over, pulling Chris off her and pushing him away. He must have banged his head at that point, though I didn't see that.'

'So you admit that it was you who pushed Chris into the desk?' interjected Claire.

'Yes, but only to stop him from manhandling a young, female member of staff. It was appropriate force for the situation.'

'And yet the boy had to be taken to hospital to have stitches put in a head wound,' replied the head acidly. 'I gather that Mr Kirkpatrick has had reports of you being increasingly volatile with your classes over the last week or so. Is that a fair description of things?'

James flashed a look towards Richard, who looked awkward. 'I've got cross sometimes, maybe more than usual, but I certainly haven't lost control at any point. All of us sometimes say things we don't mean to, but I haven't been unprofessional or inappropriate in anything that I've said or done since starting here.'

'And yet Chris Marlowe ended up in A&E.'

James looked around the room. The head looked angry, Richard looked sad and Claire was as unreadable as ever. Shit; they thought he'd snapped and that Chris's injury was the result of him losing it, not him stepping in to rescue a colleague. 'What did Josie and Chris say?'

The head picked up a piece of paper, looking at it as she spoke. 'Chris says that he was talking with Miss Small when he heard your voice and was suddenly hurled across the room. The next thing he knew he was waking up in a pool of blood.' *Suddenly hurled across the room*: James couldn't really blame Chris Marlowe for making it dramatic, but it didn't sound good put like that. 'Miss Small says that Chris was arguing with her and then you came in and...' the head searched the paper for the precise phrase, '"yanked him away, pushing him across the room". That doesn't sound an appropriate response to a conversation, Mr Hogan, no matter how heated it was.'

'It wasn't just a conversation!' exclaimed James. 'I've told you: they were fighting. Chris was grappling with Josie. What was I supposed to do, let a well-built sixteen-year-old boy – a young man – assault a slightly built female colleague?'

Claire leant in and whispered something to Mrs Cranbrook, who nodded before answering James.

'But neither of the other parties to the incident mention the so-called fight.'

So-called? She didn't believe him. Why hadn't Josie told them about it? None of this made sense. 'Fight, wrestling match, call it what you like. They were grappling, Josie told me afterwards that she had tried to stop Chris from walking out by stepping in his way, that's when he got physical. When I looked in, he had her arms pinned and was using his physical strength against her. It's awful that Chris hit his head like that, but it was bad luck – it certainly wasn't due to excessive force on my part.'

'Well,' said the head. 'This is all very difficult. We're all aware that you came to us with something of a mark already on your record. When I try to make sense of the conflicting accounts, I can't help but be swayed by that knowledge. One last chance for you to be completely honest: was this part of a developing pattern of you losing control with your students? As Claire pointed out, your reactions in this meeting are hardly a model of restraint.'

A developing pattern of losing control? Was that how she saw it? He took a deep breath, forcing himself to keep his composure. 'Okay, I accept that I've been more vocal with students in the last week or so, but only within reasonable professional standards. As for this, this has nothing to do with that. I was calm and in control the whole time. I knew exactly what I was doing and I felt – I still feel – that it was a proportional response to the situation.'

'You've made that clear, Mr Hogan. I think you should go home. Consider yourself suspended from duties with full pay until I can get to the bottom of all this.'

James sat back in his chair and took in what had just happened. He wanted to rage, to scream that he had done nothing wrong, but losing his temper now could only make things much, much worse.

'I'll walk you to your car, James,' said Richard.

'Yes,' said Mrs Cranbrook. 'Someone should see you off the site.'

As soon as they were away from the office, Richard spoke. 'I'm sorry, mate, I feel awful about this.'

'What was all that about me getting increasingly volatile?'

'Josie came to Claire and me last week, saying that you'd been shouting more than usual. She was worried and wanted us to look out for you. I told the head and said I'd keep on top of it. If this hadn't happened it wouldn't have been a problem.'

'But a pattern of losing control?'

'I never said that; that was Claire. The problem is that your account is at odds with the other two. That makes it look like you overreacted and put a boy in hospital, then made up the fight to cover your back. I'm in your corner on this, but the head isn't buying. It did go down the way you said, didn't it?'

James stopped and turned to face Richard. 'Yes! Are you saying you don't believe me now?' He could feel his pulse quickening again, a knot of anger rising in his chest.

Richard put his hands up in a calming manner. 'Look, if you tell me that's what happened, absolutely I believe you, I've known you long enough to trust your word. It's just that your statement is the odd one out and I'll be honest, it doesn't look good.'

'I can't understand why Josie isn't giving the full story. Should I talk to her, see if she can clarify things?'

'Absolutely not.' Richard's tone made it clear that this wasn't negotiable. 'The worst thing you could do right now is to make contact with Josie – or Chris and his family, for that matter. How would it look if people said you were pressurising witnesses? I'll talk to her and see what's what. All you can do is to go home and wait this out. Are you okay to drive, or shall I sort you a lift?' James dismissed Richard's offer and drove himself home. On the way he kept thinking about Josie's statement. He thought about Claire helping Josie to write it up. Had Claire taken the opportunity to twist the narrative against him? Had

Claire decided he was potential competition if ever Richard were to move on? Was this all about Lady Macbeth taking out a rival for the throne?

*

Back at home, James's mood wasn't good. He knew he'd done nothing wrong, but the facts were that he had been suspended from work pending an investigation into an incident where a child was badly injured. He knew he wasn't a danger to the Swifts, or any other children for that matter, but the responsible thing to do would be to inform Alison as the club welfare officer. But what if Alison said he couldn't be with the Swifts until things were resolved? He might miss training on Wednesday night, or – worse – the big game with Redbridge. He was torn; he wanted to do the right thing, but how could he miss out on the culmination of such a brilliant season, especially when one last win would mean promotion and finishing above the Hawks?

When Ros got home James ushered her into the kitchen, away from the kids, and explained the day's events. Ros put her hands to her face and he saw her eyes glistening.

'Oh, Jamie. Are you going to lose your job again?'

'No. At least, I don't think so. I don't trust Claire an inch, but Richard is on my side. All I can do is sit it out and trust him. You know I didn't do anything wrong, don't you?' That snapped Ros out of teary mode.

'Of course I do. You're a lot of things, but you're certainly not violent, especially with kids.' She moved across the kitchen and leant into him. 'Now hold me, you idiot.'

'Okay, I'll try not to cave your head in.'

'Don't even joke about it.'

*

Once Ros had processed the news, James asked her what she thought about telling Alison. Ros didn't hesitate.

'You have to tell Alison, there isn't even a choice.' James nodded. He had already come to the same conclusion. The clincher for him was when he reflected that Kieran would probably try to keep it quiet; reverse WWKD, as ever, made it an easy decision.

'Right, well, no time like the present. I'll give her a call.'

Alison picked up after a few rings.

'Hi James, what can I do for you?'

'Well, hopefully you can thank me for letting you know and say there's nothing to worry about. I've been suspended from school.'

'What?!'

James quickly filled Alison in. He said he fully expected to be restored to work with no sanctions once the school had fully investigated, but for the time being he had been suspended.

Alison did a lot of listening. She asked a few questions to clarify things, but mostly she just let James talk as she built up a picture of what happened. Eventually, James felt he'd said everything he needed to, and Alison had stopped asking questions.

'So,' said James. 'What do you think?'

There was a pause, then Alison spoke in a slow, careful voice. 'I'm not sure. I'm going to get in touch with the County FA for advice.'

'Seriously? Is that necessary? I mean, you do believe that I didn't do anything wrong, don't you?'

'Of course I do, James, but it's not that simple. I know you wouldn't deliberately hurt a kid, but I can't make this decision as your friend; I have to do it as the club welfare officer. If you've been suspended from work for putting a child in hospital, how does that look if the club keeps giving you access to work with kids?'

'You mean you're suspending me?' James couldn't keep the shock and frustration out of his voice.

'I mean I'm going to talk to the County FA and see what they advise, but it might well come to suspension, yes. I'll phone them tomorrow morning and let you know how it goes.' James sat there in shock after Alison rang off. He knew he hadn't done anything wrong, but that wasn't how it could look to someone who hadn't been there to see it. Why wasn't Josie telling the truth about it? What was she playing at? If he wasn't careful, he could see everything he'd got back in the last few months snatched away from him again.

CHAPTER THIRTY-SEVEN

The following day, with nothing else to do, James walked Poppy to school. Poppy was chatting away, as ever, but even her never-ending conversational flow wasn't enough to distract him; his mind kept returning to that classroom. Why hadn't he just stayed out of it, left Josie to fend for herself? Immediately he dismissed that thought: she had needed help; he had done the right thing. But why had he thrown Chris so hard? Why towards a desk? He had got away with so much over the last few months – Kieran's exhaust, the Kenny Harrison photos – now he was in trouble all over again. The fact that this time he was innocent would be no consolation if he was charged with Actual Bodily Harm. What had Detective Sergeant Hails said about not getting the benefit of any future doubt? The photos might be brought up again. James felt that familiar tension coming back as he remembered his long night in the holding cell. He couldn't go through that again.

His day didn't improve once he was back at home. His mind kept circling the same questions over and over again. Why wasn't Josie telling the whole story? James knew that Richard was trying to talk people round for his sake, and he was certain that Claire wouldn't think twice about hanging him out to dry, but why was Josie letting him dangle?

The phone rang, shaking James out of his demoralising line of thought. It was Alison.

'Hi James, how are you doing?'

'Well, I've been better. What's the news?'

'Not great. The FA have recommended that we suspend you from all footballing activities until the school resolves everything. When they clear you, I can lift the suspension, but as things stand, you can't go to training on Wednesday, or to the match on Sunday.'

'But...'

'There is no but, James. You know we have to take safeguarding seriously. Keep me posted on any new developments, and let me know if there's anything I can do.'

Ros phoned a couple of times during the day, checking to see how James was. In between, Richard called. He had spent a significant part of the day in meetings with the head and the senior leadership team, sifting through everything over and over again. Chris was still off school, so Richard hadn't been able to talk to him. Josie felt awful about the whole thing, apparently. She was wracked with guilt and kept saying that it was all her fault. James and Richard agreed she was as much a victim as anyone else, but neither could understand why she was making him look like the bad guy.

James was still trying to work that one out when there was a knock at his front door in the middle of the afternoon. Warily opening it, he saw a short policewoman.

'James Hogan?' she asked. James thought he picked up a note of accusation in her tone. Had the school got the police involved? 'I'm PC Birnham. Your school told me you were at home today. Can I come in?' James readily agreed, if only to prevent the neighbours from seeing him being grilled on the doorstep by the police.

PC Birnham declined a cup of tea and settled herself on the sofa. 'Do you know a man called Kieran Butcher?' she asked.

'Yes, we both manage teams for Stoneleigh Youth Football Club.'

'Were you aware of his car trouble a few months ago? Someone put cement in his exhaust so the engine would seize up and die.'

Yes, James was aware. He was also aware of how sweaty his palms were, and he hoped he didn't look as guilty as he felt right now.

'Yeah, everyone knew – I mean, it was all over the club. Was it really sabotage, not just a regular breakdown? We all thought he was making a bit much of it, to be honest.' He didn't feel very honest saying that.

She was looking him in the eye and he forced himself not to look away. 'It was definitely deliberate. I know how serious kids' football can get; Mr Butcher makes a compelling case for that being the saboteur's motive.'

James wasn't sure how to respond to that, and an awkward pause hung between the two of them. She maintained eye contact as James tried not to shift in his seat, before she finally broke the silence. 'Of course, if he's right, we'll find the culprit in the end. It's amazing what forensics can turn up these days.'

How much did she already know? Was she toying with him, or was he just being paranoid? He felt like he was in an old episode of *Columbo*, gradually being manoeuvred into exposing his guilt. PC Birnham was getting up from the sofa and making for the door.

'Oh, just one more thing,' she stopped and turned. 'Was Kieran Butcher really passing off a Town player as one of his boys?'

James relaxed; he was happy for scrutiny to fall on Kieran rather than him for once. 'Yes. Kieran will do anything to make sure his team wins, even if it's against the rules.'

'And what lengths would you go to, Mr Hogan? Maybe to win a bet with Kieran? You spoke to some of my colleagues recently, didn't you? Something about taking photos at Town's academy?' He'd underestimated her, been wrong-footed by a superior opponent.

'I, er, well, yes…'

'Your bet with Butcher certainly gives you a motive for the car. If I had any fingerprints, I'd say it was looking pretty conclusive.' James felt pinned by her gaze. She had emphasised "if", did that mean she had them, or that she didn't?

'And I found a fascinating collection of materials dumped in an alleyway, which was quite the treasure trove for fingerprints. What do you think I'll find when I compare those prints with the ones my colleagues took from you the other week?'

'Why would the stuff from Northumberland Street match my fingerprints?'

PC Birnham smiled and stepped back towards the sofa. 'Who mentioned Northumberland Street? Maybe you should tell me all about it.'

*

That evening, as James was putting the kettle on, he had another phone call. It was Claire.

'Hello?' James was hesitant in answering.

'Hi James, how are you?'

Claire was the last person he wanted to talk to. He considered saying so, but curiosity got the better of him; what was she playing at? 'Frustrated. I just want to be in school and teaching; I didn't do anything wrong.'

'Can I be candid?' asked Claire. Candid seemed to be her default option around the English department office and she didn't usually ask permission; he wondered what she had to say that necessitated this kind of run-up. 'The problem is Josie. She found it really difficult to get her account down after the incident, and not just because of the shock. She's afraid of getting in trouble for the situation you walked in on. You claim that she was grappling with Marlowe?'

'Yes. His arms were around her and she was struggling.'

'She wouldn't let me put that down in her statement. I think she's sacrificing you to protect herself. Are you...' She paused, as if carefully measuring her words. 'Are you sure it was conflict that you saw? It couldn't have been something else: something sexual rather than aggressive?'

James stopped and thought for a moment. Could it have been that? No, that was ridiculous. He tried to recall the conversation between Josie and Chris: the raised voices, the escalation of anger. It wasn't the way Claire was suggesting, was it? It couldn't be. Could it?

'Are you still there, James?'

He snapped back into the conversation. 'Yes, I'm still here. No, absolutely not. It was definitely an argument about schoolwork that turned into a fight; there was nothing sexual. Anyway, I can't imagine Josie would even look at one of her students like that.'

'Young teacher, not that much older than the students. It's happened before. Are you sure you can't be persuaded otherwise?'

'I'm sorry?'

'Look, I'm going to level with you. I know Richard is your friend, but he's not the most dynamic head of department in the world. I wouldn't be surprised if the head thinks she could find better. When she dumps him, I want his job. I'm not worried about you; even without this business, your past makes you damaged goods. Josie is no competition right now, but in a couple of years, she might appeal if the head wants a young, enthusiastic head of department who can be moulded. I can make all this go away for you, if you help me take Josie out of the game. Change your story, say you didn't tell the truth sooner because you were protecting a friend and colleague. Let's make this Josie and Marlowe's problem rather than yours.'

'But that's not what happened.'

'So? No one who was there is going to back you up. Josie is afraid of losing her job for letting the scuffle escalate; Chris gets in as much trouble for fighting Josie as for copping off with her. They're not going to change their stories, and if you don't change yours you look like the psychopath. You're a good teacher, James. I'd be happy to have you working under me when I ease Richard out, but if you insist on taking the blame for this, I won't shed any tears for you. Change your story and work with me, or stick to your guns and be the fall guy. Your choice.'

Long after Claire rang off, James just sat there holding his phone. Thoughts were scrabbling for position in his mind like players jostling for a last-minute corner. He didn't want to go to prison. What about his family? What was the right thing to do for them? Even if he avoided criminal charges, losing his job would badly affect them. The best thing for them was for life to carry on as normal; Claire's plan made that possible.

What about Josie? James hadn't done anything wrong, but neither had she. If he said she'd been intimate with Chris, her career would be finished. Could he afford scruples on that? Shouldn't he put himself and his family first? It was wrong to stitch Josie up – though she didn't seem to mind doing it to him – but wasn't it just as wrong to let his family suffer? Particularly as he hadn't done anything wrong this time? And even if he did decide to get himself out of this, was it smart to trust Claire, to give her something to hold over him? Did he want to stay on at Cole Hill if it meant being Lady Macbeth's lapdog? It felt like whatever he decided, he'd end up on the losing side.

*

James went to find Ros, to tell her about Claire's proposal.

'The devious cow,' remarked Ros. 'What did you tell her?'

'I didn't, and she didn't push the point. I think she's going to wait to see what I do.'

'And what are you going to do?'

He hadn't known the answer until then, but suddenly it seemed clear. 'What do you think I'm going to do? It might mean trashing my teaching career – again – but I can't throw Josie and

Chris under the bus for an illicit affair that only exists in Claire's twisted mind. I'm going to stick to my story, trust Richard and hope someone else blinks.'

Ros crossed the room, held James tightly and whispered, 'I knew you'd decide that. I just wanted you to hear yourself saying it. You're a good man, James Hogan. I'm glad I married you.'

'Even with my career in tatters again?'

'Even then.'

*

It felt good to make the decision. Even though it might all go wrong for him, at least he felt like himself again. Looking back, he couldn't believe some of the things he had done in the last few months. No matter how good his intentions, James knew it had to stop. He didn't recognise the man who had done those things and he didn't want to recognise him. Simon was right: if principles don't cost you anything, they don't mean anything, and this was more important than the names of chocolate bars. This was the hill he was going to make his stand on, and if it turned out to be a last stand, then so be it. Whatever the likes of Kieran and Claire thought, life wasn't a zero-sum game. He couldn't control what other people did, but no one could force him to make innocent bystanders suffer for his success. A Stephen King quote came to mind, which he thought he could use in a pre-match team talk with the Swifts, if he ever got to give one again.

James phoned Richard, filling him in on everything Claire had said, including her assessment of her head of department. They agreed that Richard shouldn't let Claire know he was on to her, not yet anyway. Richard said he had been talking with Josie; reading between the lines Richard agreed that she seemed afraid of the consequences of telling the truth. Maybe Claire had encouraged her in that thought, all the better to play James and Josie off against each other. James reluctantly agreed that Richard should be the one to let Josie know what Claire had proposed, and to persuade her that the truth wouldn't reflect as badly on her as she feared.

*

The next morning, James's phone rang again at around half past ten. It was Richard. 'Good news, mate. I spoke with Josie after I got off from you last night, and having slept on it, she's gone to see the head to revise her statement. She's pretty embarrassed about it all, but she's going to tell the whole story. Chris Marlowe is back in today, so I'll see if he'll change his tune, but even if he doesn't, two teachers backing each other up should make a big difference. I'll make sure the head knows about Claire's role in all this too. Don't be surprised to hear from Mrs Cranbrook later, but don't let on that I've given you a heads-up.'

Sure enough, an hour and a half later, James's phone rang again. Everything had been sorted, and James was free to come back to work the following day. The head didn't go so far as apologising, but she did say they now accepted that James's account was accurate. James resisted the temptation to unload his frustration at how he'd been treated, thanking the head for letting him know and saying he was looking forward to coming in the next day. He didn't say that he was looking forward to the Redbridge match even more, but it was his first thought. He dashed off a text message to Alison telling her that he had been cleared, and got an almost instant reply saying that she was lifting his suspension with immediate effect.

James was relieved, but there was still a cloud hanging over him. Once that policewoman had tricked him into revealing that he knew more about Kieran's car than he was letting on, everything else had rushed out like a torrent. Not only the car-tampering; he had told her about the borrowed phone, the photographs of Kenny Harrison, even his suspension from school and what had led to it. She had listened intently, letting him ramble on without interruption. Now that he had been cleared, he wished he hadn't been quite so open with all his other secrets, but they had flowed out of him like absolution. He had put himself entirely in her power; all she had to do was say the word and his teaching, his coaching, his whole life was gone. He had half expected her to arrest him there and then, but she didn't. She just thanked him for his candour, made her excuses and left. He hoped that would be the last he saw of her, but he had a feeling he wouldn't be that lucky.

*

The locker-room door opened and Amber Gould walked in. Shift patterns had kept her and Hayley apart since the protest march, and this was the first time their paths had crossed since Andy was released. Her eyes narrowed when she saw Hayley, and she glanced around to check there was no one else tucked away in a corner.

'So, Wood's lawyer jumped straight onto the question of bodycam footage. It's as if he knew we hadn't actually seen his client doing anything before we grabbed him.' Her voice was sharp, and Hayley felt like there was an air of accusation in the statement.

'Yeah, I heard. Still, it's not really a surprising line for them to take, is it? Sounds like the lawyer was just doing his job.'

'What I want to know is who else was doing his job for him? The request for footage came not long after I told you all about it. Why are you trying to undermine my arrest? Sarge tore strips off me for not being more careful.'

'More careful? You more or less admitted that you knew Andy hadn't done anything wrong. There's a difference between being careless and fitting people up!'

'Oh, don't be so naïve. What you call fitting people up, I call doing my job. We'd all be better off without trouble-makers like Andy Wood stirring things up. Just because he's your boyfriend –

yeah, I found that out – doesn't mean he can go around protesting left, right and centre.'

So she was going there, was she? 'Well, for a start he's my ex-boyfriend, but that's got nothing to do with it. Whoever he is, he was making a lawful protest. We don't get to pick and choose who is allowed to exercise their legal rights.'

'Well, we should. Your problem, Birnham, is that you're happy just to accept things as they are. If you want to get things done, sometimes you have to cut a few corners. It's all about getting the result and it doesn't matter how you get there. I don't intend to still be pounding the beat by the time I'm your age: I'm going to be a detective, making a real difference. That means I need to get noticed. What I don't need is some no-talent plod turning the Sarge against me. Just keep out of my way in future – one day you'll be calling me ma'am and taking my orders. You don't want me as an enemy.'

With that, Amber swept out without giving Hayley the chance to reply. Hayley allowed herself a wry smile; it felt good to have struck a blow against Gould's crusade for arrests at any price, and great that she had pissed her off in the process. But it felt best of all that she'd been able to help Andy to get out of trouble that he really didn't deserve. The only way it could have been better was if she had a way of properly exposing Amber to the Sarge. If only her own bodycam had been running while Gould was running her mouth off at her, then Sarge would see for himself what she was really like – the lengths Gould was going to, the corners she was cutting – and her ambitions as the high-flying one-to-watch would be seriously derailed. Sometimes the truth just has to be brought into the open. Which brought her back to the question of what to do about James Hogan.

CHAPTER THIRTY-EIGHT

Friday was a day of awkward interactions. James was under no illusions that the school rumour mill would have been on overdrive for the last few days. Students were furtively whispering and pointing in the corridors, while staff were split between overdoing their welcome or acting like they thought James had got away with something. Josie seemed to be keeping out of James's way – quite an achievement, given the proximity of their classrooms. She kept her distance at staff briefing and avoided the department office at break. Claire was more aloof than usual, barely acknowledging James when she passed him. The rest of the department was happier to see him, although, once again, they only wanted to talk about the incident. Simon and Dean were full of questions; Moira was quieter, interested but less pushy. When she did speak, it was to make an observation rather than to ask a question.

'Josie is devastated by all this. I think she felt caught in the middle and just didn't know what to do. She's feeling awful, James. Be gentle with her.'

Simon snorted. 'Be gentle? She nearly ruined James's career. I wouldn't be all that forgiving about it.' Moira just looked at James and ever so slightly raised a questioning eyebrow. James wasn't sure how he felt about Josie and her part in all this, so he took a non-committal sip of tea and said nothing.

The encounter with Josie finally happened. James was sorting out a pile of books in the walk-in-cupboard, when Josie opened her door to it. She froze mid-step in the doorway.

'Hi,' said James, surprising himself with the amount of warmth in his voice.

'So, you're still talking to me then?'

'Looks that way.'

The words rushed out of Josie like an unblocked sink. 'I'm so sorry, James; I never meant to get you in trouble – I never thought things would go this far! I remembered you saying that if you'd got physical with that boy at your old school, there'd have been no way back. I was scared of losing my job, my career.'

'So you decided to let me lose mine instead?' The frustration of the last few days came out in James's voice, which was harsher than he'd intended now. Josie's head dipped and she broke eye contact.

'I hadn't thought that through. I didn't think. First, Claire persuaded me to leave the fight out of my account, then she said that if I changed my story, it would just make everything worse. Once Richard laid it all out for me, I knew what I had to do. I'm sorry it took me so long.' She looked up, her face a mixture of hope, shame and fear. James held her gaze for a long moment before answering.

'Don't worry about it. You got there in the end and there was no harm done. Thanks for clearing everything up, even if you did drag your feet a bit. Still friends?' He held out his hand to her.

A smile chased the fear from Josie's face. 'Still friends,' she replied, accepting his handshake. 'And Richard told me what Claire said to you.'

'Yeah, that put me in my place. Apparently I'm no competition and you're the bigger obstacle to her plan to take over the world. That's me told.'

Josie laughed wryly. 'I don't see how she works that out. As the last week shows, I've still got a lot to learn. Thanks for not going along with her, though – I wouldn't have blamed you, after the way I've behaved.'

'You might not have blamed me, but you wouldn't have respected me anymore. And I wouldn't have respected myself. Sometimes doing the right thing is more important than the outcome; it's not all about results.'

*

Sunday arrived in a rush. James had never seen so many spectators at a Swifts match. There was a larger than usual contingent of Swifts parents, grandparents and siblings, plus the injured Ryan and Rory. Several of the Hawks players had also turned up to watch, some with parents in tow. Ron and Kieran were both there, although neither of them made any effort to talk to James. There were just as many there to support Redbridge too.

Hayley was on the touchline, worried as ever for Jayden. Redbridge had a couple of injuries and he was in the starting line-up again. Apparently at training Matt had been drumming into the boys just how important the game was. Her eyes wandered away from the Redbridge lads to the Swifts end of the far touchline. There he was, James Hogan. With everything he had said to her she had enough now to take him in. If she'd been on duty today she'd have been tempted to arrest him on the touchline, although Jayden would have been horrified and embarrassed in equal measure. Then again, Hogan seemed genuinely upset about the whole thing, and not just upset to have been found out – she prided herself on being able to tell the difference after all these years in the job. His moment of madness may have lasted for a few weeks, but she was pretty sure it was over now. Even so, if the local newspapers got hold of this story of feuding football managers, being the copper who got to the bottom of it would be a feather in her cap and go a long way to getting some better assignments from the Sarge. She'd wait for Monday then pay Hogan a visit.

Fans were starting to arrive now – she knew a lot of the dads tended to leave it as late as they could, just in case they were asked to step in as linesman – and she noticed another familiar face with the Stoneleigh fans, slightly withdrawn from the others. She edged a little closer, hoping she wouldn't be recognised.

*

James called the Swifts in for the team talk.

'Stephen King – great centre-back for Spurs, dodgy knees – once said "the place where you made your stand never mattered. Only that you were there and still on your feet". You guys have been amazing all season, making a stand no matter what got thrown at you. I was going to give you a big talk about making one last push, giving it everything to get that last win, but do you know what? That's not the point. Just recently I've lost sight of what it's all about. Sunday mornings are meant to be about you lot enjoying your football. Football is a game – something we play – it's supposed to be fun. I've made this all about results and I shouldn't have done. I mean, don't get me wrong, I want you to try to win, to try your hardest – the trying is where the fun is – but let's not worry about whether or not we pull it off. The way you've played this season you've got nothing to prove; not to me, not to anyone. Whatever the league table says, you're already champions for me, every one of you. I don't care whether it's us or Redbridge that gets promotion. Just go out, do your best, and enjoy it.'

*

Jayden was having a hard time of it. He was playing at the back, and the Stoneleigh player he was up against was fast and skilful. If she hadn't been so concerned about Jayden, Hayley might

325

have enjoyed the game – there was lots of good play and the two goalkeepers (that girl again) were probably the best players for both teams. Despite a steady flow of opportunities – some of them, judging by Matt's reactions, Jayden's fault – neither team could break the deadlock. Jayden didn't come back onto the pitch for the second half, and she could see him sitting cross-legged, head down amongst the players' bags and water bottles on the far touchline.

A Stoneleigh defender lost control of the ball and Flynn seized on it, threading a pass through to Milo who fizzed a shot just wide of the post. If that had been a Redbridge player giving the ball away, Matt would have roasted them, but Hayley noticed that Hogan's response was very different.

'Head up, Charlie. Keep playing. You've got this.'

Hogan wasn't the only Stoneleigh coach to grab Hayley's attention. On the supporters' touchline Kieran Butcher was grumbling whenever Redbridge missed a chance.

'Unbelievable. That one was on a plate – what do Redbridge have to do to score?'

'It'll come,' replied the older man next to him. 'It has to – we can't let the bloody Swifts finish above us.'

'What if they actually went up? Having that clown Hogan in a higher division than me would just be embarrassing.'

'He's been embarrassing you all season, son. Are you sure he wasn't behind that business with your car?'

'Hogan? No chance – he hasn't the balls for something like that.'

'Well, soon enough none of that will matter. Once you're chairman, you can forget about that stupid bet and just shut his team down anyway. There won't be anything he can do about it.'

Hayley decided to stick close to Kieran and his dad, in case they said anything else.

*

With just ten minutes to go, the deadlock was finally broken. Luke made another great save, giving Stoneleigh a corner. The tall Stoneleigh midfielder went to take it. With everyone jostling in the penalty area, he bypassed all of them by pulling the ball back to the edge of the box. Charlie, the one who Hogan hadn't bawled out for giving the ball away, stepped forward without breaking stride and swung his foot at the ball. He got it just right, and it crashed high into the net. Before Charlie had the chance to react, he was engulfed by his team-mates. The Stoneleigh fans – all except for the Butchers – erupted on the touchline. For all Redbridge's efforts in the remaining minutes, nothing was getting past the girl in goal and the game finished as a one-nil defeat for Redbridge. At least Jayden hadn't been on the pitch when the goal went in, so nobody could say that was his fault.

*

'Does this mean we're promoted?' asked Dylan as the Swifts congregated around James after the final whistle.

'I don't know, it depends on the other result. If Weston Park have beaten the Royals, then yes, we'll finish second and go up.'

'Well, that's us up then,' said Josh. 'No one beats Weston Park – no one but us!'

James let the team go to receive the congratulations from their beaming parents. He couldn't remember ever seeing them so happy. Poppy headed straight for Sam, gushing about how brilliant she had been and how she proved that girls make the best goalkeepers.

*

James and Joao chatted happily as they carried the nets back to the lock-up.

'So tell me more about this new job of yours, Joao. It sounds like a pretty well organised sports club to have an academy.'

'Not a sports club, Mister James, sporting club. Sporting Club de Portugal. I work for their academy.'

James's brain registered the new information but was having trouble accepting it. Sporting Club de Portugal, wasn't that...?

'You work for Sporting Lisbon? The Champions League club?' Joao grinned and nodded. 'I thought you worked for some local sports centre, organising stuff for ordinary kids like our lot. Back home you work with elite players?'

Joao shrugged. 'I work with kids like our lot, just ones who happen to be very good at football. Kids are kids and coaching is coaching – the basics are the same.'

James was reeling. No wonder Joao had made such a difference – he was a proper, professional coach at a proper professional academy – one that had produced the likes of Luís Figo and Cristiano Ronaldo, no less. His departure would leave an even bigger hole than James had realised. It looked like James had better start learning the Level Two stuff as soon as possible.

'Wow, that really is a big promotion, no wonder you're pleased. Thanks for everything you've done this year. We couldn't have done this without you.'

'Not me, Mister James. It was the players who did it, and they did it for you.'

'I'm not sure about that, but next season they'll get to do it all over again – in the top division.'

Except they wouldn't. When James checked the website later, he saw that the Weston Park versus Royals game had been recorded as a walkover to Royals, giving them the three points they needed to finish in second place. A wave of conflicting emotions competed for control, before one muscled the others out of the way: James roared with laughter. As well as the four points the Royals had won against the Swifts, James had also had a hand in both Royals victories over the Hawks – one by sabotaging Kieran's car and one by letting Kieran play Kenny for a second time. If James hadn't been so intent on meddling, he may well have finished above the Royals after all. Part of him wanted to mourn the realisation, but the bigger part just found it funny. After all, it was only kids' football. There were more important things in life.

*

The following week at work, Richard saw James passing his classroom and beckoned him inside. James came in, closing the door behind him on Richard's request.

'I told the head all about Claire's suggestion that you change your story to drop Josie in it.'

'Wow, what did she say?'

'Not a lot at first. She asked a few questions, weighed things up, then just said, "Right" and asked her secretary to have Claire come to see her immediately. When Elaine said that she thought Claire was teaching, the head just snapped, saying she didn't care and she wanted Claire in front of her now. I asked if I should leave, but she said no. She wanted me to witness what was about to happen, and she wanted Claire to know that I had witnessed it.

'When Claire arrived the head played it really cool. She thanked her for all her help in resolving your situation last week, which Claire seemed to take at face value. Then she asked what Claire's thoughts were on career progression. Claire gave the usual flannel about wanting eventually to move into senior management, but being happy where she was for the time being. She said she was keen to learn from me before looking to apply for head of department jobs in due course. Then Cranbrook asked why, if she was happy to learn from me, had she told you that I should be pushed aside. Claire blustered for a bit, saying that you must have misunderstood, but once she realised the head knew what she'd said about Josie too, she knew the game was up.

'Cranbrook tore into her for a bit, then suggested Claire start looking for jobs elsewhere. She didn't have the evidence to force her out, but if Claire didn't agree to move on, she would start looking for it. She could certainly guarantee that Claire wouldn't be considered for any senior roles at Cole Hill. Claire wanted to stay on here until she found a head of department job, but Cranbrook wasn't having it. She said that Claire's despicable behaviour wasn't going to be rewarded with a move up the career ladder. The head would only give a good reference for an ordinary teaching job or, at most, another second-in-department position. She wanted Claire out of the school by the end of the year, or she wouldn't get any kind of positive reference. By the time the meeting finished, the two of them were looking daggers at one another. Afterwards, Cranbrook told me to let you know that when the time comes she'll look positively at an application from you for the second-in-department job.'

'You and me running a department again – it sounds perfect.'

'You haven't heard the best bit yet, just as Lady Macbeth was leaving, do you know what I said?'

'Go on.'

'I said I was washing my hands of her.'

CHAPTER THIRTY-NINE

Today was the day; everything would be settled one way or the other. Today was the AGM and the showdown with Kieran.

James had no idea which way it would go. You could take an educated guess about the coaches' votes – Lynn thought more were on their side than Kieran's, for what that was worth – but there were far more parents than coaches, and who knew how they would see things? The other worry was the business with Chris Marlowe. Alison had been discreet about the club suspension, but if news got out, Kieran could paint a very unfortunate picture which could sway a lot of votes. Either way, James just wanted to get it over with. Part of him wanted to back out – he didn't think he deserved to be the club chairman, not after everything he'd done, but he knew that if he dropped out now Kieran would take over, which would be far worse. Whatever James's flaws, he was certainly better than the alternative.

The day at school dragged, with James distracting himself from what lay ahead as best he could. Josie wished him luck at the end of the last period before he made his way home.

James tried not to let Ben and Poppy see how tense he was about it all. As the family ate their evening meal together, James was quieter than usual. He wasn't sure if anyone noticed; Poppy, as ever, chattered away and filled every available gap in the conversation. When James got ready to leave, Ros gave him a kiss and wished him luck.

'I wish you were coming too,' he said.

'Well, someone has to stay and look after the kids while you're out becoming a towering political colossus. You'll be fine – you don't need me.'

'I might need your vote.'

'Relax. One vote won't make much difference. There can't be that many people at the club who don't realise what an idiot Kieran is.' James wasn't so sure. He knew how many idiots there were in youth football – he'd become one himself for a while.

*

Lynn had told James to arrive in plenty of time, and once he got there she kept him busy, introducing him to different parents. Some shook his hand enthusiastically and said that they were going to vote for him, while others were friendly enough without giving anything away. James tried to put the calculations and predictions to one side and just focused on coming across as a normal human being, something Ros had spent years telling him was beyond his powers.

Danny Peters made a beeline for him, wishing him luck and commiserating on the Swifts missing out on promotion. James explained what he'd subsequently learned: Weston Park had scratched their last game because most of their players were attending trials at Town's academy. As they were already champions, they had nothing to lose from forfeiting the game, although obviously it had a big impact on the other teams in the league.

By the scheduled start time, the Dunsinane room was packed. James was glad to see no one disguising themselves with tree branches – no chance of Birnam Wood marching in to seal his doom. The landlord said something about having too many people squeezed in, but after Lynn mentioned beer sales he dropped his objection. There was a row of tables at one end of the room for the committee, and even a microphone for their use.

'We won't need that, will we?' baulked Ron when he saw it.

'No harm in having it, Ron,' replied Lynn. 'Just in case we need to make ourselves heard over your adoring crowd.'

Ron was keen to rush through the preliminaries, but it wasn't all that simple. Howard, as ever, took his time, going into the minutiae of the finances. He pointedly commented on the outstanding fines for £60, plus more to come once Kieran's latest misconduct charge went through. He explained that he fully expected the guilty manager to pay those fines personally, rather than the club covering the cost of his appalling behaviour. After that, Howard invited questions, but he'd been so thorough – and boring – that nobody wanted to prolong things. Eventually, Ron took to his feet.

'I've been chairman of the club for twenty years. In that time we've grown from a small local club with just a couple of teams to one of the mainstays of the Town league, with teams in almost every age group and a decent collection of titles and cups to our name. But just because I'm stepping down, it doesn't mean the end of the Butcher era. With my Kieran ready to step up, the club can go from strength to strength in the coming years.'

There were some cheers from the crowd at this remark, but also some low muttering. It was hard to tell how the crowd was split between James and Kieran, but the divide was certainly there.

'Right, how do we do this election business?' Ron asked Lynn. 'We've never needed one before.'

Lynn took the microphone and addressed the meeting. 'First, we need to establish which committee posts are being voted on. Ron, as he said, is stepping down as chairman and we have two candidates – so far – to replace him. Kieran Butcher, nominated by Ron and seconded by Howard Gristwood, and James Hogan, nominated by myself and seconded by Alison Hines.'

Howard immediately put his hand up and interrupted Lynn.

'May I say something at this point?' Lynn passed him the microphone and indicated for him to go on. 'I did second Kieran's nomination back at the start of the season, but since then I have decided that he would be entirely the wrong person to take the club forward. I wanted to make it clear that he no longer has my support.' James wondered for a moment whether there would even need to be an election; if Kieran didn't have a seconder…

A voice rang out from the floor. 'Well, if you don't want to second him, I will.' It was Tony Dagnall, the under-fifteens manager. So that was that.

'Thank you, Tony,' replied Lynn, taking charge again. 'Do we have any more nominations?' There was no reply, so Lynn carried on. 'And any nominations for any of the other posts? Does anyone fancy taking my job and spending their evenings emailing a dozen different club secretaries every week? No one? Oh well, worth a try. Can I assume that all the other current post-holders are happy to be re-elected unopposed?' She looked across the committee table and received nods of confirmation from Alison, Howard and Dave. 'All in favour of re-electing the current secretary – that's me – welfare officer, treasurer and ground manager en masse?' A sea of hands flew up. 'Votes against?' There were none. 'Carried. Now on to the election of the new chairman.'

Both candidates were given the chance to briefly make their case for being chairman. Kieran went first, bullishly presenting his credentials and boasting about the time the Hawks had spent in the top division, the way they had helped to build the club's reputation with the rest of the league. It was clear that there were plenty of people in the room who were lapping it up. Kieran finished by saying that all he had ever wanted was what was best for the club as a whole. His dad had drummed that into him over the years, and he was determined to keep driving standards up, making the teams better and achieving more success on the pitch.

Then it was James's turn. Like Kieran before him, he came to the front and took the microphone.

'To be honest, for a lot of this season I've felt like a wolf in sheep's clothing. There have been times I've been so caught up in my Swifts competing with Kieran's Hawks that I lost sight of what this club is all about, what it should be all about. Kieran thinks the club is a trophy cabinet, that it's all about winning things, which is ironic from a Chelsea fan.' James was encouraged by the smattering of laughter and carried on. 'And it *is* important to think about the club's reputation. But the club exists for the boys and girls who play for it, not for its own sake and certainly not for the chairman or the coaches. Yes, we want our kids to play to win, but football is about more than just winning and losing.

'The Swifts aren't *my* team, they don't exist to fulfil *my* ambitions; I'm *their* coach, it's *their* team. This is about kids playing football, enjoying it and growing as a result. Growing as players, but also growing as people. The reputation this club should care about is our reputation as a place where parents know that their kids are happy, well-treated and safe; where they won't be picked on by bullying managers, or cast aside if someone decides they're not good enough; a place where children's happiness is more important than a league table, or a shiny trophy, or a coach's ego. That's the club I want to lead, and that's why I'm standing to be chairman.'

More applause, but also disgruntled murmurings from the old guard.

Lynn took back the microphone. 'Right, we've heard from the candidates, now it's time for the vote.'

'Hang on a minute,' came an aggressive-sounding voice from the floor or the room. 'I've got something I want to say.' Everyone was looking around to see where the interruption had come from, and James saw that it was one of the parents from the U15s team.

'It's all very well Hogan banging on about kids being safe, but my daughter goes to Cole Hill school, and apparently you were suspended recently for beating up a year 11 lad. What have you got to say about that?'

The momentary silence gave way to a rumble of murmuring as people reacted to the shock news. James was aware of every eye on him, and for a moment the room spun.

'And Hogan was going to just keep that quiet and not tell anyone?' added Kieran, sneeringly. 'You can't trust him.'

A few more voices added similar sentiments. James's stomach churned as the anger in the room rose: his worst fears were coming true – the business with Marlowe was going to bring him down just as he had the goal in his sights.

Alison called for the microphone, and quietened the crowd.

'The club knew all about this,' she began. 'There was an incident at Cole Hill school which resulted in a year 11 boy being hurt. The school, as a precaution, suspended James while they investigated, and I suspended him from all football activities while the school looked into the matter. That's standard FA procedure and no indication of any wrongdoing on James's part. As it happens, James was completely cleared by the school in just a couple of days with no questions remaining against his conduct.' James thought he heard someone muttering something about no smoke without fire before Alison continued. 'Once the school was satisfied that James had no charge to answer, I was able to lift his suspension. James, can you add anything, just to put everyone's minds at rest?'

James tried to surreptitiously control his breathing as he made his way back to the microphone. He took a moment to get his thoughts in order before he started to speak.

'It was a year 11 lad physically attacking a young, female teacher. All I did was step in and pull them apart, but unfortunately the lad hit his head on a desk as I pushed him away and he needed stitches. The school suspended me while it investigated, but as Alison says, they found that I had acted entirely appropriately.'

The latest murmurings didn't sound as darkly accusative as before, but the initial revelation may still have done some damage. He handed the microphone back to Alison.

'Excuse me. Could I just add something?' James couldn't place the voice, but when he saw the face it took him only a moment to recognise that woman police officer, the one who came to his house. What was she doing here? Was she about to spill the beans about his role with Kieran's car?

'My name's Hayley Birnham, my son was playing for Redbridge this season and I'm looking around for a new team for him, so I thought I'd come along tonight to get a feel for what kind of club this is. Would it be okay if I said something?' There were a few shrugs from the committee members, so Lynn indicated for her to come forward and take the microphone.

'I'm a police officer, and I'd like to confirm that we have no concerns about Mr Hogan regarding his recent suspension from work. But there's something else I thought you should all know about.'

James felt his stomach churn: she was going to tell them about the car, then arrest him at the worst possible moment. This wouldn't just cost him the vote, it would cost him his career. And he didn't even want to think how Kieran would react when he heard what James had done.

Hayley continued. 'I was at the Swifts versus Redbridge game, the last game of the season, and I was standing close to Kieran Butcher. Seeing as he made such a big thing in his speech about wanting the best for the club, you should know that I heard him saying he wanted Redbridge to win, not the Swifts.'

The room broke out with a buzz of chatter, as people confirmed with their neighbours that they had heard Hayley correctly. Kieran's voice cut through the hubbub.

'Come off it, love – no one's going to believe that. I'm Stoneleigh through and through, have been since I was a nipper. You can't go around making allegations like that without any proof.'

Hayley smiled sweetly back at him. 'If it's proof you want…' She pulled out her phone, flicked it a couple of times and held it up against the microphone.

The voice on the phone was Kieran, albeit in uncharacteristically quiet mode, as if he didn't want to be overheard. 'Come on, Redbridge, you can't lose to the fucking Swifts,' he muttered.

It was followed by Ron's unmistakable tones, similarly hushed. 'Well, you did. It was in your own hands and you messed up. Now all we can do is watch and hope they blow it too.'

Hayley stopped the audio file and the room fell silent, with all eyes switching between Kieran and Ron. It was Ron who gathered his wits first.

'It's not what it sounds like. Emotions were high. It was the week after the Swifts had cheated their way to victory against the Hawks thanks to a dodgy referee…'

Lynn interjected. 'A referee appointed by the league at your personal request, Ron. I was at that game and he was a lot fairer than your ref in the previous match.'

'We had to finish above them,' added Kieran. 'Everybody knows we're the better team. It would be embarrassing if they went above us on the last game of the season.'

'Embarrassing for who, Kieran?' asked Dave. 'For the club as a whole, or just for you? What does that say about your real priorities?'

Ron started to protest further, but a voice from the crowd – James thought it was Gabe's dad – called to move on to the vote, with others expressing their agreement.

'Okay,' said Ron, reluctantly. 'Votes for Kieran please.' Tony Dagnall was the first to raise his hand, and several others followed, including Ron and Kieran. Lynn quickly counted round the room.

'Twenty-seven,' she concluded.

'And votes for Hogan.' Ron couldn't keep the contempt out of his voice as he said James's name. Lynn counted again.

'Forty-one.' A large number of people (probably about forty-one of them) cheered wildly.

'Wait a minute.' It was Kieran, stepping forward and shouting over the noise. 'I've got some proxy votes here; parents from my team who aren't able to attend tonight.' He waved a pile of papers which he had taken from his coat pocket. 'They're all voting for me, and there are twenty-one of them. That makes forty-eight votes, which beats Hogan.' He handed them to Lynn.

A buzz swept around the room; nobody was sure if what Kieran was doing was in the rules. Did proxy votes count?

Ron turned to Lynn and asked, 'Am I still the chairman at the moment?' Lynn nodded. Ron spoke into the microphone. 'As chairman, I'll allow those votes. In that case, I declare that...'

'Not so fast, Ron,' Lynn was flicking through the pile, 'some of these people are here in person.' She started reading out the names. 'Rob Furlong – he's over there. Phil Gatwood, he's here too. You can't vote in person and have a proxy vote too.' By the time Lynn had gone through the pile, Kieran had lost a handful of his proxies. 'That makes it forty-one to James and only forty to Kieran. Now you can declare the result, Ron.'

Ron's shoulders slumped. Through gritted teeth he said, 'I declare that...' He paused, reluctant to actually say the words. 'James Hogan is the new chairman of Stoneleigh Youth Football Club. God help us.' The room broke into excited cheers again.

With James now in the chair, they ran through the rest of the meeting. Under *any other business*, Howard brought up the issue of the outstanding fines and the meeting voted by a large majority that Kieran should be liable to reimburse the club for them, despite a bitter, foul-mouthed counter-argument from Kieran. James suspected that they might find it difficult to actually get him to pay up, but that was a problem for another day.

Once the meeting ended, Lynn went to the bar while lots of people wanted to congratulate James. A few of the old guard, Tony and Nick among them, were more interested in commiserating with Kieran and Ron, but most of those present were focused on the future of the club rather than the past.

As soon as he was able, he headed across to Hayley Birnham, standing awkwardly on her own. 'I was surprised to see you.'

She grinned in reply. 'I bet you were.'

'For a moment there I wasn't sure which way your intervention was going to go. Why did you tell everyone about Kieran but not say anything about me and his car?'

'Well, as I said, I'm looking for a new team for my Jayden. Having seen both of you on the touchline this season, I know which one I'd rather have coaching him – if you'll have him, of course.'

'Even knowing what I'm capable of, with the car and the photographs and everything?'

'Look, everyone makes mistakes. You've done some pretty extreme things, but I think they were out of character. You know what you said about being a wolf in sheep's clothing? I think it's the other way round – you've been more like a sheep in wolf's clothing, if you ask me. I joined the police because I wanted to make the world better. I soon discovered there are limits to what one person can do, but we still have to do what we can. In this instance, how I decide to do my job determines whether you get to keep yours. I think everybody at your football club and everybody at your school is better served if we just forget about Kieran's car. I'm the only one who knows about the fingerprint match and I'm happy to keep it that way. Arresting you won't make the world any better for anyone, will it?'

'I'm not sure Kieran would agree, in fact, he'd be livid if he ever found out.'

'That's the only downside of all this. We don't get to tell him.'

MINUTES OF STONELEIGH YOUTH FOOTBALL CLUB COMMITTEE 10TH JUNE

Present: James Hogan (Chairman and U13s manager), Lynn Carpenter (Secretary), Howard Gristwood (Treasurer), Alison Hines (Welfare Officer), Dave Grey (Ground Manager).

Treasurer's Report: Howard reported that we had a brief cash-flow problem, but now that players are signing up for next season, we are once again sitting pretty on top of a big pile of cash, all ready to start paying out pitch fees and the like. Some fines have been paid for last season, although those responsible for the offences have not yet reimbursed the club – see below.

Welfare Officer's report: Alison confirmed that Kieran Butcher has been given a four-game ban and a £40 fine for his abusive behaviour to the referee in the last Hawks game of the season. This adds to the £60 fine that the club has already paid due to Kieran's fielding of an ineligible player for the Hawks on two occasions. Alison has informed the County FA that Kieran is no longer a manager at this club. They have thanked us for paying the £60 on Kieran's behalf, but said not to pay the new fine: quite apart from his suspension being carried over until he has a new team with which to serve the ban, Kieran will remain suspended until all fines are paid and until he has reimbursed Stoneleigh YFC the £60 for the earlier offences.

Teams report: We have entered the following teams for next season's league competition: U16s, U14s, U13s, U12s, U11s, U10s, U9s, U8s, U7s. Sadly, last year's U12 Hawks team has now folded. Several players decided to move on and find new clubs rather than play a second season out of the top division. Of the remainder, some asked if they could switch to the Swifts. The resulting shortage of players meant that Kieran Butcher felt unable to put together a competitive squad. Apparently, Kieran has approached a number of other local clubs with a view to bringing his remaining core of players over and managing a new combined team, but news of his four-match suspension (and the behaviour that led to it) has acted as something of a disincentive for those clubs. We all feel desperately sorry for Kieran, obviously.

James Hogan reported that a number of girls, including his daughter, are expressing interest in starting a girls' football team at the club. It was agreed that this would be an excellent development and that launching an U10 girls' team – hopefully the first of many girls' sides at Stoneleigh – had the full support of the committee.

Any other business: The committee wished to minute their congratulations to Chairman James Hogan on the news that he has been offered the job as Second in the English department at Cole Hill School, starting in September.

LC

FOUL AND FAIR
DISCUSSION QUESTIONS

- What has been your experience of grassroots children's football, as a player, a parent or as a coach? How authentic was *Foul and Fair* to that experience? Has reading the book made you think differently about your attitude to children's football?
- Who was your favourite character in the book? Why?
- '[Paradise Lost] is about holding onto what's right even after you've got everything hopelessly wrong.' (Maddie, p129). How does this statement relate to James' actions in *Foul and Fair*? To what extent did the various literary references in the book add to your enjoyment of it?
- How well do you think Hayley and Andy dealt with co-parenting? Did Hayley make the right decisions when juggling her responsibilities as a mother with her responsibilities as a police officer?
- What purpose do the football matches serve in the book? Are they there for more than just telling us the result? How do the Swifts change over the course of the book? How does James change as a coach?
- 'The Swifts aren't my team, they don't exist to fulfil my ambitions; I'm *their* coach, it's *their* team.' (James, p335). Is James right? Is it the coach's team, or the team's coach?

- What did you think of James's first Swifts training session in chapter 2 when you read it? Did Joao's analysis in the pub make you see it differently? What do you think Kieran's training sessions would be like?

- Which is more important – children being encouraged to win, or being encouraged to have fun playing? Is there a balance to be struck rather than all-or-nothing one way or the other?

- 'I mean, it's great that girls are getting into football now, but girls' football isn't proper football, is it?' (Kieran, p161). How common are attitudes like Kieran's? Women's football has become increasingly popular in recent years. What obstacles still exist for girls who want to play the game?

- 'Sometimes you have to bend the rules to do the right thing.' (Pikey, p126). 'It's all about getting the result and it doesn't matter how you get there' (Amber, p321). Is there any difference between what Pikey and Amber are each arguing here? Do you agree, with either or both of them?

- 'Principles and morals are sometimes a luxury that people can't afford' (Ros, p181). 'Principles that cost you nothing mean nothing; sometimes you have to take a stand.' (Simon, p229). Which of these statements do you agree with more? Why?

- Is Hayley right to say that James is a sheep in wolf's clothing for much of the book? In the final reckoning, did he deserve to get away with it?

- 'The problem with the "it's all about winning" brigade is that they never understood that not everything that counts can be counted.' (p238). What counts in football that can't be counted? More widely, what counts in life?

ACKNOWLEDGMENTS

Foul and Fair was an idea that, if you'll excuse the pun, I kicked around for several years before finally managing to get it onto the page. It went through several versions, although the core story of James vs Kieran, Swifts vs Hawks, was there from the beginning. That first attempt was written before my first novel, *Dead Man Singing*, although Hayley Birnham's strand of the narrative didn't arrive until much later, when *Dead Man Singing* was on the verge of publication.

They say that first novels are autobiographical; this is technically my second novel, but as I've just explained it's also sort-of my first. My official first novel certainly isn't autobiographical – I've never been a rock star, faded or otherwise, I've never faked my own death or set up as my own tribute act. *Foul and Fair* occupies more familiar territory for me: much of the story was inspired by my own experiences as a grassroots football coach, with West Moors YFC in the Bournemouth Youth Football League. While James's story is very different to mine (I've never broken the law in pursuit of victory, honest!) there are many instances where I've borrowed from reality for the book. A couple of the Swifts' matches are based on actual games my West Moors team played, and most of Kieran's worst excesses are things that I either witnessed other managers do or which I was told about by first hand witnesses. Unlike James, I didn't regularly use literary quotes in team talks, although I will admit to having once deployed the Dylan Thomas one, much to the amusement of my players.

I should stress that none of the characters are modelled on specific people. Kieran is an amalgam of several different coaches, a composite of all the worst examples of a certain kind of football coach. I was concerned I had made him so much of a monster that he would seem unrealistic, but several people have assured me that they have met Kieran themselves. The fact that these people live in different parts of the country, encountering their respective Kierans years apart from one another, suggests a universality as satisfying from a writer's point of view as it is depressing from a footballing one. Apologies to any real-life football coaches called Kieran – the name was chosen because I didn't know any of you. James Hogan's name was picked in honour of the great Jimmy Hogan, one of the trailblazing forefathers of modern football coaching who I first encountered in the pages of Jonathan Wilson's excellent book *Inverting the Pyramid: The History of Football Tactics*. Beyond the fact that they are both football coaches, there is no particular resemblance between the characters. Joao isn't based directly on anyone, but he looks and speaks very much like my Portuguese friend Claudio Vasconcelos who was on the same FA Level 2 coaching course as me. A handful of incidental characters are named – with their permission – after friends of mine. Their reactions to this ranged from a cheerful 'yeah, why not?' to mystifyingly giddy excitement. Fulham fans of a certain vintage may have also noticed a few names from the lower-division past sneaking into the book too.

Several people deserve thanks for their part on my coaching journey. I probably wouldn't have taken the first step into coaching if Ed Keech hadn't been willing to take the journey with me. He was my partner on the touchline at West Moors, and I couldn't have wished for a better co-manager, or a better friend.

As well as enjoying the good moments together, the lows were more bearable for our shared gallows humour, and I like to think we got the balance right between taking things seriously and not taking things overly seriously. Martin Dighton (then at Dorset FA, now at Coaching UK) along with Alex Browne and Andy Harris, were responsible for leading the courses where I learned to coach. Martin also read early passages from the book and helped to fine-tune some of Joao's training sessions. Prior to all that – several years prior – he coached my eldest son at FA Skills sessions in school holidays and was the first grassroots coach I saw who made me think, 'that's how it should be done', so he's been an inspiration in more ways than one. Thanks, Martin.

A number of friends read and commented on the initial (pre-Hayley) version of the story (then going by the title House of Red Cards). Apologies if there's anyone who I've forgotten after all this time, but thank you to Steve Goddard, Dave Moloney, Lou Porter, Pete Bone, Brian Rice and Jez Horgan. Steve Broadway read a much later version – the first to bear the name *Foul and Fair* – and it was his feedback that gave me the confidence to recognise that the book was finally ready to be submitted to my publishers. Two friends of mine consulted on the police aspect of the book. Dave Gorman (no, not that one) advised on matters around James's arrest, while another serving officer friend of mine, who prefers to remain anonymous, steered me through some practicalities in Hayley's strand of the story. I should make clear that any inaccuracies in terms of the law or police practice are entirely down to me, not them. Another friend – who shall also remain nameless – gave me worryingly expert advice on how to sabotage a car.

My thanks, as ever, to the fantastic team at The Book Guild. Daniel Burchmore oversaw the production process, calmly ensuring that all the moving parts came together in plenty of time. Ian Skewis' copy-editing tightened things up, as well as saving me from an embarrassing Jane Austen-related faux pas, and Chelsea

Taylor once again worked her magic with the cover. It's just a shame that she's named after my least favourite football team, but I'll continue to overlook that if she keeps producing wonderful covers for my books. Thanks too to Rosie Lowe for co-ordinating the team and for saying 'yes' to the book in the first place.

Becoming a football coach has been one of the most satisfying things I've done in my life. My players at West Moors YFC made the seven years I spent coaching them an absolute joy. None of the individual players in *Foul and Fair* are directly based on real life individuals, although a DNA test might find traces of some of my lads mixed in with one or two of the Swifts, particularly when on the pitch. We weren't necessarily the best team (although we had our moments), but I never saw a more hard-working, committed set of boys and I wouldn't have swapped them for any of the more successful teams we came across. On more times than I can remember, I arrived at training in a low mood and left buzzing after a great session. Seeing individuals developing as players and – more importantly – as young men was a joy, and I'm certain that I got more out of coaching them than any of them got from me. Some of them also amazed me with how much they progressed, in both short and long term. I've heard too many volunteer coaches dismissing children, writing them off as 'never going to be good enough' or 'not going to carry on playing football'. There were boys at West Moors who proved that way of thinking wrong. Once you stop seeing football as only being about the top professional ranks – a level far beyond realistic ambitions for most of us – it's an important truth that football is for everyone. Some of the West Moors boys who would have been easy to dismiss or discard in their early days had become dependable, accomplished players by the time we reached under 16s. It's enormously satisfying to know that those boys have years of pleasure playing the game ahead of them. They taught me something about not writing people off, about giving people the chance to fulfil their potential, whatever their own potential might be. Not everyone is going to be a star player, but everyone should get the chance to play. Thanks, lads, it was a privilege to be your coach.

I got lucky with 'my' parents at West Moors too. It's generally accepted among grassroots coaches that the worst aspect of the job is dealing with parents, but I can honestly say that for the most part ours were supportive and helpful rather than pushy and complaining (or maybe they just kept the complaints for when I couldn't hear them; if so, I'm grateful for that too!) One of the reasons I haven't – yet – taken on another team is the nagging suspicion that I couldn't possibly be as lucky with both players and parents a second time around. I should also mention the other members of the West Moors Youth Football Club committee – a group which bears no resemblance to the committee depicted in these pages, other than the fact that our meetings were generally held in the pub. Some of the people who I served alongside are still involved in running West Moors, and it's very good to know that the club is in such safe hands.

Finally, I want to thank my family. Once again, my mum has been hugely supportive of this book. She loved the pre-Hayley iteration of the story, and I hope that this new version meets with her approval (I think it will: she's very discerning). My wife Ann and my sons, Peter and Dan, all had to put up with living with me while I was creating an entire fictional football season and talking about little else. It's great to share my success with them now, although their idea of sharing my success involves constantly telling me how boring my books must be and scoffing at the idea that they would ever actually read them. No matter how well my books do, please rest assured that there are three people with the self-appointed task of making sure that I don't get too big-headed. They're very good at it too.

Ann also put up with several years of our weekends being organised around football fixtures, and with large amounts of kit – cones, balls, bibs – cluttering up the house, not to mention the ubiquitous presence of the beads from astroturf pitches in our carpets. The boys were less bothered by all the football, as they were part of it. I coached Dan for several years, and I stepped in to fill a gap coaching Peter's team for his Under 16 season, so both of them have had to put up with me on the training pitch and the touchline as well as at home. I think they both survived the experience and even enjoyed it, although you'd be hard pushed to get them to admit to the second half of that statement.

Finally, thanks to you for reading this book – I hope you enjoyed it. My experience of publishing *Dead Man Singing* has helped me to understand just what a difference it makes to an author when people say that they have appreciated their work. If you've enjoyed *Foul and Fair*, or if you want to keep up to date with whatever comes next, please feel free to get in touch via my website – www.stevecouch.co.uk. Football teams need their supporters, and that's true of authors too.

ABOUT THE AUTHOR

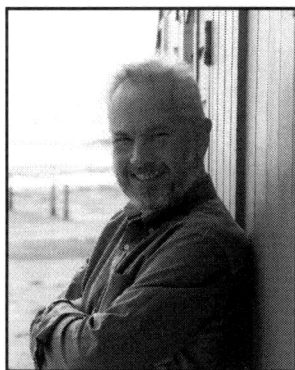

Steve Couch lives in Bournemouth with his wife and two sons. He is an FA Level 2 football coach, and a former team manager and club chairman of West Moors Youth Football Club. When not writing, he coaches small children in local schools and large men at MAN v FAT Football in Bournemouth. *Foul and Fair* is his second novel.

Steve shares a birthday with Nick Hornby, the Football League, and Paul McCartney's first solo LP. He is a lifelong supporter of Fulham Football Club and a goal-poaching fox in the box.

For more information, please visit www.stevecouch.co.uk